World-Ripper War

Book 3 of the Mad Tinker Chronicles

By J.S. Morin

ISBN: 1939233232
ISBN-13: 978-1-939233-23-3

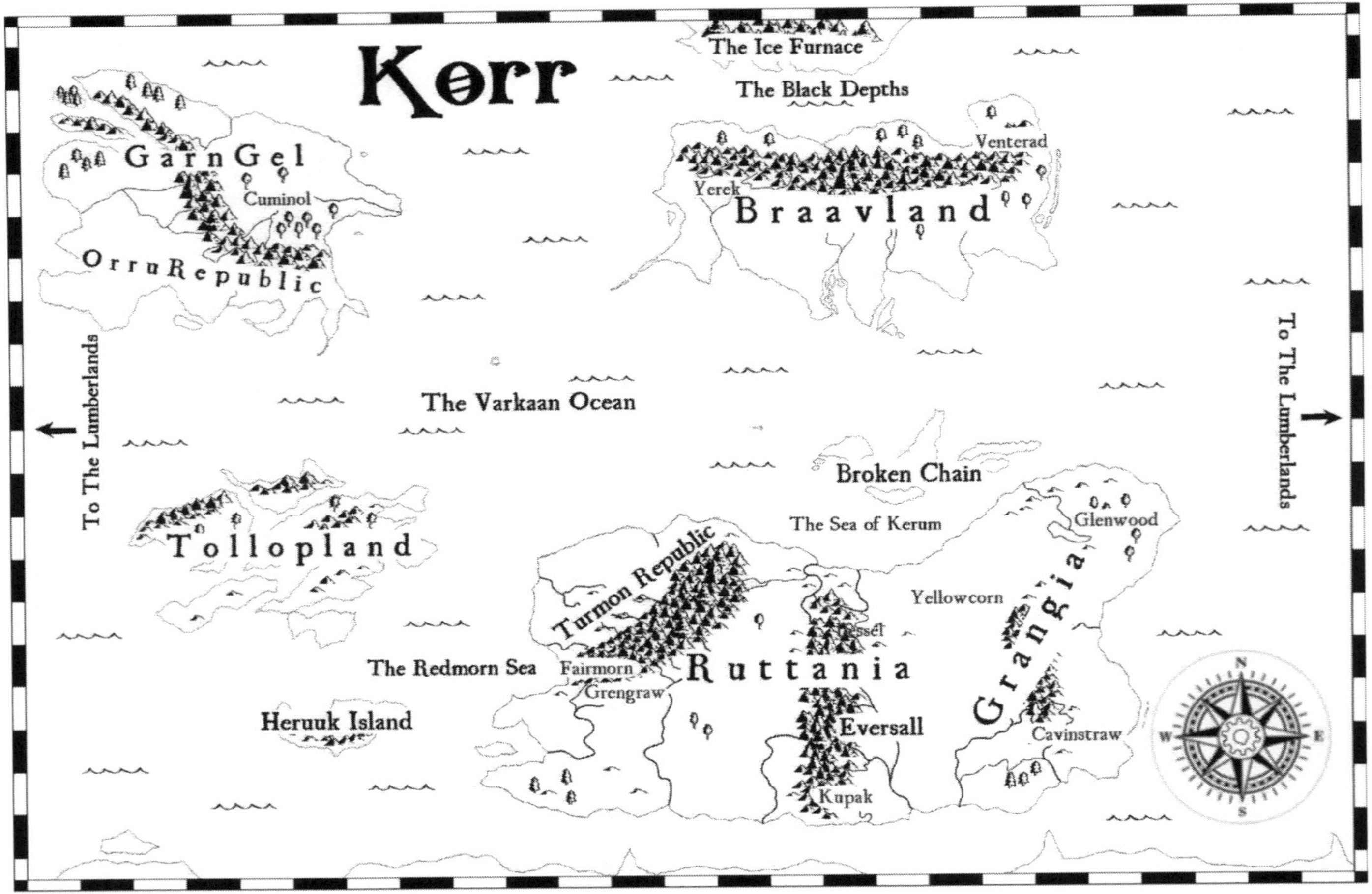

Korr
The Ice Furnace
The Black Depths
GarnGel
Cuminol
OrruRepublic
Braavland
Yerek
Venterad
The Varkaan Ocean
To The Lumberlands
To The Lumberlands
Broken Chain
The Sea of Kerum
Tollopland
Turmon Republic
Glenwood
Yellowcorn
Grangia
The Redmorn Sea
Fairmorn
Grengraw
Ruttania
Eversall
Kupak
Cavinstraw
Heruuk Island
N
E
S
W

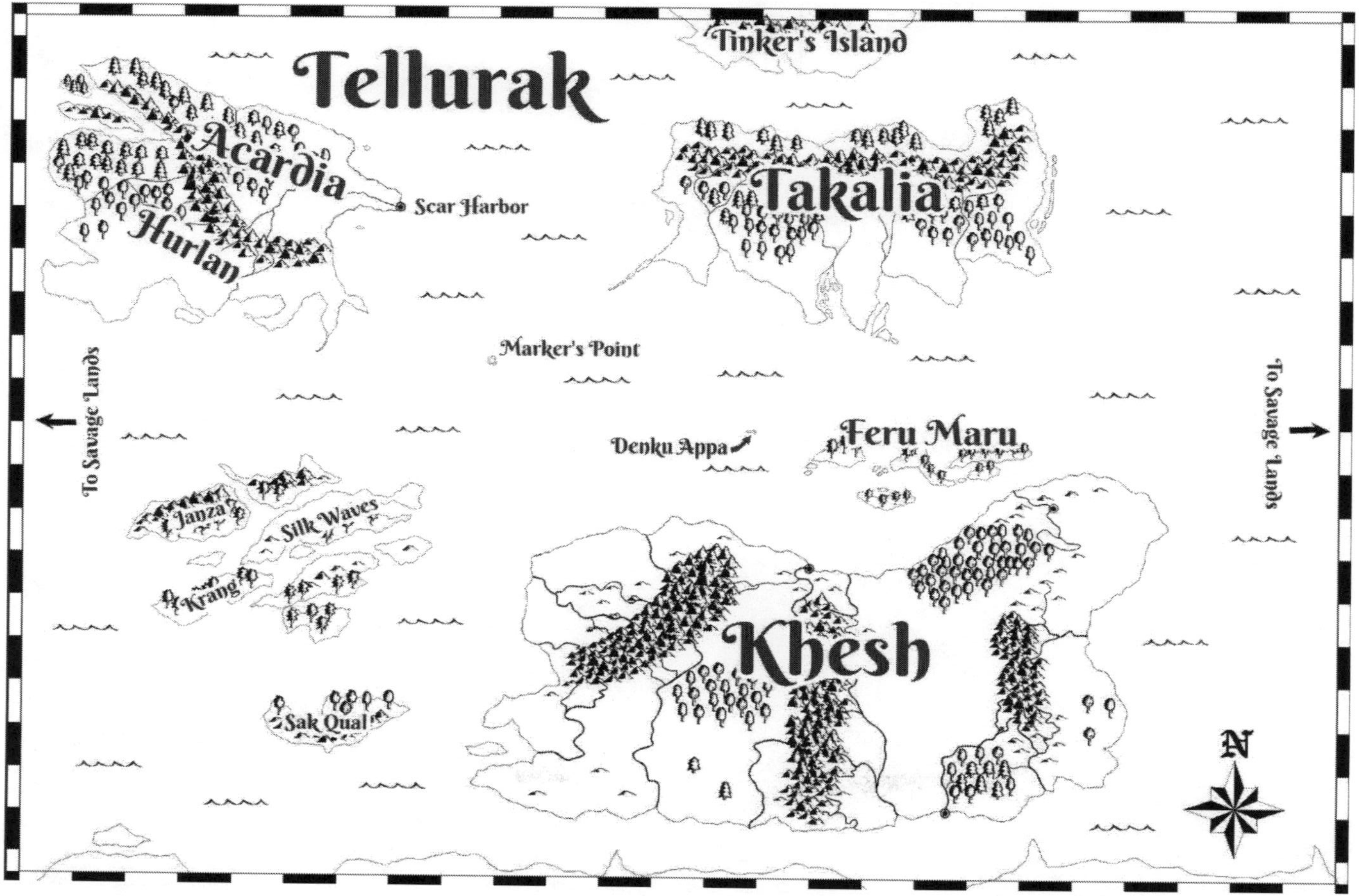
Tellurak
Tinker's Island
Acardia
Hurlan
Scar Harbor
Takalia
Marker's Point
To Savage Lands
To Savage Lands
Denku Appa
Feru Maru
Janza
Silk Waves
Krang
Khesh
Sak Qual
N

Chapter 1

"I've built so many things; I could never have picked a favorite. It turns out, that's because it wasn't a thing I created, but a place, that I cared about most." -Cadmus Errol

Home had become just a word. At best it was a memory, but it had no meaning as a real place anymore. The *Jennai* was a place for war, for camaraderie, for planning. It was no fit place to settle and feel cozy and warm, loved, safe, and familiar. There was purpose, responsibility, and anger in plenty. There was also a strangeness but not brought about by the place, but by the change in population.

Rynn of Eversall was General of the Human Rebellion, commander of all forces aboard the *Jennai* or acting afield in the name of the rebels. But alongside her was Madlin Errol, her twin from Tellurak, not native to Korr but there nonetheless. They shared one another's thoughts and memories as always, but there was no longer the distance of a world apart to separate awareness. She was just one among many such refugees from Tellurak and the now-deserted community of Tinker's Island They had come to Korr, twinborn and one-worlder alike, and now lived together in the ever-expanding airship.

The skies were clear and bright, but a storm raged below them. Never before her time aboard the *Jennai* had it occurred to Rynn that when the storm clouds gathered their fury, a pleasant sun still shone above them. The oddest thing was hearing the thunder under a clear sky above. Lightning flashed among the clouds well behind them, the sort that never made it to the ground. Each time the thunder arrived less quickly than the last as the storm drifted away until the low rumbles were drowned out by the crash of flesh and metal on the *Jennai's* central plaza.

The wide-flat stretch between the joined airships of the *Jennai* had become a tournament ground for the rowdier elements of the rebellion. Two crashball fields had been painted onto the steel plate floor, interwoven with the landing guide marks for the liftwings that used the plaza as an aerodrome. While the *Jennai* was at rest, fixed in a point in midair, six or more games would take place throughout the day. Spectators gathered along the sides of the plaza or looked out from the windows cut into the sides of the vacuum tanks that once kept the airships aloft. Now runes carved all over the vessel provided magical levitation to perform the same duty.

Rynn's suite overlooked both the plaza and the skies around them. She had moved up to the vacuum tanks of the front left ship—the original *Jennai*, named for her mother—and her quarters at the nose wrapped around left to right, with glassed windows giving her a panoramic view. Careful observation had shown her that even with the curtains open, glare prevented anyone seeing in from below.

Keeping a distracted eye toward the crashball match, she unpacked her latest creation.

The manufacturing facilities on the *Jennai* were limited. Despite salvaging everything of value from Tinker's Island, there was simply not enough room to install it all. Until they had a new landward base, most of it would remain in storage. But being a general gave her privilege and she took it. This was to be the fifth modification to her mechanical leg, each better suited to her than the last. Every iteration took a period of breaking in, of course, but after that, the designs grew sleeker, more compact, more responsive. The one problem that Rynn had yet to overcome was the persistent limp caused by the asymmetry of having one leg of flesh and one leg half mechanical.

This was her attempt to change that. Rynn removed her tinker's leg and set it aside in a rack by the bedside, joining its predecessors in obsolescence. With a damp cloth, she wiped away the sweat and grime that built up where the straps had covered her skin for days since the last time she'd removed it. Hobbling on one leg, she retrieved the latest model from its crate. This version had two legs. The left was like the prior models, an improvement here or there, but otherwise little different. The right was a hollowed shell, with reinforcements at each joint and similar arrangements of springs to cushion impacts and stabilize. Instead of making movements for a limb that was no longer there, it would amplify the leg she already had. Both legs were physically stronger than were her own, and now she had the means to balance the forces between left and right and stop lurching around the ship like—well, like a girl missing half a leg.

The whole arrangement slipped on with some difficulty. Rynn had grown accustomed to having one leg free to help orient and balance herself as she struggled to buckle on the lower bindings of the other. Instead, she had to fight with the tinker's legs moving as she twisted around to reach each buckle and clasp. She tried for several minutes before collapsing against the side of her bed to catch her breath.

"I can do this," she muttered. Much as she knew the truth of her statement, she questioned the cost. It might take her an hour to get everything into position, plus the possibility that the awkward contortions required would foul her initial adjustments to the straps.

Her determination was short lived because, as always, her thoughts were not solely her own. Madlin knew of her consternation. Rynn could not have hidden it from her twin if she tried. Madlin had just excused herself from watching over Cadmus's shoulder as the Mad Tinker searched for a suitable hideaway for their new base of operations. The old tinker was being obstinate about the selection; nothing less than perfection was going to suit him. Madlin knew she was unlikely to miss much, and Rynn knew it as well as if she had been standing there. In the same way, Madlin knew Rynn was sitting on the floor of her quarters flopping around in a pair of unruly legs that wouldn't buckle on.

Rynn settled in to wait, aware of Madlin's progress from the hull on the far side of the plaza, through the crashball field during a break in the action, and into the hull where Rynn awaited. If nothing else, the mutual awareness made impatience more palatable.

When Madlin arrived, there was no knock. She simply entered. Both of them knew she was there, and why. No greeting passed between them. Talking was pointless when they were thinking each other's thoughts, seeing through one another's eyes. In such proximity, there were just two minds inside a single space.

Madlin helped Rynn onto the edge of the bed and took the legs in hand one at a time, like a cobbler or a blacksmith fitting a shoe. She tightened each strap and marked the holes with an awl. She felt when each was pulled tight enough to balance comfort with responsiveness. Rynn wiggled each joint as needed, and once she was secured above the knees, Madlin helped her to her feet to stand with the wall for support. Madlin finished with the rest of the buckles and even the belt that came up around Rynn's midsection to join the two tinker's legs securely together. Rynn could have managed that last part herself, but Madlin was already there with tools in hand.

Had it been anyone else, even Sosha or Jamile, there would have been some sense of embarrassment. She was half-dressed, half-whole, exposing her weakness and deformity, her inability to so much as dress herself in the legs she had fashioned.

Rynn waited as Madlin installed the outer casings, protecting the inner mechanisms of both legs whether they were mechanical or living. When she finished, Rynn stood with arms outstretched to test her balance. It was hardly necessary. With practice of having done several modifications, she had grown accustomed to balancing on new legs and keeping the center of her mass still and steady. She eased herself into a crouch, testing the feel of her full leg against the half.

"Much better," Madlin said, echoing Rynn's thoughts.

"Stop that," Rynn scolded, though she knew it wouldn't dissuade Madlin in the least. She twisted around with her feet planted and fixed Madlin with a glare. "Don't I have some work to do?"

Madlin smirked. "I don't mind you snapping at me. It gets you out of my head for a few seconds."

Rynn looked down and ran a hand along the new covering for her good leg. "Thanks."

Madlin picked up a pair of baggy trousers. "Here, get yourself dressed." She tossed the garment to Rynn. It flew erratically, too loose and floppy for aerodynamic flight. Rynn lunged for it and stumbled, her movement not yet intuitive.

At the first surge of panic—the kind that accompanied any trip, no matter how minor—Madlin shot out an arm to steady Rynn. "I'll need practice before I walk around the ship."

"Just stay away from the edges for a few days," said Madlin.

"You won't get rid of me that easy."

There was no goodbye. They both knew that Madlin was departing, where she was heading, and why.

No man or woman, given five words to describe Cadmus Errol, would omit "brilliant"—or some derivative—among their count. Of those who knew him well, few would have failed to include "stubborn" or "obsessive." For eighteen hours each day at the least, he sat at the controls of the world-ripper machine. The chair that supported him had been purloined from the dining hall in the first-class section of the airship *Cloudsmith*, which was now the front right quadrant of the *Jennai*. The seat was cushioned velvet, upholstered in red. Over the long hours of his occupation, Cadmus had left the surface scuffed threadbare and imprinted with the contours of his backside. Anyone else chancing to find the seat in one of its infrequent moments of vacancy would find that it never quite felt right beneath them.

The fingers working the controls did so with no conscious thought. Cadmus's eyes rarely strayed from the viewing frame to the numbers around the dials, and if they did, it was only to mark them down when he found something of note. The desire to move the view translated itself in some corner of the tinker's brain—wherein some small mental machine had no doubt been constructed for that exact purpose—into the movements necessary to achieve that motion. The view sped over a barren plain, brown and scattered with rocky and dead scrub plants, traveling at speeds that nauseated most casual onlookers. But Cadmus had inured himself to the sensation of motion that came with staring through the lifelike window to other parts of the world. Or to other worlds. For now, the Mad Tinker was scouring Korr for suitable bases of operation, but he would look to Tellurak and Veydrus as well. A single-world solution put less strain on the dynamo that ran the world-ripper, making for more reliable transport and easier rescues should the need arise. There was always greater risk crossing worlds.

Cadmus paused the view and stretched, cracking his neck and flexing fingers held too long in the shape of a dial. Risk. Everything was a balance of risk and reward now. Every decision could be the one misstep that doomed the rebellion, just as one misstep had cost Erefan his life, leaving Cadmus without a twin. It was a game they were playing, but a deadly one. The location of their new headquarters had to be someplace where no one would look for them.

"Taking a break?" Madlin asked, sneaking up behind Cadmus mid-stretch. He shot a glare over his shoulder mid yawn. "Desolate pile of nothing, huh?"

"Eastern Lumberlands," Cadmus explained. "Off the tradeways from the western logging camps, picked over and abandoned."

"And nothing remotely like a place to build a workshop."

Cadmus grunted and started the viewer moving again. Madlin stood for a while, watching.

"I've had an idea, you know."

"What's that?" Cadmus asked.

"May I?" Madlin slid in beside him at the controls, crouching next to his seat.

Cadmus relinquished the controls with some hesitation. It was just Madlin, but he trusted so few others to touch the machine that a protectiveness came over him whenever someone tried. Madlin reached past him but adjusted only the angle of the view, not its location. In the evening sky of the Lumberlands, both sun and moon shared the sky in equal measure, neither at their brightest. She centered the moon in the view frame.

"Am I crazy?" she asked.

Cadmus furrowed his brow. "Probably. But what are you suggesting?"

"Who'd think to look for us there?"

"The moon? Do you have any idea how far away that little ball of rock is?"

Madlin nodded. "A lot closer than Tellurak."

"It's not as simple as that. The machine works on relative location. The moon is constantly moving. It would be a nightmare to keep steady enough to transport goods. Not only that, it's just a barren rock. It would be haloed in blue if it had air around it. There's no water, no animals; nothing can live there."

"I've got this all worked out...mostly," said Madlin. She took a pencil and a sheet of paper from the console—Cadmus always kept a supply close at hand—and began to sketch. "I've had plenty of time to think lately, and I've knocked this idea around in my head enough that it's got bruises. The moon moves, but astronomers know *exactly* how. They can predict its location years ahead of time. We can convert that to equations and from there to a mechanism to adjust the net location of the dials—build that right into the guts of the world-ripper."

"I suppose …" Cadmus allowed. Madlin took the lack of resistance as permission to plow ahead.

"There's probably no caverns since there was never flowing water to carve them. Instead, we steal an auger, a big mining one that barely fits through a world hole. We carve out a warren from this side, just sticking it through the hole and extracting the rock. We're over sea, so we just dump the rock overboard. Air's going to get sucked in from Korr but not enough to breathe."

"A minor problem," Cadmus muttered sarcastically.

"We've got three world-rippers in pieces, just waiting to install once you get off your arse and pick a spot for them. I plan to use all three. Two of them will stay open on a semi-permanent basis, on opposite ends of a canal we'll create, targeted a few inches apart and facing opposite directions in a river. We'll get fresh air from the top half, fresh water from the bottom. We'll wire fence the openings, so animals don't get through. The third world-ripper will keep to its normal function."

Cadmus's eyes went blank. Madlin knew the look. There were calculations going on within that skull, merits being assigned values and drawbacks being subtracted. Probabilities for any eventuality were assigned and factored into the equations. It was all rough math, but it was what kept the Mad Tinker ticking. He needed the numbers.

"Even if they think of the moon, he'll never find us," Cadmus murmured.

"It's settled then. Start planning the modifications to the machine. We're claiming the moon as our own."

Chapter 2

"If you are reading this, please tell them I am sorry." –Anonymous inscription, carved on the wall of a cavern beside a skeleton

Harsh spark light kept the gloom of darkness away from the caverns below the farthest reaches of northern Korr. The gloom of melancholy that had settled over the outpost was not so easily expunged. A contingent of thirty-five had manned the hidden facility, thirty-four kuduk and a single aging daruu. Now only five remained. A few had died in the ferocious assault that had taken them by surprise from the other world. The rest had succumbed to the deprivation that came with being stranded in a desolate wasteland of ice and rock. The caverns and the few pieces of heating equipment kept them warm enough, but nothing grew, nothing lived, above on the surface. The supplies that once had stocked the larder had dwindled to the point where even rationing was just a stalling tactic.

When the first day had passed with no aid, it had been discouraging. The first week brought desperation. The end of the first month had wrung the hope from the last of them, until only the hardiest remained.

"Would you stop that pacing?" Draksgollow snapped in a weary drawl. "You wring the strength from me just watching you."

Kezudkan ignored the request. The old daruu plodded around the idle machines and discarded tools of the outpost's workshop. With each step, his joints ground like a mortar and pestle.

Draksgollow raised his voice. "I said—"

"I heard you," said Kezudkan. "I just see no reason to heed you. It's your fault we're in this mess in the first place. If you'd engendered a smidgen of loyalty among your workforce, they'd have opened a world hole and retrieved us."

"Me? You're the one who had us attack that human settlement. We could have opened a hole, blasted their machine to scrap, and closed it. Done. Finished. Back to mining worlds for our fortune."

"And they'd have rebuilt, if we didn't kill off all Erefan's associates and destroy every copy of his production notes," Kezudkan countered. "Can you really be that shortsighted?"

"Shortsighted? Look what your brilliant planning has gotten us: starving at the top of the world, halfway past nowhere. Forgotten."

Kezudkan stopped in his footsteps and turned to regard Draksgollow. The half mechanical kuduk tinker had become a wretched thing. He slumped in his seat, a rotogun lying idle below a dangling hand, ready in case he decided to split the rations one way fewer. The fire had gone out of Draksgollow. His recriminations were bile and vitriol with no hint of resolve to lend them strength.

There was no point in answering. There had been no point in starting the argument in the first place, but it happened daily at the least. Draksgollow blamed Kezudkan. Kezudkan blamed Draksgollow. Each day there were fewer workers to overhear the bickering. One day Draksgollow himself would succumb, and the bickering would end. Perhaps today was that day. He certainly looked ready to give himself over to despair and let starvation win.

The thought that any of the kuduks would outlast him never occurred to Kezudkan. Old and infirm though he was, he was daruu. He was of the rock. Stronger and hardier than any kuduk could imagine, he would harden to stone before starvation ever took him. For while the foodstuffs they had stocked for the outpost had been for everyone, the stone itself could sustain Kezudkan for some time. It was a hollow nourishment, no better than broth, though much more substantive in the belly. But it kept the pangs away, if not the craving for real food. It also accelerated Kezudkan's ossification. His ancient joints wanted nothing more than to cease their lifelong toil and rest in one position, and his diet of nothing but stone only sped the process. Still, it was better than the gnawing feeling of his own guts devouring him from within, as the kuduks must have been feeling.

And so, to keep the ossification at bay, Kezudkan paced.

Hours passed uncounted. The fitful rage of a hunger-mad worker had smashed the only working clocks. The unchanging illumination of the spark lights made the caverns a monotonous prison. There were old mining tunnels to meander along, a whole workshop to tinker in, a surface world to explore. But facing the approach of death, tedium with companionship was preferable, even if that companionship was surly and bitter.

The mind was capable of many tricks. The want of something could make it appear before you when your mind oozed its way free of brain flesh. The desert heat was notorious for mirages, as were the trackless waves known for beguiling sailors adrift at sea. Hunger could put ideas in a man's mind just as surely. Kezudkan knew these facts, and so it was with a scientific dispassion that he beheld the first signs of his own madness.

A shimmering spark crackled briefly in the air before splitting wider and forming a hole in the middle of the workshop. Through it, Kezudkan saw the factory where Draksgollow's machinists had been working on a new world-ripper before their present misadventure had thrown their plans through a sausage-processor.

Kezudkan glanced away and continued his pacing. Dementia be dratted, he refused to be wrung free of his senses so easily.

"You see that?" Draksgollow asked from his chair.

That was enough to give Kezudkan a sniff of hope. "I might."

"Hullo in there?" a harsh voice whispered through the world-hole. "Come on, we haven't got lots of time."

Kezudkan steered his pacing more purposefully, aiming his ambling waddle for the world-hole, delusion or no. "Who's there?"

"Anvernus, sir. We've had a bit of trouble getting to you. Just get through quick and we'll explain."

Draksgollow stirred in his chair, but failed to rise. The steamworks that kept half of him animate had cooled and could not be restored to functioning without repair. "He'll need a carry," said Kezudkan. "I'm in no condition."

Avnernus shouted to others on his side, and three kuduk workers hustled through, tucking away pistols in their belts and vest as they came.

"What's this all about?" Draksgollow asked as his workers hoisted him to his feet. He dangled limply from their shoulders.

Kezudkan did not wait for any answer. Whatever the reason for the furtive, armed rescue, he preferred to deal with it from the civilized side of the world hole. He stepped through and into the welcoming dimness of Draksgollow's workshop.

"This wasn't a majority decision, sir," said Arvernus. "But we want things back the way they were."

"Just what's been—"

"There's no time, sir," Arvernus snapped. There was a hunted look in his eyes. Kezudkan stepped away from the world hole and backed himself against the control console of the machine. The cane that was his constant companion found its way into a sword-like grip in Kezudkan's hand.

"It's night," said Kezudkan. "This isn't working hours. What's going on?"

"There's no time," said Arvernus. The kuduk worker stared through the world hole as Draksgollow was dragged through. He moved to the controls and put a hand to the switch that would shut off the machine.

"There are three more still back there," Kezudkan noted dryly. He suspected by Arvernus's manner that no delay would be forthcoming. "Just a couple chambers down the main tunnel."

"There's no—"

"No time, yes, I know the refrain," said Kezudkan. "But we're saved now. It seems that whatever problem you're having with the machine, we can remedy them should anyone else be stranded."

"It's not the machine. It's Tolby."

"Tolby?" Draksgollow discovered newfound strength of voice as he heard the name. His bearers carried him through into the Cavinstraw Deep workshop but did not set him down immediately. They kept him on their shoulders and carried him onward, heading for the far exit of the workshop.

"He's taken over since Mr. Draksgollow has been gone," said Arvernus. He pulled the switch, and the machine no longer bridged the span of over half of Korr. He pulled another, and the room went dark as the world-ripper did. "We've got rooms in the city. We'll get you there. Don't worry."

"This Tolby fellow, he live in the worker barracks?" Kezudkan asked.

Arvernus shook his head. "He's taken over Mr. Draksgollow's suite."

"Well, then," said Kezudkan, setting the tip of his cane firmly against the floor. "It looks like I'll be having a word with Mr. Tolby." He trundled off down a different corridor from the one the workers were using to carry off Draksgollow.

"No," Arvnernus whispered harshly. "We'll regroup, come back in force." Kezudkan ignored him. After several more entreaties, the loyalist kuduk gave up and attended to his employer, leaving Kezudkan free to roam the halls.

Despite his apparent rashness, the old daruu was far from reckless. There was no tell-tale clop of cane as he walked, not any great sound from his heavy footfalls. The stone of the halls gave way like wet sand beneath his tread; the tip of his cane left shallow indentations. Kezudkan's old ears were a poor judge, but he doubted anyone behind a door would hear him approach.

The worker barracks were a warren of free rooms provided to Draksgollow's more miserly workers, who preferred a few saved coins a month to respite from their workplace. Never one to show interests outside his business, Draksgollow lived nestled among them, though in finer accommodations. The halls were plain stone, worked with a desire to remove obstruction, not create anything of beauty. It was not a distinction that the kuduk drew, but Kezudkan saw no reason that the creation of a simple passageway had to have been ugly. It was a simple matter of finesse with the stone that came intuitively to the daruu.

It was that intuition that Kezudkan was counting upon. As he ambled down the corridor, he paused at each door. All of them had frames made of grey-painted steel set into the stone wall. With a gentle hand, Kezudkan wiped at the rock, causing it to flow and shift like clay over the door handle of each door. By the time he reached the end of the corridor, every other door in the barracks was sealed shut.

Kezudkan took a moment to ponder his entrance. Trying the handle, he found the door locked. The steel was no finer than the rest of the doors along the corridor, but like those others it was solid and thick, at least an inch of metal barring his way. He nodded. Putting a hand to the stone beside the door, he felt his way inside, to the heart of the stone. Would it mind, kindly, removing itself from his way? The stone was only too happy to comply. It receded from the steel frame holding the door in place like a sea at low tide. With the tip of his cane, Kezudkan toppled the door inward.

The crash of metal on stone was fit to wake statues. The room's occupant gave a wordless cry and scrambled upright in his bed. A paltry light from the corridor back-lit Kezudkan. His own shadow hid the kuduk's features from him.

"Get out of here!" the kuduk shouted. "Who are you?"

Kezudkan was already lumbering over the fallen door and closing the distance to the kuduk traitor. The kuduk lunged over the edge of his bed, but Kezudkan's cane caught him on the way down, barring him across the collarbone. Feeling under the edge of the bed with a boot toe, the old daruu fumbled with something concealed there and finally kicked a rifle into the light.

"Is this what you were after?" Kezudkan asked. He pointed to the rifle. The kuduk made a stretch to get around the obstructing cane, and Kezudkan made no move to stop him. Instead, he rested a foot atop the weapon. When the kuduk's fingers tried to pry it from the floor, the rifle might well have been bolted to the stone.

"It's you. How'd you get back?"

"I swam," Kezudkan replied. "How is it that you thought you inherited this place when we had an equipment failure? You were *supposed* to have opened a world-hole and brought us back. Even if I hadn't heard him tell you in no uncertain terms, you ought to have been clever enough to figure that part out for yourself."

"I just ... I mean ... I can explain everything."

Kezudkan lifted his cane, along with the kuduk draped over it. He deposited Tolby into Draksgollow's bed and used the tip of the cane at the kuduk's throat to hold him down. "Oh, I think I understand without requiring explanation. You thought you could dispose of us, take everything for your own, and be as rich as we'd planned to be. Admit it."

The kuduk gave a sickly smile, lost in the scraggle of an unkempt beard. "No hard feelings, I hope, Mr. Kezudkan?"

Kezudkan pressed down. Tolby gagged and clutched at the cane with both hands. Just as it seemed that the kuduk would free himself from the cane's crushing tip, Kezudkan leaned into it. The gagging turned horrible, the kuduk frantic. "No. None at all."

After a moment, the kuduk fell limp. Kezudkan gave a final shove, then allowed the cane to return to its normal duties. With no further need for stealth, he clopped his way back to the door, pausing momentarily at a tray of last night's dinner leftovers. There was a half a fruit tart remaining. Though there was no pride in the act, Kezudkan broke away a corner that bore no tooth marks and shoved it into his mouth.

"Best I've had in weeks," he muttered to himself as he went to find himself something to go with his snack.

Chapter 3

"A newspaper is ten percent bitter truth, with a thick candy coating of comforting lies." –Ed. L.T Stratta of the Eversall Deep Herald, in a letter left to his son

The public house smelled of ale and fire-blackened beef, overpowering the smoke from the lamps that kept the dark of the deeps at bay. The walls were irregular, with slathered on plaster coating rough raw stone beneath. The jags and nooks cast strange shadows in the lamp light, but they seemed quaint rather than sinister. Raucous laughter broke out often over the constant murmur of jumbled voices. Stories passed over tables of friends packed so tightly together that lifting an elbow required the cooperation of a neighbor. The crowd at The Bearded Man was in a boisterous mood.

A thin lad, dressed in a brown coat with sleeves too short for his arms, squeezed his way among the tables with the skill of an aleman. A few called out to him from tables he passed, and he suffered good-natured grief for the jostling he caused along his path. Kupe was known. It was all anyone needed in The Bearded Man.

"How's it, Kupe?" a man asked. He was black haired and sweaty, with a grin that was missing a tooth in front.

"Smellin' sweet, Mull. Wrap your eyes around this," said Kupe. He slapped a newspaper down onto the table. Everyone at the table stared at the picture of an aerodrome hangar with no airships.

"Nice one, kid. What's it say?" Mull asked.

Kupe could read a bit but relied on what he had heard secondhand. "This here's the Glenwood Gazetteer. 'Bout a month old now, but lookie that there aerodrome. Heisted it good, it says. Knocks didn't like it, so they hushed it up, but the papers got word out."

"Davlin sent you to rub our noses in it?"

"Somethin' like that," said Kupe. He stuck a shoulder in between two older freemen and wedged himself into a spot on the bench across from Mull. "Wanted me to remind you about your bet."

Mull shook his head. "Ain't that easy."

"You're just rustin' up cuz you ain't never thought we'd get proof."

"Proof?" Mull scoffed. He smacked the paper with the back of his hand. "A flashpop of some building in a sky, lotsa letters we can't neither of us read. Go hammer screws."

Kupe frowned at Mull but saw no slack in Mull's sweat-glistened face. He was still sober, without enough ale in him to make him either belligerent or gullible.

There was no trick of wordplay Kupe knew to push or pull Mull where Kupe needed him to go. "Charsi!" Kupe shouted. He half stood from his seat and craned his neck to scan the crowd. "Charsi, come here a minute."

A head popped up, turning this way and that to see where the call had come from. Charsi was young, with the milk-white complexion that certain among the deep dwellers developed from a lack of sun. Her eyes were the color of the sky, the closest that most of the regulars at The Bearded Man got to seeing real blue; they browsed the patrons with a practiced glance. Kupe held up an arm, and she nodded in his direction and stood. With a gentle slap on the shoulder or a murmured word, patrons squirmed and leaned to clear a path for the girl. After all, she owned the pub.

Sidling up to Kupe, she slid an arm around his shoulder and kissed him atop the head. "Welcome home, Kupe."

"Thanks." Kupe blushed but otherwise kept coy. He gestured to the newspaper on the table. "Mind readin' this for us simple folk?"

Charsi frowned down at him. "You know your letters."

"Not in front of everyone," he whispered from the side of his mouth. "I ain't got an hour to read it to 'em."

Charsi rolled her eyes but picked up the paper anyway. " 'Rebels attack aerodrome,' says the headline. 'A brazen, daring heist resulted in the loss of eight single-seat liftwings, a twenty-crew battle liftwing, and a vacu-dirge.' Wow, that's something now, ain't it? 'Official reports are mum on casualties, but witnesses who spoke to Gazetteer reporters on condition of a-no-nym-it-y'—bloody kuduks and their fifty-tenar words—'claim that at least thirty soldiers from the garrison were killed, and the crew of the battle liftwing lost.'"

"Oil and fire," Mull muttered.

"Believe me now?" Kupe asked. "Thanks, Charsi."

"You can thank me proper over a drink after closing," Charsi replied. She put him in a headlock and squeezed affectionately. "Been worried nights over you. Davlin put you up to that trip?"

"Wasn't a put-up job. I volunteered. Ain't like it was real danger, just a bit of freeman travel. I had tickets whole way out and back. Real proper."

"Thinkin' the knocks wouldn't like seein' that paper you brought back with you."

"That they wouldn't," said Mull. "They'd have sniffed trouble, and they'd have been right to."

"He's right, Kupe. Davlin's a trouble-brewer," said Charsi "Couldn't make a machine does it better than him."

"Come down to the church with me tonight. I'm sure he can change your minds, both of you."

"You know how to sweet-talk a girl," Charsi replied dryly. "You know I can't be leaving this place to run itself. I trust my folk with the till, but they'll run this place right off the tracks if I'm not around."

Kupe put an arm around Charsi's waist and pulled her around to face him. With so many eyes around, he played at being a proper gentleman and kept his own eyes high, though she was a full head higher than him while he sat. He slipped a finger under the string of a necklace she kept concealed and tugged it free for all to see. It was little more than twine with a plain copper ring as its only adornment. It was an old tradition, but it was a mourning keepsake for the kin of freemen lost to slavery. "Davlin makes the kind of trouble that'll get your pa free one day. Ain't that worth a night off to go listen to him?"

"Davlin's gone off his nutter, boy. Gunk he's spewin' ain't even proper for a priest to be thinkin'."

Charsi ignore the comment. "All right, Kupe. Just for a little while."

No church of Eziel was kept in grand style. Cuminol Deep's was converted from a failed mine that had been rerouted down other tunnels, leaving several short shafts abandoned. Human slaves had carved the tunnels, and the priests had left the bare, ugly work of their downtrodden flock unchanged after the miners moved on. To them, it symbolized the struggles that so many humans faced. It also saved a good deal of coin on hiring masons.

The guards at the door had let Kupe pass with merely a nod. He was known. He was also a friend of Davlin. Mull and Charsi met no resistance either, for Mull was a thunderail coalman and well respected among the deepers of Cuminol, and Charsi was known to every man with a taste for ale. It was a church guard's duty to know what faces belonged to the devout, to the loyal, and to the shaver. Some just made their work easier than others.

Inside, the tunnels buzzed with conversation as worshipers filed in to find seats. The main tunnel crossing stood as the hub of the church, with a low dais meant not to elevate the priest at sermon, but to allow his voice to carry over the rows of eager ears. Kupe led Mull and Charsi past the altar and dais, giving a nod to Davlin as he stood watching over the incoming flock. They picked their way through the crowd and found seats down one of the side tunnels. The benches were plain steel, shin high, and kept well-scrubbed and free of rust by the initiates.

"I had no idea so many folk came to sermons," Charsi whispered as she settled herself to Kupe's right.

Kupe lifted his palms. "Well, here they are. Not everyone makes it down to the pub, and most of the ones that do ain't regulars here. You get the gossip and the gripes. No offense, but you're the drain where folk dump the slop from their souls. This is where you get filled back up with hope."

Mull grunted, eavesdropping from the far side of Kupe. "Liked him better when he stuck to takin' alms and buyin' bread with it."

Kupe shushed him and pointed toward the dais.

The crowd quieted as Pious Davlin took his place in view of all. He wore plain spun robes dyed brown and with a hand-make look to them. Conversations died away and all eyes turned in his direction. Davlin was no imposing figure, bald atop and greying at the temples, stoop-shouldered with his eyes cast down. He wore a beard—as any good human grew—close-cropped and flecked with grey.

"I see more faces than last week," Davlin said, his voice echoing down the silent tunnels. His face spread in a smile. "You're spreading the word. Good. Hope is still the strongest weapon we have. But hope alone will not be enough. Soon, we will need the sort of weapons that spill blood." There was a low murmur from the crowd. Davlin raised his voice. "This day is long in coming. We have waited under foot and boot, bent with the weight of our enemies bearing down upon us. Our people are rising. We have found the strength and are beginning to stand up, not to squirm from under those boots but to throw them from us.

"Look to your left and to your right. Those are your brothers and sisters. We are all kin. We will stand together, united against our common foe. Cuminol must also look to its north and south, to its east and west, above ground and below. In every city, there are more of our kind, freemen and slaves alike. They are our brothers and sisters also. They are our kin. Their fight is our fight, and they have already begun to fight back. In Ruttania and Grangia, the forces of freedom have begun to take back what was stolen so, so long ago."

There was a rumbling in the crowd in the silence that followed. Davlin let it percolate for a minute and more before he continued. "I hear the questions you ask among yourselves. What was taken? How do we fight back? I am not a soldier, what can I do? I will tell you ..."

Davlin delved into history then, speaking from the old texts, long kept hidden by the priests and priestesses of Eziel. He told the stories of the great wars with demons and dragons, fey creatures and followers of black-hearted gods. At length he told of the struggles against the daruu, the last remaining threat to mankind after all the other wars had been won. The rise of the kuduks was a great surprise to many. Kupe smirked as he picked from the crowd those who were attending their first sermon since Davlin had dredged up the old texts and read from them again. To think of a kuduk as nothing more than the bastard children of humans and daruu cast them in a wholly new light. They seemed less the superior people and more the ungrateful children of the elder races. Lastly, Davlin spoke of the great war, of the defeat of mankind and the supplanting of the daruu.

"It is time to remember old ways. We have grown numerous and strong. Under the light of Eziel's gentle teachings, we have persevered when we might have been forgiven a loss of faith. We have bottled our anger instead of letting it drip and leak from us in pointless small revolts. It is time to remember the Eziel that strode beside us into battle, the one whose teachings are sharp enough to draw blood. Join hands and speak the invocation with me:

"Lord Eziel, grant us vengeance upon our enemies. Let us share our strength as comrades and become fearsome to our foes. I am your servant, teach me to kill in your name."

The congregation murmured along, many silent because they did not know the words. Davlin repeated them, and a few new voices joined in. The chorus grew louder the third time as the words sank in, and the newcomers began to absorb them. Kupe felt his heart pump. To his left, Mull clung to his hand with a man-shy timidity, still seeming self-conscious. To his right, Charsi's hand was slick with sweat, trying to squeeze the blood from his fingers. By the time Davlin repeated the invocation a fifth time, the tunnels thundered with the voices of the worshipers, new and old alike.

"Here we cleanse our hearts and gird our souls for battle. Outside these walls, let none know our heart or purpose. The time draws near. You will each be given your part to play. Go in peace and brotherhood."

A heady crowd rose unsteadily and began sorting themselves out the doors of the church. Kupe had heard the invocation enough times that he kept it in his heart, not to be carried off each time he heard Davlin speak it anew. He helped Charsi to her feet and waited for Mull to collect himself.

"I had no idea," said Charsi. She clung to Kupe's arm as if she'd imbibed too much from her own wares.

"It gets in you, that's for sure," Kupe said, helping her pick her way among the benches. "We can talk more later when it's quiet."

"But I've got so many questions."

Kupe nodded. He caught her eyes with his own and held them briefly, men and women pushing past the pair as they stood idle in the flow of foot traffic. There was a fervency there, a hope blossoming like a color-petal plant from the skies. He could hardly wait to see her again later. But business pressed. "I'll see you to the door, but Mull and I have some things to discuss with Pious Davlin."

"What sort of things?"

Kupe grinned at Mull, who stood uncomfortably waiting for the pair to say their goodbyes. "Mull's our new inside man at the thunderails."

At the back of the farthest reaches of the back tunnel of the church, another couple sat. To all appearances they waited for the crowd to thin before pressing through, but they were no natives of Cuminol, nor any other place in Korr.

"Quite the speech. Gets the blood running hot," said Juliana. She wore a plain wool dress dyed grey as stone and straight from the seamstress. It was less apparent when she sat, but she towered over the Korrish women. The tallest she had met only came as high as her nose.

"I take it you followed along? I didn't hear you chanting the invocation," Kyrus replied. He wore a workman's coveralls, but had at least taken the trouble to rub them with grime to make it looked as if he worked. Though well taller than Juliana, men Kyrus's size were not uncommon among the stock-bred humans, though he was thinner of limb than the crashball players and heavy laborers that were common among the very large.

Juliana shrugged. "Sure. Easier reading the stuff than listening to it, but daruu isn't so bad to pick up. So, you going to join the rebellion, be a hero?"

Kyrus shot her a glare that would have had a sensible creature soiling itself. Juliana just snickered. "I'm no hero. Look at what these people are doing? They have nothing—or at least very little. Yet here they are, ready to stand up and fight against the people who control the whole world."

"You could make it easier on them."

"I could sully their victory, steal away their purpose and resolve, let them remain soft and beaten, but under a kinder master. No. There were real heroes in this crowd. I don't know who they were—they don't even know yet themselves—but someone here will shape a new future for our kind."

"Their kind. They're really not *our* kind anymore."

Kyrus sighed. "No, I suppose not. Our kind are enough of a problem as it is. I'm not going to worry about them today, though."

"Will they listen?"

Kyrus gestured to the church around them "I wish they could have listened to *this*. But they'll listen to me. I won't leave them a choice."

Chapter 4

"It takes a thick skull to play crashball. You start lettin' ideas into your head; you might think twice about playing at all." - Gemno ("Hayfield"), star sweeper for the Steam Rats Crashball Squad

"Lord Eziel, grant us vengeance upon our enemies. Let us share our strength as comrades and become fearsome to our foes. I am your servant; teach me to kill in your name."

Rynn spoke the words along with everyone else on the plaza, in a slow chant so that all the voices merged together into a single sound, far greater than any long voice could have managed. It was more than symbolic; it was demonstrative. The Human Rebellion was more than individuals. Pious Rascal, who Rynn could never seem to think of him as Henlon, kept his emphasis on the communal purpose being what would bring them victory. Rynn knew that it was helpful, but she suspected that coil guns and other rune-tech were going to prove the difference in the end.

"Rise, and part as brethren," Rascal said, his voice carrying over a crowd that had fallen silent at the final word of the invocation. "We have the work of Eziel to attend."

Rynn levered herself up from one knee, the posture everyone on the plaza had taken during Rascal's sermon. The supports in the tinker's legs made the kneeling easier on her than on probably anyone else in the rebellion. It hardly felt different than standing. With the springs and air pistons helping, the rise was cumbersome but not taxing in the least.

The crowd began to thin immediately. Most of the rebels had duties to resume. There was still construction going on over most of the ship. With every added floor inside the old vacuum tanks, the crowding in the crew quarters lessened. The liftwing hangars were taking shape, both in ease of use and in readiness to launch in haste. The cramped workshops cut through walls and set up more of the equipment that had been salvaged from Tinker's Island. The *Jennai* was a great clockwork beast, being built from the inside out.

But not everyone had duties that pressed, and those who had odd tasks went about those as well. Certain idle and rowdy rebels loitered on the plaza, waiting for it to clear. After all, the plaza was painted with the boundary lines for two crashball pitches. The would-be player shifted nervously, trying to avoid the eye of their general as she watched them linger. A few guilty souls took themselves to find some useful occupation instead of waiting until they were among the lonely few left to explain why they hadn't left the plaza.

Rynn took a quick count of the remaining rebels. "Sides of nine, friendly touch, no tackling," she called out. Those who had been taking care to study the sky or gaze up at the windows of the vacuum tanks suddenly realized that their general meant to play. Rynn felt exposed standing in the midst of a group of her troops, out of place for the first time she could remember aboard the *Jennai.* Every one of the players seemed clipped from newspaper flashpops of crashball matches. Tall, broad, muscular, they exuded a jovial violence just milling around waiting for a match.

"I bet we could round up better than that for a friendly," Hayfield shouted over from the sidelines. He was among a number of well-wishers who clung to the games but didn't get involved. He drew eyes away from Rynn as he crossed the painted lines that separated prospective players from spectators. With a solid decade over the next oldest player in the plaza, his arrival signaled a change in the tone of the game. A few other hangers on slipped over the barrier of white paint that might as well have been a chain fence just moments earlier. Too young, too small, too timid, or too female, these others had found reason to steer clear of the miners, soldiers, and freight handlers who dominated most matches. Now they joined Hayfield and Rynn with the prospect of a gentler game.

"C'mon, old timer," one of the barrel-shaped lads complained. "We need to steam off a little. Can't be havin' kids and girls out here."

"There's two pitches painted," Rynn said. "We can have a game of each. We can play friendly here, and you boys can knock each other's teeth out on the other."

A certain sort of lad never liked to be compromised with. There was a bit of a bully in many of them that liked when they could bull and bluster their way over obstacles, getting their own way. Such a lad might have been inclined to tell a girl of nineteen years and half his size that she could well clear off his pitch and take over the free one. A slightly smarter sort remembered that he would be arguing with his general, a woman who could order him to the fore of a charge, have him tossed off the ship, or just shoot him herself. It wouldn't have been the first time she'd done it.

The lad nodded. "Awright." He jerked his head toward the other pitch and led his goons to the other playing field.

Her goons. As much as Rynn looked down on their oafish antics, those goons were soldiers of hers, the sort who could brawl with kuduks—knockers or militia—and win. If they haunted the plazas and the bars aboard the *Jennai* in their off hours, it was a small price to pay when it was time to raid.

Someone tossed Rynn a crashball, and she juggled it before latching on and taking hold of it. It was an oblong leather-wrapped ovoid with a wood core and a layer of wool padding between. Rynn had only handled one a few times in her life. She was no athlete. The only serious attempt she'd made to play crashball was a children's game in the tunnels of Eversall Deep when she was eight. She'd ended up with scraped knees, a twisted finger, and a bloody nose. Ever since then, she had steered clear of the game.

They ended up with twenty-four players. Rynn and Hayfield took captaincy and chose sides. As they took turns picking, Rynn wondered just how late she would have been picked if she wasn't on a team by default. She certainly wouldn't have picked herself (or Madlin, had she been among the candidates) over anyone waiting to be selected.

Once the two teams had been selected, they flipped a five-gorm to see who would take the ball first. Hayfield flipped, and Rynn called 'sky' before it landed—sky-side up. Hayfield's squad huddled up in their half of the pitch and prepared to kick away to Rynn's.

Rynn and her team spread out in their half, ready for wherever the kicked crashball headed. "Let's have a nice clean one, everyone. No broken bones. You might need one of theirs backing you up with a coil gun in hand someday soon. Keep that in mind when you're tempted to tackle."

Hayfield handled the kick himself. There was a dull thud as his boot connected with the ball, sending it tumbling end over end into, arcing through the air into Rynn's half. Rynn saw a parabolic arc in negligible wind. She figured its flight at landing somewhat shy of a symmetrical arc, accounting for wind resistance. It wasn't heading her way but over her head and to her right. She bounced on her tinker's legs to get ready to spring into action once someone fielded the kick.

There was a slap and a thud as a skinny lad tried to catch the kick, and it bounced off his hands to the plaza. The oblong shape made predicting bounces nearly impossible. Four of Rynn's players scrambled to corral the crashball as Hayfield's team barreled down on them. Had they been playing full contact, a flubbed catch on the kick was a prelude to carnage as both teams fell on it like packs of wolves. In a friendly, Rynn took up her duty trying to block the path of her opponents, knowing they had to avoid body to body contact.

The sight of a man bearing down on her kept Rynn hunkered down and ready to spring away. He was mechanic in his coveralls, and not nearly the size of the players who'd opted for the rough game, but more than Rynn could have fended off had he wanted to bowl her over. She kept her arms out in front of her, elbows slightly bent as she'd seen other players do and wondered if she ought to have lugged a few more sacks of wheat flour in her life. There was no tool to help her, nothing but her own flesh against her opponent's. In that moment she saw the appeal—for those lads with arms like thunderail pistons. Strip away the money and artifice, and you were left with animal combat. Of course, there were rules to keep it civil, but Rynn had always relied on wit and tinkered machines over brute force. As Hayfield's team closed in, the plaza shook under their feet. Instinct told Rynn to take cover, to dive out of the way and bring her arms up to protect her head. The arms stretched out to take an impact drew closer and closer to her body.

The mechanic veered aside. Rynn knew her job was to sidestep and block him off, force him even farther out of his way, but she leaned away from him instead. *The legs can't move laterally that fast.* It was an excuse for later, nothing she believed. Another of Hayfield's players brushed by to her left. Rynn spared a glance over her shoulder and saw that her squad had recovered the ball and were passing it back and forth to keep it away from the onrush of opponents. It was a peculiarity in the friendly game that would never have stood up in full contact. Forced to go around one another, Rynn's players kept Hayfield's at bay simply by forcing them off their intended path, tossing the ball to a free teammate when the opponents got too near. Played so wide and loose in a contact game, one team or the other would have knocked a path clear to score or steal before long.

Rynn looked to Hayfield's side of the pitch and saw that only two players had stayed back as safeties. No one was paying her much mind either. She took two hopping strides to get a feel for the plaza floor, then raised an arm and waved to her team. "To me!"

It had been the thing to do. She was no great fanatic of crashball, but she knew the call. She said it without much thought to what would follow. The teammate with the ball heeded her. Whether his general's voice held some thrall over him, whether he took pity on the left-out player, or whether he naively believed in her ability to score, the ball lofted her way. The oblong crashball wobbled through the air with the narrow ends to the sides, like it was trying to paddle a canoe. Players from both teams turned to watch its flight and to follow its course. Rynn was suddenly the center of attention of twenty-three other players.

Rynn judged the ball in flight and shuffled her feet to position herself under it. She tried to ignore the pounding boots growing closer by the second and kept her attention skyward, on the little glint of open air between the *Jennai's* forward vacuum tanks. It hung in the air for hours, it seemed, growing larger rather than nearer. *Too fast. Step aside.* Fielding the ball on a bounce was a dice roll as she saw with the kick. She had to try.

"Oomph."

The ball hit Rynn in the chest, and she cradled it against her body as it knocked the breath from her lungs. To her credit, she held it tight and regained her composure before looking to see how close the pursuit had come. Too close.

Rynn tried to twist, but the bulk of the tinker's legs made it into the movement of a compass—one point stabbed into the paper as the other swung in an arc. Once she got her legs lined up, it was time to field test them. She ran. All the joints of the legs were spring stabilized, which was nice for stopping the momentum of the heavy steel mechanisms, but it was also meant to store energy on the move. She couldn't manage the churning piston run of a normal human sprint but bounded like a two-legged deer once she worked out the gait after three steps. Higher and higher she bounced with each stride, longer and longer each bound until she reached the limit of what her muscles could manage with the load of the springs. The two player's Hayfield's squad kept back took an optimist's angle to cut off her charge and found themselves left in Rynn's wake as she sped between them like they were statues.

She heard the shouts of encouragement as her own teammates broke off pursuit and cheered her on. There was no one to stop her from crossing the score line. She pressed on, full steam ahead until she reached the far painted line of the pitch and broke into an exultant grin as she scored.

Slowing proved to be a different matter. Rynn eased off her sprint, but forward momentum carried her onward. At each bounding stride, the springs in the tinker's legs returned much of her kinetic energy to her. Leaning back to ease up, she felt her balance faltering and stumbled to catch herself.

The edge of the ship. It was too close. The *Jennai* was massive, with the plaza running the full length of the ship, but it was still finite. And Rynn had rediscovered that fact in alarming fashion. There were no safety rails or nets at the end of the plaza; its core function was as an aerodrome, not a sporting stadium. Even non-tinkers have a sense of certain applications of physics, quick scratchwork within the brain that tells them how to aim a rifle or catch a crashball. Rynn's internal scratchwork needed neither her exact velocity nor her distance to the edge of the airship to tell her she was about to pitch headlong into the sky.

The only way Rynn foresaw went against her body's preservation instincts. It became a test of will; her instincts told her to keep herself from falling to the unforgiving steel of the plaza against the reasoning that it would hurt far less than a fatal fall from above the clouds. Rynn let the crashball tumble from her hands and braced herself as she put her feet together and used the muscles in her foot to catch a toe on the plaza floor. She felt the instant panic of falling, putting her arms out to cushion her fall. Rune-balanced for weight though they may have been, her tinker's legs still carried their mass like the steel constructs they were. Rynn slammed face-first to the ground, dragged down by the mass of her legs to hit far harder than she'd have liked.

Rynn's arms did nothing to cushion her impact as far as she noticed. She blacked out as she hit the plaza's edge, just a few feet from empty air. What could only have been seconds later, she blinked her eyes open, feeling the blood gushing from her broken nose.

The crashball wobbled along and plummeted over the side.

Madlin cringed and held her hands to her nose.

"What's wrong? Rock catch you?" Cadmus shouted over the grating of the auger and its steam engine. The auger's bit reached through the open world-hole and into the guts of Korr's moon. It dumped moon gravel into a chute that ran down into a newly cut hole in the bottom of the *Jennai*, dumping the extramundial stone debris into the Sea of Kerum in a fine shower.

"No," Madlin replied. She was standing by the head of the auger, but she was wearing goggles and helmet, and none of the large fragments were being ejected in her direction. "Rynn's a clumsy idiot is all." She checked a counter on the side of the auger, the numbered dials each turning slower than the one to its right. "Stop there! Three hundred twenty-five feet, two inches. You went over a bit."

"We'll deal with the variance," said Cadmus. Madlin was possibly the only one alive who could pick the sarcasm out of his assurance. They were within a twentieth of a percent of their target length for the pass. The auger kept running, but the noise cut down sharply as Cadmus pulled the world-ripped back the way it came. The auger scraped the edges of the hole it had cut, but was otherwise spinning idly.

Madlin clutched at her elbow as she watched the numbers reverse, counting back toward the zero mark where they'd begun the tunnel. She tried to hold up the sketched plans for the lunar hideaway, but sharp pains in her arm kept her from bending it properly. Sharp *imaginary* pains, she knew, but they were troubling her no less for it.

"She hurt badly?"

Madlin gritted her teeth. "Still has all the parts she had this morning." She could feel the eyes on her, though Madlin and Cadmus were alone in the world-ripper room. Guards had been posted to keep work on the lunar expansion under wraps. Its actual location was to be a secret shared only by the two of them. The actual eyes were on Rynn. Curious, gawking eyes, too scared of doing wrong to do anything of use for her. They were all just waiting for Jamile or Sosha to show up and do the work for them.

Rynn stumbled into her room in a daze and slammed the door behind her. She'd ordered her way free of Sosha's ministrations as soon as she'd wrung out an admission that she was in no more immediate danger. The loss of blood had made her lightheaded along with the blow to the head itself. She had a welt where the side of her forehead had struck, and a bandage wrapped tightly around her face, packing her nose with gauze to set the break. Her left arm was splinted and swollen; Sosha said she'd have to wait for the swelling to subside but was fairly certain it was broken. Numerous scrapes and friction burns stung from antiseptics. Bloody Eziel, even her chest hurt from the impact of the rusted crashball.

It seemed the only part of her that came through unscathed were her legs. Armored in the tinker's legs, she hadn't gotten so much as a scratch or bruise on them. So all in all, a successful field test followed by an unforeseen disaster attributable to user error, not design.

"Bet you wish you knew a shielding spell about now, huh?" Dan asked.

Rynn flinched and snapped her head to see what Dan was doing in her quarters. Mistake. Rynn squeezed her eyes shut against the dizziness and waves of pain from moving her head too fast.

"Wud you want?" she demanded, her voice muddy by the bandage over her nose.

"Some trick with those legs. I saw the whole thing from up here."

"How long you been up here?"

"I watched that little festival in the plaza," Dan said with a shudder. "Nice cult you've got there. Not my style, worshiping dead gods."

"Wud you know 'bout gods?" Rynn was too weary to throw Dan out or yell for guards—what little good those might do—so she sat herself down on the bed and hoped to get the conversation over with.

"I probably believe in Eziel more than you do," said Dan, "but the gods are long gone. I mean, thousands of winters gone. Whatever gets you rebels off your arses and fighting again though, right? But that's not why I'm here. I want to know when you're sending me back to Tellurak."

"You sure you dun wanna fight for us here?" Rynn asked. "You're good at it."

"I'm more of a war god than Eziel is these days, but that's not the point. The food here is dog shit, most of your people don't speak a civilized language, and this airship was interesting for about a day and a half. This isn't a warship or even a vessel anymore. It's a backwater garrison stationed in the middle of nowhere."

"I thought you liked the idea of having airships." Rynn tried to pinch the bridge of her nose to alleviate her headache, but the bandage was too much in the way.

"Yeah, sure. Real ones though, not this spit-pasted monstrosity. So when can you get me back to Tellurak? I need to find out what became of Tanner. For his own good, and for my peace of mind."

Rynn sighed. Just talking was exhausting her. "Couple days. Promise."

Dan stared at her. She couldn't tell whether he was trying to formulate an argument or trying to decide whether she was lying. "Fine. You should get some rest though. You look like shit someone stepped in. Maybe you should consider a full armor suit."

Chapter 5

"I left the Academy early not because I had nothing left to learn, but because that had nothing left to teach me." –Rashan Solaran

The cramped, stone-walled classroom smelled of old paper and chalk. Glass-paned windows stood guard against the entrance of fresh spring air and the scents of grasses and flowers. Summer crept up slowly on Kadris, seat of the Kadrin Empire, at the southernmost extent of the civilized world. Danilaesis Solaran was never one for frolicking in the gardens or roughhousing in the grass with the other boys, but a discontent brewed in him at being cooped up on so fine a day.

At the front of the classroom, Wenovin droned on about stars, sketching the night sky in white chalk on the black slate hanging from the wall. For the major stars, he listed the name in both Kadrin and Arcane, and explained the etymology of each. Each had a story, a lore, a history, a use in navigation or in reading omens. It was rubbish, every bit of it. Madlin had undone the class with one simple revelation from the astronomers of Korr.

"The sun is a star, the closest by unimaginable margins. The other stars are just like it, but seen from afar."

The Korrish knew better. They had better telescopes, better methods, better thinkers, quite frankly. It was so painfully obvious when he saw the work that went into their machines. Magic had made Veydrans lazy, Kadrins in particular. If they could see the stars well enough to steer a ship, that was all that mattered—and few enough Kadrins were sailors, with their sprawling empire webbed with roads.

Crack!

Wenovin's wooden pointer slammed against Danilaesis's desk, startling him from his mind's idle wandering. "I asked the name of the topmost star in Tansha's Tear," said Wenovin. "Would you be so kind as to tell us?" There was a tittering from behind Danilaesis, Cara and Inivise as always. They were peasant-bred and whip-smart, but neither was sorceress enough for him to pay them any mind outside of the classroom. Inside it, they tormented him with their inanities.

Dan rubbed a hand across his face, trying to force the sleep from his eyes. "Piss off," he muttered.

"What is that supposed to mean?" Wenovin demanded. He towered over Danilaesis, something the sorcerer could only manage because he was the one standing. It was intended to be intimidating, but Danilaesis found him wearying instead.

Danilaesis considered the question a moment. It was a direct translation from Acardian, so any meaning ought to have come along with it, but he could not formulate a proper definition, now that he thought about it. At length, he shrugged.

"A sixth year ought to know to be more judicious with his words. Schoolboy taunts are a nasty habit for a boy who considers himself fit to be warlock."

Danilaesis had been staring off at the walls as he thought and had not turned when speaking to his instructor. He raised a dead-eyed glare to Wenovin and watched the Fourth Circle sorcerer stiffen. "Considers?" he asked. "Are you lecturing on star names or spoiling for a draw, Wenovin?"

"That's Sorcerer Wenovin, Danil—"

"Warlock Danilaesis. If you're going to pull formal ranks here, let's have it. My grandfather can spew on until he turns grey again that I'm not, but I *am* a warlock. Go back to your droning and leave me in peace."

Wenovin slunk over to the blackboard with his head hung but a hard set in his eyes. Axterion would hear of their exchange, Danilaesis knew. Wenovin was too much a coward to confront him, and too weak a sorcerer to take up the challenge of a draw. Until Axterion's rejuvenation, everyone had been too weak to oppose him openly.

Danilaesis looked down at the idle scratchings his quill had traced during his mind's wanderings. Numbers, equations, and simplistic diagrams were scrawled haphazardly all across it, with nary a word reflecting Wenovin's lecture. It was a combination of algebraic gymnastics that were just on the cusp of his understanding and formulae that he had seen in Korr and nowhere else. The latter were memorized and copied, but he had no means of puzzling out their meaning. Mathematics was tedious, his least favorite of subjects after etiquette and genealogy. The thought that he would need to plumb such depths of it as Veydrus might never have seen was something he dreaded.

But the world-rippers were powered by mathematics. If he was to master their secrets, he needed to know how to operate one on his own. He needed to find a way to learn just enough to get one working, but the only sure way he could think of was to consult with Rynn, Madlin, or Cadmus. They were the only ones he had access to in Korr who didn't seem completely dim, but none of them would be inclined. Madlin and Rynn would want magic in exchange, and he wasn't sure he was ready to trade that yet. Cadmus would as soon teach kuduks how to use the world-ripper as him. For all the help he had been, the Mad Tinker was skittish around him. Magic was daruu to him, which Danilaesis found vaguely insulting since the daruu had Sources like rocks and the sorcerous ability to match. Rune carvers they might be, and brilliant ones, but they were nothing like Kadrin sorcerers.

The lecture continued on around him. In front of him, Wenovin babbled, and his chalk tapped and scratched on the blackboard. Behind him, whispers of gossip passed among his peers—at least in age. There was no quiet in which to lose himself, but Danilaesis shut out the noise and lost himself in his own mind. *Considers himself a warlock*, he scoffed mentally. He let the classroom become a battlefield, his ponderings his only opponent. The rest faded from his hearing.

With a clear head, he considered how he might take advantage of his hosts in Korr while he was marooned there.

Maybe I don't need to know how it operates. Just how the dials aim it. He would need a plan, but he was in no real rush. Getting one of the machines for his own use was important, crucial even, but it was not urgent.

It was not until he was jostled by one of his classmates pushing past him that Danilaesis realized that the lecture had ended. He blinked a few times to bring himself back to the world around him. He was going to be one of the last to leave, it seemed. With a glance to the nonsense that covered his note paper, he leaked a bit of aether into it and set it aflame. Taking it between thumb and forefinger, he lifted it from the desk before that caught fire as well, and watched it disappear into ash in a matter of seconds.

"Showoff."

It was whispered, but Danilaesis caught the word in his ear. He failed to recognize the voice, but he had his guesses. Cara and Inivise were huddled close as they walked, heads nearly touching. Nothing witty came to mind that would refute the comment without making him sound like a braying mule, but there were other ideas that crept into Danilaesis's head. He kept his place as he watched the two peasant sorceresses depart, taking his measure of them as he did every stray chance he had to glance at them unawares. Lowborn and poor, a few summers of Academy life had flowered them into proper young women, worth the time to linger after and watch. Close as cousins they were, too. He wondered if he could split them by taking an interest in just one.

Danilaesis saved the idea for later; he was busy with too many roiling thoughts in his mind to add another just then. Still, as he walked to history class, he could not help wondering which of them he would choose if he did.

"Warlock Danilaesis!" the voice called out from down the hall. It was evening, and Danilaesis's day of lectures was at an end. He had studying to do, but it would be his own research and nothing he had been assigned. Mind-sore, groggy, and stiff from long hours sitting in hard seats, he was hardly in the mood for anyone shouting his name. Those sorts of messengers usually meant someone wanted him to go somewhere—usually Empress Celia or his grandfather.

"What is it?" he asked, not concealing his weariness.

"A letter has just arrived for you, warlock," the messenger said as he approached. It was petty, Danilaesis knew, but he was placated by the use of his proper title. The messenger knew how to lick a boot or two to get his job done. Danilaesis took the sealed envelope and turned it over in his hands. It was plain paper, the seal pressed into the wax was just the tip of a sword. That alone was enough to tell him who it was from, even if he hadn't been secretly hoping for such a missive.

The messenger stood at military attention as Danilaesis looked the letter over, not willing to open it in public. It seemed odd that the man would wait since he had not announced the sender and thus could not be waiting to take a reply. Letters were an entirely different matter from spoken messages. A single, amused sniff escaped Danilaesis as he realized the man expected a coin for his efforts. He didn't carry coin since no one ever asked him to pay for anything. It was one of the many small privileges of being a warlock from a wealthy family.

Danilaesis ignored the messenger and walked away. Once he was safely ensconced in his room with the door locked and the wards armed, he broke the seal and read:

Dan,

Not sure how long this letter will take in getting to you. Sorry for any worries in the meantime. I didn't trust the Errol girl to make good on getting me off that rock, so I made my own arrangements. Stalyart took me in, and I'm safe and sober (fig. of speech, of course) on his ship Merciful. *If you want to meet up, I'm sure you can find a way to contact him or me.*

-T

It was written in Acardian, a simple precaution for which Danilaesis was grateful. The annoyance was that he did *not* have a way at hand to contact Tanner. Magic was not the cure-all that Tanner suspected it was, at least not in Danilaesis's hands, nor Dan's. Rashan might have known how to find a lone man somewhere out at sea with his magic, or perhaps any number of other sorcerers long dead. The Errols' machine could make short work of a search as well, he supposed. Dan shook his head.

Patience. Tanner was fine, which was a greater ease on his mind than he would have expected. He felt no great love for the sword-wielding lout, but Tanner had been a companion for long enough that Dan was used to his presence. With no immediate danger, there was little reason to rush to a rescue Tanner didn't need.

Dan held the note flat in his palm and set it aflame. He watched it burn, his shielding spell flickering as it kept the heat from scorching the skin of his hand. *Problems are so much simpler when they can be burned away.*

That evening, Danilaesis strode the halls of the palace, past guards who stiffened at his approach. He was neither invited nor barred from the royal chambers; the guard captain had long since abandoned hope of corralling him under the rules that governed everyone else when they visited the imperial palace. Though he wore his warlock's garb, all trimmed in black, he felt like an impostor without Sleeping Dragon sheathed on his back.

Blast you, grandfather. You had no right to take it.

The sword hung at waist level in mid-air, in the front courtyard of the palace. Danilaesis had to pass by it every time he visited. Twice he had tried to snatch it from the air, but both times the aether construct Axterion had placed around it stopped him from so much as touching it, resisting him with greater and greater force the closer his hand came to the hilt. On the second attempt, he caught palace servants stopping to stare at his efforts, snickering behind their hands at him. It took an act of will to ignore the sword each time he passed by it, but Danilaesis despised being mocked.

He knocked on the door of Empress Celia's private chambers. The ornate doors were meant to be impressive, but Danilaesis had never cared for them. The gold leafing and red lacquer seemed gaudy. His family's estate was not quite so richly appointed, but it was done with better taste, in black and silver. The Solaran Estate runed theirs better as well.

When there was no quick answer to his knock, Danilaesis forced the door. He had done it enough times that he knew just where to apply a bit of pressure to cause the wards to fail and leave the lock unprotected for a moment. There was a gasp from within.

"What are you doing—" the servant's words were cut off in her throat as self-preservation warned her that it was the warlock barging in on her empress.

Celia lay on her side, facing away from the door, the bare skin of her back glistening with oils. She was nestled among a vast pile of embroidered pillows, propped up in languorous comfort as her servant kneaded the tension from her. A chalice at the bedside in easy reach of the empress told that she sought her ease inside as well as out. "Do they no longer teach manners at the Academy?"

Danilaesis caught himself staring for a moment, then remembered himself and shut the door. "They do, but I've always preferred my uncle's form of diplomacy. Manners are for enemies and strangers, and I always found them a bit false among friends."

With a sigh, Celia took up the chalice and drank deep. Wine was ill advised when carrying a child, but Danilaesis had stolen sips of her wine often enough to know it was little more than water scented with grape. She would have to drink a bucket of the stuff before Danilaesis would fade from her worries. "So you would presume us friends?" she asked. The servant girl resumed her work on Celia's back, digging fingers into the muscles and working them loose as Celia made quiet noises of approval.

"Of course," said Dan. "Our lives may be different. I still have lessons every day; you have to sit long hours on the throne listening to nobles prattle. I spill the blood of our enemies to protect the empire; you spill your own to provide it heirs. You take your pleasures with Tia atop you; I'd prefer to—"

"Where is this leading?" Celia asked. Dan watched as Tia blushed. Like all the palace servants, she was enspelled to remember nothing of conversations among her betters, but she was listening in as they spoke.

"We have our common problems as well. Axterion is becoming a bother."

"We have a powerful sorcerer at the head of the Imperial Circle once more. I find it more of a blessing than a bother."

"And when he contradicts you in front of the court?" Danilaesis asked.

Celia held up a hand, and Tia paused her ministrations, wiping her hands on the hem of her dress and sitting back on the bed away from her empress. Dan smirked and moved to the side table where Emperor Sommick kept a selection of expensive liquors. The chambers were Celia's alone, but when the emperor visited on official business, he needed strong drink. Pouring himself a chalice of brandy, Dan waited for Celia to decide how she would answer.

"Leave us," Celia ordered. Despite the fact that Tia was no threat to remember anything that was about to be said, there were elements of decorum and embarrassment to consider. The servant girl nodded to the empress and rose to leave. On her way past, Dan winked at her, causing her to flush anew. She was peasant comely, which meant she was plain but well-formed; Dan only teased for her reaction, not with any intention of following through on it.

When the door closed, Celia's demeanor shifted. She rolled over to face Danilaesis, clutching a pillow in front of her for modesty. "How can you be sure he wasn't watching through the girl's eyes?"

Dan shrugged as he took a swallow of the brandy. Something in the fermenting of it was a magic all its own; the brandy did not burn until it was halfway down his throat, where it caught fire like a dragon's breath. "Can't live life fearing. I'm not afraid of the old buzzard. So answer my question: you going to put up with him talking above you at court?"

Celia stretched out a hand, and a dress lifted itself from the back of a chair and drifted over to her. With a glare, she convinced Dan to turn his back as she clothed herself.

"Should you be levitating things with the babe?" he asked.

"I've borne three children, and I, the babe's Source ,will be fine with a bit of magic around it. Just don't *you* go pulling any reckless tricks."

Dan sketched a bow, chalice in hand. "I'm no fool, Your Highness."

"Axterion is a nagging pest. He knows everything, or so he'd have us think. Every plan and plot we hatch, we've left a dozen holes that only he can see. He was always sharp tongued before, but it makes me wonder whether his newfound youth has restored his wits or merely emboldened him further."

Danilaesis chuckled. "I never thought he could get crankier, to be honest. But now that he doesn't have to worry about anyone overpowering him, he's become a hog at a tea party."

"Seems to run in your family," Celia observed. She took her own chalice from the table and refilled it from a pitcher. Danilaesis lowered his brow, but kept silent as he took another swallow of his brandy. "What would you have me do?"

"Prepare for a war with Megrenn," said Danilaesis. Celia sputtered grape-scented water back into her chalice. "Send me out on some mission to secure our border. Use me as you would an acknowledged warlock."

"Axterion would never hear of it," said Celia. She took an embroidered cloth from the bedside and wiped her chin. "He wants nothing but peace. He's sent envoys to the Megrenn for a lasting treaty."

"His idea, or yours?"

"His, but I approved it," said Celia. "I have an empire. I don't need a war in it."

"Spoken like a queen, not an empress," Danilaesis said. He threw back the last of the brandy in his chalice. It was more than a sensible gulp, and he gasped as the fire chased it down his throat. Setting thc chalice on the side table, he walked over to stand before his empress. Though just a lad, she only came to his collarbone. She could have stepped back to keep space between them, but instead she craned her neck to keep her eyes on his. Even with the sting of brandy vapors in his nose, he smelled the perfumes from the oils Tia used on her, the talc from the tinted powder on her cheeks and eyelids. She trembled slightly. "An empress should always want more."

Celia broke their gaze and turned her back. The dress was cut low, giving Danilaesis nearly the same view of her that he had seen on first arriving. "Why now of all times? You think you can force him to give you back your sword?" She sniffed. "What a price to pay for a blade."

Danilaesis felt the heady rush from Emperor Sommick's brandy. It made things seem simpler. He stepped behind Celia and put his hands on her shoulders. It took what little willpower the alcohol left him not to slip the dress loose from those shoulders. He whispered in her ear. "I get to be free of the Academy. You get to occupy that idle old brain of his with more important tasks than nipping at the hem of every decision you make from the throne. In the bargain, I'll reclaim Megrenn for you and give you Ghelk as well."

"Why do you think you can when Rashan failed?"

"Because I'm going to have the help of those Korrish tinkers, no matter what it takes."

Chapter 6

"There's only so much money you can pay a man. You just can't buy more competence than they have."–Cadmus Errol

By the light of stars peeking down between the vacuum tanks of the *Jennai*, Madlin made her way across the plaza. She pulled the collar of her jacket tightly against her neck to keep the wind from finding its way inside. Here and there a window glowed in one of the crew quarters, but the ship's bulk bathed her in shadow that was good enough protection against being spotted by anyone in a lighted room. It was a trick Rynn had learned for her in the tunnels: when trying for stealth, light around someone *else* is your friend.

The door to the cargo hold with the world-ripper was guarded, of course, but guards were not her concern. The two on duty gave a fist to chest salute as Madlin approached.

Pulling out her pocket clock, Madlin flipped it open and angled it to catch enough light to read the face. "It's 2:32. The two of you stand relieved until 4:32, two hours from now precisely. I don't want to see boot or hat of either of you until then, and I don't want to be kept waiting after. Understood?"

"Yes ma'am," they replied in unison, rather louder than she would have liked.

"No booze, and if you must sleep, you better be rusty sure you wake up in time to be back here."

Madlin waited until they were gone and slipped inside the hold. The dynamo for the world-ripper hummed at idle, but the room was too dark for her to see anything. Fumbling along the wall, she found the switch for the spark lights and closed it with a solid *thunk*. The room burst into shabby yellow light, not enough to chase away the shadows from the far corners but sufficient to see a path to the controls and the stacks of notes and maps that lay beside it.

As she sat and began sifting through the various documents for the maps she needed, Madlin was aware of the approach of her co-conspirators. She did not so much as flinch when the door opened and admitted Rynn and Jamile. Jamile closed the door behind them as Rynn shuffled across the room and took the seat at the controls as Madlin got out of her way.

"He's sound asleep," Jamile reported in a whisper.

"I know, you told me two minutes ago," said Madlin. She pulled one of the panels off the control console and looked inside. Her father had anticipated the need for non-lunar destinations and had installed a toggle switch to re-enable standard use. Aside from being buried in the guts of the world-ripper, he could hardly have made the swap any easier.

Rynn took over shuffling through maps as Madlin threw the switches one by one to turn on the viewer. When the last was activated, the view sprang to life but was a wall of blackness. A few pinpricks of light were stars, shown from where the moon had been before Madlin stopped the synchronizing device. Rynn spun dials and twisted the view around until Korr looked much like the maps spread out on paper all over the console. Clouds obscured it in parts, but it was otherwise a faithful rendition. A splint on Rynn's left arm slowed the process, but she spun dials one by one to bring the view around and narrow them down onto the region of northeastern Grangia. The maps they were concerned with did not involve Korr, however, so Rynn turned one more dial and threw the viewer into chaos as the image vanished, to be replaced by swirling blues and whites. With knowledge of the worlds at their disposal, and the coordinates for Tellurak well ingrained in everyone who worked the machine, the image resolved itself into a world once more.

The change was striking. The land and water were all in the same places as they had just been, though the clouds had moved. What was notable was the shift in color. The reddish brown of the Grangian landscape was replaced by greens and lighter browns of northeastern Khesh.

"Well, time to find Mabliss," Madlin muttered. It was something she'd have said to someone else running the machine, but it was redundant with Rynn at the controls. Still, useful or not, she could not help but comment.

"Are you sure this is a good idea?" Jamile asked.

Madlin moved to the viewer and pulled the lever that would move the auger out of their way. It was stationed on rails to be able to insert or retract through the world hole with ease. "That thing Sosha's watching over ... that isn't human."

"He's just a sorcerer. Since when have you been superstitious? We can both work some degree—"

"It's not that. I'm sure there are plenty of sorcerers out there just squeaky clean of mind and heart. That one's a twisted monster. He's got a soul like a bear trap and all the remorse of a headsman."

"Sounds like a perfect servant of the new Eziel."

"The old Eziel," said Madlin. As the two of them talked, Rynn scanned Khesh under the early rays of dawn, looking for the city of Mabliss.

Jamile closed her eyes and shook her head. "The Eziel I grew up with helped his children, fed them, gave them hope."

"There's a fat lot of hope riding on beating the kuduks."

"Hope shouldn't involve bloodlust."

"Now you're just being difficult," said Madlin. "Besides, I think we can both agree that we don't want *that* being our legacy. Dan's a menace. I don't know how Tanner stood being around him."

"And you promise you're not going to just murder him?" Jamile asked. "Much as I hate that look in his eyes when he talks about war and killing, he doesn't deserve that. Someone made him this way, and it's not his fault he turned out rotten."

Madlin held up her hands. "Hey, you want to learn magic or not? Dan's not going to teach you; we've figured that out by now. These folks are willing to help with magic *and* might have some ideas what we can do about Dan. They might lean to killing, but let's be reasonable and hear them out anyway."

"I think I found it," Rynn called out. The viewer hung over a modest city by Kheshi standards, built in the hills. Well-worn trade roads headed south and west, with smaller ones snaking out into the countryside in all directions.

"One more world over," Madlin said. She crossed her arms and waited. For all their knowledge from the mysterious books, Cadmus had yet to let them try seeking out Veydrus. The Mad Tinker had strange ideas when it came to being conservative. He'd build a machine that scratched and tore its way through the fabric of the universe and use it without a further thought. But to aim it at a world where magic was known and commonplace? To him it was folly. To Madlin it was potential.

The viewer swirled through another iteration of color and chaos before resolving itself into yet another world. Veydrus. From an airship's view or even higher, it did not look so different than Tellurak. The Kheshi city of Mabliss was gone, but another occupied the same space. It was quaint by comparison, spread out over the same hills but with trees and gardens mixed among the streets, and fewer of the roads appeared cobbled.

"No time to gawk. Let's get to finding someplace that looks official," said Madlin. Even staring through the world-ripper viewer, she could see herself in Rynn's glare. The sooner she was through in another world, the better.

The view dropped so quickly that Madlin felt her stomach lurch, and she leaned away from the viewing frame. Rynn had done it on purpose, of course. All the buildings were circular in shape, some domed, some with conical peaks. Larger structures consisted of multiple circles conjoined. The city was built around a central hub, a towering structure much taller and with more sub-circles than any other. "Looks like as good a place as any," said Rynn.

"Are you sure that's where you can find the Zayne boy?" Jamile asked. "Maybe it would be better to go somewhere less likely to be guarded and ask around for him."

"Maybe," Madlin said. "But we're in a hurry. My father wakes up like clockwork at five sharp. We need to have the world-ripper shut down and everything back the way it was before he gets down here."

"What do we do with Dan if he wakes up?"

"We'll think of something if it comes up," Madlin replied. "I don't think Dan's ever *seen* the sun in the east though. Cadmus is a bigger problem."

"I should come with you," Jamile said. She slipped beside Madlin with eyes wide and earnest.

Madlin shook her head. "You stay here to warn Rynn if Dan gets up in the night. I'll be fine."

"I can warn *you.* The two of you have to connect anyway to make a warning effective. I might as well be on the far side to lend a hand."

"You going to be able to shoot anything if we need to?" Madlin asked. It was a trap question.

Jamile surprised Madlin by drawing the coil gun from her holster. "You shouldn't even bring one of these things. What makes you think that this world of magic is going to let you get away with shooting people? Half of them are probably just like Dan. If we can't talk our way through this, Rynn's going to sneak us out. I'm not fighting wizards and warlocks."

Madlin studied Jamile for a moment. She seemed determined, her chest rising and falling with nerves, excitement, and ranting without pausing often enough for breath. Her gaze didn't falter. Madlin's did. "Fine. You're right. Either Anzik is there and agrees to help us, or we shovel coal and steam out of there."

Returning her gun to its holster, Madlin unbuckled her gun belt and hung it from one of the control levers of the steam auger. Before she'd taken two paces away from it, she found herself feeling for the gun at her hip, the absence of its familiar weight triggering a momentary panic that she'd lost it. A naked feeling crept over her. Madlin was young and unimposing, no good in a brawl and an invitation to all sorts of trouble from a certain criminal element. Chipmunk's voice, still buried inside her, told her to take just the gun and stuff it inside her jacket. *Better to invite a fight and win it, than stumble into one I can't win.* A hand reached out for the gun belt, but Madlin stopped herself.

Jamile took her by the wrist before Madlin could change her mind again. The two women stood by the viewing frame and waited. The scene was a storybook come to life. The front courtyard of a palace—by the look of it—spread before them with dew-dropped grass glistening in the first light of dawn. The rounded walls of the tower before them were easily the match of any kuduk workmanship, with seams in the polished marble visible only by the change in the grain. A phalanx of guards stood before the arching wooden door at the end of the path they would emerge onto, armed with spears and wearing chain armor covered by livery of green and gold.

"You ready?" Madlin asked softly.

Jamile nodded.

Rynn pulled the lever and the dynamo screamed at the effort of jumping them two worlds distant. But despite its protest, the dynamo was able to power the world-ripper. A hole opened and before either of them had time to second-guess how long it might last, Madlin pulled Jamile through with her. The hole closed an instant later.

The first sensation of Veydrus was the pleasant scent that accompanied the dewy grass. The second was the sound of shouting in an incomprehensible language as the palace guards came rushing towards Madlin and Jamile.

Jamile ducked and shrank back. "Maybe we should have—"

"Anzik!" Madlin shouted to the guards. She held her hands wide, showing that she held no weapon. "I am here to see Anzik."

Eight guards encircled them, spears leveled. They continued to babble loudly in a language that Madlin caught not a single word of. Spear points had better luck.

By feints, jabs, and tips waved toward the crushed stone path, Madlin and Jamile were made to understand that they should get down. Madlin knelt, continuing to keep her arms wide and looking as unthreatening as she knew how. A guard behind her put a foot to her back and forced her prone.

Struggling and grunting protests that she was sure the guards could not understand, her hands were bound behind her back. Madlin muttered Anzik's name, but with the weight of two men holding her down, she could hardly spare the breath to breathe. Her solace came in knowing that Rynn was still watching over them, and that a hail of coil gun fire was the throw of a switch away.

Strong arms hauled Madlin off the ground and set her down on her feet. A hand knotted itself in her hair and gripped tight. It was nothing like the reception she had hoped for; apparently the guardsmen in Veydrus were the proactive sorts—not gentlemanly in the least. One of the guards produced a knife. By the angle she saw it, Madlin expected it was the same one holding her by the hair. Rough words came from just behind her ear, but Madlin could not puzzle out what they meant, even from context.

"Anzik," was all she could think to say that they might understand. Had she been misled? Was Anzik a criminal or a rebel in this world? The guard behind her shouted to his fellows, and one handed his spear aside and came over. The second guard grabbed her under the chin and squeezed, his fingers digging in until Madlin's mouth was forced open.

The dagger slipped between her teeth, and Madlin finally understood. *They think I'm a sorceress.* They were afraid of her talking or gesturing to work a spell. Was that better or worse than merely being thought to associate with a criminal?

The knife seemed content to rest tip first just past her teeth. She bit down lightly on the blade to try to keep it away from her tongue, but she felt the point as she tried to keep it off the tender flesh. The guard pushed her by the fistful of her hair, and Madlin did not need to be goaded twice. She marched behind the lead guard as she was led toward the palace. Jamile was out of sight, but she could hear them talking to her and Jamile's babbled answers, barely comprehensible even in Korrish. The sniffs between words told Madlin that Jamile was crying. *You'd think she'd never been captured and threatened with death before*, Madlin thought darkly. For a girl with a formerly collared twin, she ought to have been better hardened.

The walk through the palace was harrowing. Madlin had the impression of great riches in tapestries and gilded architecture, but she was in no position to appreciate it. She was dragged past everything at a slow walk, shaking with the effort of keeping still enough that the knife did not dig into her mouth. The stairs were a labor of fear and balance. The only small grace was that the guard's grip was sure; she found herself unmindful of the pain in her scalp since a looser grip might have let her jostle, and the guard at least knew his trade in delivering sorcerers.

On the fourth floor, they traversed hallways that must have crossed between towers. When they reached a door at the end of the hall, one of the other guards knocked and stepped away. The door opened of its own accord. Madlin's escort removed the knife from her mouth and the hand from her hair. She was shoved through the door, with Jamile pushed through right after.

The room was stark, just bare walls with windows, no furniture or decoration. At the center of the room, a green-clad figure sat facing away from them, legs crossed. The figure's hair was pale brown, pulled together and tied off at the top of his head and falling in a horse's tail. The door slammed shut behind them.

"Anzik?" Madlin ventured.

"You are fortunate I warned them a foreign woman might come seeking me," Anzik replied, not turning. He spoke Acardian. "Bringing the Taklish woman was foolish."

"I'm sorry," said Jamile. "It's not her fault. I insisted."

Anzik stood and turned. The resemblance to the son of Denrik Zayne was minimal, but there. It was like seeing a beggar and a prince from the same father. The cold, stoic look of Denrik's son Jadon could have been mistaken for idiocy or shyness. On Anzik, it seemed royal. He stared at them with impassive eyes, no hint of curiosity or surprise in evidence. His features were pale, smooth, untroubled.

With a whiff of smoke, Madlin was suddenly aware that her hands were freed from the rope that bound them. She pulled them in front of her and rubbed the raw skin where the rope had bitten in to grasp her; her fingers came away sooty.

"I came because of your note," Madlin said.

Anzik watched her, but did not reply.

Madlin glanced to Jamile, who shot her a worried look in reply. Jamile's hands were free as well, Madlin saw. Whatever Anzik was up to, he saw no threat from them.

"I ... I was hoping to discuss terms of a deal," Madlin said when the silence showed no sign of breaking on its own. "Magic in return for dealing with Dan ... maybe I can throw in some weapons."

"Have you worked out a plan?" Anzik asked.

"No, not yet," Madlin admitted. She swallowed and looked around the room. She could not bring herself to keep looking into that face. *He's not blinking. Same as Jadon.* The silence grew again. "Well, the thing is, he's saved our lives—all our lives—but he's just ... dangerous. I worry that one day he'll take something I say wrongly, and I'll be dead before I know it."

"He's like his uncle," said Anzik. "But there is no force within Kadrin to oppose him. Rashan Solaran had Brannis to keep him in check, and eventually kill him. You can count on no such internecine strife to do in Danilaesis Solaran. There is even less chance of finding a suitable foe for the twin. You'll simply have to do."

"Do?" Jamile asked.

"What do you mean?"

"I'll teach you what you need to kill him," Anzik said. "The twin. There is no hope that you could deal with Danilaesis."

Madlin frowned and cast a skeptical eye at Aznik. "I saw him fight when the Korrish force came to destroy Tinker's Island. Dan is an army all to himself."

Anzik smiled. It was a small, forced thing that barely moved the muscles of the young sorcerer's cheeks and came nowhere near his eyes. "I can see Sources. I have seen both him and his twin. I am sure Dan seems quite strong to you, but here he would be just a curiosity—a weakling warlock, all bluster and little bite."

"What kind of world are we in?" Jamile asked in a whisper meant for Madlin.

"A world ruled by dragons and demons, with humans taking the scraps left between their realms," Anzik replied.

"But Dan said his people ruled half the world," said Madlin.

"Half a continent, but they consort with demons."

"Danilaesis?"

"In manner, if not in fact," Anzik replied. "He was taught by the demon warlock Rashan, an ancestor of his."

"He's descended from demons?" Jamile asked. A puzzled frown had worked itself onto her face and stuck there.

Anzik closed his eyes, the most true emotion he had shown since they arrived. "There is no time to explain the vagaries of Kadrin's twisted past. You will help us against them, but for now, you must be going. There will be no lesson today. When you seek me next, come to this room and no place else. Your twin is waiting with the portal entrance. You may leave."

Madlin blinked. "You can *see* it?" She knew in the back of her mind that Rynn had followed their short journey within the palace. The awareness of her twin was comfortably secondhand once more with a separation of worlds between them.

"My aether-vision is keener than most. Have a care where you send your machine in this world. There are others who see better than even I." To demonstrate the truth of his claim, Anzik stepped aside and swept an arm toward the waiting viewer. Rynn obliged by opening the world hole just where he indicated.

Madlin nodded to the young sorcerer—though he was probably near her own age, she felt older of late. "Thank you."

Jamile nodded her agreement. There was no reply from Anzik. The two of them stepped through the world hole, and Rynn closed it behind them.

Once safely back aboard the *Jennai*, Jamile let out a long breath, ending in a slouch. "Next time, you can go on your own. That was awful!"

"That was power."

"Dan's still asleep," Jamile reported. "Let's clean this up and get out of here."

"Kuduks aren't going to know what hit them," Rynn muttered as Madlin pulled the panel to reattach the lunar tracker.

"As you see, gentlemen," Kezudkan said, his bass voice rumbling across the assembled kuduk troops. "This new venture, of which you are now a part, will make us as rich as bankers. I don't just mean myself, or Mr. Draksgollow, but each and every last one of you." There was a stirring in the ranks as the hired soldiers muttered amongst themselves about the implications. "This machine is the key to it all. It is a one of a kind, irreplaceable, indispensable. We must all guard it with our lives."

The new Venterad Deep workshop was cleaned and refitted. Equipment gleamed with fresh chrome and wax, polished brass and brightsteel. Few of the new recruits paid any of it the least attention. Standing in orderly rows in their bland, store-bought uniforms, all heads turned toward a single point in the room, and it wasn't Kezudkan. They all looked through the viewing frame of the world-ripper as Draksgollow worked the controls, giving them a breathtaking view of the Veydran countryside. Yellow fields stretched miles wide, and forests had trees that the Lumberlands could only envy. The wood from just a few of those could set a man up for years.

"This land is not even upon the face of Korr but another world entirely. It seems much to swallow, but I promise you wonders you have not yet begun to imagine. Tomorrow you will assemble here, and you will actually go through this hole between worlds."

There were more mumblings among the troops, and they sounded worried. One soldier spoke up, putting words to the concern shared by many. "Will we have to climb down a rope?"

Kezudkan put a hand over his eyes. "Mr. Draksgollow, if you please..."

The airship's view of the landscape drifted down to a more comfortable level, twisting until it faced sideways instead of straight down. Draksgollow settled in among a grove of trees the size of thunderail cars and even with the ground.

"And open it, please."

Draksgollow obliged, and a pungent odor of rotting leaves and pitch wafted into the workshop. Kezudkan stepped through the world-ripper and back. "Just like that. No trick to it at all. Well ... no trick on your parts at least. I had a puzzle of a time getting the machine to do that." He chuckled and a chorus of nervous chuckles answered him from the ranks.

"I will see you all tomorrow morning at six, same spots you're in now, armed and armored. Dismissed."

Kezudkan and Draksgollow watched the soldiers disperse, picking their ways through the workshop and into the barracks area beyond. "Where did you dig these up?" Kezudkan asked. "Dull as eggs, the lot of them."

"I thought you'd prefer them a bit simple. The last smart ones I hired mutinied on us. Or don't you remember?"

"Well, so long as the machinists in the Telluraki shop are sharper than these. I don't want to trust my travels to imbeciles."

"The machinists know what's what," Draksgollow said. "I had to tell them otherwise when they worked it out on their own; they'd have had grounds to turn on us as well."

"I *told* you not to let anyone else know! If they know there are more machines, they might think to take one for themselves."

Draksgollow shook his head. "I told them we had countermeasures in place. So long as we make them rich, I think we'll be fine."

"Well, we'd better find some deep veins then. Treasuries, vaults, and the like. We've made a lot of promises."

"Well, we always have the machines none of the others know about." Draksgollow smiled.

Three men and a lad sat together in a private booth of one of Marker's Point's better known and oft avoided taverns. The lamps created more shadow than light, and a three-piece musician's troupe played a lively melody that kept conversations from spilling far from the tables where they belonged. It was a place for doing business more than making merriment, and were it not for the flow of ale and liquor into the patrons, there might have been little good humor within its walls.

"Can't believe I'm selling *you* a ship, Zayne," said a thick, neckless man in a grubby leather vest and three days' beard. He hoisted a tankard the size of a pitcher and offered a solitary toast before downing a huge swallow. His companion was slim and quiet, keeping his hands below the table and rarely touching his drink.

"We all have our days, Sanson. Besides, how many of you lot can claim to have sunk one of the Mad Tinker's smoke ships?" Zayne replied. He had replaced his wardrobe since arriving in Marker's Point. His shirtsleeves gleamed white, and the jacket that hung from a peg at the tableside was starched and pressed immaculately.

"Ya got me there," Sanson replied. "A lesser man, I'd say he's full 'o piss, but the likes of you ain't got nothin' to prove."

"How soon will she be ready?"

"Soon as you get me my price."

"I'll have it this evening. We'll make the exchange on deck."

Sanson's partner narrowed his eyes. "You ain't thinkin' anything, Cap'n, are you?"

"Why Jimmony, I was scarcely aware you remembered," Zayne said, breaking into a smile. "No, this will be nothing like my acquisition of the *Fair Trader*. If nothing else, I never expect the same trick to work twice. Besides, I have no quarrel with you and coin in plenty to pay for it."

"You've always been good as your word, Zayne," said Sanson. He stuck a meaty hand across the table. "It's a deal."

Zayne took the offered hand and shook it. Sanson was a swindler and a thug as circumstances demanded, but he was also a wise man. Dealing with Captain Denrik Zayne made thieves and pirates rich men; crossing him was most often fatal. "Agreed."

"Your boy don't say much," said Jimmony. "He a mute?"

The corner of Zayne's mouth twitched. "You have a problem if he is?"

Jimmony leaned away and shook his head.

"He didn't mean nothin', Zayne," Sanson said. "Jimmony won't be at the meet tonight." He turned to his companion. "Will ya?" Jimmony shook his head.

"I'm not," said Jadon. "I am my father's apprentice. I watch. I listen. Speaking out of turn is for fools."

Sanson snickered and Jimmony shot the lad a hate-filled look. At sixteen, Jadon had the height of a man, but none of the muscle or the weathered look in the face that comes with age at sea. Denrik wondered how long it would be before Jadon found himself being challenged when he spoke his mind to small-minded men.

The two ship-selling pirates took their leave and left Jadon and Denrik Zayne alone together over a pair of untouched ales. Denrik reseated himself so that he was across the booth from the boy.

"What do you think of them? Tell me," Denrik said. He leaned over the table.

"Jimmony would kill you for the coin, but not the ill-won fame," Jadon said, his manner that of a schoolboy asked to recite a lesson. "He would blame someone else, to keep his head in the retribution that would follow. Sanson blusters, but he's afraid of you. He's dealing honestly, at least with you. Possibly not with Jimmony or his other associates. You'll get your ship, and they'll get their money. Jimmony won't be there at the exchange; Sanson won't dare renege on that promise, but Jimmony will get his cut, and they'll smooth things over between them."

"Nothing's ever smooth with Jimmony," Denrik said. "That's why I put him off my ship. But go on."

"Of more import are the girls from Korr," said Jadon. "They contacted Anzik last night. They are eager to learn magic, and finally sound as if they have taken your warning about the Kadrin warlock to heart. It seems the rumors of the destruction of Tinker's Island were true, and that the twin of Danilaesis Solaran was the hero of the Mad Tinker's retreat. His actions and methods during that conflict have peeled back yet another layer for Madlin Errol to see who she truly has in her employ."

"Do they have a plan?"

"Not as such. But they have it within them to concoct one. The machine holds great promise, and I'm sure their innate cleverness will avail them."

"Excellent! This is even better news than a new ship."

"Have you thought of a name for it, father?"

"I think I have: the *False Profit*."

Chapter 7

"Yes, I read it. They got me entirely wrong." –Rashan Solaran, commenting on his biography, The Diplomacy of Fire and Steel

Steel rang against steel, the sound echoing from the stone buildings walling off the practice yard. Two pairs of booted feet scuffed the dirt, angling for position. Danilaesis wore his hair tied back, but through his exertions, strands had fallen loose to be plastered by sweat to the skin of his face. He locked gazes with a squire his own age, waiting for his opponent's next move. There was a fire there that Danilaesis rarely saw aimed his way, a determination to fight back, to stand up to him, but on a more basic level it was the best way to anticipate the squire's next attack.

Danilaesis feinted low, and the squire dropped his sword to catch the attack. Before he could even make his real thrust, the squire had already seen through the feint and countered as Danilaesis drew back his sword. Stumbling back, Danilaesis flailed his sword, catching the squire an awkward blow to the mail protecting his forearm, but he took a hit for his trouble. The blunted sword tip caught Danilaesis squarely in the sternum, driving him from his feet. Had it not been for the shielding spell—his only concession to magic for the match—he might have been gravely wounded, blunted tip or not.

The sky filled Danilaesis's vision, going black briefly as his head struck the dirt. Clouds wandered by, breaking up the expanse of pale blue. The practice yard had gone silent, leaving him hearing the sound of his own lungs sucking in air to replace what had been driven from them. A face appeared, blotting out the clouds. The squire. A gauntleted hand extended down toward him.

Danilaesis accepted the help to his feet with a nod of thanks. "Your name?" he asked between breaths. It was the first squire who had bested him in a season.

"Gallaen."

Danilaesis looked Gallaen over. They were of similar size and build though admittedly Gallaen was the brawnier of the two. Despite wearing full armor, the squire had shown remarkable agility and reflexes.

"How'd you pull off that trick?"

"Wasn't a trick, warlock," Gallaen replied. "Been watching you every chance I've got."

"Study your enemy and learn his ways," Danilaesis quoted. "You've been reading *The Diplomacy of Fire and Steel.*"

"Your uncle was a great source of wisdom, warlock."

Danilaesis picked up his sword from where he'd dropped it when knocked senseless. "Can't say that enough. You're going to go far, Gallaen. I'll see to that. Just keep following my uncle's way, and you will be a great asset to the empire. Now, let's have it again."

Gallaen settled into a fencing stance and Danilaesis mirrored him. Hoots and cheers of encouragement rang in from the edges of the practice yard, where the other squires had retreated to watch. It was supposed to have been the time of morning when the squires paired off for sparring—and Danilaesis should have been listening to lectures on spells he could perform backward in his sleep—but all duties were being shirked for the occasion.

The two combatants circled one another. There was no feeling out process; they had dispensed with that in the first bout. Now it was time to look for openings, to pick apart pacing and footwork to find an off-balance moment, or to create one. Danilaesis broke the standoff with a feint of a feint. He made a quick, tentative thrust, but followed immediately behind it with another with full intent behind it. Gallaen caught himself halfway before reacting fully to avail himself of the opening after Danilaesis's first strike. The squire backed away a step and turned aside the young warlock's sword. Danilaesis used the angle of that parry to loop his sword around for a swing that made Gallaen's next parry as difficult as possible. Three more strikes, and Danilaesis had pulled Gallaen's defenses apart, forcing the squire to backpedal and sling wild blows to keep the warlock's blunted sword from connecting.

With a determination borne of the fear of imminent defeat, Gallaen stepped into Danilaesis's reach and caught the warlock's sword near the hilt of his own. He had no leverage to disarm Danilaesis but had caught him with enough of a surprise where the warlock could not free his blade without allowing Gallaen a clear strike. The two swords scraped against one another, subtle tricks of leverage and weight balancing the blades as each tried to separate them only when they could find an advantage. Each took his off hand to bear, pressing for all he was worth.

When the locked blades worked above shoulder height, Gallaen changed tactics. He shifted his footing and brought a knee up into Danilaesis's midsection. The young warlock saw the blow coming and took his off hand from the hilt of his sword. He did not stop the blow but locked his hand under Gallaen's knee; the armored plate over that knee drove the breath from Danilaesis, but little else. Using two feet against Gallaen's one, Danilaesis overbalanced the squire and the two lads fell heavily to the dirt. The impact knocked the locked blades apart, and Danilaesis clouted Gallaen with the hilt of his sword.

"What are you playing at?" a crotchety voice shouted from the edge of the practice yard. Danilaesis knew even before he looked up that it belonged to his grandfather. Fun was at an end for the day, it seemed.

Danilaesis climbed off his defeated opponent and offered the stunned squire his hand in aid. Only when Gallaen was on his feet and gave a nod to confirm he was unharmed did Danilaesis respond. "What does it look like I'm doing? Putting good use to my time. The better I am with a sword, the less aether I'll need in battle."

Axterion ventured into the dusty confines of the practice yard of the School of Arms. He looked out of place in his black silk finery, chased in red and gold embroidery indicating his place at the height of the Imperial Circle. Stripped down to an undershirt and riding pants, Danilaesis looked perhaps too poor to fit in among the armored squires. He rested the flat of his sword over his shoulder and waited for his grandfather to approach to closer than shouting distance.

"How many times are you going to defy me and skip classes?" Axterion said. His furrowed brow now only bore the slightest flecks of grey when once they had been mottled grey and white.

Danilaesis wiped the sweat from his brow with a sleeve and shrugged. "I hadn't planned to keep count. If they were teaching anything interesting or useful, I'd stay. But I have an empire to protect, and I won't get any better at it muttering along with those dolts as they learn spells I could work silently when I was five summers."

"So, you think you're too good for spell lessons?" Axterion asked, his voice rising singsong, in the classic baiting of a verbal trap. He was so predictable at times.

"Those lessons? Of course," Danilaesis replied. "You think you can convince me to go back by beating me in another draw? By slipping some trickery by me that proves you can cast those dusty librarian's spells better than I can? You can only even draw aether because of that potion I gave you, you ungrateful old codger."

"Ungrateful? You think I'm ungrateful? I'm doing you the best favor I know, forcing a proper education into that porous skull of yours by any means at my disposal. It's like being on a sinking ship, me scooping water out in buckets, and you scooping it right back in. It's maddening. You'd think you wanted to be an imbecile with no skills but war and killing."

"Fire and steel; all else is vanity," Danilaesis quoted.

"Mule snot! It was then, still is now," Axterion replied. "Rashan was referring to efficiency in battle, not the practice of war to the exclusion of all else."

"Shows how well *you* knew him."

"I knew him forty winters longer than you, boy."

"Fine. Then I *understood* him better. He talked to me when you weren't around. He told me I was his proper heir after Iridan died. I just needed to get older and stronger, and he'd teach me. Well, after Brannis killed him, I figured it was my duty to justify his faith in me. I'm not going to fall like he did. There is no Brannis to betray me."

An uncomfortable silence followed, each studying the other. Danilaesis had been much younger then; the details faded around the edges. But he remembered overhearing arguments between Rashan and Brannis; their disagreements stayed civil while in his earshot, but it was always Rashan advocating the path of war and

Brannis seeking the clever way around. *Are* you *going to turn out to be my Brannis, grandfather?* He could only wonder if Axterion was thinking along the same lines.

"This is unseemly," Axterion said. "Get yourself cleaned up and meet me in my office in the Tower of Contemplation."

"So, no more classes today?" Danilaesis asked with a smirk.

Axterion grunted. "Like it would matter." He strode away, a path opening in the gathered squires to allow him passage.

For being one of the most prestigious rooms in the empire, the office of High Sorcerer Axterion Solaran was slovenly. In part, it was due to the inordinate number of missives, reports, and correspondence that piled high on the desk and spilled onto spare chairs, bookshelves, and impromptu towers here and there on the floor. Mostly it was due to Axterion's hesitance to allow anyone in to clean. Stacks of plates and teacups caked with remnants of past refreshments leaned against the wall nearest the door. They would be shooed out with a sorcerer's foot when Axterion grew sick of seeing them or concerned about the stability of the uppermost reaches of the stack.

The clutter kept casual guests from lingering. Anyone who wanted a seat would have to vie with reports of Academy student progress and notes from field agents from the Megrenn border for a chair. Most who visited preferred to stand rather than risk the high sorcerer's ire by damaging a page worth more than their life.

When Axterion arrived, he found his grandson already waiting for him. Danilaesis had washed and dressed, looking once more like a pompous little nobleman, rather than the scrappy squire that had been in the practice yard an hour earlier. Rather than worry over the value of the information of the contents of any of the chairs in the office, Danilaesis had thrown a stack from the desk atop one of the chair piles and taken its place.

"About time," Danilaesis remarked upon Axterion's entry. "When you said 'get yourself cleaned up and meet me in my office,' I had assumed you were in some sort of rush. I'd have stopped at the kitchens for a bite if I'd known. You want me to send for something? Sword work is hungry work."

"Slap a hand over that beak of yours," Axterion snapped. He glared at Danilaesis as he stepped past the boy and took his seat. "And get off my desk."

Danilaesis held up his hands in mock innocence as he slipped down and stood across the massive oak desk from his grandfather. "You know, you'll worry yourself to an early death. It's bad for the heart, the Korrish say."

Axterion snorted. "You think you can go about doing whatever you please, just because you've done me a favor? What good's raising you done me? You still treat me like I'm a doddering old man, just hanging on to life by his toothless gums. You never took any of the advice I gave you."

"Rashan's was always better. And Brannis was the one who listened to me, not you."

With a scowl, Axterion continued. "And now I hear from Empress Celia that you're taking to barging into her chambers?"

"Well, you have to admit, I barge everywhere I go. It's not like I'm especially welcome anywhere." Dan tipped one of the chairs until the pages slid onto the floor, sweeping aside the last few that stuck to the felt cushion. With an air of exhaustion, he slumped into the seat he'd cleared and threw a leg over one of the arms.

Glancing down at the mess Danilaesis had made on the floor, Axterion nodded. "Yes, I can't imagine why. What are you angling at?"

Danilaesis shrugged. "What did she tell you? I'm not sure it's seemly to discuss what goes on inside the empress's chambers."

Axterion scowled, but caught himself and forced his features smooth. "No, even you wouldn't dare."

"Why wouldn't I?" Danilaesis asked. "You don't think she'd rather me than that fat pig of an emperor we've got?"

"She'd twist your head in knots, boy. I don't care how strong you think your Source is. It's female magic, more powerful than anything those noble lasses and serving girls you drag into your bed can manage. And I'd advise you not to speak of Emperor Sommick in such a fashion. He may be a buffoon, a drunkard, and a glutton, but it's rude to point it out."

"Celia runs the empire anyway. He's just around to rut up heirs once in a while."

"*Legitimate* heirs. I don't want to see little princes and princesses running around glowing in the aether like miniature dragons. Do you understand me?"

"As well as I understand all those classes I skip," Dan said. He stood and gave a soldier's salute, raising a fist to his temple, then spun on his heel and marched to the door. It always did his spirits good to hang around the School of Arms. There was better camaraderie there, with sweat and bruises and occasional blood. The Imperial Academy was filled with mincing phonies who wanted the advantages of their sorcerous birth without having to fight to keep it. If they had better food, he'd spend even more of his time among the squires.

As he quick-stepped down the dizzying heights of the spiral stair around the inside of the Tower of Contemplation, he couldn't imagine the meeting having gone any better. Not only had he been given credit far beyond his intent to eventually seduce the empress, but he had steered Axterion completely clear of the actual intent of his meeting.

Me with Empress Celia? He chuckled to himself. He remembered her from before she was empress, dallying with his cousin Brannis, angling to better her lot in the empire. Thinking back to those days, it was hard to imagine trying to fill Brannis's boots. If he made a fool of himself now, he might never win her back. Better to bide his time and wait for her to come to him.

Emperor Danilaesis Solaran, First of His Name, Ruler of All Veydrus. It was a good dream. All he needed was time and Korrish ingenuity to make it happen.

Chapter 8

"What works in one world, works in the other." -Rakashi dar Fandar

It was not the most comfortable of hideaways, but it was sufficient for the time being. Kezudkan toured the finished living space for the first time since shutting himself away from the bustle and noise of Draksgollow's workshops. The furnishings were sparse, just a few chairs around a table—all formed from granite—and beds in the two private rooms. The pantry and larder were stocked, a well and pump system provided water pressure for proper hot and cold water taps, and a dynamo kept the spark lights running. All the essentials were in place, including the world-ripper and all its associated controls. The cozy touches that would transform it into a home would come over time.

"That's it, huh?" Gederon asked. "We're on our own now?" The younger daruu was Kezudkan's height already, and there was a strong resemblance in the nose and brow. But where Kezudkan was stiff in the joints and had the pitted skin of the elderly, his grandson's features were smooth as sea-washed rock and moved with the grace of a sculptor.

"Indeed. Enough noise from kuduks and humans to last me years, Geddie. Why don't you fix us something to eat while I look in on our minions?" Kezudkan turned on the world-ripper's view frame and set it a few paces from the Draksgollow's world-ripper.

By the time Gederon returned with a lunch of chicken-and-coal soup, Kezudkan was well settled into his chair, watching his kuduk partner search for worthwhile troves of treasure to plunder. "How long's it going to take him to find someplace?" Gederon asked. He was a sharp lad. After his initial shock at seeing how the world-ripper worked, he picked up on the usefulness of such a device with a quickness that made his grandfather proud.

Kezudkan swallowed a spoonful of his soup, savoring the flavor of the imported Tollopese coal. "He's getting a feel for how the humans build their cities and protect their coin. I don't expect it will be long. Sit yourself down and stop your fidgeting. You're not going to ossify at your age."

The two daruu settled in to watch the events unfold as Draksgollow worked the controls of his own world-ripper.

Much as he was loath to admit it, Draksgollow's wrist was growing sore from the search. He had been hours at the controls of the world-ripper and had nothing to show for it. Searching the countryside of what Korr would have called Garn Gel, he had found nothing but city after humble city, village after poverty wracked village. The wealth of this human nation had to accumulate somewhere, he figured. And at long last, he hoped that he might have stumbled across it.

In the view screen, the latest city he found was well up-river, farther from the sea than most humans seemed to concentrate their crown cities. The buildings were larger, better built, better maintained. Streets teemed with humans though like the rest of the human cities in the area, they were drab and broken creatures. All the same, it was the first city where there had been more than a mere token presence of armed guards. It was yet another sign that he might finally have found someplace worthwhile.

Flexing away the ache in his wrist, Draksgollow swept around the city and found the grandest of the buildings, a three-story palace of white-washed stone, ugly in the way that all human stonework tended to be—blocky, mortared, and cut with stone that never matched exactly from one section to the next. Still, it was a massive structure, and the comings and goings of a great many humans indicated that it was a hub of some sort, either commercial or governmental. Either way it was likely Draksgollow's best chance for salvaging a profit from his day's searching at the controls.

The view blurred through arched halls filled with humans as the kuduk tinker scanned for something besides lousy workmanship and stinking creatures. It was certainly a different building than the other seats of government he had stumbled through in his searching of Veydrus. There were offices filled with humans huddled behind desks, and humans waiting in lines to see them. It was similar to a Korrish bank or civic office. Many of the offices held small caches of coin at the ready, doling payments to the waiting humans or taking them in. It was all too small for Draksgollow's vision of a raid. Upper floors proved even less interesting as there were fewer humans and even less loose coin stored.

The deep. Even humans were known to burrow a shallow layer or two beneath their larger buildings, and Draksgollow was not ready to give up on the structure until he'd seen whether they had a deep beneath it or not. Drifting the view frame down from the third floor like a disembodied lift, he found one.

The lower level of the structure was darker, lit by torches at regular intervals. Something seemed wrong about them. Draksgollow stopped twisting dials, and walked over to the view frame for a closer look.

"No smoke," he muttered.

The lack of ventilation shafts had tickled some tinkering sense in his brain and pointed out the missing precaution when working with fume-spewing substances. The torches ought to have choked the halls in smoke for how many there were and how little chance for any of it to escape. Someone wanted the *look* of torches but without the unpleasant consequences. He squinted, but couldn't make out any runes carved into either the wall or the torches themselves.

"Bloody free-runed aether-spewers," he grumbled.

With a jitter in his aching hand, Draksgollow set himself back at the controls and followed a pair of humans carrying a strongbox. The sooner he found the vault where they stored their wealth, the sooner they could be gone. He would have been just as happy never discovering who aethered up those torches. It just was not worth the knowing. For a moment, he considered abandoning the search altogether, but then Draksgollow remembered his partner.

Kezudkan was a nuisance, too eager for gain and far too brave with kuduk lives on the line instead of his own. But the daruu was expecting profits, and if Draksgollow could not deliver them, Kezudkan would fine someone else who could. While he knew how to build the world-rippers, the crotchety old fossil was the only one who could tinker them into functioning properly; none of them ever worked when first assembled.

The humans in the viewing frame led Draksgollow down a layer farther—at least what passed for a layer among humans. The corridors were still lit by the same artificial torches, but guards were posted along the way, armed with bladed poles of the sort that had fallen into disuse in Korr along with the invention of black powder. *Easy enough, as long as whoever does the torches isn't around.* There was every possibility that the torches were a legacy of a bygone age, kept up by aether-tenders such as he used in his own factory. There was also the chance that torch-making was a specialized skill, unrelated to the fiery mayhem that the human rune-thrower among Erefan's rebels had wrought.

The humans with the strongbox ended their trek at an iron-bound door and were admitted by another pair of armed guards. Inside, a series of accountants of human persuasion sat piling coins and taking notes in ledgers. Promising, but not the bonanza Draksgollow hoped to find. Another door at the back of the room held more promise. Bypassing a formidable-looking lock, even for someone from Korr, Draksgollow slipped the view through to the room beyond. He grinned.

The room was filled with sturdy iron shelves, stacked with strongboxes identical to the one whose bearers Draksgollow had followed to the vault. "They even packed 'em up for us." He chuckled to himself, with no one else around to appreciate the comment.

Draksgollow was ready to round up his assault forces when something caught his eye—another door at the back.

The quick twist of a dial carried him through and into a larger chamber. Draksgollow's jaw hung slack. He blinked to tell himself he was imagining what he saw, but there it was, still there after each blink. The chamber beyond the tidy little vault was the epitome of excess wealth. Mountains of gold coins formed a landscape fit for excavation. Draksgollow had been to open pit coal mines that were smaller. The chamber dropped away, forming a valley and looking like a proper Korrish deep layer. There was no telling how deep the piles plumbed below the surface. Colored sparkles caught the eye, as gemstones and craftwork trinkets mixed among the coinage. The wealth of that single room was incalculable.

It was not going to be a quick plundering. Not at all. There was no way they would remain undetected and take one one-hundredth of the wealth from the sea of gold. It was time to bring his army and cleanse the city of humans.

"Why is he going to rush into this?" Gederon asked. The young daruu stood at the viewing frame, face nearly pressed against the wire webwork concealed behind the image. "It's not as if that much gold is going to wander away on him."

"You see, Geddie? This is why I took you on. You've got a thinker in that head of yours, and not just a bunch of hot steam like Draksgollow."

"Shouldn't we warn him?"

Kezudkan chuckled. "Now who's rushing into things? Let him try. As you said, it's not as if the gold is going to sneak off on us. We'll still know where it is. If Draksgollow fails, we'll still have a chance for it."

"There must be some formidable defense for the gold to have remained all that time."

"I agree," said Kezudkan. "I wouldn't even be surprised if this world still had dragons."

The view of the awe-inspiring cache was gone, replaced by the corridors of the human city's deep. Thirty steam tanks and a hundred hired guns on foot stood ready to receive orders. Everything about them was new, shiny ... untested. The signs of military might from the humans were next to nil, but overkill was the best sort of precaution. A small group of field sergeants had been given instruction on how to handle any rune-throwers they might run into: *Keep shooting until it stops moving, then put a couple more bullets into their heads.* It was the best Draksgollow could think of.

"You lot are going through to clear out and take control of the building you will enter," said Draksgollow. "If it's human, shoot it. If you're not sure, shoot it. I don't want prisoners, and I don't want escapees. No survivors. Understood?"

"YES, SIR." The workshop echoed with the chorus of replies. Draksgollow felt a little shiver of power hearing so many kuduk soldiers obey him. Steam tanks rumbled as the drivers started their engines.

Draksgollow put a hand on the switch that would open the world hole. "On my mark ... FORWARD!" He threw the switch, and the view turned into a hole to Veydrus—and riches beyond measure.

The halls of the Royal Palace of Azzat filled with the sounds of gunfire, steam tank chains gouging into the stone floors and humans screaming. If the primitive human weapons could have even scratched the paint on the steam tanks, the drivers would never find out. Roto-gun fire hewed down guards like practice targets before they had a chance to get anywhere near the vehicles. There were bumps in the smooth stone of the corridor when the steam tanks crunched their bulk over human corpses.

The stairs were the most harrowing portion of the raid thus far, with the incline tilting the center of mass dangerously close to tipping as the steam tanks swarmed through the human structure. Drivers leaned forward in their seats and prayed to the manufacturers that they had kept the balance point low enough. But one by one each steam tank made its way without fail. The humans fought bravely, or at least presented themselves to be bravely turned into shredded meat. They shouted unintelligible battle cries, with fury in their eyes as they charged, pointy sticks against armored roto-gun vehicles, with predictable results.

The work was growing routine by the time the convoy of destruction reached the main floor. Preventing non-combatant escapees was promising to be the most difficult task the steam tanks would face.

The ground shook. Once might have been a coincidence, but it shook again and again in a rhythm too like footsteps to be anything else.

Drivers covered their ears as a roar thundered through the palace. The thing that made that horrid scream showed itself, stepping from a side corridor with a form forged from nightmares. It stood easily twice the height of a kuduk, dark as coal ash and made of wrinkled leather. Its head was a nest of horns; its eyes red with a dull glow to them. A wide mouth parted to show fangs like thunderail spikes, and its clawed hands resembled grappling hooks.

The creature spoke, dust falling from the stonework as its voice shook the building. Its words were meaningless, but their intent was clear and unwholesome. Roto-guns fired from all angles, from steam tank and foot soldier alike. The creature threw an arm up to shield its eyes, and faint blue flashes glimmered around its skin where bullets pelted it to no avail.

"Fall back! Keep firing! Fall back!"

The creature cocked its head. "You speak daruu," it said.

The revelation was of some small curiosity to the fleeing forces. It was far less important, however, than escaping the monstrosity that shrugged aside bullets. As steam tanks backed away and spun on their chains to make their way back to the world hole, spark lanced from the creatures fingers, crackling through the steel vehicles and fusing control sticks, gears, and parts of their drivers as the heat of the unnatural spark melted the metal.

One driver, untouched by the spark assault, sped on his way, but the shaking floor behind him was his only warning before the creature grabbed the roof of his steam tank and lifted it from the ground. Chains clattered in the air as the machine fought to move with no purchase on the ground to make such motion possible. The gunner fired in a panic, but the roto-guns had no angle to aim at any part of the creature. With a snarl, it tore the guns away and threw them across the room. With its free hand, it plucked the driver free of the vehicle by his neck.

"What are you? You're no daruu."

"I'm ... kuduk," the driver replied, gasping for breath.

"What was that?" the creature asked. It relaxed its grip from lethal to merely inescapable.

"Kuduk. I'm a kuduk."

The creature put its face close and sniffed the driver. Its lip curled in a sneer. "Mixed blood. My children would never rut willingly with the stone folk. You are a foul creature indeed. Where have you come from? How did you get here?"

"Down ... down by the vaults, a hole between worlds."

"Oh?" the creature's voice still held a note of anger, but its curiosity sounded almost human. There was that lingering high pitch at the end that could be heard among the slaves, at least when they talked among themselves. "What world?"

"Korr," the driver replied. It sounded ridiculous. The week before, he had never considered the possibility of other worlds. Now he was giving directions to an otherworldly creature.

"Let us see about this 'hole' of yours."

The creature set off through the halls of the palace, still clutching the kuduk driver by the neck. When he noticed a few paces later that he had inadvertently snapped the kuduk's neck, the creature let the body fall and kicked it aside.

Draksgollow sat back in his chair, the metallic fingers of his tinker's hand massaging the muscles of his fleshy one. The last of his troops were through the world hole, and the first of the runners just coming back against the flow of foot and chain traffic.

The runner pressed himself against the corridor wall as the last steam tank drove past, then stepped through and into Korr. "No meaningful resistance, sir."

"Good. Send the next runner back when you reach the main body. I want constant updates."

The runner saluted and put his rifle over his shoulder as he hurried back through the world hole to Veydrus to catch up with his comrades. Draksgollow blew a long sigh as he found himself alone once more. *Shouldn't be long. First things first though.* It was sorely tempting to start a crew plundering, but he wanted to be sure to clear the building first. Better to hold it as a defensive structure than worry about anyone coming upon their salvage crew directly. Caution. That was one of Kezudkan's words, though he meant something different by it than most kuduks Draksgollow knew. The old daruu wanted things thought through, not rushed into half-assembled. His caution still allowed for using a machine in its technological infancy to conduct cross-world raids. Heeding the old daruu's advice seemed to be paying dividends though. The human structure would be fully within his control before long and the vast treasure vaults free for the taking.

The first of the flood of soldiers quashed Draksgollow's hopes. The distant sounds of gunfire and the gentle hum of far off steam tanks grumbling were drowned out by an awful bellow. Draksgollow had not been to a zoo since he was a boy, but he could recall no animal that could make such a noise, and he had seen no machine in Veydrus that held such a sound within it. His hired soldiers scrambled through the world hole with wide eyes and heaving chests. Most had their rifles, but not all had bothered bringing their weapons with them in flight.

"What's going on out there?" Draksgollow demanded.

Heads shook. Shoulders shrugged. "I ain't heard nothing like *that* before," one soldier admitted. "Weren't stayin' to find out what it was."

As more of his troops returned, including steam tanks that had backed their way down the corridors, Draksgollow plied his men for information, but nothing concrete was forthcoming. "I heard the order to retreat, so I did." It was the best answer he got.

The sounds coming down the hallways were horrible. Kuduks screamed, the human screams having long since ended. Spark crackled. Metal smashed against stone. A tinker's imagination held a variety of sounds and could piece them together into scenes of what might cause them. Draksgollow's could put nothing together that allowed him to diagnose the situation.

One last soldier rounded the corner, blood slicked feet sliding out from under him. The soldier scrambled on hands and knees until he was able to regain his feet. Though the world-ripper insulated Draksgollow's side from the vibrations in the floor, he could see the corridor floor shaking and heard the ram-piston footsteps approaching.

Draksgollow reached back for the switch to close the world-hole. The kuduk soldier still had several paces to make the world hole, and Draksgollow wanted to give the man a chance. When the creature came around the corner, Draksgollow's guts clenched. It was a nightmare wrapped in flesh, the sort of creature meant to chase poor sleepers through a shadowed dreamscape, only to wake them screaming when its claws tore into their flesh. This creature was nothing imaginary. Its horns threatened to scrape the ceiling; its claws were drenched in blood; it was faster than the kuduk soldier but did not appear fast enough.

Draksgollow gritted his teeth, rooting silently for the soldier to make it through in time. The creature paused in its tracks when it saw the gathering on the Korrish side of the world hole.

"You will pay for my children's lives," it roared. Its hands came up, claws pointed through right for Draksgollow, or so it felt to the kuduk tinker.

The soldier was two paces from the aperture when Draksgollow opened the switch. The hole turned back into merely a view of a distant world. Flames poured silently from the creatures outstretched hands—if those clawed appendages could even be called such—and tore down the corridor. Draksgollow and the few kuduk troops who had made it back to Korr looked on in horror as the stranded soldier was burnt to cinders before their eyes.

There were sighs of relief, and a few kuduks collapsed in fear-soaked exhaustion. Draksgollow let out a shuddering breath that he had not realized he was holding. His hands shook as he wiped a sleeve across his sweating brow.

Through the viewing frame, the creature looked all around. Kuduks backed away from the world-ripper frame as it stepped right up to the view and stood staring. Its reddened pits that passed for eyes did not betray where its gaze fell, so everyone imagined it was looking straight at them, individually. Draksgollow gave one of the control knobs a quick twist, and the view pulled back a few paces down the corridor.

The creature stepped forward.

In the air before it, letters appeared, clear as a spectacle lens and in impeccable Korrish script. Each glowed an angry red as if scorched into the very air itself.

I am Xizix, and you have killed my children. I lust for your deaths, daruu mongrels.

Draksgollow pulled another switch, and the image disappeared. Veydrus was hidden from them once more.

"What was that?" Gederon asked, pointing through to the scene of Draksgollow's workshop in the wake of the creature's message.

Kezudkan chuckled. "It was a life lesson in caution, patience, and looking a bit harder for the guardian of a pile of gold that size. Draksgollow's lucky to come out of that alive."

"But we still know where the treasure is, right?"

"Sit," Kezudkan ordered. Gederon complied, fixing his grandfather with an eager look. "Have you any idea how to deal with a creature like that? Didn't think so. Well, I don't either, and unless that changes, we look to yellower veins. Hmm ... maybe not *yellower*—doubt we'll ever find a vein that rich again—but certainly something less likely to get us all killed. No, I took something much more important from that little message."

"What's that?"

"We've got kin in that world somewhere. That creature knew of our kind. Might be worth our while finding out where they are."

Chapter 9

"You can tell a real tinker when he doesn't wash his hands before a meal. He's got grease in his blood, what's a little more in his stomach?" -Cadmus Errol

The ceiling of the cavern was cut into furrows where successive passes of the auger had left parallel circular channels. Spark lights anchored to the walls with rock bolts cast striped shadows along the ruts. It might have seemed like a Korrish deep except for a two important differences. For one, the rock was pale grey, with a chalky texture to it; no kuduk architect would think to build a city through it. The other was not apparent to anyone observing through a world hole but unmistakable to anyone present.

Madlin bounded across the world-ripper room of the new secret headquarters of the rebellion. With each step she lofted into the air head high and floated back to the floor like a puff of dandelion.

"Would you stop that?" Cadmus snapped. "This isn't a nursery."

"I don't see why we can't enjoy the gravity. Besides, it's the quickest way to get around. I've been testing it."

"Rusted nuisance is what it is," said Cadmus. He twisted himself to get beneath the control console of one of the three world-rippers that the headquarters now boasted. With six dynamos, an array of spark lights and other modern spark conveniences, and a small workshop with two of every piece of equipment they might need, the third world-ripper was the last item to check off before the base was functional.

"Is that your excuse for not being done yet?"

"I took on the least ready of the three. Of course, it's a slower job."

"I still got two of them operational and calibrated before you finished yours. Want a hand? I can show you how to—"

"If you don't mind, I've got work to do. Go ... recheck your wiring or something."

"Air getting too stale for you? I can open a hole from here now ... using one of the rippers I just fixed."

Cadmus pulled his head out from under the console. "That reminds me. If you've still got enough of a connection to Rynn, have her scramble the dials and disconnect the lunar compensator. We won't be needing it anymore. All travel will be initiated from this side."

"Oh, you know what? That would be a great idea," Madlin said sarcastically. "Let me just have Rynn reinstall it and set it back to our coordinates so she can do that." Madlin huffed. "The *Jennai* is already decoupled from the locking runes and under power. If we're going to be cooped up together in here, you're going to have to stop treating me like I'm an imbecile."

"Since when have I ever?"

"Just now. I'm not six anymore; I have this all under control."

"Just like when you nearly killed yourself playing crashball with those meat-for-brains soldiers?"

"That was field testing!"

"And how'd that work out? I could have told you that plan wouldn't hold pressure."

Madlin fought the temptation to throw a screwdriver at Cadmus. It felt feather-light in her hand, but its mass was unchanged. She could hurt him with it, just as she might on the surface at full gravity.

"Well, I guess you should have said something. If you don't need me here, I guess I'll go try out the stove and make some soup. Call me if you can't figure it out."

Cadmus muttered something under his breath as he climbed back under the console, but Madlin had to use her imagination to fill in the words.

"Oh, one other thing," Cadmus shouted, his voice echoing from inside the steel enclosure. "Figure out how you're going to generate the extra power we're going to need with only one sixth of the gravity for the waterwheels."

"Already have some thoughts," she replied. Perpetual motion with two world-rippers was one of the key innovations she had planned for the base. If she could get it working, they could cut their reliance of building aether-powered dynamos.

"You just won't like them," she added under her breath.

The crew quarters aboard the *Jennai* had come a long way in the time Dan had been aboard. Every day, more and more rooms were constructed inside the giant, hollow steel bulbs that used to keep the airship aloft, and not all of them were mere bunk-rooms. Stuff so many men into one area, and no matter how dedicated they might be to a cause, you had to keep them occupied. The workers had built in kitchens, pubs, rec halls, wrestling rings, and a firing range. Dan preferred the casino.

It was an informal title, but one of the pubs had taken to catering to the dicers and card players among the rebels. Dan found his games among the Tellurakis and the twinborn. He would be gutted before he bothered learning daruu just to talk to people he intended to be rid of at his earliest opportunity.

"Aren't you young for whiskey?" they had asked, his first night there.

"Where I'm from, they say a soldier earns himself a free drink for every man he kills in battle. I think if I'm old enough to earn 'em, I'm old enough to drink 'em." No one could argue his point, so they let him drink. It didn't matter that the story was complete manure, straight from the horse's arse. Dan was from Veydrus as far as they knew, and none of them could tell Veydrus from a fairy story.

The rebels drank well. When the world-ripper crews pillaged, they pillaged top of the line. Dan held his cards in one hand and a wooden cup of Takalish whiskey in the other. It was Tenik Faii, and nearly as old as Dan, and some of the Takalish that worked for Errol had enough class to know that wood brings out the flavor. The cards were worthless, the dwindling pile of coins in front of him were a testament to how poorly the game was running for him. Dan hadn't been cheating, mostly because he had been enjoying his drink and the bawdy humor of the soldiers.

When the jokes quieted, and the soldiers choked back laughs unfinished, Dan knew something was coming their way. He heard the thumps and tiny hisses and creaks approach from behind him, watching his fellow players' eyes.

"Can I help you, General?" Dan asked. He took a sip of his whiskey and leaned way back in his chair, hooking a foot under the table to keep from toppling over. Rynn appeared upside down in his field of vision, and he gave her a sloppy grin. *Go away. Let me drink in peace.*

"I need to talk to you about something."

"Pull up a chair. I'm sure we can make room." The table was packed, but there was no way that the men around it were going to quibble over making a space for their general.

Rynn smirked. "Last time I played Crackle with you, you killed everyone but me and the barmaids."

Dan didn't take his eyes from Rynn, but he heard the scrapes of chairs, the muttered excuses, the departing footsteps. He watched Rynn watch his fellow players slink off to other parts of the pub or remember pressing duties that needed attention.

Dan let his chair thump back onto all four legs. "You are, without a doubt, the most boring person I have ever met. Do you do anything but work? What have I done that warrants this latest interruption of my attempts not to die of boredom on this flying barge?"

Rynn leaned close, bending awkwardly without moving her legs. "I need to see you in private."

"Should have thought of that before you installed the rat trap," said Dan, nodding toward Rynn's tinker's legs. "Wouldn't have you, now. Gotta think of my safety."

"Would you quit fooling around for once?"

"Your father made it quite clear what *not* joking with you would get me. World-ripper. Black-powder. Sleeping warlock. Torch. Boom!" Dan opened a fist into a spread of fingers to punctuate his comment.

"This is serious. I need your help with something."

"Anyone bleeding to death?"

"No."

"About to?"

"No."

"Pretty sure I'd have noticed if we were under attack."

"Probably."

"This sounds like it can wait until dinnertime."

"I'm General of the Rebellion. I can't bend my schedule around your mood."

"Maybe not, but I'm drunk," said Dan, lifting his cup and downing the last of its contents. "I'll be a bit more use once I've dried out a little."

Rynn crossed her arms, and Dan could see the tendons stand out as her fingers dug into her arms. "Fine. After dinner then. No more booze for you until then." She snatched the bottle of Tenik Faii off the table.

"Dinner in your quarters. Have that chef of yours cook us up something better than the slop-line chow."

"That 'slop' is better than most of these fighters ever ate in their lives."

"Yeah, so what? I've had better and I know the difference. Vaulk and Greuder make the only real food I've seen on this wreck. I'm not one of your rebels, and I don't take orders, so if you want my help you're going to need to wipe that look off your face and try asking me for help over dinner instead of expecting me to come begging at your door after you dine like a princess."

Rynn gritted her teeth. "Fine. Dinner'll be at six."

"Six-thirty would suit me better," said Dan. Rynn scowled immediately, but Dan continued before she could object. "But I am happy to bend *my* schedule around to accommodate you."

Once Rynn had stormed off in a jangling cacophony of mechanical apparatus, Dan leaned across the table and grabbed one of the bottles left behind by his departed opponents. The label claimed it was a cheap Acardian ale, popular among the north-blooded Tellurakis, who preferred brewed to distilled.

"Mostein Hills, huh?" He eyed the bottle dubiously but lifted it to his lips anyway. Too bitter. Still, it was on the table and little else left looked any better. Downing a swig, he decided he could stomach it. Dan shook his head. "If she were a man, I'd have gutted her like a fish by now."

Madlin sat basking in the borrowed sunlight from Tellurak's Savage Lands, her chair pulled over next to the viewing frame of one of the working world-rippers. The other world-ripper she had tuned stood idle but was ready at any time if she needed it. The last, Cadmus appeared nearly done with. It lay at the far end of a semi-circular canal that ran the length of the chamber, with a viewing frame set into the floor at either end. The view was lush, filled with greenery and shimmering water from the river whose waterline was just below the top edge of the canal. The cross section of the water gave Madlin a view of the river fish as they swam unaware of the bizarre sight they were about to witness. The scene would have been worthy of a painting if not for the mesh protective screen erected across where the world hole would form, giving the frame the appearance of a fan housing.

"I didn't brew enough tea for this if you're going to be much longer," Madlin called across the room. Cadmus ignored her and continued his adjustments.

Madlin turned her attention to the wildlife, watching some movements in the underbrush and wondering whether she could catch a glimpse of what creature was concealed within. She had never paid much attention to the out of doors, and Tinker's Island had few native species. Rats, cats, horses, dogs, and birds, all other creatures were meals or stories. Madlin had eaten her share of fish but had never given them much thought as a source of amusement. The colorful creatures in the muddy shallows of the Telluraki stream were like something from a fairy story, too alien to be real. Someone must have drawn them with ink and brought them to life with magic. *I wonder if that isn't just what Eziel did.*

Madlin's philosophical musings were interrupted by a clatter from across the room. Cadmus had dropped a wrench as he pulled himself from beneath the control console. "Things going amiss over there?"

Cadmus said nothing, but pulled a switch and the first bulb around the world-ripper's frame lit. "Hah!" his voice echoed across the room. He pulled the others in succession and when the final bulb lit, his world-ripper sprang to life, showing a view out over the sea. "What are the coordinates over there?"

With the controls operating on relative location, the settings for the two would be nearly identical for what they had planned. Madlin read off the numbers from her machine, and Cadmus turned the settings on his to match. The view was from the same remote valley in the Savage Lands as far from Madlin's view as his machine was from hers. Cadmus adjusted his side until the two views were back to back.

"You ready over there?" he asked.

"Nothing left but to try it."

Madlin threw the switch, and her machine opened a hole to Tellurak. Water from the stream gushed through as if a dam had burst. In a strange sense, one had. The canal carried the water across the room, under a metal bridge that connected one half of the room to the other, covering the ends of pipes that jutted into the canal to pump fresh water out and wastewater in. It sped toward Cadmus's side where he awaited its arrival with a hand ready on the switch for the other machine.

The water level in Cadmus's view had drastically lowered. Madlin's machine was starving the stream just an inch upriver from where his looked. When the water was about to crash into the frame of his world-ripper, Cadmus activated it, opening a world-hole for the water to exit through. The water poured back into the stream bed on Cadmus's end.

Madlin let out a whoop, and Cadmus cackled and clapped his hands together. "Smell that fresh air," said Madlin.

"We need to install some rocks, to make it babble like a proper stream," said Cadmus with a critical eye on the flow.

Their elation was short lived. Once the water filled the canal, it kept rising. In the span of seconds, it was spilling over into the banks of the canal and heading for spark equipment. Prudence had made them keep the wiring off the floor when trying to harness a tiny river for themselves, but a flood was an alarming prospect when trapped in a small space with enough spark to turn them both to cinders.

"What in Eziel's name...?" Madlin shouted.

Cadmus was already back at the controls for his machine. "It's the gravity. Water pressure is higher on both sides than it is in here. We need to raise the world-holes."

Madlin rushed to her own controls as Telluraki water washed over the soles of her boots. "Blast it, you're right. I worked out the setup without taking the gravity change into account. Who knew the moon would be like this?"

"Cap it," Cadmus said. "Worry about it after we stop this flood." Cadmus brought his side completely out of the water, turning his end into a drain pipe. The water level in the canal began to drop.

When Madlin was able to adjust the controls on her end, she brought the hole halfway out of the water, and the flow into the canal lessened and stabilized.

"Sorry."

Cadmus looked down into the canal. None of the pipes were underwater, meaning no pumped water until something was done about the civic engineering of their new headquarters. "Well, you're the one who's going to mop it up."

Madlin looked out her end of the setup, then across to the hole on Cadmus's side of the room. "I can only imagine what this must look like to the animals out there."

"I imagine they see two idiot humans, trying to flood the moon of another world with their stream water."

"Yeah, I'll get working on a solution to the gravity problem."

Rynn felt foolish. She fidgeted in her seat, trying to find a comfortable position. Her tinker's legs were the best thing she'd built since her injury; they'd changed her life. But there were still deficiencies to the design and sitting was one of them. For reasons she could not quite explain to herself, she had washed and changed in preparation for dinner. Nothing she wore was fancy or even particularly ladylike—she owned nothing but coveralls and loose-fitting, comfortable garments—but she was scrubbed clean to the freckles and her clothes smelled of laundry soap.

For Dan? The question nagged at her. She tried to justify it to herself as a visit of state. Dan was as good as an ambassador to Veydrus. He was influential, powerful, and she was planning to ask for his help. *He's all that ... but ... DAN?* He was also spoiled, vicious, and violent. Her boys liked the idea of putting holes in a few kuduks here and there, but there was never the *glee* in their eyes that she had seen in his at the prospect of a force invading Tinker's Island. There was never the wanton bloodletting as Dan had shown at the card room in Buou.

There was a knock at the door. In a panic, Rynn mussed her hair—which she had just finished brushing—lest Dan get the wrong idea. "Come in."

"Thought I'd come half an hour late," Dan said as he poked his head in, "but I figured I'd kicked enough dirt on your boots for one day." He slipped inside and closed the door behind him. They were alone.

"Thanks," said Rynn. "You're one of the few left around here who ever does. You're better at it than the gang I ran with."

"Well, there's always a line you can't go over," Dan said as he sauntered to the table. "Back someone into a corner, even the scrawniest cat will fight back. Me? I just don't worry about that line."

"But you just said—"

"I said you'd had enough, not that I was worried about pushing you too far. Nice spread, I must say. Your bandits pop off to a royal cupboard for all this sparkling finery?"

"This?" Rynn asked, waving a hand over the table set for two. The plates were polished obsidian, chased with gold. Forks, knives, and spoons all shone in immaculate brightsteel—which did look a little like silver at a casual glance, now that Rynn thought about it. "These vacu-dirges were classy rides before we filled them with sweaty human soldiers. This junk all came from first class. Kitchen staff went a little off the tracks when I told them I needed a table set for two in ... my ... quarters." Rynn swallowed. She had gone off the tracks a bit herself.

Dan smirked and slid into the chair across from her. "You don't say. Well, you're looking a lot better. Wouldn't hardly know you broke your nose a week ago."

Rynn fumbled her hands under the table and gave a nervous laugh. "Well, I can't grow fingers back, but I'm not exactly made of glass."

Dan flexed the fingers of his left hand. "Yeah, the skin color took a while to get right, but you'd think I grew up with these. Perks of being a mighty sorcerer, am I right?"

"Wouldn't know. You keep refusing to teach me."

"Well, I'd teach Madlin if I was going to teach either of you. She's got a better Source for it. But you need a real teacher, someone who can get you the guidance you need. Not some lucky, gifted warlock who can barely explain what he's doing."

Rynn stopped fidgeting. "You'd really do that? Help me find a teacher?"

Dan shrugged. "I've got all kinds of political power in Veydrus. I could get you instruction at the Imperial Academy. They'd plunk you in with the eight-year-olds, and you wouldn't know the language, but they could teach you real magic in a few years."

"Pass."

The food arrived just then. Though they were still rebels and soldiers, a number of the *Jennai's* crew were full time kitchen staff, from cooks to servers. She was glad that the two who carried in their meal were relative strangers to her. Given a calm moment's thought, Rynn could have put names to both of them, but her thoughts were anything but calm. She was glad that Greuder hadn't delivered the food personally, or she might have turned red as the tomato soup that was their first course.

As soon as the door shut behind the servers, Dan spoke. "So, what was it you needed to see me about?"

Rynn took a mouthful of piping hot soup—burning the inside of her mouth—to try to compose her approach. "Blasted stuff is boiling!"

"Yeah, I've heard you can blow on it to fix that," Dan remarked dryly.

Rynn huffed and took a sip of ale to ease the burning. "Well, the *Jennai* is completely reliant on runes for levitation."

"You're better off, believe me."

"Oh, I agree. But I've been thinking ... how do we land? I was hoping you knew a reverse rune for levitation. One that makes gravity, maybe?"

"Gravity? The bloody blades is that?"

"You know, the force that keeps us all from drifting off into the sky? Makes the world go round the sun?" She almost added that the moon does the same, but the less talk of moons, the better.

"Why would we need a force to hold us down?"

"Eziel, damn your backward little magic world! Any two objects attract one another; the larger and heavier the object, the more they attract."

Dan shook his head. "Nope, that can't be true. I find I am much better attracted to small women than large ones."

"It's ... is ..." Rynn put a hand to her forehead. "Never mind. Just ask your grandfather—you mentioned once that he was clever—or your teachers at that academy. Someone in your witchcraft world must have puzzled out celestial mathematics, and if they're half as lazy as you, they immediately found a way to do it with magic."

There was a moment's pause where Dan furrowed his brow with his head cocked to one side. "I am getting the impression you think Korrish are smarter than Veydrans."

"I imagine we've damned well had to be. We've had to work for everything."

"Envy is ugly, isn't it?"

They ate in silence after that. Rynn could think of no recovery from the cliff she'd had thrown the conversation off. It amazed her that Dan could keep his silence for that length of time. *Did I actually hurt his feelings?* It seemed implausible. Dan had never shown signs of having complicated feelings before. The boy was little more than a machine that sorted people for future rutting, killing, or exploiting. Bruising his ego would be like stomping on a shadow.

"Thanks for the dinner. Better food than the rest of your crew gets, that's for sure." Dan stood and wiped his mouth on a cloth.

"Dan, just try. Please?" Rynn asked. "If you can find a way to use runes to create gravity, I'll take the world-ripper off duty for as long as it takes to find Tanner and get you to him."

"Blackmail, huh? I was wondering if you even *remembered* I wanted off this boat."

"No, it's not blackmail, it's ..." Rynn searched for a word.

"About time you grew the stones to play bare knuckle—figuratively, anyway. I'll see what I can do."

Chapter 10

"Having a gun pointed at you teaches you to value your own life. Pointing one at someone else tells you who you are." –Pious Henlon (a.k.a. "Rascal")

Kupe had never held a gun before. As a boy, he had imagined toting one of the knockers' scatterguns, but in his imagination it had never been as heavy as the real thing in his hands. It was no scattergun—those rarely hurt kuduks, from what he had been told—but rather a rifle. Where Davlin's people had gotten a hold of it, who could say? The rifle bore the mark of the Glandrek Company, which Kupe had never heard of. Guns were a subject where he was just beginning to learn what he didn't know.

All around him, similar wonder and discovery was taking place among the humans of Cuminol. They were the ones who had backed up their brave words after Davlin's sermon and shown up for duty. One of the acolytes had a crate filled with various implements of war and was doling them out like loaves to beggars. That was the sort of thing that the priests *used* to do, before they started talking about the old ways.

Kupe was assigned to a squad with nine other would-be rebels. Davlin made the assignments himself, and he broke Kupe and Charsi into separate squads. Kupe wasn't sure whether it was intentional. No one else was asking questions about who they were teamed with, and he wasn't about to be the troublemaker. At least Mull was with him as squad leader.

There were no uniforms, no badges, nothing knocker-like about the whole operation aside from being armed. Each of them covered their faces with whatever they could manage—scarves, handkerchiefs, hoods, goggles, or even just thick-smeared grease and soot. The squads filtered out into the maintenance tunnels, places Kupe barely knew existed, always taking them for granted. Regular tunnels—the sort with trolleys and shops and houses—those Kupe knew back and forth. As a news hauler, that was the oil that kept his business moving. People, places, happenings, he bought and sold those. The newspapers didn't make a lot of money from the humans; most didn't read, and a single newspaper could get passed among a circle of friends, then spread by word of mouth as gossip. It made Kupe enough money to get by, and it kept him known. It hadn't gotten him into too many sewers, water treatment ducts, or spark routing junctions. It was a part of his education that he was about to fill in, it seemed.

Mull had ordered a tunnel-rat ahead to act as scout, a boy named Murfy. He was small for his age, skinny, and with twitchy eyes that never looked long in one direction. Kupe had seen him around, but didn't know much about him. Murfy wasn't a reader, wasn't a gossip, and wasn't a girl—the three sorts of people Kupe paid the most attention to. Tunnel rats were thieves and scrounges. Not many humans minded because they spent more time on the kuduk layers than bothering fellow humans. It was simple practicality though; you don't steal from the poor because there's no coin in it. Besides, the kuduks had the monopoly on wringing coin and labor from the humans.

"What's the smell in here?" one of the other squad members asked. Kupe didn't know her name.

"Everything," Murfy answered. "C'mon." He waved for them to follow. Oil lamps lit the passage, fed by an aging and rusted tangle of pipes that reminded Kupe of a bowl of noodles.

"Where we headed?" Kupe asked. He didn't want his to be the first question, but since that valve had already been opened …

"You don't need to know," Mull snapped. "Just keep up and don't get lost."

Kupe gritted his teeth. He'd snookered Mull into this rebel business, and now the old coalman wouldn't so much as tell him where they were going. How was Kupe supposed to rebel if he didn't know where he was going?

The sub-tunnels wove endlessly through the stone of Cuminol Deep. There were inclines and dips; sometimes they climbed ladders. Kupe had tried to keep a mental map of their journey in his head but had hopelessly tangled it. It didn't even seem possible that Cuminol was big enough to account for how long they'd traveled.

"Keep up. No stragglers," Mull called behind him in a whisper that echoed down the tunnel. The comment wasn't meant for Kupe, who had been managing to match Murfy's pace, but for a pair of slaggard desk-sitters who had joined the rebels. Mull's whisper was comically loud to reach them at the back of the pack over the sounds of their footsteps and the gear they carried. If any kuduks were in the sub-tunnels with them, there would be no element of surprise.

"Ain't too far left," Murfy said.

The tunnels rumbled. The tunnels had rumbled to some degree all throughout the squad's journey, but this was different. No boiler, factory or trolley could cause the rhythmic thrumming in the stone around them the way the thunderail could. They were approaching the depot, and a thunderail was arriving.

"What?" Kupe asked. "We knocking off a thunderail?"

Mull pulled a pocketclock from his jacket and squinted at it in the feeble lamp light. "Yeah. And we're a minute behind. Pick it up!"

Murfy set off at a more vigorous pace, Mull close behind. The rest of the squad hurried to keep up. It sounded like a riot in the tunnels. How could anyone miss such a racket going on just a few paces below the railyard? A shriek of tortured metal cut the air and jabbed into Kupe's ears, making him wince—the thunderail's brakes. Even deadened by the rock above, it was an impressive sound.

"Third car from the end," Mull said as they stopped at a ladder leading up. "Grab what you can run with and get back down here. We've got four minutes. Shoot what you got to, and no more. This is a heist, not a war."

Not a war, Kupe echoed in his thoughts. *I wonder if Davlin knows that.*

Kupe was in the middle of the pack as they crowded up the ladder. The climb was awkward with a rifle in his hands. There was a strap to sling it over a shoulder, but Kupe didn't trust a strip of sturdy cloth with clip-hook ends to keep his only weapon with him. He had never been properly armed before, and he had a premonition that he would need it before the heist was over.

When Kupe emerged from the maintenance tunnel, the railyard was already in turmoil. It seemed that the rebels had already been spotted, and the freighters and laborers were running for cover and screaming for others to do likewise. Kupe had run like that before when knockers came shaking down human-run establishments looking for criminals. Guilty or not, when the knockers came, sensible humans scattered. Now the kuduks were on the other side of the guns; some humans were as well, but they were in no real danger, not that they knew that. Kupe knew it, though. Those kuduk-serving shavers might be cowardly collaborators, but they were blameless in the greater war. Davlin had made sure to pound that into the rebels' heads in his sermons. Kupe tried his best to ignore them and look for signs of knockers as he ran for the thunderail.

The third car from the end was a freight car, nothing special standing out from the others in a long line of similar cars. Up front were the passenger cars, pristine and shining. The squad could pocket some heavy coin there, Kupe knew, shaking down the passengers. The gambler in him wanted to break off from the squad, let them carry off whatever was in the freight car while he went and made himself a half a year's wages in minutes. He felt the weight of the rifle in his hands. Davlin had entrusted it to him as he had entrusted weapons to so many other rebels. It had been for a reason, and it wasn't to make one human rich—even the sort of rich that lasted for half a year.

A shot rang out. It came from the front of the thunderail. Kupe and several of his fellows whirled, rifles to the ready, to see who was shooting at them. Nobody. It was another squad of rebels, taking on a knot of club-wielding knockers near the engine.

Of course. Davlin knows the front is where the coin is. He didn't forget. He assigned another squad. Kupe's momentary lapse into greed was washed away. The rebellion wasn't going to waste a prime opportunity to part the traveling kuduks from their ill-earned coin.

"Move! Move!" Mull shouted. There was no place for stealth in the operation, not anymore. Kupe ran for the third to last car, finding that he had fallen to the back of the pack.

The next crack of gunfire was louder, closer. One of the rebels at the front of the charge collapsed. Another rifle report, and another rebel fell to the ground. The gunfire was coming from their destination, the third car from the end of the thunderail.

A momentary panic fell over those nearest the fallen fighters. They stared down at the bodies, ignoring the weapons in their hands. Two more were cut down by the next wave of fire. Kupe's eyes widened and the edges of his vision grew fuzzy.

All he saw were the two kuduk soldiers—not plain old head-knockers, but large-as-life army troops—stationed on the front and rear platforms of the car. They wore plate iron vests and helmets like inverted bowls. Their rifles looked similar to the one in Kupe's hands. The soldiers seemed to know quite well how to use theirs. Kupe raised his own to fire back, and heard the *pling* of his shot ricocheting off the iron vest of the soldier he had shot.

"Rush them!" Mull shouted, his voice carrying over the commonplace din that settled in between shots. The railyard was a battlefield, with at least one end of the thunderail fighting back for all they were worth. Kupe had no thought to spare for the front end of the thunderail. He saw that the soldier he had fired at was swinging a rifle in Kupe's direction.

Kupe was never a tunnel rat. His eyes didn't dart around on their own. He wasn't the skittish sort. Bravado was his preferred image, with an easy swagger and an insouciant smile. That was how he liked people to see him. That image was so much trash and broken glass when someone pointed a rifle in Kupe's direction. He dove to the ground, scrabbling on hands and knees to put something solid between him and the kuduk he had shot. He heard a shot ring out and winced, expecting to feel a stabbing pain, but there was nothing of the sort. Sparing a glance back, he saw that the rebels had followed Mull's order and rushed to overwhelm the soldiers while they still had the numbers for that sort of tactic. Kupe scrambled to his feet to join in, pleased to find that he had kept hold of his rifle the whole time. It seemed that there might be some hope for him as a soldier yet.

By the time Kupe got to the car, both soldiers were dead. Dragged to the ground. Shot at zero range. He tried not to look down but had to in order not to trip over the corpse. The ruined face, the red beard, they were images that would come back to him in nightmares, he just knew. He swallowed back his lunch as it tried to escape. Kupe pulled down his handkerchief and took a deep breath, free from the stifling cloth.

Inside the car, Mull was acting as freightmaster. Rebels shouldered past one another, rifles slung over shoulders and arms filled with boxes and crates. There should only have been six of their squad left, by Kupe's count, but more than that number were already inside. Another squad had joined them for the plundering.

Mull caught Kupe's eye and pointed to a stack in front of him. "Kupe, take that crate there. If you can manage it, take two."

Kupe nodded. "Yessir!" It felt respectable taking orders from a human boss for once. He slung his rifle over a shoulder and hefted the crate. It was only the size of a bundle of newspapers but weighed like stone. "What's in here? Bricks?" Kupe felt stupid when he looked more closely and saw that the crate was labeled. In plain, stenciled letters, it read: MUNITIONS 0375IN, ROTO RATED.

"Shut up and haul it out of here. Knockers'll be here any minute."

Kupe nodded though no one was paying him any special attention. He grunted and shifted the ammunition crate into a better grip in his arms, then squeezed back through the crowd and out. On the front platform of the car, Kupe glanced down to check his footing. The dead soldier had been dragged out of the way, a smeared

red trail marking his passage. When he looked up, thankful not to have been forced to look into the corpse's face again, a flash blinded him momentarily, accompanied by a popping sound that he would know anywhere.

Newspaper flashpop! The realization echoed in his head. When he hawked papers, Kupe bragged that the *Cuminol Chronicle* got to crime scenes faster than the knockers. It was no idle boast, and it was being proven again at Kupe's expense. *I'm naked!* It was an exaggeration brought on by panic, but Kupe's face was exposed when the flash bulb popped. He wanted to reach down and pull his handkerchief up; it was just around his neck. But there was the matter of a crate filled with munitions, occupying both his hands.

There was no hiding. With all the rebels' attention focused on plunder and the potential for knocker reinforcements to arrive, putting down his crate to take a shot at a news reporter seemed ludicrous. Kupe at least looked to see who had gotten him, to see who had exposed him as a rebel. He knew everyone at the paper, kuduk and human alike, even the cranky old daruu who owned the newspaper. If he could catch them before they published, he might be able to find a way to convince them not to run a flashpop that showed his face. It was a longshot, but Kupe was known. Being outed as a rebel was doubly bad for someone like him. He wouldn't be an anonymous human face in the newspaper, his name would spring to mind. He'd have to go into hiding. He'd be ruined.

The camera fell away from the reporter's face, a thin plume of smoke rising from the flash bulb. It was Charsi. *What is she doing here? Was this her assignment?* Kupe had no time to ponder. He and the rest of the squad ran for the sub-tunnels.

Rynn sat working at her desk, a pile of messages and reports pushed aside in favor of a fresh sheet of vellum. A ruler, compass, and pencil were all she needed right then. It was a sanctuary in a world that ended where the off white of the vellum gave way to the wood grain of the desk. Within that rectangle of space, her power was absolute; nothing happened there but what she wished. Unlike the *Jennai,* which seemed to obey her orders with fingers crossed behind its back, crew and all.

There were times when the whole of the rebellion seemed designed to vex her. Simple instructions were botched with regularity. The welders veered from her plans. Soldiers played crashball instead of training. Even the parts from the workshop were defective now and then, something she had never given much thought on Tinker's Island, under Cadmus's watch. Wherever she went, a small pocket of attentiveness followed her. None of the crew wanted Rynn of Eversall, General of the Human Rebellion, to see them lax in their duties. But months on, the rebellion was growing stale for some—no longer the joyous freedom of throwing off kuduk rule, but the dogged, dreary march of daily life working as pieces of a larger machine. Not every cog could see what the whole was doing; it just spun along, teeth tugging the same chain, link after link.

Rynn could sympathize. When she had been just a lookout for Hayfield's gang—had it possibly been Rascal's, all along?—all she cared about was spitting in some kuduk eyes, pocketing some coin in the bargain, and getting to work the next morning with no one the wiser. If she needed a night off, a sly word to one of the gang and she was free; they'd plan around her or not go out themselves that night. Now, there was nowhere to go, no escape. The world-ripper made it possible to *go* anywhere, but it needed her, and through some paradox that prevented her leaving it.

Madlin and Cadmus got their freedom, but now I'm the only one who knows how to work it. There were others who had been trained in the device's use. Some of the mechanics could even make simple repairs when something broke down. But when it came right down to it, the only one who could strip it to the bolts and get it working, no matter what, was Rynn.

A knock sounded at the door. Rynn looked up from her work, but said nothing. It was a test. The door opened—someone had failed.

Rynn slapped the pencil down against the desk. "Did I say to come in?" she asked, her voice mixing exasperation and sarcasm.

"You've got a new batch of papers," Sosha replied, hoisting the bundle of newsprint she carried as evidence to back her claim. "Forty seven minutes, start to finish."

Rynn cocked her head and nodded, impressed despite her annoyance. "Not bad. Leave them on the chair." While gathering newspapers from across Korr was good practice for the world-ripper trainees, the papers themselves were of less concern. It was merely proof that the operator had dialed in the locations of cities across the world and opened discreet holes to snatch the papers.

"I think you're going to want to read the *Cuminol Chronicle* today."

"Why's that?" Rynn asked. She resumed her work on the vellum.

"The rebellion hit a thunderail there," Sosha replied, slapping the paper down atop Rynn's pile of mostly unread reports.

Rynn looked at the paper with a frown. "We didn't have anyone on that. Did we?"

Sosha shook her head. "No, we didn't. We're not the only rebellion around anymore, it would seem."

"Must be Rascal's people. From what he's told me, the Church of Eziel was poised and waiting for someone to throw the first punch. They must be shoveling coal on our fire." Rynn squinted at the flashpop and adjusted her glasses. "Some poor sop got his face in the news. Sloppy."

"I read the article. His name's Kupe, and there's a hunt on for him."

"Let me guess …"

"Can we look for him?" Sosha asked.

An idiot. Just what we need around here. No, that wasn't the right way to look at it. *Another face for the rebellion—one besides mine.* Rynn studied the flashpop more closely.

Kupe stood there staring blankly from the dingy grey page, a crate in his hands, its label too small to read. He was older than her, but still young, and not bad on the eyes. A flashpop like that was bound to get pilfered by other papers; a human face for the kuduks to see. *It could work.*

"Fine. Just make it clear that we're not going to be rescuing every brick-headed clod who gets himself caught in the papers."

It was off hours in the steel mill. The furnaces never went cool, but the workers were gone, save for an understaffed group of night watchmen more concerned about thefts than simple trespassers. Since robbing a steel mill would involve heavy, steam-powered equipment, most of the watchmen dozed through their shifts.

Beneath that negligence, a squad of human rebels had taken temporary refuge in the quenching room. It wasn't all that far from the railyard, less than a mile of tunnel and a layer down, situated on the outskirts of Cuminol with vent access to the sky. The steel mill used plenty of water, so water lines from the main civic pumping station ran directly to it. The maintenance tunnel had been ankle-deep with stagnant water from various minor leaks—the perfect cover for bloody boot prints.

Kupe sat on his prize. The small wooden crate was battered and worn from years of use, packed and repacked with munitions and dragged across half of Korr no doubt, but it was sturdy enough for a seat. With a wire brush and a pail of water, he scrubbed the soles of his boots clean.

"Ain't never thought I'd see the day I considered throwing away good boots," he muttered. "Gonna be watching my own tracks for weeks, checking for blood."

Kupe wasn't the only one who had been stepping in blood, nor was he the only one cleaning his boots because of it. The brushes were from the mechanic's shed, meant for scrubbing rust from pipes and beams. Some poor steelworker was going to come to work to find his tools flecked with blood come morning.

"Ain't never had boots nice as yours," Murfy commented. The boy was wearing soft-sole shoes, the kind that only made noise if you scuffed your feet walking. Kupe hadn't even heard Murfy come up behind him. The boy never seemed to stay put.

"Well, Kupe, you're a fighter now, not just a news hauler," Mull said. "Don't want to be breaking in a new pair when you're running from a knocker."

"Them weren't knockers," said one of the other rebels.

Mull nodded. "Yep, them were soldiers. We hit us an army shipment, sure enough. Them crates is full of—"

"Bullets," Kupe finished for him.

Mull pushed up the brim of his cap. "Fancy boy, eh? Can't help rubbing your reading in people's faces? Well, if we're going to be shooting these here rifles, we're going to need bullets. Lotsa bullets."

Kupe felt the weight of his rifle against his back. He had only fired it once and hadn't so much as put a dent in the kuduk he had aimed at. "So … we shoot a bunch of kuduks so we can steal bullets, so next time we can shoot more of 'em."

"Ain't all of it, but yeah," Mull replied. "We'll keep ourselves fed, armed, clothed—you want new boots, next time we're in the markets, just grab a pair. Bust me if that didn't feel good, watching them stone-hearted blighters take it for once. Makes me wonder why none of us did this years ago."

"Yeah," Kupe said, agreeing for form's sake. He couldn't shake the image of that kuduk soldier with the ruined face. Had he been slower, or the other rebels hadn't been there to save him, Kupe and that soldier could have reversed places. It was a humbling feeling, having your life dangled in front of you like that.

"How long we gotta stay down here?" one of the rebels asked.

"Early-clocker's'll be on shift 'round about five thirty. We gotta be back in the tunnels by then," Murfy said.

Mull flipped open his pocketclock. "That means we bolt our arses to the floor for another two hours and change."

"Wish we'd snagged something to eat," one of the rebels groused.

"Wasn't our assignment," Mull replied.

Murfy slinked into a corner of the room, cheeks bulging. Kupe might have been the only one who noticed him, but he didn't care enough to say anything. He was known. Who was he to snitch on a tunnel rat who knew enough to bring along food. That was how kids like Murfy got by, thinking of survival, first and last. Kupe could always bum a meal at one of the public houses if he had to; that was the sort of thing that being known got you.

Kupe was lost in thought—idly wondering if it was worth trying to wheedle a share of Murfy's food for himself—when he wandered into a waking dream. At least, that was all he could imagine at first, when a giant window opened up in mid-air. The window, or whatever it was, was larger than the maintenance tunnels Kupe and his comrades had spent the day traversing. Through it, there was a large, metal-walled room, with a line of human soldiers leveling pistols toward Kupe's squad.

"Bloody, rusted—" Mull began, backing away from the window.

A woman slipped between the soldiers to stand in front. She wore baggy coveralls and a pair of wire-rimmed spectacles. In one hand she held a newspaper, in the other a pistol of her own; she pointed it right at him. "You Kupe?"

Kupe's eyes went wide and a sudden dizziness crept over him. It was the second time today that he'd found a weapon aimed at him. He wanted to deny her question, to claim he'd never heard of any Kupe. But his tongue was a sack of coal in his mouth, and he couldn't make it form words.

The woman with the gun flipped the newspaper around and showed him the flashpop above the fold. It was the *Cuminol Chronicle*, and the headline read: REBEL RAILYARD RIOT. The flashpop showed a thunderail car with human rebels crowding out the door, carrying crates and rifles, their faces covered in scarves, hoods, and masks. A lone human stood out, barefaced and gawping, in the fore of the image. "This sure looks like you. You're even doing that face again." The woman gestured to him with the pistol.

"What do you want?" were the first words Kupe managed to put together. Everyone else had the sense to keep their mouths shut and edge away from the strange scene.

"Listen, whoever this Kupe is just got made by the papers. If he wants to live through the month, he can come with us. Life's going to get pretty full of knockers for him if he keeps around Cuminol."

"Who are you people?" Mull asked.

"My name is Rynn, Rynn of Eversall, General of the Human Rebellion."

"General?" Mull asked. "Since when do we have ranks? Davlin's in charge of the rebellion."

"Sounds like someone I ought to talk to," Rynn replied. "For now, how about you all come through, and we'll give you a lift to where you need to be. I can't imagine you lot will be welcome when that mill opens."

"Who said we were going with you?" Kupe asked. He glanced to Mull, looking for support for his stand. None of Kupe's squad had their rifles out, having been taken by complete surprise.

Rynn aimed her pistol for one of the coolant pipes, a monstrosity of plumbing more than two feet across. When she pulled the trigger there was no *bang*, just a crackle of spark and hissing from the barrel, but the pipe rang with the impact. Water spurted from both sides as her bullet punched a hole clean through it. She fired five more shots, and the pipe looked like a fountain, water spraying in all directions.

"How did you—"

"We're the pro leagues, Kupe," Rynn said. She gestured to the crate of bullets at Kupe's feet. "Where you're going, you're not going to need bullets."

Chapter 11

"No society has developed without the invention of tea. You can tell that humans are savages at heart by the nasty things they brew and drink." –Kezudkan Graniteson

Kezudkan sipped at a cup of tea, savoring the nutmeg and crushed limestone. The cozy little boarding house he had commandeered had come with an elderly daruu woman who knew how to brew a proper drink. Kezudkan suspected that she doted on him because she hadn't met a daruu her age in decades, but his own interest began and ended with the tea.

Tea was a gentleman's thinking aid. No great thought in the history of the world had been conceived with any lesser drink. It warmed the guts and soothed the mind, instilling a calmness that allowed the world to crystallize to perfect focus. The better the tea, the better the likelihood of achieving that malleable state of mind. It had taken days of sampling to find a housekeeper who could make a cup such as the one in his hand.

That monster spoke our language. It was the burr that had rubbed his mind raw since the disastrous encounter through the world-ripper. There were so many possibilities. The scientist in Kezudkan could not deny that some of them were implausible, but his mind refused to shake its hold of them. *It could be aware of our world, able to open holes like the machine's. It could have studied us; we may have drawn its ire, and it knows where we live.* It was the worst scenario Kezudkan had imagined. *It could be a scholar itself. We attacked its home; perhaps its normal demeanor isn't so … monstrous. In that case, a more subdued overture might be accepted, a chance to clear clogged pipes and sift out bad bearings.* Optimistic drivel. Only a mud-brained idiot would expect to weld up a crack such as that. Barging into a man's—thing's?—home with steam tanks was not the sort of thing you could mend by penning a heartfelt apology. There were plenty of other theories knocking about in Kezudkan's head, ranging from the creature being created by daruu to being daruu itself. But the tea. The tea helped clear away discordant thoughts, and let Kezudkan see the most probably reason: *That world has daruu.*

The beauty of the daruu language was its immutability. Kezudkan had read of the old human tongues. If the daruu language was carved of stone, the human tongue was scratched into the mud of a riverbank, never settled, never constant. That monstrosity that spoke the daruu language could only have learned it from an original source, whether from living daruu or from the study of their works. Somewhere beneath Veydrus, there would be deeps.

The door opened. "Care for a top-up?" Mrs. Bas-Siltson the innkeeper asked. She carried a silver tray with a teapot, a delicate steam rising from the spout and carrying with it the scent of limestone.

Kezudkan sipped the last of his cup and smiled to Mrs. Bas-Siltson. "I do believe I would. You are most kind. This was exactly what I needed."

Draksgollow sat at the controls of the world-ripper, scanning through mile after mile of unbroken rock. "Tell me again why we're even bothering to look?" he asked. "I thought we agreed up front that we wouldn't be plundering from our own people, if we find them in other worlds."

"I believe we have brethren here, yes," Kezudkan replied, standing before the viewframe. "But I think we've been charging in blind."

"Like a flanker taking the ball against three defenders, instead of passing?" Draksgollow asked.

Kezudkan twisted around to display the furrow of his stony brow. "Is that some sort of ball crashing metaphor?"

Draksgollow waved his hand back toward the view-frame. "Just forget it."

Kezudkan turned his back and continued. "This endeavor might benefit from local knowledge. If we can find our people, they might be more than willing to tell us more about their world. Our predations might enrich us while weakening their enemies. It could be greatly beneficial to all concerned."

"And all this is because of some tea?" Draksgollow sounded skeptical. "How do you know that creature doesn't have the ability to puzzle out languages? Maybe it uses magic."

"Oh, I considered that, among a hundred other theories. But I have heard nothing of creatures such as that thing visiting Korr. It is far simpler to assume that it learned our language from its own world." It grated on even his own ears, referring to the daruu tongue as being shared by the kuduks. Kuduks never had a language to call their own, and had merely made the obvious choice, when the alternative was one of the myriad, amorphous human languages.

"And why start in Braavland, anyway? Piss poor geology for deeps. Their deeps have got five times the support structure that a nice solid deep like Cavinstraw needs. You'd think this primitive world might not have worked out how to even build one in a place like that."

Kezudkan tapped his cane against his shoulder as he pondered. "You know … you may have something there. Perhaps a geological search might yield better results than a thorough progression through the locations of all Korr's deeps. Let's try one I *know* is built in stable rock—Eversall."

"Now, you've hit the vein," Draksgollow replied. He sat forward and perked up; his hands moved more briskly over the controls. There had been no attempt to disguise the kuduk tinker's boredom.

Kezudkan rattled off the coordinates. Wherever they set up a world-ripper, he figured out their location relative to Eversall Deep before calculating all the other locations he had recorded in his log books. While it was certainly a convenient mathematical aid and the lynchpin of all his inter- and intra-world movements, he always felt a bit easier in the stomach knowing where home was. Nothing upset his digestion like being adrift, cut off from the stones that were as much a part of him as his own feet. It was a feeling he could not convey to the kuduks who worked for him. Perhaps when he found the daruu of Veydrus, they might be sympathetic to such sentiments.

Cuminol—or at least its sister in Veydrus—was at higher elevation than Eversall, so Draksgollow ended up approaching it from the sky side. When the view stopped blurring and Draksgollow left it still long enough for Kezudkan to get an idea of the place, the city was spectacular. Nothing but stone. Despite its deplorable exposure to the weather and sun, the sight warmed Kezudkan's heart. A towering wall rose against the foothills and plains, clearly meant for defense in a world unknown to artillery.

Smooth stone. No human or kuduk hand could have crafted it so finely. "Bring us in closer. I want a good look. How did we even miss looking here when we were searching for our gold?"

"You said it was a drain on the dynamo, as I recall," Draksgollow replied. "You found a mountain busting at the seams with gold and didn't look past it."

"Indeed. It seems I was remiss."

Draksgollow took a scenic path, showing more showmanship and artistry than Kezudkan was wont to credit the tinker. They ascended as if by cable gondola, sweeping up toward the city from the hills below. Kezudkan felt his spirits lifted by the grandeur. As the viewframe crested the wall, his jaw went slack. The buildings within were stone, the flat, ugly, blocky constructs that humans built. It was better than Korr's humans had ever managed, but it was nothing like the elegant simplicity of the wall. The effect was magnified by the presence of a second wall, overlooking the city, built just as mightily as the first. It held back the glacial snow and ice that were absent in the upper reaches of the same mountain range in Korr. But whereas Korr's denizens vented forges and ore smelters through chimneys in the mountain, keeping the ice from building, the inhabitants of Veydrus simply walled it off.

The city between the two walls vexed Kezudkan sorely. It was like finding a gold nugget, only to discover that it was merely a thin plating of gold over lead. Why would anyone who could build walls such as that, build a city so rudimentary?

"You gone kinda quiet," said Draksgollow. "Something wrong over there?"

Kezudkan nodded. "Everything. None of it fits. The walls look like daruu work, but the city itself could not be. Not unless my people have designated this a children's playground. I could have stacked stones better at five."

"Yeah. Wasn't gonna say anything, but you're right. Who knows, maybe the daruu here aren't what they used to be. Old walls, new city?"

"Ghastly thought. Bring the view nearer the wall; I want a closer look."

Draksgollow complied, drifting the viewframe right up next to the wall, close enough to reach out and touch had the world-hole been open. "Runes all over it. Bust me, someone spent a lot of time carving that thing."

It was true. The wall looked textured from a distance, but now that they were so close, it was plain that the whole surface was adorned with runes. Kezudkan squinted at them, trying to focus on individual patterns. Even by daruu standards, he was well-read on the subject of rune construction. But as he followed the connections, he found himself lost in the complexity. For long minutes he stood tracing a single grouping, looking for a beginning or an end, but found none. "This is beyond me," he admitted. "It would seem that while their stonework might be a subject of debate, the runecraft of whoever built this wall is superior to anything Korr knows."

"You can tell that from just a quick glance?"

"I could tell that as soon as I couldn't fathom an end to it," Kezudkan replied. "I may not be the foremost expert on runes, but I'd wager that you couldn't fill a trolley car with men with more rune knowledge than I. This … this was done by people who rely on runes, not science, and have plumbed a depth we wouldn't dare."

"It's just a wall."

"Perhaps. But perhaps that proves the point all the better. What casual power, choosing to rune a wall to stop a glacier, rather than melting it away, or better yet, simply not building a city here. And the power of the runes. Do you have any idea the weight of ice and snow bearing down upon it?"

Draksgollow stared blankly for a moment, eyes twitching back and forth at calculations that Kezudkan could only imagine. It was mathematics the old daruu could manage himself, but it always amused him how Draksgollow ground numbers up in that tinker's brain of his. *Just like Erefan used to do.* The memory immediately soured his mood.

"Yeah, I've got a notion," Draksgollow said. "Still, you want to keep looking? I didn't see anyone out in the streets, but we didn't look hard, and it looks like there's fires going. Someone's living here."

"Indeed," Kezudkan replied. As Draksgollow lowered the view from the glacier wall, Kezudkan noticed a gate set into the mountainside. "Wait! Stop there."

"What? You want to look inside the mountain?"

"These primitives have no lifts. If they have deeps, it stands to reason that they would have tunnels and ramps heading down."

"Fine," Draksgollow huffed through pursed lips. The view slid smoothly through the solid gate and into a tunnel beyond. The walls were roughly carved in barbaric human fashion. Kezudkan fought down the urge to order Draksgollow to stop and shut down the machine. He needed to know.

The tunnel curved around and down in a single loop of a grand spiral. Without being there, Kezudkan could only estimate, but it seemed as if they were doubling back to an area directly below the sky. The bottom of the tunnel was guarded by four human guards armed with spears. What lay beyond them caused the old daruu to overlook that distasteful fact.

They built a deep. These humans built themselves a deep. There was no mistaking it. As in the city above, the construction was all distinctively human: drab, square, and utilitarian, with ill-fitted stone mushed together with mortar. It was, as near as Kezudkan could tell from first glance, a single enormous cavern, defying everything structural engineering said about deeps. There were a handful of pylons running floor to ceiling, big around as a thunderail engine, but by Kezudkan's estimation, they should not have been enough to support the weight of the city above.

"Rusty blood," Draksgollow swore. "Those buggers built themselves an actual deep. Ain't nothing of our kind around here, mine *or* yours."

"Agreed," Kezudkan muttered, staring at the scene in the viewframe.

"Face it. This world's just like ours, except here it was humans that won the great war. Your kind ain't nothing but old walls and monsters' memories. That thing must have been ancient."

There was a clack, and the viewframe went dark. Kezudkan spun—his old back protesting immediately—to see Draksgollow throw the remaining switches, powering down the world-ripper. "What are you doing?"

"Getting some sleep," Draksgollow replied. "Got no more patience for paving your daruu memory lane tonight." The tinker stood, the hiss and whirr of his mechanical joints echoing in the quiet left behind as the dynamo spun to a halt.

As Draksgollow left, taking with him the few onlookers who gathered any time the machine was active, Kezudkan went back to looking at the viewframe. It was nothing more than a webwork of warm copper wires, cooling rapidly in the chilly air. When the sound of kuduks faded, Kezudkan abled over to the door, locking it shut. Sitting himself at the controls, he turned the world-ripper on once more. It was time to see what sort of deep these Veydran humans had managed.

"What are we doing here anymore, Kep?" Draksgollow asked. He sat across the dinner table from his old mechanic, as close to a friend as the tinker had among his employees. "I didn't sign on to hunt for lost daruu legends, or fight monsters."

"Too right, boss," Kep replied, just before biting into a sausage skewered on the end of his fork.

"Rip my rivets out, I didn't even plan on plundering. I figured, maybe a few easy mines, places we already knew were rich in gold and silver. Maybe if we wanted to branch out, we'd get into lumber. Good money in that if you own land with trees."

"Naw, wood's good for paper, but raw boards make my skin itch."

"What's the good in being rich if we get ourselves killed in the process?"

"Ain't none," Kep replied.

Draksgollow took his anger out on a chicken leg, ripping the meat from the bone with his teeth. "That old daruu's down a tunnel with his back to the cavern. He can't even see what we could do with these machines. We could change the world."

"Sounds like more work'n it's worth." Kep took a hunk of grey ash-bread and bit into it.

"What's work? Ain't this all been work? I lost good men. You wanna tell *them* it ain't work? We crack our backs building the machines, keeping 'em running right. Good men went into those other worlds to bring back riches."

Kep nodded along. "A lot of them didn't come back."

"Can't we take a bit more … long-term approach? Maybe get rich *and* make names for ourselves? Right now, we're looking like the villain from one of those festival day pageants. Robbing, robbing, robbing … just because it's easy and they can't stop us."

"'Cept that time they did," said Kep.

"And that's just the thing. Why are we taking stuff, risking more run-ins when the owner catches us hitching a ride on his thunderail and boots us off? That sort of risk just doesn't sit right in my belly."

"That or the beans," said Kep.

"I'm not getting my britches twisted over morals here," Draksgollow said, pointing a finger at Kep.

"'Course not," Kep agreed before helping himself to a chicken leg.

"It's just good business. I want coin, but I want someplace to spend it, too. What good's being rich when the world's gone flushed itself down the sewer drain?"

"It's them rebels. World weren't perfect before, but it's a sight worse now."

"You know, we lost a steel shipment? Thunderail got boosted last week. Rebels didn't haul away the steel, but the thunderail went off the tracks, and it's trapped in a wrecked car."

"Can't read a paper without seeing some gloom and drear about 'em."

"Well, Kep, who says we have to be the pageant day villains for that daruu? We can get those machines running on our own. Kezudkan's rebel tinker managed it; why not us?"

Kep scratched his head. "Well, the old guy seems to have a way with the things."

"I'm not suggesting we cut him loose or anything like that. I just think maybe we don't *need* him anymore. Maybe we let that thought drift into the miscast skull of his and see if we don't get a bit of leeway. I'm growing tired of chasing his fancies around three worlds."

Kep ran his fingers through his beard, a nervous twitch. "That Kezudkan, he seems like the wrong sort to go knocking at."

"So am I."

The human city was small, relative to the deeps of Korr. Certainly the large central cavern was immense, but that was the extent of the livable space. There were no tunnels lined with homes and shops, no grand factories, stadiums, theaters, each with their own cavern. All there was of the human deep was there, almost as if the humans had been so ambitious in their excavations that they had gone too far, then decided to use their primitive masonry to replace the lost rock that could have been left for buildings.

Around that central cavern, however, were mines larger than Kezudkan could have dreamed humans would delve. Considering the lack of technology, the humans had either greater skill at mining that he would have credited them, used magic in the digging, or had been at it for a very, very long time. A simple, macabre fascination took hold of the old daruu. Despite its infestation with humans, and occasionally larger, human-like creatures that he could not put a name to—perhaps some cousin race, or a tribe of humans that had simply outgrown the rest—he was enrapt. Here and there he would recognize a vein or iron, or a seam between two strata of rock that he knew from Eversall Deep. A shop should have been here; a trolley crossing there; over that way would have been the tunnel to the lifts. He got his bearings by the moment and marveled at the differences from the Eversall he knew to the strange, twisted tunnelscape that the humans had created.

Wandering through the night in another world, Kezudkan lost all sense of time. He would have been pressed to remember that he even carried a pocketclock. But his untold hours of meandering took a sudden turn when the tunnels changed. There was a heavy steel plate set into the wall, with words engraved in two languages. On the one side, closest to the tunnels he had traveled from the human deep, the words were gibberish. Gracing the other side, in immaculate daruu runes, was written: "Human territory. Do not cross without leave."

The tunnels beyond were polished smooth, glossy in the faint light that the world-ripper's search mode provided. Where the human tunnels had been an irregular arch swept through the rock, these new tunnels had flat walls that curved gracefully above head height to meet at a gentle peak. Kezudkan had not seen the style before, but the workmanship was undoubtedly his people's.

"Draksgollow, you mechanical wretch, *this* is what I was looking for!" Though no one was there to hear him, it felt good to say it aloud.

Kezudkan followed the tunnel, down, down into the bones of Veydrus. It seemed at first that the tunnel complex was deserted, for Kezudkan went miles without seeing signs of his kin. The thought that struck him was how similar the tunnels were to the human mines, when he realized that was just what they were: mines. Rather than leave the tunnels to languish as had the humans above, the Veydran daruu chose instead to finish them as proper corridors.

With a steam engine determination, Kezudkan pressed onward. His fingers and wrist grew aches from countless twists of the world-ripper's dials. But he was used to aches; what part of him did not ache from time to time, either from use or idleness. It was a losing game to try to avoid them all. Daruu often quit at Kezudkan's age—quit everything. The stiffening of the joints was only painful if one tried to move. Many were the elderly daruu whose next of kin discovered a virtual statue. Not Kezudkan.

At long last, the mine tunnels gave way, and beyond them was a city unlike anything the daruu of Korr could have dreamed. It appeared as a single piece of stone, shaped into tunnels, buildings, statues, fountains, stairs, and everything else a deep needed. There was no sign of a seam, a crack, or an awkward corner anywhere. The runes carved everywhere were not the magical sort he had seen on the walls protecting the human sky far above, but bore the names of streets and shops, all exquisitely formed as if they had been pressed into the stone, not chipped or carved.

Some few among the runes did bear magic, for that was the cause of the ambient glow that lit the whole of the deep. Soft, pervasive, and a gentle blue-white, it spilled from runes along the tunnel walls, ignoring the rule of shadow and pouring into every corner and doorway. All these wonders Kezudkan took in at a glance and promptly shoved aside.

Daruu. *My people. So, so many.* Kezudkan knew perhaps three dozen of his own kind personally, scattered across Korr. Many were kin, a few were old friends, and the rest acquaintances he had met throughout his career. They did not, as a rule, gather. He had never seen ten of them in the same place before, and the last time he had seen more than three at once was at his father's memorial farewell. His sister had been there, along with his grieving mother, his daughter and her husband, and his two grandchildren. The Veydran deep teemed with them. They strolled the streets, alone or in mixed pairs; they came in and out of shops; they sat on benches in a plaza that surrounded a multi-tiered fountain. His first inclination had been to try to get a chalk-board census of the daruu population, but that was a human's errand. *Too many to begin counting.*

Kezudkan studied his otherworldly kin. In face and body, he could not tell them from his Korrish brethren, though their coloration was matched to this particular deep, which would have had them all look like natives of the Eversall area. The clothing they wore appeared to be entirely metallic. A copper mesh of tiny linked circlets seemed to be in fashion, with fewer daruu wearing steel or iron; one young daruu gentleman wore silver. All were adorned with plates of solid metal, usually on the shoulders, and sometimes at the elbow or chest. None wore footwear of any kind, their bare feet getting to feel the stone of the deep beneath them. *I haven't gone barefoot since I was a lad. Was it kuduk foolishness that made it undignified to go without shoe or boot? Bearded vermin! What else have they corrupted?*

With the Veydran daruu's signage, navigating the deep was a trifling matter. It was layered and interconnected, each section bearing a harmonious balance that the Korrish deeps strove for but never quite managed, never too much nor too little stone for support between. At intersections and upward-sloped tunnels, signs pointed the way to various landmarks and districts. He found that he liked the sound of Royal Palace Way, and followed it.

Through twisting tunnels, bedecked with murals and bas relief on every surface, he followed the sign and others like it, seeing ever more opulence as he went. No longer was it rare to see precious metals worn as garments, and many daruu wore jewels worked into their clothing as well.

By the time Kezudkan reached the palace, he saw guards in uniforms of full gold armor. The interlocking plates covered every inch of their bodies, save for a slit at the eyes and a few holes to breathe through. Only by body shape and context could Kezudkan even guess that there were daruu inside the suits. Stretching from floor to ceiling of an otherwise toroidal cavern, the palace acted as an immense pillar. The entrances were halfway up, thin bridges of stone that should not have supported their own weight except by magic. Each radiated from the palace like spokes of a wheel toward the surrounding tunnels.

Oh, how secure they must feel, buried beneath a mountain, with such limited access. My appearance inside their walls will be such a shock. The thought amused a giddy part of Kezudkan's mind too numbed by lack of sleep for sense. *Appearance? Blast me, I must be an atrocious sight.* With that realization, the weight of that night's exploration settled upon him and took hold. He took note of the effort it was taking to keep his eyes open; he noticed the slouch in his posture as he sat at the world-ripper's controls. *Not tonight.*

There were times for haste, and introducing yourself to a lost civilization was not one of them. Kezudkan's drowsy mind was good for little else at the moment, but it knew that much. He scribbled the coordinates on a piece of paper and shoved it into the pocket of his vest. In so doing, his fingers brushed the pocketclock he had forgotten. Pulling it out and giving a flick of the wrist to open it, he saw the time; it was nearly four in the morning.

It took an effort of will, but Kezudkan kept his gaze from drifting back to the image of Veydrus in the viewframe. He shut down the machine before the temptation grew too strong and spun the control dials back to all zeroes, so that neither Draksgollow nor his underlings would know where he had seen.

More privacy next time, he promised himself. *Can't be certain how long it will take to meet the daruu king … or emperor, or whatever they call him.* He flipped off the spark lights on his way out of the workshop, then hesitated a moment in the dim light from the corridor beyond. Struggling out of his boots, Kezudkan walked back to his accommodations barefoot, feeling the stone against his flesh.

Chapter 12

"It is only by the application of advanced sciences that we achieve flight." - *Ebner Jornuss, inventor of the first vacu-dirge airship*

The *Jennai* hung motionless in the air, parked just high enough above the swells of the Sea of Kerum that the ship was in no danger of getting hit by one. They were positioned well off any of the standard shipping lanes and far from any coast. Per General Rynn's order, they were located in the least likely place for anyone to spot them. The edge of the airship was lined with crewmen enjoying the view. Some held fishing lines or the end of nets hung far down into the dark ocean below, in the hope of catching something worth eating. The trackless seas were sparse with life as far out as they were, but it did not stop some of the rebels from trying. More daring were the ones who went down the rope ladder to swim in the early dawn hours when the sun was not so blinding on the water.

Apart from all those, buried within the holds, were Rynn's apprentice world-ripper operators. All of them had been certified to work on their own by now, but they needed the practice of finding their bearings anew each time the rebel airship stopped. With their coordinates relative to the *Jennai*, there were a series of calculations to rediscover all the locations in Rynn's and Erefan's logbooks.

"How far does it move each time you spin one?" Dan asked. He stood with his hands resting on the shoulders of Kaia, the operator currently stationed at the world-ripper's controls. The two of them were the only occupants of the hold. With the novelty wearing off, Rynn had finally managed to stop the machine's standard operations from becoming a theater performance.

Kaia swallowed, her muscles tense beneath Dan's fingers. Dan looked over her shoulder at the control panel, catching a faint whiff of fragrance from her hair that reminded him of cinnamon. "Don't know, exactly. Dials get more particular to the right and move it less. More just a feel though."

Dan glanced down at a sheet of paper, covered in pencil-scratched calculations. "Looks like a lot of ciphering for a 'feel.' Think you could explain what that all means?"

"Well, we take where we are and subtract where we were. Then we can just add that to whatever the logbook says, and there you have it."

Dan squeezed, and Kaia winced. "No, I don't quite think that I do. How do you add and subtract places?"

He could feel Kaia tremble in his grasp. "General Rynn gives us a start, with sextant readings," said Kaia. "It's enough to get us close, then we scoot the view until it's lined up again. It's all there in numbers. North, south, up, down, and world."

"World?"

"That's the easy one," Kaia replied. "Zero is here in Korr, and those numbers there are Tellurak and Veydrus. If … if you wanted, I could send you back right now."

Dan smiled, even though he knew Kaia couldn't see it. He patted her on the cheek. "Not yet, but I'll remember your offer. We can just keep that between us, right?" Kaia nodded. "Good. Now, I think you have some newspapers to gather."

Reaching over the frightened woman, Dan pulled the switch. The surge in the aether was obvious to him as the view turned real. The back room of the little news stand that had been a vivid painting a moment ago was now just a few paces away. With a tug of aether, Dan levitated the day's edition though to the hold of the *Jennai.* "I'll leave the rest to you."

"Please, *please*, Rynn, don't let him know I said anything."

"Of course not," Rynn agreed. They were meeting in the pantry of one of the adjunct dining halls, the sort of volume eatery that was below Dan's standards for culinary fare and devoid of the moral hazards that drew him like a rat to rubbish. No one gambled or drank much in the rearmost dining hall; soldiers and rebels went there, ate, and left. "Dan's starting to grind his welcome thin. I don't know what things are like where *he's* from, but around here, I take care of my people. As a precaution, you're going to spend a few days with Madlin and Cadmus."

Kaia gaped. "Really? I thought no one was supposed to know where they are."

"We don't want word leaking to the kuduks," said Rynn. "But that doesn't mean I'd rather risk your life than let you in on the secret. Just … keep it to yourself when you get back. Got it?"

"Yes, ma'am." Kaia let out a long breath and seemed to deflate a little in the process. She had been ready to burst before Rynn's reprieve.

"Make yourself scarce today—real scarce—and meet me at the world-ripper at eleven tonight." Rynn pulled her coil gun from its holster and handed it to Kaia. "Tuck this away. If Dan comes looking for you, shoot first."

I've put this off too long.

"I'm worried, Rynn," said Jamile. "Do you really trust him any more than Dan?"

Rynn slouched in the water, letting the suds drift up near her chin. Her tinker's legs were in a tangle on the bed, where Jamile was scrubbing away the grime from days of use. Much as they had become a part of her, it felt good being free of them for a while. "I don't see how they're anything alike, aside from both being sorcerers."

"Something didn't feel off to you when we talked with him?"

Rynn held up her hands, dripping and with bubbles clinging to them. "Fine. He's a bit of a square bolt. I haven't known too many sorcerers, but I'm guessing that ignoring physics probably isn't good for a healthy brain. He's still got it together better than Dan though."

"Stone calling the steel soft," Jamile muttered.

"Have you got a better idea?" Rynn asked.

Jamile stopped scrubbing. "He's a nutter, and he's awful, but he hasn't *done* anything. I mean, nothing we wouldn't ask one of the soldiers to do, if they could. It's just … he *does* seem to enjoy it a bit too much."

"That's the problem. Or one of them at least. I could win a war with ten of him, but even one might be enough to get us all killed. We're juggling dynamite."

"Why give Kaia a gun? Won't that just provoke him?"

Rynn shrugged, her bare shoulders poking out of the water. "It was to calm her down a bit. She was a wreck. Dan's not going to find her, not as long as you've got Sosha keeping an eye on him … You *are* still keeping an eye on him, right?"

"I'm not exactly cut out to be a spy," Jamile replied quietly, putting her head down to resume her work.

"Jamile!"

"I didn't lose him, but he knows I'm following him around. He … he's been sending me drinks."

"Trying to get you drunk and slip away, no doubt," said Rynn.

"Oh, I haven't touched a single one of them, even though the barkeep keeps giving me looks."

"Good girl," Rynn said, pointing to Jamile with a dripping finger.

"So …" Jamile let the word hang a moment. "Getting all prettied up to meet Anzik again?" She broke into a sly smile.

Rynn sat up in the tub. "It's not like that!"

"What's it like, then? You bathe less often than the welders, and you've hardly taken these mechanical legs off since you first put them on."

"I finally feel like a whole person with them. I can walk without hobbling around like a broken wind-up toy. They take too long to put on to be taking them off at night." She shrugged.

"Why now, then?" Jamile asked. "He's about the right age for you. Older than Dan."

"Oh please. Dan? His delusions aside, what would make you think I'd—"

"You're a girl, Rynn. You're not clockwork inside. It was bound to happen sooner or later."

"I am going," said Rynn, "to meet with a very influential sorcerer from another world. I am the chief representative of the Human Rebellion, and I ought to present myself as such."

"Oh, so a dress, then?" Jamile's eye gleamed. "Perfume? Maybe some earrings and a necklace."

"We don't have anything like that on board."

"It would take half an hour pillaging with the machine," said Jamile. "And I imagine Madlin's dresses would fit you with a little help from a seamstress."

"I'm a tinker. I'm a soldier. That's how I'm going to meet with Anzik," said Rynn, trying to add an edge of finality to her words. "Plus, I'm thinking he's not the sort who pays much attention to dresses and perfume."

Jamile slumped. "Well, you might be on to something there."

"Come on," Rynn said, reaching for a towel. "Help me out of her and back into my legs. I've got work to do."

"Where'd you end up hiding all day?" Rynn asked.

Kaia handed back the coil gun she had borrowed. "My brother's quarters. He and his bunkmates agreed to spend the evening drinking, courtesy of General Rynn … I hope you don't mind."

"No, that was good thinking," Rynn replied. "That's the last place Dan's going to prowl. Ladies' quarters maybe, but not in with the men. Anyway, he's going to bed. Sosha's keeping an eye on him."

"You sure Madlin and Mr. Errol aren't going to mind?"

Rynn smiled. "Madlin already knows. You're a welcome guest."

Kaia fidgeted, sparing glances at the inert viewframe. "But what am I going to do there? I don't want to be in the way."

"Oh, don't worry. They'll find plenty for you to do. If nothing else, they've got world-rippers of their own for you to practice with."

"Oh. I suppose I could do that. If they don't mind."

Rynn put a hand on the Kaia's back, guiding her toward the machine. Hisses and creaks emanated from beneath Rynn's coverall trousers with each step. "It's all worked out."

Lowering herself to the floor was a challenge for Rynn. The tinker's legs gave her support and a gait that felt natural; they were even stronger than her own flesh-and-bone legs. But they lacked agility, especially the subtle twisting of ankle and knee that made crouching and squatting possible. Rynn used the edge of the control console and the chair to help herself down.

Beneath the console, behind a key-locked panel and tucked in among a myriad of levers, gears, and miles of spark circuitry, there was a small clutch lever. Rynn pressed it closed and the gears on the underside of the control dials began to move.

"What are you doing to the machine?" Kaia asked, peering into the console past Rynn's body.

Rynn snorted, trying not to laugh aloud. *I'm about to hurl you into the core of the moon. Don't worry, even though it's a moving target a quarter million miles away, we've got the orbit figured out and dialed into the guts of the world-ripper.* "Wait five minutes; then, ask Madlin that same question."

Kaia helped Rynn to her feet, then watched as she took the controls. After a few scratchwork calculations, Rynn started spinning dials. "Wow," said Kaia. "I thought I was getting good with those, but you've obviously been at this a lot longer."

"You ever seen Cadmus work this thing?" Rynn asked. Kaia shook her head. "Just watch. He can wave the viewframe around like he's pointing a finger. Flip those switches." Kaia complied, and the viewframe sprang to life.

The scene was off by several paces, and Rynn adjusted the targeting until she and Kaia had a proper view of Madlin and Cadmus's kitchen. Kaia licked her lips. "Is that it then? The secret hideout?"

"And for the time being, your new home," said Rynn. She pulled the final switch, and the moon was right next to them.

"Should we … should I wait for them?" Kaia asked. She leaned one way and the other, trying to peer around through the world-ripper for signs of her hosts.

Rynn took Kaia by the shoulder and looked her straight in the eye. With the inches of height the tinker's legs added, she even managed to be the taller of the two. "Listen. You're a valuable member of the rebellion. You're being assigned to this remote headquarters to work in operations, not just to hide. You have the skills to be of use to both of them. Once I close this hole, Dan can't get anywhere near you. Once I've dealt with the problem, you'll be eligible to return to the *Jennai* …" Rynn smiled, "if Cadmus and Madlin can spare you."

Kaia nodded, though Rynn could still feel the nervous tension in her muscles. On a sudden impulse, Rynn pulled her close for a hug. "You're going to be fine. Now, get through."

Picking up her pack, Kaia nodded to Rynn and stepped through the world-hole to Korr's moon. After a single step in the fractional gravity, Kaia spun with a shocked expression frozen on her face. Rynn wagged a finger. "Madlin will explain." She pulled the switch and closed the hole.

Rynn's sigh let the worry siphon out of her like fouled oil. Squirming her way under the machine again, she disengaged the lunar orbit compensator. Nothing in Dan's life had given him a sniff of mechanics. Without someone to spoon feed him the process, he'd never figure out how to find the moon with the world-ripper. With Kaia safe, a dark cloud passed from Rynn's heart. There had been a temptation to use her as bait, a pawn in some half-formed ploy to trap Dan, one which she had purposely sabotaged before she could finish devising it. Rynn had never seen Dan play chess, but she suspected that he was the sort who flicked captured pieces off the board with the attacking piece. He was not the sort who treated pawns with care.

With an undignified grunt, Rynn hauled herself into the chair and paused to catch her breath. *More flexible, better joints, maybe lighten the next ones a bit more.*

Relaxing at the controls, she dialed in the coordinates from memory. She didn't trust writing them down anywhere Dan—or her father—might have found them. While Cadmus was safely tucked away in the second headquarters, Dan was a constant worry. He might not understand how the machine worked, but apparently he was intent on remedying that fact.

Well, that's why I'm doing this, after all.

The machine sprang to life once more as Rynn reached her destination coordinates and closed the switches. Unlike her slight misfire on Madlin's lunar workshop, this time she found herself staring into the meditation chamber of one Anzik Fehr, Veydran sorcerer and potential ally. He was present in the chamber, sitting with his back to the viewframe, as still as if he had been carved there. At least, she assumed it was him; his form was completely robed, and his hood was up.

Last chance to back away, Rynn told herself as she slowly reached for the final switch. *It's either the sane one with the pirate for a father, or the crazy one who kills for pleasure—so far only our enemies, but you never know…*

Rynn pulled the switch and connected the two worlds. Anzik did not so much as flinch.

"Hello," Rynn called through the hole, standing and walking toward where Anzik sat. She wondered whether she should disturb him further if he was so deeply set in his meditation.

"You have returned," Anzik replied. "Good. Come through."

"Thanks," Rynn replied, stepping across the hole into Veydrus. "I hope I didn't interrupt anything."

Anzik climbed to his feet and turned to face her. "Of course you interrupted. Nothing truly begins without something else being interrupted. Had I not been meditating, I would have been sleeping, or studying, or consulting with the ministers or even just thinking. I am never doing nothing. This interruption is both welcome and long overdue."

"Sorry," said Rynn, "I didn't think it was a decision to be made hastily."

"Once made, it cannot be unmade," Anzik agreed, nodding. "Close your device, so we can have some privacy."

"The door to the machine is guarded. Dan is being watched in his sleep. Unless he wakes up, the world-hole will stay open. If he does, someone will come in and close it and scramble the coordinates."

"Stranding you here?" Anzik showed the faintest sound of curiosity, the hint of a raised eyebrow.

Rynn smirked back at him. "I've made arrangements."

"Very well," said Anzik. "You have decided to ally with Megrenn, then." It was not a question, but the conclusion of an equation Anzik had figured out. "What terms do you propose?"

"You help me get rid of Dan, we both gain …"

"Agreed."

"I supply you with the knowledge of how to build coil guns, you supply materials and a workforce, and we split the production yield fifty-fifty. Your people made cannons once, according to Tanner. This would be more complicated, but you've got a lot more potential workers than I do right now."

Anzik paused. "You would need to supply considerable aid in explaining the manufacture of those parts. The coil gun is beyond what Tellurak knows. It is far beyond what Veydrus knows."

"How long do you think it would take to train your people?" Rynn asked.

"Several summers," Anzik replied. "You'd have to start with young apprentices, those whose minds might still stretch themselves around new concepts."

Rynn held up her palms. "Whoa, whoa, wait a minute. Summers? You mean you expect me to spend years getting a workshop up to speed? Not happening. I've got a rebellion to run, I can't be—"

"I agree," Anzik said. "My own people would be a poor choice. Megrenn, Ghelk, Safschan, Narrack, all the members of the Megrenn Alliance lack the skills you require. Our smiths can forge beautiful weapons, but you must know the limits of smithing."

"Of course, but what are you planning to do about workers, if you don't have them?"

"My father once bargained with the goblins, to make him Acardian style cannons," said Anzik.

Rynn took a step back, the creak of the stabilizing spring in her mechanical ankle glaring in the quiet of Anzik's chamber. "Goblins? You're going to bring me goblins?"

Anzik looked down at the floor and shook his head. "No, I'll tell you how to gain their help yourself."

"I don't like the sound of this. I thought I'd be helping humans, not monsters."

"I don't know what your world says of them, but I know Tellurak's concept of the goblin is erroneous," said Anzik. "They've made them into night story villains, crawling creatures living in dark nooks and shadowed corners, attacking naughty children. I tell you, this is far from the case."

"Fine then, what are they?" Rynn crossed her arms.

"They are small, delicate creatures, weak but quick. In a wrestling contest, you'd best their greatest warrior. Sparring with blades, you'd never touch one. They aren't great fighters though; they rely on cleverness. They are quick learners. Goblins don't live as long as humans, so they have to be. My father taught them to build cannons in a season."

"That's not encouraging," said Rynn.

"They had been using catapults before that."

"Oh." The difference between a catapult and a cannon was like the difference between a pick axe and a steam-chisel.

"He taught them large-scale casting, better alloys of metal, how to make black powder …"

"And your people … ?"

Anzik shook his head. "Far beyond our craftsmen."

Can't keep this rebellion going with kindling. Time to throw coal on this fire. "How many goblins can you get me?"

"Depends how well you impress their god," said Anzik. Rynn's eyes shot wide. "Don't worry. They don't worship actual gods." Rynn let out a breath. "They worship dragons."

Dan crept through the corridors of the slumbering airship undetected. Rynn was a fool if she thought that Sosha could keep him under constant watch. The girl had succumbed easily to his sleeping charm and would awake knowing only that she had nodded off while on duty. Avoiding the few nocturnal denizens of the ship was a simple matter when Dan could see their Sources in the aether, even through walls. *Pathetic. This whole world could fall to a few resourceful sorcerers.* Dan paused. It was worth considering, now that he thought about it. He shook his head to clear it of wandering notions. *Later. I have to see what they were hiding first.*

It was amusing in a way, the childish subterfuge of the human rebels, thinking that they were working some sly plot behind his back. Rynn had kept him from returning home for some reason he had not yet fathomed; the easy assumption was for protection. *I'd make the best coinblade this world ever knew. Why not just pay me to fight for you?* Dan didn't know the price he'd ask. But he knew he was worth every eckle of it—or whatever they called money in Korr. He had shown his worth in the defense of Tinker's Island. But that assumption was almost *too* easy, too simple for the trouble they were taking to keep him away from certain places at certain times. The misdirection, the guard—using a pair of pair of same-worlded twinborn was brilliant, he had to admit—all of it told the suspicious part of Dan's mind that something more was going on. He intended to find out what.

As always, Dan's first instinct was the world-ripper machine. It was the heart and fist of the rebellion. It took a mighty and daring sorcerer to work a transference spell—more skilled than Dan or Danilaesis, he was forced to admit. The world-ripper not only mimicked the effect, it exceeded it, allowing detailed surveillance and extended transit, not just an instantaneous swapping of two bits of the world. It also had no trouble transcending worlds, something that only his cousin Brannis had ever managed, so far as he knew. *Once I get that thing figured out, I'm going to pay those Megrenn scum a nice surprise visit. Then the goblins … then the ogres …*

Dan's musings kept him occupied as he skulked through the *Jennai.* Keeping himself hidden was just not enough of a challenge. The door to the hold with the machine was locked and guarded. Another sleeping charm and a bit of fiddling telekinesis made short work of both problems. Once inside, he shut the door and found himself alone. *Odd. Where's Kaia?* It was her shift, and she had been the most pliable of Rynn's world-ripper navigators. *If you told anyone …* Dan was tempted to hunt the girl down and demand to know why she had missed her shift. No explanation would be good enough, he suspected, to make him consider sparing her life. She was supposed to tell no one and acting peculiar was just a coward's way of signaling that something was wrong.

But something stopped Dan. The controls. The operators were meticulous about returning all the dials to a null setting when they finished with the machine. Not this time. Whoever had last used the machine had left it in haste, failing to wipe out the evidence of the last destination. Taking a step toward the machine, Dan caught himself short. What had that old buzzard Axterion said about coincidences? *"Two oddities are more than doubly odd." Something like that. First, the girl is gone. Now, someone left the coordinates behind to find. Why?*

A trap felt likely. He had only to think back to the death of Erefan for evidence of how the device could have been rigged to kill him. Though he hadn't witnessed the explosion, he had heard third-hand how the daruu, who had owned Erefan, had set it to explode. Of course, Erefan lacked shielding spells but depending how much black powder had been used, Dan might still have been at risk. He ripped the panels off the control console, heedless of the damage to the lock that Rynn had installed and poked his head inside.

Spark was a mystery to Dan. He knew that lightning sought metal—Danilaesis had learned as much at the Imperial Academy—but how it could be tamed to do tricks was too abstract, even for a sorcerer. The tangle of copper wire was like a magpie's nest, an insane collection of bits someone happened across and stuffed together. It shouldn't *do* anything as far as Dan could see. But while the innards that belonged there were meaningless to him, it was what did *not* belong that mattered. Black powder wasn't dangerous in small quantities. You could hold a pinch in the palm of your hand and ignite it, with nothing more than a burn for your trouble. The amount he'd worry for his life over … well, Dan assumed that he couldn't fail to notice someone storing that much black powder underneath the console.

Nothing. Hmm. It was unlike Dan to find that his suspicions were unjustified. The worlds were filled with intrigue and betrayal, all sitting just below the point where average people took notice. Dan had seen his share of it, had started his share of it. He normally had a good sense of when something was a set up. *There's always the chance someone was just careless …* No, it was too convenient, too perfect.

Other possibilities flicked through his head. Perhaps the view would open to something he was meant to find irresistible. Wait for him to go through and they could strand him; Dan knew enough about spark to know that Rynn could disconnect the power remotely—how was a mystery, but it was enough to realize that *she* knew. A straight-out ambush seemed unlikely, since he could see his destination before taking the step of turning the image into a hole between worlds. *Why they can't just call it a 'gate' or a 'portal' is beyond me.*

It struck him. *What if someone is already through?* It would make sense to leave the coordinates dialed in, especially if it was an operator who had gone through. Any idiot could work the switches to turn the machine on and off, but someone paranoid about being left on the other side might not trust just anyone to find them again. There was only one person aboard the *Jennai* who came to mind when Dan considered that scenario. *Rynn.* She was both an expert with the machine and thought that everyone else—save her absent father—was unqualified to use it. A wicked grin spread across Dan's face. *I bet you went through, and Jamile is supposed to sneak back here and open the portal back up to let you in again. Sosha watches me, Jamile works the machine, and you get a secret meeting wherever those coordinates are.*

Dan nodded to himself. It fit. It sounded like the limit of Rynn's deviousness. It just wasn't enough to fool him. Seating himself at the controls, Dan activated the levers one by one until the viewframe sprang to life. *So, where did you go, Rynn?*

Dan gaped, eyes staring. Thoughts of Rynn trickled out the corners of his mind like drool. Sitting in a circular room of fine-cut stone sat Anzik Fehr. *Checkmate.* So it seemed Rynn had gone to meet Anzik Fehr and bargain with Megrenn. Whether she was in Megrenn or somewhere aboard the *Jennai* was no longer relevant. His most hated rival was sitting with his back turned, not a half dozen paces away—even fewer if he walked to the viewframe and activated the switch with magic.

Patience, he cautioned himself. Axterion's lessons sank into him like water into hardwood. They beaded up on the surface of him, but given long enough, they seeped in. Dan knew that Anzik was stronger than Jadon Zayne, his twin. Just because he could overmatch Jadon did not mean he would fare as well against the stronger twin. Dan opened the door to the hold just a crack, enough to reach through and snag a coil-gun from one of the snoring guards. The runes were well-powered, and the steel balls it used in place of bullets were racked up in a neat line behind the barrel, ready to fire.

Time to die, Anzik Fehr.

Walking to the viewframe, Dan took careful aim at the back of Anzik's head. He was a poor shot with Tanner's pistol, but at such close range, even Dan couldn't miss his mark. With a glance over his shoulder, he pulled the switch and activated the world-ripper. And fired.

The shot tore through Anzik's head without the barest hint of resistance. Dan squeezed the trigger a second time, then a third, not willing to risk any chance of survival. It all happened in the blink of an eye, and when that blink had ended, Dan knew he was in trouble. There *should* have been a hint of resistance, even from so mighty a gun. A twitch, a spasm, a spray of blood and gore, something should have happened.

"Thank you for coming," said Anzik, his voice coming from beyond Dan's field of view. With no further warning, Dan felt himself yanked through to Veydrus by means of Anzik's magic; the coil gun pulled free of his hand and thrown back through to Korr. He turned to break free and dive for the airship but only managed to turn himself around in time to see the switch opening by telekinesis. Korr vanished.

"Where are you?" Dan demanded, switching to aether-vision as he suspected he would get no helpful answer. The false image of Anzik was so obvious, so plainly constructed when viewed in the aether. He watched as Anzik let it unravel.

Anzik emerged from around a corner, entering though an open door. "This has been a long time coming."

"You think I'm afraid of you?" Dan snarled.

"Irrelevant. You've lost," said Anzik. "I don't care whether you spend your last moments in terror or rage. I just care that you expire."

Dan spared no more time on chatter, throwing himself bodily at Anzik. Unarmed as he was, he still liked his chances against the Megrenn sorcerer in fisticuffs. It was the key advantage to being a warlock, the ability to maintain calm and focus while struggling between life and death. Though Anzik was older and full grown, Dan was in fighting shape and half a head taller. It didn't matter.

The ground pulled away beneath Dan's feet as he was lifted and hurled across the room. A flash of shielding magic flared as he struck the stone wall. Anzik shook his head. "Not here. Aboard the *Fair Trader*, I was the one on the defensive, the weaker, the cornered. This is your turn." Dan struggled, but Anzik pinned him against the wall without so much as moving a muscle.

"I'll kill you," Dan promised. "Danilaesis will avenge me. I'll burn Veydrus to cinders just to see you die in the flames."

"Perhaps," said Anzik, his voice calm against the hurricane of Dan's rage. "Perhaps one day I will stand across the battlefield from Danilaesis Solaran, and you may have your chance for revenge. But I suspect that I will one day stare down at the smoldering ruins of Kadris, wondering where your body lies amid the rubble."

Dan thrashed, struggling to draw aether as Anzik sucked the room dry with his superior draw. "Rynn put you up to this, did she? What deal did you strike with her?"

Anzik thrust with his telekinesis, and Dan's bones cracked. The fury in his eyes went dull and his muscles slack. Anzik let the corpse slump to the floor. "I can't see what I could possibly gain by telling you," Anzik replied.

Rynn was sitting in a dimly lit kitchen, sipping at a strange brew of tea under the watchful eyes of a pair of nervous cooks when Anzik returned for her. She had felt the shockwaves, the subtle force beneath the surface of reality that told her magic had been at work. It reminded her of the Battle of Tinker's Island except this time, it seemed, Dan was not victorious.

"It's done," said Anzik.

Rynn felt an emptiness inside. The room, the people, the idea that Dan was really dead, none of it seemed quite real. *What kind of a monster am I turning into?* Dan had saved her life multiple times—once from Jadon and his father, even. He had taught her magic, taken the collar from her neck, had helped power the Tinker's Island world-ripper. Even when he had tried to bed her, it had been in the block-tongued way of an adolescent boy who was all optimism and awkwardly misplaced self-confidence.

"Your father told me he was like a rabid dog," Rynn said.

Anzik said nothing in reply.

"Isn't this the sort of thing I was worrying *he* would do?" she asked.

"Prophylaxis is often difficult to reconcile," said Anzik. "For me, he had already earned his death. He has killed more of my people than you can know. He intended to kill far more and made no secret of it. It is the Kadrin way, at least among their sorcerers. They view all as theirs and would take it if we do not oppose them at every turn."

"Does he know?"

"He is no fool. His twin will blame you, of course. You are committed to my cause now, insomuch as you have made an enemy of the Kadrin Emprie. With your help, they *will* fall."

"So what now?" Rynn asked, setting aside the cup of tea.

"Now, I prepare you to bargain with a god."

Chapter 13

"Vengeance must be pursued in both worlds to be effective." - Rakashi dar Fandar

The door to Axterion's chambers burst open, cracking against the wall. A howl of aether followed in its wake, trailing a young warlock who strode in with a sword slung across his back. Danilaesis marched over to Axterion's breakfast table, scowling fit to scare off demons. The not-as-elderly-as-he-used-to-be sorcerer sat sipping sugared wine as he ate a morning meal of roast boar and eggs. His look of mild reproach was a rock in a storm sea.

"You left orders that I can't move our troops?" Danilaesis shouted, lifting spread arms. "How am I supposed to—"

"You're not supposed to anything," Axterion snapped, the mild expression hardening. "You've no place yet commanding troops, let alone the movements of the whole imperial army. Now, what's this all about?"

"They *killed* me!" Danilaesis screamed. He grabbed the sword from his back and whistled it through the air. In an instant, Axterion's breakfast table was dashed to splinters, his breakfast splattered across his clothes and onto floors and wall.

Axterion had watched over Danilaesis often when he was a young boy, his mother absent and his father too busy to pay him attention. Servants and tutors had been no match for the boy's mischief and magic, so it had fallen to Axterion to wrangle and raise him. In all those summers of caring for Danilaesis, he had never raised a hand to the boy. The surprise on Danil's face was obvious when Axterion grabbed his wrist in one hand and his throat in the other. His newfound youth had given him back a strength he had not known in ages. Never a burly man, Axterion still held more meat on his frame than did his grandson, with a man's grip.

"Get a hold of yourself," Axterion snapped. He could smell the brandy in Danil's sweat, and wondered how long the boy had been awake to have been drunk already. "You're disgracing us both." He flung Danilaesis back, then waved a hand to slough the foodstuffs from his shirt and pants. With a second's pause for thought, he gestured to the door and it slammed itself shut. "Now, skip to the part where this all starts making sense."

Danilaesis seethed, his breath coming in long, hissing gasps. "They. Killed. Me. *He* killed me!"

"Who?"

"Anzik Fehr," Danilaesis replied. "That little sewer rat tinker and him used that portal machine to ambush me. And after all I did for her and her scraggly rebel oafs."

Axterion's blood went chill. He had heard a similar tale when his wife—who had been twinborn—had died in Tellurak. He put a hand up to his mouth, rubbing the raw stubble of a beard that grew there. "We'll make them pay for it. Just … not while they expect it. Too soon. Haven't you heard that revenge ages like cheese?"

"I want you to teach me the transference spell," said Danilaesis, his breath calming. "Not the book version; I know enough to understand that the best versions of anything never get written down. You must have a better spell for it tucked away in that rotting old skull of yours. I'm going to appear in the Ghelkan royal court, walk over to Anzik Fehr, and …" Danilaesis thrust his sword through an imaginary opponent … "skewer him like a piglet. Then … then I'm going to do what Brannis did and transfer world to world. And then I'm going to do the same to Denrik Zayne while little Jadon watches, and *then* I'm going to beat that little wretch with my bare hands until he's nothing but crow food."

Axterion let Danilaesis finish his rant and run himself out of breath again. "I can teach you a better version than you'll find in the libraries. But I'll also teach you something far more valuable, if you're willing to learn."

"What's that?" Danilaesis asked, narrowing his eyes.

Danil had been the victim of many cruel twists of words by his tongue over the years, but this was not to be one of them. "I'd like to teach you how to be a proper bastard, the kind Rashan could be, when he wasn't solving all his problems with brute magic. The kind of sorcerer that doesn't need to take every problem head on, sticking his neck out. If you want your revenge, you're going to want to live to see it."

Danilaesis nodded slowly.

"And *then*, we're going to show them what happens when someone kills a Solaran."

Chapter 14

"The words on one man's lips can put swords in a thousand hands." -Illiardra

Rynn stared at the sheet of vellum. It wasn't blank, but only held the faintest hints of what would eventually come to life within its creamy white confines. The pencil was a bar of steel, too heavy to move. Each time she tried, Rynn attempted to picture teaching a goblin how to read the schematic she was creating. It didn't help that Rynn had only vague notions of what a goblin looked like, just a few bland adjectives from Anzik, who was not the most poetic of storytellers.

The enemy of my enemy is my friend … but what about the enemy of an insane acquaintance I betrayed? The rebellion will get by. It might take years, but we'll get them enough weapons to fight back in earnest. As much as she told herself that, the words felt hollow. She had been a slave so short a time, been forced to carry the stubborn collar on her neck a while longer. In all, it had been a few months of her life taken from her. And while she'd hated her job working for Mrs. Bas-Klickten at the university, she hadn't been treated badly by most standards. For her to ask miners, farmhands, and brothel slaves to wait "just a few years" seemed callous.

For better or worse, Rynn had cast her lot with Anzik and his goblin labor force. They had only two small workshops, one aboard the *Jennai*, and one with Madlin and Cadmus on the moon. Even thinking about it made Rynn shake her head. *Not only have we settled the moon, we've industrialized it.* But even if they produced nothing but coil guns—and Madlin and Cadmus were doing nothing of the sort, far too busy with projects of their own—they could only produce ten or twelve a day. Supporting construction and expansion of the *Jennai*, servicing the small fleet of liftwings, and Rynn's personal projects to improve her tinker's legs, they weren't even yielding half that number on a good day.

Rynn pushed aside the vellum and decided to go for a walk. She had never been fond of them, but once deprived of the ability to walk, she had learned a new appreciation for the simple pleasure of meandering around the ship under her own power. She greeted her rebels when she passed them in the corridors, but they seemed to sense the distance between her and where her thoughts were traveling. *I'm going to meet a god.* It was an unsettling thought. Anzik's reassurances that it was "just" a dragon changed little. Rynn knew something of dragons from stories, but they had always been simple villains, either animalistic brutes to be slain by knights or riddling tricksters to be outwitted by peasant heroes. Anzik's description made them seem more like … well, like gods. They ruled over the goblin people, taking tributes of gold and food, setting down laws and issuing decrees. In exchange, the goblins gained the creatures' protection—absolute protection—against neighboring nations and races.

Anzik had told her of the one dragon he had in mind, had even told her its name, but it was just a blur of confused syllables in Rynn's head—she hadn't quite followed as he said it, and doubted repetition would have made it any clearer. She was to lay out her proposal: a force of science and technology capable of striking down their foes, in exchange for a three-quarter share of the proceeds—Anzik had been willing to take a mere quarter out of Madlin's share for acting as a broker. *Why would it take such a deal?* It seemed unfair, or it would from behind Rynn's spectacles if their positions were reversed. She would have to trust Anzik's knowledge of the creatures since no storybook she had ever read talked about how to conduct trade negotiations with dragons.

Rynn's wanderings went undirected, at least by her conscious mind. Her subconscious seemed to have had a plan though and didn't inform her of it until she stumbled into the common room of the crew deck where her former gang-mates were relaxing. Kupe was with them, having been remanded to Rascal's custody.

"How's it, Rynn?" Buckets asked.

Rynn smirked. "You picking up Cuminol slang, now? Don't let this yokel ruin you."

"Grab a chair. Have a pint," Hayfield offered, gesturing to a keg of pilfered Telluraki ale. The labeling on the side was in Acardian, at which point Rynn stopped paying attention. Madlin's taste buds could handle Acardian brews, but it felt too bitter for Rynn.

"I came to see how Kupe was doing," said Rynn. It sounded better than admitting she happened by absentmindedly. "So how *is* Kupe doing?" she asked him.

He shrugged. "Rascal's been newsing me on this oversized gang of yours." Kupe looked around the room. "Pretty packed car you're hauling." He lifted his mug in Rascal's direction. "It ain't as blush-faced drinking with a Pious when you ain't been going to his sermons all your life."

Rascal chuckled as he finished a swig of ale. "His Pious Davlin is an old badger. Never met him, but I heard enough over the soft wire. Miracle of Eziel that he ever managed to preach the patient litany. He was a crashballer and a bare-knuckle fighter when he was younger. Served in the Garn Gel militia when they had that scuffle with the Orru Republic. Preaching was supposed to have been his penance for all that." Rascal shook his head as he looked up to the ceiling. "If only they knew."

"Is them legs of yours gettin' quiet-like, or am I just getting' used to 'em?" Pick asked. He sat in the corner with his feet up on the keg.

Rynn felt a sudden flush without knowing why. "I … well, I do keep them oiled, and I've made a few adjustments."

"I seen you with your runey-guns and your goggles and your gizmos," said Pick, tallying on his fingers as he listed each item "But I still can't stuff it into my head that you ain't all girl under them trousers."

Hayfield slapped Pick in the shoulder with a backhand. "Kinda way is that to talk?"

Rynn crossed her arms. "You're sweet, Hayfield, but I'm no wicker dolly. Pick can imagine whatever he wants up under my trousers cuz that's the only way he's ever gonna see."

They all shared a laugh at Pick's expense though Rynn noticed that Kupe seemed to be forcing it.

"Hey, you seen the papers today?" Buckets asked when the mirth faded.

"Which one?" Rynn asked. "I've seen a bunch."

Rascal reached over and grabbed a folded newspaper and tossed it to Rynn. "Glenwood Gazetteer, evening edition. Look at that silly mug they've got front and center."

Rynn unfolded the paper and flipped it around right-side up. "Kupe, you're famous." The image of Kupe from the *Cuminol Chronicle* had been reproduced larger, and the rest of the flashpop had been cut away. The headline read: "Rebels Growing Brash, Lead Daytime Heist." News of the rebellion was spreading across Korr.

Kupe smiled weakly. "Yeah … just like you said. Dunno why they had Charsi snagging flashpops, but she got me good."

"You boys been getting his boiler stoked?" Rynn asked.

"They been fillin' his head with stories older than me," said Buckets. "I told him about our smash'n'run with those old museum coins."

"Don't worry," Rascal said. "We'll make sure he can talk like a proper rebel."

"You remembering all those stories?" Rynn asked.

"Yes, ma'am," said Kupe, perking up with an earnest imitation of military discipline.

Rynn rubbed her chin and regarded Kupe with an appraising eye. "Let's go find out."

The image in the viewframe was dim. The mine tunnels on the far side were lit by a few lanterns not even connected to oil lines, just hanging from simple hooks pounded into the rock walls. Crowded along those walls were a collection of filthy, haggard, well-armed humans.

Kupe stared at them like they were a museum painting. "Where are the kuduks?" he asked.

"You really want to see?" Kaia asked. She had returned shortly after Anzik had disposed of Dan. The moon's low gravity was too much for her to acclimate, and she had been more than willing to cut short her apprenticeship under the Mad Tinker.

"Dontcha think I oughta?" said Kupe. "If I'm gonna have to convince them I'm some big rebel hero, I can't be lettin' my face hang out when I see them kuduks they took."

Behind Kupe's back, Rynn nodded to Kaia. "Go ahead. You know where to look?"

"Yeah," replied Kaia, "I scanned the whole mine after I read about 'em in the Gazetteer. A hundred and eighteen humans—mostly miners—and eleven kuduk hostages." Kaia slid the view through the mines, doing an excellent job of following the tunnels rather than plowing through solid rock. While both methods worked, Cadmus had always appreciated the skill required in mimicking a pedestrian's viewpoint throughout such a short traverse. Apparently it was rubbing off on the operators he trained.

Past all the grim, soot-blacked faces of coal miners turned rebel, there was a short side tunnel. Rynn guessed that it was either a failed shaft or had been excavated for some other purpose than extracting coal because it only ran fifty feet before dead ending. There, in the gloom of a tunnel lit only by stray light from the intersection, sat a group of disheveled kuduks, all chained together. All wore quality garments, good, respectable kuduk-made cloth in unfashionable workman's cuts. Faces and clothes all bore stains, though with little light it was hard to discern whether it was blood, soot, or a mix of both. Every kuduk was male and looked to be of working age, none young enough to be apprenticed, nor old enough to have retired. Their beards had been hacked off lopsidedly, by the look of it, with a knife.

Kupe took a step back. "I'm not sure I can do this."

"Beer," Rynn called over her shoulder. One of the soldiers by the door was ready with a mug in hand. She had talked with Rascal and knew that Kupe might need some liquid bravado.

"I ain't thirsty," Kupe objected, refusing to take the mug when the soldier offered it.

Rynn took it instead and forced it into his hands. "This isn't about thirst. This is about getting your nerve up and making these miners see that they're part of something bigger than one riot and a few hostages. You read that article?" Kupe nodded. "Well, once the knockers feel like they've got enough backup, they're going to go in with bullet shields and scatterguns, and not a rusty one of these miners is going to survive."

"But," said Kupe. He looked down into the mug. "But we … but you could just make a hole where the knockers are at, blast 'em all to bits and bolts? Or just make one right here, let 'em all escape."

"Escape where?" Rynn asked. "This is their home. Besides, do you see a lot of empty beds on the *Jennai*? We haven't got room to save everyone. You have any idea how many humans there are in Korr? Even if you just counted the ones who've boiled over and are ready to fight back, I could build a dozen ships like this, and they'd overflow it. Once people see the rebellion heating up, more and more are going to get up the courage to join. We're not trying to collect this fire; we need it to spread. So bottoms up, hero."

It took the full mug and another two just like it before Kupe declared himself ready to "go rile up some diggers," as he called the miners. Rynn had only known Kupe for a week, and had never gotten drunk with him. She had been playing on faith that the beer would loosen his tongue and steady his hands long enough to be inspirational. So long as he looked like his flashpop and could walk around shaking hands and slapping backs, that was all the rebellion needed. But while Kupe the Sober was a pleasant, shy young man, Kupe the Drunk liked attention. When the world-hole opened, he strode into the midst of the miners like a conquering hero come to accept drinks and kudos at his hometown tavern.

"How's it, brothers?" he called loudly, projecting without shouting, but making sure all who saw him could hear him as well. There was a brief commotion, with many of the miners reaching for weapons at what appeared at a glance to be a raid. But picks and shovels aren't weapons that a nervous man fires while retreating, and the miners didn't have but three guns among them.

"What the bloody tunnels is this?" one of the miners asked. He brandished one of the few firearms the miners had acquired, a stubby revolver of the sort that skittish kuduk foremen keep stuffed in a pocket to prevent—well, to prevent what had just happened to them.

"Quench it, Lipp. Don't you see who that is?" another miner said, pointing at Kupe. "That's him. The flashpop. Rebel hero of the northerns."

Yup, that's him. The flashpop. Rynn hid her smirk, but none of the miners were paying her much heed. Kupe was flooded with a slew of questions: if it was really him; if it weren't really him, would he say; how were things up north; were they preaching the new Eziel yet? Kupe didn't have much trouble catching the lobbed questions of a friendly audience.

"So what' it like killin' them knockers?" a miner asked. Kupe stopped short, a flat look on his face.

Come on, Kupe. This is one you should have gotten out of Rascal and Hayfield.

Kupe ran a finger through sweat-slick hair. Though air was wafting in from the *Jennai*, the mines were like a furnace. "Well, can't rightly say," said Kupe. *Oh no!* "Ya see, there ain't much time for feelin', what with the runnin' and the shootin'. Man with a gun in his hand's got a job to do. That's just how it is. You stop and feel stuff, well. Maybe one of them knockers takes his chance at you. Gotta keep your head on it, else you might end up missin' a head." There was a chorus of chuckles at Kupe's grim joke.

Rynn let out a trapped breath. *Good enough recovery.*

"How come you look like a plated fish in that flashpop? You ain't looking like you got a head in, there."

Kupe grinned sheepishly. "I was just lucky is all. That flashpop was taken by a pretty slip of a thing. Can't blame a man getting his eyes twisted around sideways by a girl? Piss on them knockers before I'd let 'em have a shot at me, but I ain't made of stone."

Rynn and a few of her soldiers stepped through, falling into a respectful position behind Kupe as he and the miners shared a laugh at Kupe's expense. "This here," said Kupe, hooking a thumb over his shoulder, "is Rynn of Eversall. She's the boss of the big rebellion. All us little guys owe it to her that we're getting' our way with the kuduks these days."

"A girl?" one of the miners exclaimed. "I heard of Rynn, but I always pictured him a brotherish sort, sweeper's build, maybe even a blocker. I ain't followin' no boss that—"

A click sounded, and shot hissed past, burying itself in the wall a foot from the miner's head. "Go ahead and look. That's a half-inch ball bearing you're not going to find; it's lodged a foot into the rock. It'll put a half-inch hole into anything you point it at, from knockers to steam tanks. I came up with them. I made the first one, and I killed a half dozen knockers the first time I tried it out. You boys play your cards right; I'll be leaving a few of these for you to help you out."

"So long as we call you boss?" the miner asked.

"Something like that," Rynn replied. "I'm not in this for money or power. I'm in this to win. I run things because I don't want brick-headed mules like you lot running amok. A mine? Really? You got nothing down here but room and no back door out. Smart rebels would have holed up someplace that has food, supplies, a couple or more ways out. Lucky for you boys, I came along."

"Where you get off tellin' us what's what?" another of the miners demanded. He was Hayfield's size, with skin caked in soot where lines of sweat hadn't washed it away.

"I've been at this years, mostly on a smaller scale. But I've fought the kuduks—soldiers even, not just your average, everyday head-knockers from Judicial Enforcement—and let me tell you, you've got a lot to learn."

A lean miner with a limp ambled forward, pointing one of the miners' few guns in Rynn's direction. "What's to say we don't just take them fancy guns of yours, and you leave without a hole in you?"

"For starters," Rynn replied. "I've got eight hundred soldiers, all of them better armed than the whole lot of you. You wouldn't get spit out of us, and we'd let you get steam-rammed by the knockers when they get here. Plus, you're pointing a Millstone Valley 800-K at me, and those things aren't accurate past forty feet. You've got to be a good sixty away, and even if you do hit me, it probably wouldn't put me down before I turned you into a steam manifold. On top of all that, it would be doing the kuduks a huge favor, and I don't think you'd be willing to do them any favors after how they've treated you."

There were murmurs of agreement with that last sentiment. Rynn had spent enough time among various rebellious humans to know that the one trait all of them had in common was some deep-seated grudge against the kuduks. Rynn's army didn't get many shavers with wage complaints among their number. Most of her rebels had been slaves or had family who'd been taken.

The miner lowered his gun, nodding with a clenched jaw. "Aww right. Say we do call a bootlace of a thing like you boss? What then?"

"I get you boys some proper guns, show you how to use them, and tell you how to turn those knockers that're on their way into sausage meats," Rynn said. A few scattered whoops of enthusiasm sounded from the crowd. "But first, we've got to have a talk about prisoners."

Rynn, Kupe, and a few of the *Jennai's* soldiers followed as the miners brought them to see the kuduks in person. Rynn pretended that she didn't already know where they were heading and managed not to look dismayed when she saw the kuduk wretches that were chained in the dead-end tunnel.

"These were the ones that didn't get away when we took over the mine," explained a miner who called himself Raddert. He had been as close as the miners had to a leader since the riot.

"Unchain them," said Rynn.

"We can't be—"

"Where are they going to go?" Rynn asked. "They look in any condition to rush us?"

Raddert nodded to the miner with the key. "Dunno what you're up to …"

Rynn looked the kuduks over. The miners had brought lanterns, so there was enough light to see the hatred in the kuduks' eyes. It was clear that they had been mistreated; a few could barely stand. Nothing but pride and that stereotypical kuduk toughness was holding them up. She picked the one who looked to be in the best condition, an ornery-looking fellow with a few stray tufts of black beard and cuts where the rest had been taken. He was also the largest of the kuduk hostages.

"You. What's your name?" Rynn asked. The kuduk said nothing. "Your *name*!"

"That's Baedrek," Raddert said, when it was clear that Baedrek wasn't going to answer. "He's one of the foremen."

"All right everybody," Rynn called out to the crowd that had gathered behind them. "What's Baedrek done to you? Just shout it out; we've got no fancy rules here."

"He's knocked out me teeth." "Clubs us when we ain't working to his liking." "I got a rib he busted, ain't never been the same." The litany went on until Rynn shouted for quiet.

"I've heard enough," she shouted to the crowd. In one smooth motion she drew her coil gun and shot Baedrek dead.

There was a moment of stunned silence. The kuduks, stoic and defiant a moment before, shrank back against the far wall, putting as much distance between themselves and Rynn as they could.

"What'd you do that for?" Raddert asked. "Now, we got us one less hostage."

"There aren't going to be any hostages," Rynn replied. "Hostages are a one-time gamble. Maybe you get something for them, maybe you get a bloody standoff and all wind up dead. It's a loser's play, and I'm not going to let you make it. These kuduks," Rynn gestured with her gun, "you're going to pass judgment on them. Now, maybe every last one of them's done you wrong, wrong enough to deserve a bullet. If that's the case, so be it. But if there're innocents in among these men, you're gonna send them home."

"It don't sit right with me, sending kuduks free when we got 'em caught fair and even," Raddert replied.

"Let me ask you something. If the kuduks were trying to kill off every last human. If they did nothing but hunt us, chain us up, and kill us, do you think more of our kind would fight back?"

Raddert put a hand to his chin and squinted at Rynn, trying to puzzle out where she was leading him, no doubt. "I believe they just might."

"But they don't. They leave most of the freemen alone, so long as they play by kuduk rules. Why make more enemies when you don't have to? Well, Raddert, why are you going to try to convince every kuduk alive that we're a threat, an enemy they can't deal with except by killing us all? We don't need them *all* dead, just the ones who fight back. Just the ones who've already earned it. The rest … I'd rather they were just watching from the cheap seats."

In less than half an hour, it was all over. Of the eleven hostages, three shuffled through the throng of humans, deemed not to have done anything worth killing over. One was the mine's quartermaster, generally accounted a good sort; another was a cook's assistant; and the third, the mine owner's nephew. The nephew was the hardest decision for the miners, who saw a young man that had grown up privileged at the cost of their sweat. In the end, Raddert and his fellows decided that it was not justice to condemn the boy for his family's crimes.

Rynn left them with thirty coil guns and a detailed plan for the defense of the mines once the kuduk reinforcements arrived plus suggestions on how to carry the fight to the rest of the deep. Raddert and his men handled the weapons clumsily and the battle plans with even less deftness. Still, with thirty coil guns and the element of surprise they brought, the rebel miners should have been ready for anything the kuduks would bring.

Back in the hold of the *Jennai*, Kaia shut down the world-ripper. Rynn had dodged around questions of her arrival when speaking with the miners. They were simple folk, and Rynn had little patience for dealing in technical details with laymen. Her biggest worry had been the distraction of the world-hole appearing in their midst. Kupe had done his part in both distracting the miners and winning their trust.

Kupe slumped into a slouch when the machine went dark. "Woo. Glad that's done." He was sweating and red-faced, but the glassiness had left his eyes. He was starting to sober up.

"You did good," said Rynn. "Not great, but good."

"Yeah, maybe," said Kupe. He pointed a wagging finger at her. "But you … you're something else. How's a cute thing like you end up tougher'n a fella like that Raddert? And that one with the pistol … I'd a pissed myself if that'd been me he was pointin' it at."

"You go around wearing tight-laced dresses and tailored blouses, a man gets a nice look at the shape of you," Rynn said. She rapped at her midsection, producing a solid *thunk*. "You go around in loose coveralls, nobody's going to notice if you wear an iron plate underneath."

Kupe chuckled. "Still, you went in front of that whole group, sober. You bargained 'em up like a bunch of alley rats that owed you. Guess that's why they made you General, am I right?"

Rynn smiled, but her eyes stayed somber. *Raddert's a nobody. Let's see if I can fare as well with a dragon.*

"I should be the one to go," Cadmus said. He perched on the edge of one of the kitchen chairs, across the table from his daughter. A sparse lunch of cold ham and warm cheese lay between them.

Madlin shook her head. "It's the communication. I can still talk through Rynn."

"Who won't be here."

Madlin threw up her hands. "The rebellion needs her. It's the same reason she can't be the one to go. We'll send Jamile here to sit with you, and that will keep the chain connected. You'll still get your updates."

"I just don't like the idea of you being under the power of a dragon."

"You think I like the idea?" Madlin asked. "You have to admit, we've got it good here. Gravity aside, this is halfway to paradise: no bothers, no kuduks, a good sized workshop all to ourselves, and three world-rippers."

"Technically two of them are needed full time bringing us air and water," Cadmus replied. Madlin glared at him. He held up his palms. "But I see your point. It's just … you're all I have. I want to keep you safe. If you die off in Veydrus, no amount of vengeance can bring you back."

"If I die because of that rusted dragon, I expect you to cook up something *good* for a vengeance."

"It won't be the same around here without you," said Cadmus. It was as close as Madlin expected to get to a concession.

"It'll only be a few months, hopefully, and you can check in on me with the world-ripper. I'll be leaving tonight."

Chapter 15

'Fancy fabrics and a bit of paint on your face won't make you any less a tinker." -Cadmus Errol, to Madlin—age 12

The streets of Zirom were wide enough for ten people to walk abreast. The Kheshis took this as a sign that twelve could fit, if everyone pushed to get where they were going. Madlin followed Jamile through the crowd in the marketplace, finding the juxtaposition of their usual travel order vexing.

"How did I let you talk me into this?" Madlin asked, speaking Korrish so that none of the natives would understand her. She preferred sounding foreign to sounding insane. "I have to meet with a dragon eight hours from now."

Jamile checked a pocketclock and looked back over her shoulder at Madlin. "Eight hours, sixteen minutes. I know; I won't let you be late."

"I understand bargaining with mine owners and trying to soften their heads up a bit," said Madlin as she squeezed between two Taklishmen to finally catch up with Jamile once more. "But what's a dragon going to care about seeing me in a dress?"

Jamile took Madlin by the wrist and towed her to the edge of the crowd, pressed against the side of a florist's shop. "It's not about the dress, or trying to distract the dragon with your charms—let's face facts, Madlin, you haven't got many—it's about not looking like a tinker fresh in from the workshop."

"You'll just use any chance to try to get me to dress up."

"You're in charge now, Madlin," said Jamile. "It's not like no one pays attention anymore. I hear gossip, you know." Jamile set off once more, hugging the sides of buildings.

"What sort of gossip?" Madlin asked, hating herself for not being able to leave the question alone. Jamile was baiting her. She could tell.

"About how you're so much like your father, you dress like him," Jamile said, not slowing her pace.. "How you've got no man in your life at your age."

"I'm not that—"

"That you ought to spend more time looking after the food supply than the workshops."

"I delegate that stuff to—"

"That you don't really want to be general at all." Jamile did stop just then.

"How come you never told me any of this before?"

"You're a hard woman to tell things like that," Jamile replied. "I rehearsed it for days. Sosha and I drew lots to see which of us would have to do it."

"It's not like I'm some knocker with an itching fist," said Madlin, frowning. "What would I possibly do?"

"Stop talking to me for a month, throw me off a moving ship, feed me to a wizard from another world, or just put a nice bloody hole in me," Jamile replied, counting with her fingers.

"I would never—" Madlin said, but caught herself short. She had been about to protest that those had been kuduks, and that they all deserved what they got. But Jamile's examples were carefully chosen—probably rehearsed, as well—and every one of the incidents she alluded to had involved a fellow human.

"Face it, Madlin. You've got a temper like a stick of dynamite."

Madlin swallowed and couldn't meet Jamile's eye. The "not talking for a month" had been her after Jamile had been forced to cut off Rynn's leg. "Sorry."

Jamile threaded her arm through Madlin's and squeezed. "See there? No harm done, and I'm all in one piece. Now, let's have us a look."

Madlin looked up and saw a sign overhead that read: Jinlo's Creations. Through the glass windows, sculpted wooden figures wore the latest in Kheshi women's fashions. Madlin took too long a pause to formulate a response, and Jamile took that chance to drag Madlin inside by the arm.

How do I let myself keep getting trapped like this?

"How may I help you?" an elderly Kheshi woman greeted them. She wore a conservative dress of midnight blue, along with pearl earrings and necklace. It told Madlin that they were in an expensive store, not that coin was ever an obstacle for her.

"My friend needs a dress," said Jamile. Madlin found herself impressed at how far Jamile's Kheshi had come. There was a heavy drawl of Takalish to it, but the words were all correct.

The old woman looked Madlin up and down in her sweat-stained white blouse and trousers, her calf-high boots that hadn't seen a wash or polish—ever—and her gun belt. "I … cannot … help … you," the woman said, using the slow cadence that natives reserved for foreigners and idiots.

"Listen," said Madlin, cutting in with her fluent Kheshi. "Have you got something nice I can wear out of here today? Nothing with too much flash or sparkle, just something …" Madlin struggled for a word that would hold Jamile at bay without getting her anything too extreme, "… dignified."

The old Kheshi seamstress pursed her lips, the wrinkles around her mouth deepening. She tugged at Madlin's blouse a few different ways, then took a measuring tape and wrapped it around Madlin torso at various heights. She shook her head, though it spoke more of consternation than refusal. "A young girl should be shaped like a peanut, not a bean. There would be too much alteration."

You burlap-mouthed old nag. You're one to talk. You're a coat rack made of bones. Did you soak that dress in perfume or did you just bathe in the stuff? A dozen other spiteful thoughts bounced around Madlin's head, but nothing made it past her gritted teeth. "I'll pay triple."

The old woman's eyes widened but then she shook her head slightly. "Sorry, can't be done." Madlin could almost see the numbers in the old woman's head as she turned from seamstress to huckster. It disgusted her at times how easily some people turned base and predatory when they smelled easy money.

"Ten times," Jamile said, throwing kerosene on the fire of Madlin's negotiation.

Why do I even care about the money? I can dump trade bars in this place until the doors won't open.

The old woman's eyes gleamed—but in a perfectly polite and deferential way, Madlin was sure. She looked as if she was about to accept when Madlin beat her to it. "Forget it. We're going."

Madlin took Jamile by the wrist and yanked her along on her way out of the store. The press of bodies in the marketplace was a welcome relief compared to the cloying condescension in the seamstress' shop. She let go of Jamile and plowed through the crowd with no particular destination in mind.

"What happened?" Jamile asked. "I think she was going to accept."

Madlin stopped, letting the crowd jostle to avoid running into her as she disrupted the flow. "And what? Get some dress I don't want at ten times the price, from a woman who thinks I'm shaped like a bean? You know what? I think I'm going to show that rusted, leaking dragon just what I'm made of."

As Madlin started into the crowd again, she Jamile muttered something. "What was that?"

Jamile sighed. "I said you should send Rynn if you want to show off your tinkering."

Madlin glared at her. "I think I liked it better when you kept secrets." She led them down side streets and thoroughfares until they were clear of the marketplace, with room to breathe and stretch their arms and walk without bodies bumping into them on all sides.

When they turned down a deserted street, Madlin came to a halt. She looked both ways for bystanders, and found no one; she and Jamile were alone. The signal was simple; Madlin held up a hand with four fingers extended, then two, then three. It was her birth date, less the year, and it let Cadmus know that they were done shopping.

It appeared as if the world hole was opening in one of the boarded up buildings. Madlin and Jamile hopped through, into the reduced gravity of Korr's moon, and the hole shut behind them seconds later.

"What happened?" Cadmus asked. "I couldn't tell a blasted thing either of you said." In a lower voice, he muttered to himself: "Wonder if I can get sound to come through …"

"I changed my mind," Madlin said. "I'm done playing at dresses and politics. I'm going to show that dragon who he's dealing with. I'm not General Rynn, and I'm not some princess, or queen, or diplomat. I'm Madlin Errol, the Mad Tinker's daughter, and a tinker myself."

Jamile looked at her with worried eyes. "You're a bit mad yourself, I think."

"I still hate this whole plan," Cadmus grumbled. He sat at the controls of the "spare" world-ripper, the one that was not opened constantly to the remote jungle that provided them both fresh air and water. The once sparse room, with its bare lunar stone and rough cut walls, had been transformed into something loosely resembling a home. Jamile had only been there a day, but had already ordered crewmen to supply them with rugs, wall hangings, and decorative tables.

Jamile stood by Madlin's side a half pace back as Madlin watched the image in the viewframe. She had changed into fresh clothes, but looked every bit the tinker. She wore a pair of modified night-seeing goggles, set with hinges to let the tinted glass flip up and leave a set of lenses ground with Madlin's spectacle optics. Her blouse was freshly bleached, her trousers brand new and fresh from the tailor. While she wore her old boots, she had given in and allowed one of the rebel crewmen to give them a buff and polish. At her hip she wore her gun belt slung low, with a fully charged and loaded coil gun tucked inside. The pack Madlin held slung casually over one shoulder was a strongbox with straps riveted on, carved with levitation runes; the latter was the only thing keeping the weight of the gold within from crushing her. It swung about like a trolley car due to the mass within but weighed less than Madlin's gun belt.

On the other side of the viewframe, Aznik Fehr stared at them. It was uncanny how closely he had judged where the viewframe was aligned. He stood there still as if carved, barely showing any sign of breathing. Madlin watched, waiting to see if he ever blinked.

"If you've got a better plan, now's your last chance," said Madlin, not taking her gaze from the view of Veydrus. "But it's got to replace a workforce of thousands and get us a new consulting sorcerer."

Cadmus thought a moment. "I'm going to bring Kaia back here. We'll set up a rotation to watch you in case you get into any trouble. Give the signal, and we'll pull you out of there."

"The first day, maybe two, fine," said Madlin. "But I'll be gutted if you're going to watch me at all hours. A girl needs her privacy now and then, you know. If nothing goes wrong in a day, just wait for word through Rynn if I need anything from you."

"I just hope that will be quick enough," Cadmus replied.

Jamile perked up. "I'll have Sosha glued to Rynn. The instant she says anything, you'll know it."

Cadmus looked to Jamile and smiled. At least, Madlin credited the twitch of the corners of his mouth as a smile. "I'm trusting you on this, Jamile. You've done well by Madlin, and I'm counting on you to keep her safe."

"Can you get on with this?" Madlin snapped. "We're on a schedule, and this isn't even the dangerous part."

Of course, I've already had to have us kill one sorcerer.

When Cadmus pulled the switch to open the world hole. Anzik did not react. The only sign he was even aware of the change was that his gaze adjusted to look in Madlin's direction, a change of perhaps three degrees.

"Are you prepared?" Anzik asked.

Madlin nodded. "Yes, come through. Is there anything you wanted to bring with you?"

Anzik held out a hand and a satchel drifted from an unseen corner of the room and into his grasp. Without word or hesitation, he stepped through into Korr. At that instant, the first step into the lunar hideaway, Madlin saw that impassive visage falter. For a brief moment, a wide-eyed look of puzzlement crossed the sorcerer's face. "What is this place?"

"Korr's moon," Jamile replied. They had never discussed telling Anzik the truth of their location, but neither had Madlin or Cadmus given orders that he not be told.

If there is anyone less prone to idle talk, I haven't met him. I suppose what's done is done. There were times when Jamile seemed hopelessly naïve, but Madlin was beginning to wonder just how much of that was a conscious rebuttal of the secrecy and minor deceptions that she and her father played at constantly of late.

"Ah," Anzik replied. "That explains it." He swept the room with a perfunctory gaze, eyes pausing only momentarily at each of the other world-rippers, giving little consideration to the rest of the main chamber. He stopped entirely when his eyes settled on Cadmus. "Thank you for hosting me. I find your suspicion understandable, but your quarrel with my father's profession should not carry over to me. Denrik Zayne is a deplorable man, whose company I keep out of duty and because for all my prowess, he still knows far more of magic than me. His twin, Jinzan Fehr, was a great man, if not a good one. Circumstance changes a man, taking the same actions and lauding them in one world, condemning them in another. Think how you would be judged, should your enemies know how you raid and plunder with these machines."

Cadmus stared into the sorcerer's eyes. Despite being seated and physically shorter than the young sorcerer, he still seemed to loom over Anzik. "Pretty speech. You rehearse it long?"

Anzik tilted his head. "I did no such thing. I saw your displeasure at my presence, assumed that it was based on my parentage, since I have had no dealings with you and nothing but favorable encounters with your daughter. I drew the analogy that seemed best suited to improve our working relationship."

Cadmus grunted.

"What do you need from me to navigate?" Anzik asked.

"Can you just tell us where the dragon lives?" Madlin asked. "We're pretty good at finding things."

"I fear we may lack a geographic reference," Anzik replied. "There is no settlement in Tellurak that correlates. The city is in along the eastern edge of the westernmost mountain range in Khesh, but it's wilderness as far as you would know it."

Cadmus stood and walked to one of the non-decorative tables, one that had been in the chamber since it he and Madlin had first moved there. It was strewn with maps and notation papers. Shuffling through the piles, Cadmus pulled out a pair and laid them across the rest of the mess. Both showed the southern continent that Anzik was describing, one showing Korr, the other Tellurak. "Can you point it out on here? I just need a place to start looking."

Anzik peered down, his eyes flicking to and fro around the maps. He stuck a finger down on the map of Korr. "That looks closest."

"Ebrinn," said Cadmus, nodding to himself. "Fine then. We go to Ebrinn."

"Is that one of the ones underground?" Anzik asked. "Madlin has explained about your subterranean cities."

"It's got a deep and a sky," Cadmus replied. "I'm to understand that dragons live in the deeps?"

"Not as you would know them," Anzik replied. "It's a much simpler cavern complex. There are goblin settlements surrounding it that might be analogous, but I don't expect that Fr'n'ta'gur's lair will remind you of home."

"Fr'n'ta'gur … that's certainly a mouthful," Madlin said. She repeated it twice more. "I'm not going to offend it if I gargle-mouth its name, will it?"

"First, remember that Fr'n'ta'gur is male. 'He,' not 'it.' That will certainly be cause for offense," Anzik said. "Other than that, I suspect it would do little more than lower his opinion of you. A fluent pronunciation might impress him, but a poor one should not prove fatal."

"And you're sure that he'll speak Korrish?" Jamile asked.

Anzik remained facing Madlin as he replied. "I have been able to confirm that your world's major language is in fact spoken in Veydrus. It is the language of the stone folk, the daruu. Fr'n'ta'gur would be inexcusably remiss in being ignorant of it."

"Wait, what?" Cadmus asked. "Your world has daruu? Since when?"

"Since always," Anzik replied. "We have little time for history before we send Madlin on her way, but I would be willing to fill you in on Veydran history in the coming months."

Cadmus rubbed at his chin. "Just tell me one thing first: how do your people get on with them?"

Anzik shrugged, though it was little more than a twitch of his shoulders. "We have hardly any dealings with them. My father fought them, briefly, when they allied themselves with the Kadrin Empire. Their numbers are few and they live in isolation. In my world, they are not a major factor."

Cadmus smirked. "Guess we beat 'em on one world, at least."

"Two, I suspect," Anzik said. "Tellurak might well have had stone folk at one point, but wiped them out entirely."

Madlin watched the viewframe trek across Veydrus with detachment. Her eyes faced the images as they rushed by, but never passed them along for her brain to process. If ever there was a time when she would need to be at her best, it was now—or rather, very soon. Thinking ahead to her negotiation, she rehearsed her introduction.

"I am Madlin Errol, representative of the humans of Korr, a world much like this one. I have come to bargain for your aid" … no, that's not right … "I have come to forge an alliance to our mutual benefit." Should I be more formal about the introductions? There was no solution in sight, for anything she said would be wrong. It was just a matter of *how* wrong. Fr'n'ta'gur would view her as an inferior creature regardless.

"There," Anzik said, pointing to a spot in the countryside, nestled against the side of a mountain. "That's it."

Madlin blinked and shook herself from her stupor. The goblin city was a sprawling, wooden shantytown, with haphazard streets and no uniformity among the buildings. *It's just like Khesh*, Madlin thought with a wry smile. The rolling, irregular landscape had the same effect on goblin city planning as it had on the Kheshis, it seemed. *Maybe they aren't so foreign after all …*

That thought lasted until Cadmus was able to bring the view closer, and Madlin was able to make out the inhabitants. The goblins were spindly creatures, all limb and head. All were some combination of green and grey that varied from goblin to goblin. While the streets of most large Kheshi cities teemed with chaotic market-goers, there was a remarkable sense of purpose to the goblin streets. Though equally packed with bodies, there was a distinct flow, with no sign of jostling or turbulence, just a steady, laminar flow of traffic.

"We are looking for a building on the northern outskirts," Anzik said. "That's where we'll find your sponsor."

Anzik had explained that she could not just pop in on Fr'n'ta'gur unannounced. If the dragon did not kill her on sight, his priests would. So even though the world-ripper could deposit her right inside Fr'n'ta'gur's sanctum, she would be going in with an escort who had arranged for her visit.

Madlin flinched as Jamile's hands took her just above the shoulders, where the muscles connect to the neck. "You're tight as a stuck valve," she whispered, fingers kneading the knotted muscle. "You can still back out." Madlin shook her head and shrugged Jamile away.

Anzik directed Cadmus as the two of them hunted down a particular goblin. He was, Anzik had said, as close as Veydrus had to a proper tinker. Madlin was skeptical, but as they passed through the city, she did see more technology than she'd found elsewhere in Veydrus. The goblins had pump wells, cranes, lifts, and even a drawbridge walkway that spanned two of the larger buildings on either side of the narrow river that ran through the town.

"That's it," Anzik indicated, pointing to one of the few buildings with a stone foundation. In fact, the whole first floor was stone-walled. Most of it appeared to only be a single, oversized story, but from one corner a taller section jutted skyward three more floors.

"Can't we just go have a *look* at the dragon first?" Madlin asked.

Anzik shook his head. "I can sense when you're looking at me through the machine. If Fr'n'ta'gur has a keener sense of the aether than I do, he might take offense. Top floor, please."

Cadmus took the cue, and the view entered the building at the top floor. Inside, Madlin saw an obviously ancient goblin. He was grey-haired and hunched at the shoulders, his skin mottled with a grey so pale it was nearly white and so loose that it dangled from his bones. A pair of spectacles perched on his nose, with lenses thick as Madlin's finger. He paced the room, which held a bed and desk, with every other surface covered in paper, from books to loose sheets of scratchings.

"Do it," Madlin ordered. Cadmus pulled the switch.

A musty odor pervaded the lunar hideaway as the two worlds connected. The goblin made several clacking noises and hopped away from the world hole, showing surprising agility despite its obvious age. It glanced around and found Anzik, chittering away at him for a moment. Anzik replied in a language Madlin couldn't understand. It boded ill, the two of them talking indecipherably. They could have been conspiring to have her killed, for all she knew. When the conversation went back and forth several times without any way to know what was being said, she butted in.

"You, goblin, do you speak my language?" she asked, pointing to eliminate any confusion as to whom she was addressing.

The wizened old goblin looked up at her. Though Madlin was average height for a woman—at her most optimistic—she towered over the creature. "Unfortunately, I do," he replied. The vowels were clipped, but present, unlike the language he had spoken a moment before, which sounded more like a defective machine's sputtering and clanking than real words. "I must force my tongue to these horrible shapes, all because you are dumb as an ox horn."

Madlin scowled down at the creature. "What's your name?"

"K'k'rt." The goblin smirked at her, surprising her with the human-like mannerism.

"Kukroot, I'm Madlin Errol."

"K'k'rt," he said, correcting her. "No mooing between syllables. And I know who you are. You and I are going to have quite an interesting time, I think."

"K'k'rt," Madlin repeated, trying to mimic the goblin sound.

K'k'rt stuck out his lower lip and nodded. "Better. You may not be hopeless. Now, get rid of this hole in my house and send your lackeys away. That one, too." He pointed to Anzik.

Madlin stepped into Veydrus and nodded to Cadmus. Their eyes met. It was as much of a goodbye as either of them wanted, perhaps even too much of one.

Madlin saw him reach for the switch, but the hole disappeared at his first tug upon it.

K'k'rt collapsed into a chair in one corner of the room. "About time. I hate waiting. Care for some tea?" Nestled among a stack of papers was a teapot and cups. K'k'rt held a hand to the side of the teapot, and seconds later steam whistled through the spout.

"You're a sorcerer?" Madlin asked.

"More common among my people than yours, but few are worth a wet sock at it."

Madlin accepted a cup of tea which she had never officially requested. "And you?"

"Worth a whole drawer full of wet socks," he replied, grinning.

"You seemed like you were in a hurry a moment ago," said Madlin. "Now we're just waiting and sipping tea?" She tasted hers and found that it had a Kheshi flavor to it. *Local ingredients*, she suspected.

"Yes, I was impatient to meet you," said Kk'k'rt. "For your meeting today, you are going to be late."

"What?" Madlin sat bolt upright in her chair.

K'k'rt chuckled. "I am sure your sorcerer friend warned you not to offend Fr'n'ta'gur. Your lateness will not bother him. Time passes differently for dragons. Today is a blink's blink, less than nothing to him. Had you arrived tomorrow, we might not even have drawn his attention to your late arrival. No, we are doing this for his priests."

"We're provoking them … intentionally?" Madlin asked. She hoped that skepticism wasn't lost on the goblin. "That doesn't sound prudent."

K'k'rt chuckled once more. "You're a human about to bargain with a dragon. If you were the prudent sort, you'd have thrown someone out a window for suggesting this plan. No, you are willing to take risks. Bah, scratch that out, you *like* risks. Only a few humans have ever tried this sort of thing. That sorcerer's father was one. That's why he can't have any part of this plan from here on. He got a dragon killed, listening to his plans. I don't think it was his intent, but it happened, and dragons are cautious creatures."

"So why upset the priests?"

K'k'rt took a sip of his tea, looking Madlin over. "You're going to be here a while, perhaps a season or two, perhaps the rest of your life, if you're unlucky. The priests run most things around here. You don't want them running you, too. If you work for Fr'n'ta'gur, they might think you fall under their purview. We're going to let them know, starting today, that you do not. You are going to ignore their schedule for your visit, and we are going to see Fr'n'ta'gur anyway."

Madlin pulled off her goggles and rubbed her eyes. She was suddenly getting a headache. "So … politics."

K'k'rt chuckled. "Ah, you have them in your world, too? Pity, I hoped I might find someplace quiet to retire once this is over."

Madlin's first impression was that of a Telluraki mine. The side of the mountain was slashed across with roads and lifts, loomed over by cranes, and dotted with arched entrances, supported with wooden beams. As she and K'k'rt drew closer, she saw that there was a single, far larger, entrance, right at the base of the mountain, large enough to sail one of her father's steam ships through, had there been enough water to float one.

Leadership had accustomed Madlin to having eyes follow her wherever she went, but the trip through the goblin city made her feel like insects were crawling all around her feet. Strange, inhuman eyes watched her, staring up from navel height from every direction. The windows of multistory buildings grew pairs of curious eyes as well, taking in the strange sight of a human in their city. *I wonder if they've ever seen one of my kind in person before.* Jinzan Fehr had made his bargain with a different dragon, who ruled another city.

"Remember," K'k'rt muttered to her in Korrish. "No deception. No lies. Fr'n'ta'gur is far too clever to fool, so be blunt and truthful. He—"

"He will sniff out any lies by the scents I give off, drive teeth like thunderail spikes through my guts, and swallow me before I've finished bleeding out," Madlin finished for him. "I've envisioned my death a half a thousand times since I agreed to this plan. Now, clamp that valve of yours shut unless you've got something useful to tell me."

K'k'rt just chuckled.

A gaggle of goblins in purple robes greeted them at the main entrance to the dragon's lair. While she was still fuzzy on the details of goblin behavior, it was no trick to tell that they were angry with K'k'rt. The elderly goblin tinker laughed off their objections, chittering and clacking right back at them. After several minutes of this, K'k'rt had his way.

"Follow this one," he said, pointing to one of the priests. "Her name is Nk'pt'n."

"No way I'm remembering that," Madlin muttered as she followed the priestess—and Madlin only had the tinker's pronoun use to tell her the goblin was female—down the tunnel and into the mountain.

The tunnel was primitive in construction, with the stone chipped and chopped away, leaving scarred, ugly walls that would never pass the mason's code, even in the poorest human layer of a deep. The floor was worn smooth by untold goblin footsteps, with one exception. All along the way, there were great gashes in the stone, two to three paces long, and a few inches both deep and wide. *Claws! Eziel defend me, this thing did this with its claws—his claws. Blast it, got to remember that.* The edges of the gashes were worn smooth as well, and there was no debris settled into them. For such a raw piece of stonework, the tunnel was immaculate.

Madlin's guide led her down deeper into the mountain, through twists and forks, ignoring side passages altogether. *Our destination isn't a side passage sort of place, I suppose.* Whatever lit them, Madlin could only assume was magic. There was no clear source for the somber light all down the tunnel, and it never grew brighter or dimmer.

At long last, the tunnel widened into a vast cavern. The stonework was better here but still primitive. It had the look of a natural cavern that had been expanded by the occupants. Here the magical light did fail, illuminating the entrance and not much beyond it. If Madlin's estimate of the size was correct based on a guess at the shape, she was only seeing the nearest twenty percent or so.

"Fr'n'ta'gur!" the goblin priestess shouted. It was strange to hear from one of the tiny, chittering creatures, but the goblin's voice reverberated through the chamber. The priestess bent in half at the waist, eyes to the floor, and scuttled backward out of the cavern.

Madlin waited.

In the silence left in the wake of the priestess' departure, Madlin thought she could hear something, a rhythmic rush of air. She strained to tell what direction it was coming from; all she could tell was that it came from the darkened end of the chamber. *Breathing. I can hear the thing … the dragon's breath. It must know I'm here. Should I say something? Should I wait?* K'k'rt had mentioned that patience was a draconic virtue, not a goblin one. If the goblins were lesser creatures to the dragon, could she set herself above them by displaying self-restraint? She waited longer.

Madlin had no polite means to tell how long she stood there. Reaching for the pocketclock she carried seemed like an inexcusable rudeness. But there was no sunlight, no wall clock, no routine of workers bustling about that she could use to at least estimate the time of day. It could have been half an hour; it might have been more than two. Finally, she could stand the wait no longer. Her feet were growing numb, and an ache was creeping up her back.

"Fr'n'ta'gur?" Madlin said loudly. It was not a shout, but merely an attempt to project her voice across the chamber. "I am Madlin Errol, representative of the humans of Korr, a world much like this one. I have come—"

A noise deeper than any Madlin had heard echoed through the cavern. It sounded like a slow chuckle. "And another one loses," Fr'n'ta'gur said. The voice had a presence all its own. Madlin felt it thunder through her, though by the tone it was neither shouting, nor angry. "Still I find no mortal creature possessed of greater patience than Fr'n'ta'gur. You did better than I expected human, and you bring me a unique gift."

Madlin had forgotten about the pack slung over her shoulder. Even magically lightened, the strap had spent so long digging into her skin that it was a relief to sling it to the floor. "I am glad you appreciate it. This is a token of my people's appreciation." Madlin popped the lid and turned the chest so that the contents faced the unseen dragon's direction.

"A pittance," said Fr'n'ta'gur. "Drag it to the edge and dump it in. No, I referred to a human who speaks only the daruu tongue. I find that fascinating."

"Um, which way is the edge?" Madlin dared ask.

The cavern flared into light. A soft yellow radiance shone from above, bathing the cavern in golden shimmering. Madlin stood upon a precipice, several paces from a sharp drop into a sea of gold coins. Madlin had grown up wealthy, and Rynn as a pauper. Neither had ever considered the worth of money in detail until the rebellion. Madlin always had so much that prices and payments were just abstract numbers; Rynn, so little, that stealing was more practical. But when Madlin stared in gaping wonderment at the treasure the dragon lounged upon, she wondered if she could purchase all the world with it. *We'd ruin the economy. Gold would be worth less than coal for the same weight.*

It was a testament to the power of seeing that much gold that it took several seconds before Madlin registered the presence of the dragon. The cavern was too large; it had to be playing tricks with her eyes. The great reptilian beast was longer nose to tail than the *Jennai.* It defied logic. It was impossible; a creature so massive should collapse under its own weight.

"I see you are suitably impressed, human with a daruu's tongue," said Fr'n'ta'gur. It waded through the sea of gold until its head crested the precipice, looming over Madlin. "Now tell me, what bargain do you wish to strike with me?"

At one point along the walk to the dragon's lair, Madlin had wondered why they let her keep her coil gun. Seeing the beast up close, she understood. What could her weapon do against such a creature? She could stand upright in one of its nostrils, walk between its teeth. *How do these creatures not rule the world?*

"Oh my, I think I may have broken this one's little brain," Fr'n'ta'gur remarked.

Madlin drew her coil gun, held it up, then set it on the ground in front of her. "I want more of these made. I understand your people are the best workers in Veydrus." Her voice trembled, but she didn't stumble over her words, at least.

"So, we are conducting simple commerce," said Fr'n'ta'gur. It yawned, and Madlin covered her nose and mouth to ward off the carrion stench. "I had hoped for something more interesting from a human with a daruu tongue in her."

"I want to conquer my world with them, and if you keep a quarter of the ones your goblins make for me, you can conquer yours."

The corners of the dragon's mouth curled up, and its lips parted. "Better. And for form's sake, let us discuss why I should not devour you and let my clever worshipers dissect your little machine to find out how it works?"

"Because your world is a backwater," Madlin said. *Bluntness, right K'k'rt?* She swallowed, feeling a bit dizzy. Whether it was from her gamble or from the lingering smell of the dragon's latest meal, she couldn't say. "My world runs on machines and science, and this is a top of the ladder piece. My world can barely make them, and I can't make them fast enough for my army. Your world won't know what to do about these. One goblin can pack as much punch as a cannon."

Fr'n'ta'gur made a grumbling sound that could have been either a purr or a growl. "I like cannons. You have met K'k'rt, my cannon-maker?"

"He helped arrange my visit," Madlin replied. "And cannons? Please. Cannons are unwieldy and slow. If you'll allow me …" Madlin reached down and retrieved her coil gun.

"By all means," Fr'n'ta'gur replied.

Madlin flipped down her goggles, took aim at the floor, and pulled the trigger. A shower of rock dust blew into the air as a crack echoed from the far reaches of the cavern. The sound was lost in the deep, guttural laughter that followed. "Oh, wonderful. Simply wonderful. You can show my tinkers how to make more of these?"

Madlin nodded. "Yes, and in return for that knowledge and training your workforce, you can keep one quarter of them."

"The quarter share will be yours," Fr'n'ta'gur corrected her. "And only because of my gracious nature." The dragon bellowed in another tongue, and Madlin raised hands to cover her ears. Goblins poured into the room in purple robes, throwing themselves prone on the cavern floor in neat rows behind Madlin. The dragon gave them instruction in that same alien tongue, clicking at his worshipers like a municipal clock gone haywire. The goblins scattered as quickly as they arrived. "You will have thirty-five thousand workers at your disposal, Madlin Errol of Korr. You will be my guest until I am satisfied with your end of the bargain."

Madlin looked up into the colossal eyes of the dragon, catching the reflection of the sea of gold below. She took a deep breath to steady her nerves. "Thank you, Fr'n'ta'gur."

Chapter 16

"I can feel my grandfather when I touch the stone of this place. He touched it and left a part of himself." –Kezudkan Graniteson

Kezudkan looked at himself in the mirror, a habit he had largely abandoned in his later years. It depressed him, more often than not. His face lacked the range of expression it once had as the muscles beneath grew harder and less pliable. Cracks and small crevices lined the skin around his eyes and mouth, and he was too proud to mortar them like an old woman. Still, he was dressed to compensate, in a red and gold brocade jacket, and a dark velvet vest over a starched white shirt beneath. He bought a new cane for the occasion, real oak with a solid gold handle and tip. In his vest, he carried a pocketclock of his own design, made over a century prior and still keeping time like a thunderail conductor.

The feel of the stone on my feet. Neither shoe nor boot covered the old daruu's feet. While he wanted to greet his distant kinfolk in his native garb, he was eager to embrace their local custom of unshod feet. With a final glance at the mirror and a grudging nod of approval, Kezudkan set out for his secret workshop.

It seemed as if workshops were becoming disposable commodities. He had the one in his Eversall Deep estate for more than a hundred and sixty years, but in the past six months, he had honestly lost count of the workshops he had set up, only to see them abandoned, destroyed, or overrun by kuduks. Draksgollow was insidious, overpopulating the workshops with his own hired help, stuffing them so full of bustling, bearded bodies that a daruu had neither the time nor space to think properly.

This one was different, he hoped. Tucked away in a remote corner of Tellurak, in mines that Erefan had abandoned, he had finally found the last place the human tinker's allies would think to look. *Not one for looking back, that one. He'd mine a vein, and never bother sifting the ore from the rock, just moving on to the next vein.* He used to think Erefan was entirely predictable, but he had been wrong enough times to question his guesses now. Whoever had taken over Erefan's little rebellion had yet to find him, but he had no doubt that there were standing orders to hunt him down.

Gederon was waiting for him when Kezudkan arrived, attentive at the controls of the world-ripper. His nephew was decked out for the occasion as well, on the assumption that the daruu of Veydrus might want to see the machine. The viewframe was dark.

"How are we today, my boy?" Kezudkan called out as he entered. His voice boomed through the workshop, reflecting his mood. Booming summed him up quite nicely, he felt.

"All set and dialed in, Uncle," Gederon replied. "Just saving spark until you were ready."

"Good lad, Geddie," said Kezudkan, "always thinking. How do I look? Fit to see a king?"

"Never met a king, but you look like you're ready to make a speech for an award." Gederon tugged at the collar of his suit.

"Well, in theory, a king is more important than an awards committee. Though depending on the award, some of *them* might dispute that." Kezudkan chuckled and Gederon mimicked him amiably.

"Where is the view parked?"

"I picked one of the long bridges to that middle part. It looked more important than the others."

"Fine, fine," said Kezudkan. "Open it up, and let's have a look."

Gederon's hand hovered over the first of the switches, hesitating. "Are we going to end up living there?"

"Why would you say that?"

"It's just … well, you've been different since you saw it. You're acting fifty years younger, like you got a new girl or something. Maybe you like it there so much, you want to stay, and maybe you convince mother that I ought to go with you."

"Hadn't crossed my mind," said Kezudkan. He looked into the dormant viewframe and pictured the daruu city instead of the web of copper wires strung across. *Would I be happier there?* It was impossible to know until he had met his kin. "Perhaps. I've always said you were cleverer that your parents. Might be that you know my mind better than I know it myself."

"So, you haven't talked to mother about this?"

"Your mother and I discussed an apprenticeship, nothing more. Now, if you please …" Kezudkan swept a hand toward the viewframe.

Gederon nodded and pulled the switches, until the view sprang to life. It was just as the boy had said. The view hovered above what appeared to be the main walkway into the palace. Kezudkan stood there admiring the view for some time, a tear welling in his eye. *So beautiful. So perfect.* It was the kind of palace he would want if he were king, the kind of city he would build around it. *Except marble. It would need more marble to be a proper palace.*

"Want me to open it?" Gederon asked. *Impatience. Polite impatience, but just another sign that I'm getting old, and the world is filling with young daruu behind me.* Filling wasn't the proper word, he knew, because Korr was anything but filled with daruu. Filled with kuduk, perhaps. Even filled with humans though they only counted because they could talk. Might as well say that the world was filled with cows, or fish, or clouds.

"No," Kezudkan replied. "Not here. I don't feel like answering my way past gate guards. If there is one constant I can expect between all worlds, it is that the dregs of any organization get stuck on guard duty, and will have to pass me though a chain of command a mile long before I can talk to anyone of importance. That is, of course, if they don't kill me as a spy or a madman first. No, let's snoop around the palace first; see if maybe we can find a likely candidate to introduce ourselves."

"You're going to introduce me, too?" Gederon asked, a hopeful rumbling in his tone.

Kezudkan furrowed his brow. "Figure of speech. You're not apprenticed up enough to be greeting kings."

"Sounds like a failure on your part. Shoddy education, I'll tell mother …"

"Got your father's wits, but your mother's idiot tongue. I'd have to spend hours explaining to that sister of mine what a king is."

Gederon put on his best school recitation voice. "A king is a hereditary ruler, chosen because one of his ancestors was good at both politics and killing people. Usually he convinces his subjects that winning the wars that got him the throne was a sign that some god or other sanctioned—"

"Top marks for history, now close the valve on it. I'm hoping this Veydran king is a reasonable sort, or this could be a very short trip. You know the signal for a quick escape hole as well as you know your kings?"

"You grab your cane by the middle, either hand," Gederon replied.

"If I drop it and start to run, you can consider that a signal, too."

"You running, Uncle? I'd be laughing too hard."

"Nice to know I'm in safe hands," Kezudkan said dryly.

"I could hop over and snag one of Draksgollow's goons to watch the controls for you."

"I think I may be giving you the wrong sort of apprenticeship," said Kezudkan, smiling despite his best efforts not to encourage the lad.

The halls of the palace were rune-lit stone. Nothing hung on the walls or covered the floors. The stonework itself was decoration enough. Not a surface was flat or unadorned. Bas relief covered every inch of the walls; if they stopped for long enough, Kezudkan suspected they could learn much of the daruu history in Veydrus from the scenes depicted. The floors were textured mosaic tile, fitted tightly together from different types and colors of stone, then fused together by daruu magic. *Oh, how I'd have loved working on those when I was young enough to crawl about on my knees all day.*

A few daruu roamed the palace, all bedecked in metallic finery that made Kezudkan suddenly self-conscious that the only gold in his coat was the thread. *My native dress*, he kept telling himself. *Got to be true to my people.* He tried to decipher the roles or duties of the palace staff, but it was all in vain. For all he knew, he could be looking at messengers or members of the royal family. No one in the structure gave any hint of subservience, performing menial labor, or giving orders.

There was an order to the palace, in layout if not among its inhabitants. At first, it seemed like a maze of corridors, with too few branches and irregular angles. But Kezudkan puzzled it out. "It's a defensive layout. Stones know who'd attack this place, but if you look, it's designed to divert foot traffic away from somewhere central. Quit trying to follow the corridors, and just find me the middle of the place."

Gederon complied, plowing the view through walls as he went. "Got an idea where we're headed?"

"It's a palace. Whatever it is designed to protect seems to be at the center. It's the one direction these corridors seem intent on preventing us from going. What would a palace be protecting?"

"A king?" Gederon asked.

"Precisely! It's what I'd do if I was a king and living in a palace."

"What's living there got to do with it?" Gederon asked. "If you're king, it's your palace."

"Yes, but if I had a residence somewhere and a formal throne in the palace for royal business, I wouldn't make it so muddy hard to get there. I'd be spouting mad by the time I got to my throne each day, and I'd probably order too many executions and get myself overthrown."

"Is that how kings worked? Execute too many people, and they throw you over?"

"Overthrow is the technical and polite term for a king's subjects switching tracks on the whole execution business. They rid themselves of a despicable monarch, and someone else takes a crack at being king for a while."

"What if he's not despicable? Do the subjects ever make a mistake?" Gederon was full of questions. It was a hazard of youth, but Kezudkan's mood was still intact, and he was feeling amenable.

"My boy, while I don't doubt that there might be exceptions, there are good reasons we don't have kings. Despicability was practically a requirement. Not that you couldn't bargain with them, mind you. I think I've got plenty to offer if I say so myself."

"This what you're looking for?" Gederon asked.

Kezudkan turned his attention back to the viewframe. The scene within certainly looked the way one might imagine a daruu palace throne room. It was a perfectly domed room, the whole of the ceiling clad in gold and dotted with sapphires in what gave the impression of a night sky. *Curious choice in décor, certainly.* The center of the room sported a tiered dais, five steps high, leading to a single stone chair. Seated upon that stony throne sat a daruu far younger than Kezudkan's imagination had led him to expect. Unless the daruu of Veydrus aged differently, the king before him could not have been much older than eighty. Nowhere in Korr would allow a daruu to hold high office younger than a hundred and twenty. *Another of the downsides to hereditary rule: hereditary timing.* You can tell a king when he can die, but you cannot prevent him dying before then, overthrow or no overthrow. The next in line is whatever age he happens to be at the time, ready or not.

The king was far from alone in his throne room. He was attended by two servants holding food-laden platters and a third with a pitcher to refill his goblet. All around the dais, daruu in finery gathered in small groups as other servants glided among them with trays of refreshments. There were nearly as many women among the group as men, more women than Kezudkan had seen gathered in one place, all bedecked in the finest precious metals. Silver seemed to be in fashion among the women, as were rubies. Kezudkan was a grandfather, and few of the daruu women of the court looked to be even a quarter of his age, but an age-old longing returned at the sight of them in their exotic dress.

"Uncle?" Gederon prodded.

Kezudkan glanced around the room. Workshop. He looked back to the viewframe, Throne room. The contrast was glaring, dissonant. *I can go there looking like a backwater peasant from another world, but I can't show them this mess.* "No. Well … it is, but we're not opening a hole yet."

"Why not? Feet taken a mortar?"

Kezudkan waved away the notion. "Just look at this place, and tell me we won't disgust the lot of those daruu in there."

Gederon gave a quick glance around the room. "We won't disgust those daruu in there."

Kezudkan waggled his cane in his nephew's direction. "Time for that smart tongue to be put away. We've got a coal pit to paint."

While technically some of Erefan's old mines once held some amount of coal, they did not actually paint the workshop. Kezudkan and Gederon—mostly Gederon—swept up the debris that neither of them normally took notice of. With a bit of welding gas and a few spare lengths of piping, they constructed a frame. It took a quick jaunt via the world-ripper to find draperies that looked suitably royal-friendly, but in the markets of some bustling Telluraki city, they scared the wits from a gaggle of human shoppers and snatched an entire bolt of red velvet.

By the time they were finished, the view *from* the world-ripper was at least not so embarrassing compared to the view through it. The pipe-work frame acted as a curtain rod, and the draperies blocked the view of most of the workshop from the viewframe. All anyone in the daruu throne room would see would be a backdrop of red velvet, like the curtains at a theater. *I suppose this is a theater of sorts, playing the world out before us. Cracked and slurried veins! I could have made my fortune charging kuduks to watch the show, and never told them that it could open for real.*

Gederon arranged the viewframe to the exact coordinates they had found before. The king's court had finished their meal, and the courtiers had rearranged themselves into a proper audience for an audience. A pair of daruu stood at the base of the dais, with the king's full attention fixed on them. Everyone else present looked on from neat rows of stone seats, arrayed in a semi-circle in the king's field of vision.

"Were those benches there before?" Kezudkan asked, eyeing them suspiciously.

"I didn't notice any. But I wasn't looking for benches, last time," Gederon replied.

"Magic. Must be."

"Feet getting all gooey with mortar again?" Gederon asked, smirking at him.

"Listen, lad. I'm about to walk into the throne room of our distant kinfolk from the world of Veydrus. I am neither an orator nor a diplomat, just a crazy old tinker with delusions of grandeur. If this works, it will be the single most significant achievement for our people since the great wars. If it doesn't, we might both be in for a rather unpleasant demise. So pardon my caution, but I do not intend to step into that throne room on a whim, or because you're prodding at my pride with a sharpened nail, or because I can't stand the wait a moment longer. So if you would kindly dunk your head underwater for a few minutes, I'd like to think this over."

Kezudkan watched for minutes that stretched into hours until every joint threatened to stiffen solid. He studied the expression on the king's face, cursing for the hundredth time since building the world-ripper that he could not read lips. He knew nothing useful of Veydrus, especially when it pertained to his kin there. Who were the supplicants? What were their pleas before their king? He tried to imagine professions for them, but their garments and mannerisms gave him too few clues. What he *was* able to gather was that this daruu king seemed even of both hand and temperament. There was no rancor in his countenance, no frown, no sneer. The young king exuded a calm dignity, and his subjects—however they were who approached him—treated his judgment with respect.

"Good enough," Kezudkan announced at last. "We'll open the hole as soon as I can walk again." The idleness had crept insidiously into his joints, hardly paining him as they hardened. It told Kezudkan that he had hardly moved during his observation. He took a few moments with the help of his cane to hobble loose his knees, ankles, and hips. His hands never seemed quite so bad as his lower extremities; a lifetime of tinkering and writing had kept them more mobile than the rest of him.

Gederon hopped from his chair, his eagerness to be busy plain as he pulled the drapes between the viewframe and the rest of the workshop. Within arm's reach, there was a fold of fabric with a slit meant to be used as a peephole. "All set, uncle. I can see enough to be sure you're through."

"Not until I give the word," Kezudkan warned. He watched the scene in the throne room, imagining himself standing amid that waiting crowd. There was a feel to the proceedings, a rhythm he had watched and judged as he tried to decide whether the king was a man he could deal with. Lulls were the key. The bailiff—or whatever they called the one who acted in a bailiff's stead—would escort the supplicants to and from the base of the dais. In between, the court relaxed momentarily. Small conversations broke out; people shifted in their seats, came and went. Once the next supplicant was brought forth, they would all settle into respectful stillness again.

Kezudkan watched as the current supplicant was dismissed. The king lifted a hand, and the bailiff came to take a middle-year daruu gentleman in a bronze jacket back to the gallery. *Five … four … three … two …*

"Now," said Kezudkan.

Gederon was alert. Not a second passed before the thunk of the switch heralded the change in the viewframe that made the throne room a real place just a pace away. Kezudkan took a step forward, cane leading the way. No sooner had he set both feet on the warm, smooth stone of the throne room, but the pervasive hum of the world-ripper's dynamo vanished. The eerie silence that was left was short lived.

There was an outcry from the audience, a hundred different exclamations of shock and outrage. Kezudkan did not let the chaos reign unopposed. "Greetings," he proclaimed, raising his voice to be heard above the courtiers. "I am Kezudkan Graniteson, I am from a world known as Korr. I have come here by—"

"Silence!" the king commanded. Kezudkan caught himself short, feeling as if he may have misjudged the monarch. The throne room grew quiet enough that he could hear nearby daruu breathing. "What manners are these? We have a guest among us, one who claims to be from very far away indeed. I will have silence that we might all hear what he has to say. Continue, Kezudkan Graniteson of Korr."

Kezudkan bowed slightly, which was all the bowing his body was fit for. "My thanks. I have recently created a device that allows me to see and travel to other worlds, or to other places in my own. To my astonishment and delight, I happened upon this place, where I find a people who are no doubt some kinfolk of mine. I come in friendship, and fellowship, and in the hope of learning more about my own people through knowing yours."

"You speak our language," the king observed. "How is this, if you are from another world?"

"Runes are runes, and the daruu tongue cannot change while it uses the runes of our ancestors."

"Well said," the king replied. "I am King Dekulon, ninth to take this name. You will be a guest of our people. This forum is unfit for scholarly discussion, and you, elder, seem very much to be a scholarly man. I would learn of your world and our people who inhabit it. Hulara, take him to a guest room, and see that he gets some proper attire." The king raised a hand, and the bailiff came forward to remove Kezudkan.

This could have gone worse. At first, he assumed Hulara to have been the bailiff's name, but he was handed off to a woman at the edge of the room who took custody of him. She was in her late second century, smooth with just a few crevices at the corners of her eyes, her brow sloped gently back to her scalp. Kezudkan was very well inclined to follow wherever she wished to take him.

"Right this way, honored guest," said Hulara, sweeping a hand out to the side toward a side exit from the throne room.

"Thank you very much," Kezudkan replied, inclining his head toward her.

"I must say," she replied. "You have the most charming accent. Do all your people talk like that?"

Kezudkan could not have removed the grin from his face with a pickaxe and hammer. "Not a one of them. I am utterly unique."

Gederon sat with his feet on the edge of the control console, lounging in his chair. The draperies bunched at one end of the curtain rod contraption he and his uncle had assembled, allowing an unfettered view of the proceedings. A lazy hand gave a dial a twist here or there, keeping up with Kezudkan's progress through the Veydran palace. Like his uncle, Gederon had no talent for reading lips, but he was no fool, and neither as young nor naïve as his uncle seemed to think him. He watched as the daruu woman—who had to be half his uncle's age—followed Kezudkan into what appeared to be a lavish bedroom.

Stretching from his reclined position, Gederon managed to get a hand on the main spark switch for the world-ripper. With a pull, the machine went dark. "Best of luck, Uncle, but that's about the limit of what I'm willing to see. You're on your own until morning."

Chapter 17

"I didn't expect to live a long life. That's how I managed to live one." –K'k'rt

Rynn awoke from a fitful night spent on the floor of K'k'rt's little workshop, which took up the large ground floor of the tinker's home. It felt wrong, primitive. While Tinker's Island had been a bit of modern comfort in a backward world, K'k'rt's workshop was like a living museum. Outdated tools were organized in wooden racks around the room, more iron than steel in their construction. The floor was dirt, the better for dealing with molten metals, K'k'rt had told her, but knowing that did not make it seem any less a hovel. Spread upon the floor, a tarp delineated her sleeping spot. Piled with cloth to soften it, there was still no escaping the feel of the earth beneath. A single blanket of goblin manufacture was too short to cover her neck to toe, and so she had used two of them, with an awkward overlap that turned to a chilly gap as she tossed and turned through the night.

K'k'rt's chuckle greeted her. "Oh, you decided to join me this morning. Not all humans are so lazy. I know, since my own are already at work."

"You have humans?" Madlin asked. "You never mentioned having humans."

K'k'rt chuckled again. "It was a busy day. Besides, if I told you all at once, we would have nothing but silence for the rest of your time here. Yes, I have a few human workers. Refugees from Megrenn, they came with me because they did good work for me, and I let them live with my people instead of dying with their own."

"So where are they? Can I meet them?"

"You hope too much, I think. Yes, you will meet them. You will meet everyone. But they aren't going to speak your language. Maybe you can teach them, huh? Just don't let me catch you not teaching how to build spark cannons."

"Spark cannons?" Madlin echoed. A lopsided grin spread across her face. "I think I like the sound of that. So where are these humans of yours? You never answered me."

"Where is everyone?" K'k'rt asked. "Oh, they are all working, that's where." He bustled around the workshop, checking on things and moving them around. What the routine was meant to accomplish was anyone's guess.

Madlin looked around. Tables, forges, kiln, all corners of the workshop were empty save for Madlin and the tinker. "Oh, this isn't where we're going to be working?"

K'k'rt paused, like a gearworks with a rock jammed in between the teeth. Tilting his head to the side, he watched Madlin for a moment. "In here? Where would we possibly hide thirty-five thousand goblins?"

"What are you talking about?" Madlin asked. "We haven't even started yet."

"*They* have. You mentioned the basic facilities you would need. Construction began last night. I've lived with humans, so I can understand your confusion. We don't—I don't know if this translates well—sit around warming each other's cheeks."

"Huh?"

"You talk too much," K'k'rt replied. He chuckled. "Listen to me babble like a human … Talking is fine, but doing is just as important. Come, we'll get you a morning meal on our way. It's easier just to show you."

The morning meal came from a communal cafeteria, one of dozens scattered throughout the city, according to her host. Waterlogged puffed grains sounded unappealing, but they were sweetened with cane sugar and honey, topped with a sprinkling of cinnamon, and served warm. Madlin wolfed down three bowls meant to fill goblin stomachs before she became self-conscious of the stares she drew. She could have eaten three more, she guessed.

Trekking through the goblin city, Madlin attracted every eye to her. It was a small thing, but there seemed to be fewer of them than there had been the day before, and she asked K'k'rt about it.

"I think you still might not grasp what you've started here," he replied. "You will see those same eyes from yesterday, and they will see you. But not here."

She followed the tinker through town and out the southeastern gate. The guards there were armed with spears tipped with steel blades so thin and sharp they looked like they would shatter the moment they touched something. Madlin had a sudden vision of one breaking off inside her flesh after being stabbed and understood the danger. *Small creatures, so the lightweight blade makes it easier to handle. Vast numbers, so the loss of a weapon that takes out an enemy is a good trade.* She had always been the one outnumbered. She had always been the one pressed for manpower, for supplies. *Is this the mindset I'm going to have to take now?* Humans outnumbered kuduks in Korr, and if she had reinforcements from Tellurak, and maybe even Veydrus, how badly could her own forces outnumber the kuduks?

Madlin pondered as she followed the elderly tinker into the foothills. He was keeping up remarkably well, considering his apparent frailty and reliance on a walking stick. She began to suspect that he was not so infirm with age as he let on. He sped his pace subtly as they approached one rise, reaching the crest well ahead of Madlin.

"There is your answer," he stated simply, pointing down to the unseen valley beyond.

Madlin reached the hilltop and stared, dumbstruck. *Thirty-five thousand, the dragon said.* They were all there. Madlin did not try to count them, of course, but the number was plausible. Down on the valley floor, goblins and oxen were constructing what looked like a small city. "What is all this?"

"You made mention of the facilities you would need," K'k'rt said. "Forges, foundries for several metals, rune carvers and empowerers, glassworks, workshops for metalworking and woodworking, a test range, warehouses for raw materials, piecework, and finished weapons. I told them to add worker barracks and an office for you."

"You … *you* did all this?"

"Are you daft? I'm thirty-eight. I don't do real work anymore. I sketched out a map of the valley for your foremen before I went to bed last night. I laid out where I wanted everything."

"But … the planning, the details …"

K'k'rt chuckled. "If my people were your size, we'd own this world." He paused, raising a thoughtful finger to his chin. "Or perhaps we would grow lazy and busy-tongued, and spend all our energies fighting our own kind. Perhaps being smaller than the other peoples of Veydrus forces us to be smarter, to work harder."

Madlin looked out over the sea of goblins. If the green of the Katamic were tinged with grey instead of blue, it would have looked like her new workforce. *So many of them … how am I even going to teach them?* "Are you going to be my translator?"

K'k'rt's shoulders rose and fell in a silent sigh. He turned to look back at the mountain. "Fr'n'ta'gur decrees is, and so it is. But I've rounded up three scholars who speak the stone folk tongue. They're going to begin classes for the workforce. By season's end, I hope a quarter—maybe a third—will have picked it up."

"A quarter of your people can learn a new language in three months—I mean a season?" Madlin asked. K'k'rt just shrugged. "Can I ask you something?"

K'k'rt chuckled. "You've done little else," he replied.

"I met Fr'n'ta'gur. I see how fast your people work, and everyone keeps telling me how smart you all are. How come you *haven't* taken over Korr? That dragon of yours could wipe out cities. Surely you can figure out some way to protect him from anything that might hurt him."

"What do you think we're doing right this moment?" K'k'rt asked. He pointed to the valley floor. "Dragons are expansionists by nature, but they think in times we can't conceive. A hundred winters, five hundred? Tell me, Madlin Errol, how many of your people plan fifty generations ahead? How many even plan two ahead? Fr'n'ta'gur is cautious, like all dragons. He had time we don't. So what if he hasn't moved his borders in my lifetime. What are thirty-eight winters to him? He waited for a strong play, and now you've given it to him. He gives the word, and my people—who are *his* people—act on it."

"Still, it just seems like …" *your dragon is a coward.* Madlin thought better of finishing her thought aloud.

"You are new to this world. Anzik Fehr told me that the world you are from is poor in magic. Have you ever felt its touch?"

Madlin shrugged. "A few times. I've seen sorcerers fight. Anzik and a Kadrin warlock. It's like a wind running through you."

K'k'rt nodded slowly. "You felt its kiss, but never its bite. I felt magic once, *real* magic. I am a sorcerer myself of no small skill, and this power struck me like a hammer against my Source. I was across a city from it, but there was no doubt that the power of that force was greater than I wished to see from any closer."

"How did you survive?"

K'k'rt rapped Madlin in the shin with his walking stick. "Follow along, human! It was a figure of speech. I was not struck by the magic; I only felt its presence."

"Fine, you felt a strong magic. What's that got to do with Fr'n'ta'gur and the other dragons not banding together and carving up the world for themselves?"

"The demons," said K'k'rt, exaggerating his vowels for effect, Madlin guessed. If it was meant to sound scary, it was going to have to come from a more menacing creature, one not hammering at her language with a wrench. "A dragon is as strong a creature as the old gods made, but the demons made themselves even stronger, against the wishes of the gods. Certain human sorcerers are dangerous as well, but it is the demons above all others who the dragons fear."

"Nothing personal, Kukaroot, but I think I'm heading back to my own world as soon as this is all done. Any place where something the size of Fr'n'ta'gur fears the inhabitants is someplace I might not want to stay on a long-term basis."

K'k'rt turned to watch the workers in the valley below. "Perhaps."

"Perhaps what?" Madlin asked.

"Perhaps I, too, may not stay long."

"Are they always like this?" Cadmus asked.

"Yes," Anzik replied.

The two of them stood in the lunar headquarters, not looking at one another. Each had their eyes fixed on the viewframe where Madlin and K'k'rt watched the construction in the valley. Had the viewframe been inert—as it had been first thing in the morning—they would have found some other way not to look at one another.

"Could use workers like that."

"You are."

"Are you going to go on like that all day?" Jamile asked as she bounded into the room with a tray of pastries. "I thought I told both of you that you're going to be civil while we're cooped up together here. I've a mind to bring in a proper household staff."

"Kaia quit after a day," Cadmus pointed out. "Just too strange here. Most minds can't adapt."

Jamile landed beside Cadmus with the false grace that one sixth gravity can give a body. She offered him a choice of tarts or turnovers, all filled with strawberry. "Well, look what we've got here," she said, pointing to Anzik with her free hand. "A spare warlock with nothing to do but start at a machine all day."

"Sorcerer," said Anzik, not turning to look at her.

Jamile rolled her eyes. "Fine, we've got a rusted sorcerer hanging his face all over the place and eating our food. Why not have him fix up gravity so it feels like back below? Hmm?"

"We asked Dan the same thing, and *he* couldn't do anything about it," Cadmus replied. "Why would I bother with this one? We've adapted just fine."

"Yes, but Dan didn't really try. I think he just didn't want to—"

"Danilaesis Solaran is a buffoon," Anzik said, a hint of venom slipping into his normally placid voice. "He is gifted with a powerful Source, a boon from the Kadrin selective breeding plans. He had the mind of an infant: spoiled, selfish, and temperamental. He knows nothing about magic save what his tutors have forced into his head, and the destructive spells he relishes wielding." Anzik turned to Cadmus with a ghost of a smile on his lips. "He is a hammer for a world of screws."

"That's a Korrish saying," Cadmus said, "Where'd you pick that up?"

"Unlike Danilaesis and his weakling twin, I absorb my surroundings and process them. Rynn chose me over him because I am the stable one, the reasonable one. Though I suspect she does not even realize it herself, she prefers a thinker to a blunt instrument. As much as she leads a rebellion, she would rather wall herself in behind a pile of books and never come out."

"How would you know?" Jamile asked. "You barely know her."

"Because I recognize me own kind."

Cadmus sneered at the sorcerer. "You've got nothing in common with my daughter."

Anzik held the Mad Tinker's gaze for a moment, then turned back to watch the viewframe.

Jamile slunk out of the room in a series of low, shallow bounds. "That's it. I'm bringing some humans up here," she muttered under her breath. "I'll go bonkers alone with those two."

Madlin walked through a procession of oxen pulling huge timbers, freshly cut from nearby forests. The smell of pitch was strong in the air, even contending with sweating oxen and the ineffable stench coming from the makeshift latrines. The ox drivers, or oxherds, or whatever the goblins deemed the one leading the beasts, seemed to steer them around her in such a way that crossing their path felt safe, despite the oxen being ten times her size. K'k'rt followed in her wake, allowing her to explore the construction site as she saw fit. He answered all her questions, introduced her to a number of important goblins, none of whom she could name a minute after meeting them, and generally provided her the only source of sanity among the well-organized chaos swirling around her for half a mile in any direction.

"Is that poured-stone?" Madlin asked, pointing to a new foundation.

"For the foundry," K'k'rt replied. "It seemed prudent."

"But I thought you said last night that your people didn't know how to make it."

K'k'rt chuckled. "Last night, we didn't. You described the ratios, and I relayed them. Clever idea, but no trick to make once you know it."

"You're telling me that your people invented poured-stone overnight?"

"Of course not," K'k'rt replied. "Your people invented it. Mine just copied. Our test batch from last night still isn't cured, but the theory is sound, so they went ahead with it for the foundation."

"But what if they got it wrong?" Madlin said, "It'll cure wrong or not at all."

"That's the beauty of our way," K'k'rt said. "By the time a bunch of humans were done testing it to see if it worked in a little bucket, we've poured a whole foundation. By the time we're both convinced it works, we're done, and the humans have a whole foundation to make. If it doesn't work, then both of us would still have foundations to make."

"But what about wasted time, labor, planning?"

K'k'rt chuckled. "You should try worshiping a dragon. Fr'n'ta'gur would have you, I think. So many small details go away when Fr'n'ta'gur says to do something."

"So … fear. You're so afraid of your dragon that you'll rush headlong into a project on his whim."

"Yes," K'k'rt replied, grinning and nodding. "I tell you this because I think I have taken a liking to you: do not anger Fr'n'ta'gur. As much as he covets your invention, as much as he might tell himself he has a new pet human to make him weapons, if he catches you in a lie or trying to double-cross him, he will incinerate you."

Madlin sighed. "I spent years at a job once, knowing that if my nightly activities became public knowledge, they'd drag me out and hang me. I guess hanged or incinerated, it's just another job with death looking over my shoulder.

"Come on. We've got more of this place to get sorted out. I think the warehouse should be closer to the new road."

Chapter 18

"The enemy of my enemy is my enemy's enemy, nothing more." –Rashan Solaran

Danilaesis ran a hand over the steel of the inner hull, feeling the rough edges of the runes, etched a hair's width into the metal. The insides of the *Daggerstrike* smelled of oil and polish. The shipwrights had taken the grounded airship into their care and had kept it well. It had not been aloft in years, for there was no one in the empire who could replenish the vast, interconnected web of runes that it took to operate the airship. Every surface bore runes of one sort or another. Runes for levitation, runes to push to the left or right, runes to strengthen the hull, runes for light within, and runes to carry the captain's orders to the hold. Too many runes. All of them linked together in a maze of connected sub-patterns, meeting at the ship's wheel. Despite having no rudder, the *Daggerstrike* had a wheel fixed in place at the helm, each bearing runes that would respond to the captain's touch.

"So this is what all the fuss was about?" Axterion asked, ducking as he came down the narrow stairwell from the main deck.

"Don't tell me you never got curious and came to see it," Danilaesis said. "All the years it's sat here, and you've managed to ignore it?"

"Perhaps you may be forgetting just how much of a creaking old relic I'd become. Down the stairs to breakfast and back up again was a day's exercise … left me winded. I wasn't in the habit of strolling the docks, gawking at derelicts."

"It's not a derelict," said Danilaesis, placing a hand against the smooth metal. He could feel the mild tingle of the runes leeching whiffs of aether from his Source. All runes would gather aether themselves to some degree; some cleverly carved wards replenished themselves indefinitely. The *Daggerstrike* was a dry creek bed. It would take more than a passing shower to fill it. "Brannis just had his head in his arse when he made it. Never stopped to think how anyone else would use it when he wasn't around."

Of course, Danilaesis knew now that his cousin Brannis had not been Brannis at all, but rather his twin, Kyrus. The Telluraki twin had been the one with magic, a Source so powerful he could be seen from halfway across Kadris, the largest city in the world. The magical accident that had switched the two of them had set off a chain of events that had rocked the Kadrin Empire to its core—and left Danilaesis with the best airship in the fleet, completely unable to fly it.

"The carvings are sound, at least," Axterion said, squinting at some of the smaller runes. "Going to take a while to get my head wrapped around this mess though. It's as if some poor fellow who'd studied a bunch of rune patterns decided to see how many he could squeeze into one ward, then kept trying to top himself. I can already see a few forced joinings, where wards at cross purposes are linked together just to share aether. Your bloody cousin was the most brilliant idiot I've ever known. Looks like he decided to make it easy to replenish by making the whole confounded ship into a single ward with a dozen functions."

"Hasn't exactly worked out that way," Danilaesis grumbled.

"Not for us," said Axterion. "But he wasn't making it for us. He made it for himself. He could manage it, and he never stopped to think that no one else would be able to force runes through this whole tangle of insanity."

"I thought he made it for Juliana," said Danilaesis. "That's why he made the *Starlit Marauder*, so she'd have one she could replenish herself."

Axterion harrumphed. Growing younger had not robbed him of the capacity for proper old-mannerisms. "Lot of good that did us. Girl's probably off in Elok with it."

Danilaesis waited. His grandfather pored over the runes, walking around the interior of the ship with his face practically pressed against the steel walls. Once in a while he would grunt, or mutter something to himself, but otherwise silence reigned within the ship. Eventually, the waiting became too much for him. "Well?"

"Well, what?" Axterion replied, not taking his attention from the runes.

"Can you make it fly again?"

"You mean can I refill the runes," Axterion corrected. "I could levitate this thing around the harbor under my own control. Could I get it to fly like a proper airship? … Perhaps."

Danilaesis spread his arms. "Well. Then do it. You're the mighty old wizard returned, right? Prove it."

Axterion turned and raised a single eyebrow. It was neither as bushy nor as grey as it had once been, so the effect was not nearly as challenging as Danilaesis had once found it. "Do not goad *me*, boy. You're out of your circle on this one. For over seventy summers I was High Sorcerer, and I sat in that maddening Inner Sanctum with those persnickety old rascals, engaged in debates set off by a misplaced connotation or a poor choice of wording. I kept the peace by goading and not being goaded. I was the rock in the sea, the kind that you put a lighthouse on because you know that short of the gods' return, it's not going to budge a finger's breadth over the next hundred winters."

"Can you do it or not?"

"I'll try," said Axterion. "But I'm going to need your help."

Danilaesis perked up. He gave the nod of an officer receiving the order to take command. "I'm ready."

"Good," said Axterion. "Because this is going to be perhaps the most difficult task you have ever faced." He let a gravelly undertone slip into his voice. "This may be beyond you. If you fail, it could be your doom."

"I'm not afraid," said Danilaesis. "What do you need me to do? Where should I be?" He looked all around for a likely place his grandfather might station him, trying to guess by the layout of the runes.

"Listen carefully, because I don't want to repeat it."

Danilaesis nodded.

"I am going to need you to … leave me the dead blessed gods alone for an afternoon," Axterion snapped. "Brannis did this by brute force, but I'm going to have to wheedle my way through these wards. I'm going to be juggling forces that could snap back and crush me like a walnut shell. If I don't lose my concentration, I think the worst that might happen is I destroy the ship. I get some precocious whelp yammering in my ear, I might just kill us both."

Danilaesis glared at Axterion, hopes of a glorious partnership dashed. "Have it your way." He stormed out of the ship, stomping across the deck to make sure his grandfather heard every footstep.

In a tree-shrouded glade, surrounding a pond, a small community of tiny homes basked in the midday sun. A sweet breeze carried the scent of fresh blossoms across the pond's surface, sending ripples across the shining water. No smoke poured from chimneys, though a few of the houses bore them; they were there for architectural sake, not for function. The inhabitants needed no food, felt no chill. Not that there was any threat of chill on a pleasant spring morning. Those who dwelt in the glade at the heart of Podawei Wood were immortals—demons, in the common parlance.

Philosophy and idle study were the prevalent forms of entertainment. For beings with no bodily needs to attend, entertainment was the only activity that mattered. Not every immortal lived in the isolated community, cut off by choice from mortal struggles. Some few snuck among the mortals, lived among them, amused themselves by pretending to be mortal themselves. One was an outlier. While all the others eschewed ties to the mortal lands, one among their number had staked his claim and ruled a continent. Far from distraught at the constant upheaval in mortal society, he took his mortal subjects under his protection, giving stability and permanence to their civilization.

His name was Xizix. The others regarded him as a madman.

Acceptable behavior among the immortals was never codified; it was just understood. Wherever the immortals—sensitive creatures when it came to aether—felt a strange tingle that foretold the imminent arrival of Xizix, they knew those mores were about to be stretched to breaking.

He arrived with a crash like a thunderclap, appearing in the air above the shores of the pond, his dread wings spread, casting a grotesque shadow on the pristine grass. "What are we going to do about *this*?" Xizix asked. In one clawed hand he clutched the shattered hulk of a Korrish steam tank. "The incursions grow. My own lands have suffered the outworlders' trespasses. I have felt them in the dragonlands and among the daruu as well."

For all the faults his fellows found with him, Xizix was always a source of great interest. In seconds, a crowd had gathered around him. Creatures of all shapes and origins—mostly humanoid—popped in via magics that prudent mortals feared to work. Others walked from their studies, be they in their homes or the surrounding forest. One boiled up from the ground like a geyser, forming into a squat, marble-skinned creature with gemstone eyes.

"We have felt the portals," said Illiardra, one of the most respected of the immortals, who often spoke as de facto leader of the anarchic colony. She was willow slender, with light brown skin and a mop of tangled green curls. Through those curls poked two ears—human-like but grown so long that they drooped over—and a pair of delicate horns that twisted around and framed her face. She had eyes so large they made her look innocent and naïve, but she was neither. "Some of us are old enough to remember when they were not unheard of."

Xizix growled. Most of the immortals knew him well enough to ignore the theatrics. He was no threat with all of them gathered together though he was among the strongest of their number. "We should put a stop to it," he said. He dropped the steam tank on the shore with a crash of metalwork. The broken heap looked profane amid the idyllic beauty of the glade. "No good can come of allowing this to continue."

"No good?" Illiardra asked. "You lack imagination. I can see many forms of good that we might enjoy. Think, if the other worlds open up to us once more. The places. The peoples. How long has it been since any of us set foot in another world, except one trip through our own gate."

"That is *your* rule, Illiardra," said Xizix.

Another of the immortals stood forward to speak. Bvatrain was the eldest among them; no other could remember his origin. With coal-black skin and a body like a martial statue, he showed no sign that Xizix intimidated him. "We limited the gate because it was the only way between worlds. It was precious, last of its kind. If the mortals of the other worlds have discovered how to link them once more, perhaps it is time to lift those restrictions."

"Bah," replied Xizix. "You think to play at travelers' games. Trips to our own mortal kingdoms no longer amuse you, so you look to sneak off to the other worlds? Or worse, you might let them sully the world we have with filth like this." He kicked the wreck of the steam tank. "I say we put an end to the incursions."

"And how would you do that?" Illiardra asked. "There are at least eight different origins of these portals."

Xizix furrowed his brow, a jarringly human mannerism for a creature twice the height of a man, with glowing red eyes and leathery, ashen skin. Illiardra was sensitive beyond reason, her perception of the aether transcendent. Xizix grinned. "I have it. Some of you must be raving in those vacant skulls of yours, looking for a release from this prison of boredom. Go. Volunteer. Become rulers of these worlds, and keep the separation between them in place."

"No."

Immortals turned in unison toward the speaker. He appeared at the back of the assembly, a normal human, though tall for his kind. He wore outlandish clothing in the literal sense; his attire originated in Korr.

"So, you found what you were looking for, Kyrus?" Illiardra asked.

Kyrus strode through the immortals' ranks, a path opening up before him as he approached Xizix. "There will be no conquering mortal worlds, no demon overlords. I won't allow it."

"I thought you had learned the lesson of Tallax, Kyrus," said Illiardra.

Xizix bellowed a deep, throaty laugh. "Power is power. You couldn't imagine a babe like this one could resist it. So what now, Tallax the Second? What fealty do you demand of us?"

"Do as you will," Kyrus replied. "Look in on the worlds, travel there, mix among the mortals. Just do not rule them. Do not close them off from one another again."

"A half measure of kingship," Xizix replied. "As soon as you make laws for us, you have stepped off the cliff."

"I can fly," Kyrus replied. "And my offer stands. Something vast is happening among these three worlds, something the mortals ought to work out amongst themselves. Let them be. Xizix, you are an exception. If the mortals threaten your lands again, by all means, repel them."

"How generous of you, master," Xizix replied, his sarcasm dripping ichor. He stepped closer, until he loomed over Kyrus.

Kyrus looked up into those eyes with their pale red glow. "Why the show? You worry for your people, your children. Protect them, and leave the rest of the world to its own ends."

"There are more than those three, you know," Bvatrain remarked.

"I know of twelve," Kyrus replied.

"There are more than twelve," said Bvatrain with a smile white as starlight.

Kyrus shrugged. "Whoever wrote the books only cared about twelve."

"Books?" Illiardra asked. "What books?"

Kyrus held up his palms before him and a stack of six books appeared in each. "Twelve books, too. I can't say whether it's coincidental. I have no idea who wrote them, but they were meant for interworld travelers who needed to work with local materials. It's … a survival guide of sorts for exmundiates."

"Exmundiates?" Bvatrain asked.

Kyrus gave an abashed smirk. "What else would you call people living on a world besides their own?"

"Pilgrims?" Illiardra offered.

"Observers," said Bvatrain.

"Invaders," said Xizix.

"You're welcome to these," Kyrus said, holding them out. "These are copies I've made, faithful to the smallest detail. I have no idea what the material is, but I was able to duplicate it."

Illiardra held out a hand, and the books floated toward her single file. Bvatrain picked one from the air and opened it. Other immortals followed suit until Illiardra was left with a single volume. Pages turned and immortal eyes devoured the information contained within.

"This changes nothing," Xizix said. He had taken none of Kyrus's books. "You think you can buy our compliance?"

"I'm buying you off with a bone to chew on. Sate your curiosity—maybe not you personally—but the rest of you, enjoy the worlds out there. Or don't. Just leave the mortals in peace, or in war, or whatever they choose for themselves."

"How is your Juliana?" Illiardra asked.

"The same," Kyrus replied. "And I credit you for more subtlety than this one." He pointed over his shoulder to the red-eyed demon. "But don't think you can threaten her. She is fine. I shared the secret with her, and we plan on spending our eternity together. She has been a great help in resisting the lure of Tallax's folly. It would be a shame for all of us if I were to lose her strength and support. A great, great shame."

"I understand," Illiardra replied.

"I mean no harm to any of you," Kyrus said. He looked to Xizix pointedly. "To any of you. I expect that in a thousand years; you may be the only link to my origins. Some of us may even become friends."

"Unlikely," Xizix replied. The towering demon vanished in a cloud of smoke.

Kyrus sniffed. "Tawdry theatrics." Then he was simply gone.

Sleeping Dragon felt like a willow switch in his hand. Danilaesis whipped the blade through the air with a *whoosh* at each pass. The hilt was solid, comfortable, the leather-wrapped grip conforming to his hand as he had grown up with it. It gave the impression that it was weightless, or nearly so, but the business end would fell trees and bite into stone. He worked through the same set of slashes and thrusts he always did, the practice routine that his swordmaster had created just for this one weapon. Practicing with plain steel or even wooden weapons was good for both his combat reflexes and his fighting instincts. Fighting without using magic for anything but personal safety built muscle on his frame and expanded his lungs. Now though, on the eve of war, it was time to reacquaint himself with the weapon and style he would use when lives were for the taking.

Arrogant old bastard. Thinks he doesn't need my help. The sword swished through an imaginary Megrenn soldier and his comrade. *When the bloody part of the war smacks him in the face, I'll be the one picking up the army and carrying on.* He leaped and brought his blade down in an overhead chop that split a giant stripecat's head down the center; phantom gore splattered him. *Just watch. He's not going to be able to do it. He'll come out here making excuses, saying how it's only because of his vast skill and experience that he wasn't blown to pieces.* Danilaesis leaped, cresting the top of a city wall cutting through two merlons to kill the archers cowering behind them. *Won't be long now.* Before gravity pulled him back to the ground, he formed a small aether construct, just a flat spot anchored firmly in mid-air. He kicked off against it, flying backward. He made no flip or spin; Uncle Rashan had warned him against vanity in fighting. Arcing to the ground, he held *Sleeping Dragon* before him to shield himself from arrow fire. He hit the turf on one knee, panting, and steadied himself with a hand as he caught his breath.

The *Daggerstrike* was only a few paces away. The whole area was cordoned off by imperial soldiers, though their orders contained no provision against the crowd that gathered to watch Danilaesis practice. He smirked to himself but did not acknowledge them. *Let them look. They all wish they could be me. When we go to war, they'll sleep better knowing that I'm on their side.* If any sorcerers were watching, they would have been far more interested in the esoteric events taking place in the ship's interior. From the outside, only the most aether-sensitive of commoners would even have been aware that great magic was taking place within the hold. The peasantry liked the glamor, the flash of a warlock. They always had.

Historians had hated his uncle Rashan. For over a hundred winters, the warlock had been absent from the empire, gone off to learn how to be immortal, Danilaesis always supposed. He had never asked about the details of his sabbatical. But during those hundred and two years, Rashan Solaran had been believed dead, and the historical accounts of his life and deeds clucked their tongues over his bloody rampage across the continent of Koriah, carving a larger empire out of the lands of Kadrin's neighbors. "Too many enemies," they said. "He created the threat that the Grand Necromancer came to rid the world of." Danilaesis knew better. His uncle had protected the empire, expanded it at the behest of his emperors. Grand Necromancer Loramar had been his greatest foe, an avenger of the people Rashan had conquered. In the end, he was all that stopped Loramar from destroying the Kadrin empire and turning every one of them into dead monsters. Rashan Solaran was a hero, and the people of the time had to have known it. Danilaesis would be the same, once he was rid of Anzik Fehr. Admittedly the boy was no Loramar, but he *had* used necromancy. All the reports said so. *Like father, like son.*

"Water," Danilaesis called out, addressing no one in particular. It didn't matter. He trusted that someone would get him a drink. One of the soldiers would see that someone fetched him one, or even go to find a flask himself. It was one of the privileges of rank.

The crowd gave off a constant, low stream of aether. Even if Axterion would not take his help directly, Dan wanted the ship badly enough that he wanted the old sorcerer to have the best chance to empower it for him. Drawing fresh Sources to the area was the best he could think of without being obvious.

The *Daggerstrike* was looking better. Switching momentarily to aether-vision, Danilaesis could see the aether oozing into the wards, rune by rune. He hadn't gone around the ship counting them, but there had to have been thousands. Brannis had snuck Juliana out of the city on the *Daggerstrike* the night it was completed. They had both been at Emperor Sommick's coronation, along with half the city, and before the procession had returned to the palace, she had been gone. Considering walking time down to the docks, Brannis must have empowered the runes in moments; Danilaesis suspected it was even less time than that. Axterion had been prodding at the runes with aether all morning, and looked to have managed a third of them thus far.

Danilaesis missed him. Missed both of them. Why had Rashan and Brannis destroyed one another? Was it that cooperation between two sorcerers of such power could not last? *Like me and grandfather*, he realized. *Will it come down to a battle between us, one day*? He watched the runes fill, his grandfather's Source obscured but visible among the progress he had made. *Slow, patient, wearing away at it. He is earth and water. I've got the wind and fire that faded in him a long time ago.* It was an interesting thought to occupy his idle mind. There was little else to do while he waited for one of those oafish clods to bring him some water. Well, there was one thing.

Danilaesis walked over and sat on the edge of the gangplank, halfway up, letting his feet dangle over the edge. It was a drydock, so there was no water beneath him; the *Daggerstrike* might have been shaped like a ship, but slits for archers and the drawbridge-like side gates kept it from being watertight. For all his thought of bringing the peasantry close to watch, so that Axterion would have more aether in the area, Danilaesis had been using it up himself in his sword practice.

Eventually one of the soldiers came back with a pitcher of water and a silver goblet, like Danilaesis was some foppish noble son. He drank anyway, but gave no thought to thanking the soldier or taking note of his name. Sitting there on the gangplank, Danilaesis let his own Source spill its aether unhindered. Let Axterion have *all* the help he could offer, and not just what was convenient.

Danilaesis clung to the rigging of the *Mountain's Breath*, leaning out over the bow and watched the Ghelkan countryside drift by far below. The wind whistling across his ears drowned out most of the noise of the crew, and save for the creak of the mast and spars he could imagine that he was alone and aboard a far different vessel.

In the end, Axterion had failed. It had been two days aboard his consolation ship, flown by air sailors, not by Danilaesis. It took a skilled hand to steer a ship by the air currents, a task doubly hard compared to travel on the sea, where the gusts and crosswinds were not so dangerous. Danilaesis had always wanted to fly an airship himself, and though he could have ordered the captain to relinquish the wheel, he knew that he had no hope of controlling an airship properly. Even Madlin's airships were complicated beasts, piled full of levers and wheels, little needles that twitched back and forth, pointing to numbers. He wanted the *Daggerstrike*, a ship made by a sorcerer *for* a sorcerer. It needed just one person to do everything, and it took only hands on the captain's wheel, activating the right runes. That was the sort of ship for him.

But Axterion had failed, and Danilaesis rode aboard a lesser vessel. Due to the High Sorcerer's supreme skill and utter mastery of the aether, that failure had been unspectacular, with the runes rejecting the partially infused aether, but not detonating. He had not even had the satisfaction of his grandfather making a fool of himself; that would have been something, at least, if he could not have the airship.

His uncle had always clung to the rigging when he flew. The view from atop the bowsprit was spectacular. Clinging to a rope with one hand, he had no fear of falling. The worst that would happen would be the ship would have to come pick him back up. His magic made the fall a trivial hazard. Besides, he had a strong grip, and fearing a personal failing made it more likely to occur. He leaned to the side, his arm stretched out straight, and looked straight down.

The geography of Ghelk was a topic in which he had only recently taken an interest. Danilaesis knew the cities and larger villages, the lakes and rivers, the trade routes, and the ports. They were nearing Hemuhn Lake; he could see by the glistening of placid water on the horizon.

"Turn us to the starboard," he shouted the order behind him. He squinted, trying to gauge the angle. "Fifteen degrees."

"But warlock," Captain Gelleoth objected, "We're on course for the lake. It's dead ahead."

"I can see it. I'm not blind as the high sorcerer," Danilaesis snapped back. "Turn us."

The first mate sidled up to the bowsprit and spoke in a normal tone. With the noise of the wind, it was the air sailor's equivalent of a whisper. "Beggin' yer pardon, warlock, but we has orders from High Sorcerer Axterion. We're to dump them barrels in the lake and go back."

"If he wanted blind obedience, he wouldn't have sent me along. I'm here because a commander in the field has instincts to know when a plan needs to change," Danilaesis replied. He turned to the captain. "I'm countermanding the high sorcerer's orders based on new reconnaissance. If you've a mind to object, speak up."

"Aye, aye, warlock," Captain Gelleoth replied. *Sailors. Almost as good as soldiers for distrusting sorcerers. I'm one of them, but with magic. I get my hands dirty, just like them. I don't sit in a room all day, writing orders.*

The barrels had been his grandfather's idea. Where the old tortoise had stashed them all these winters, Danilaesis never knew. The barrels looked newly made, but with the preservative runes maintained as well as they were, there was no telling their true age. Like Axterion himself, the appearance of youth was misleading. They hadn't opened one. Axterion hadn't dared. What rancid toxin dwelt within those oaken barrels, the high sorcerer had feared to expose them to air while they were still in Kadris.

"Most of their water starts in that lake," Axterion had said. *"Foul that, and the countryside is weakened."* It wasn't Danilaesis's idea of fighting a war. But apparently that was part of being a right bastard, as his grandfather had promised he'd make Danilaesis. It was some consolation that it was the first step toward a war, and not the whole war itself. The Ghelkans had wells, and smaller rivers that did not share water with Hemuhn Lake. People would get sick, or die, or do whatever it was that

the barrels' contents were supposed to do to them. But not all of them, and Danilaesis would not see it happen.

Danilaesis wanted blood. He wanted a lot of it. For every drop of blood in his twin's dead body, he wanted a death in return. Not knowing how many drops that was, he would settle for all of them. The Megrenn Alliance was more than just Ghelk. It was Megrenn, Ghelk, Safschan, Narrack, and all the smaller island kingdoms that had banded together to topple the Kadrin Empire. They had failed, but the remnants still clung together, recovering at least as fast as the empire had in the aftermath of the war.

Danilaesis's new course put in line with the city of Kehin Nim, but he called for the *Mountain's Breath* to circle in low among the outlying villages and farms. He leapt from the ship with Sleeping Dragon in hand. The peasantry did not even attempt to fight back. They fled, they hid, they begged for their lives and the lives of their children. *I'm no monster*, Danilaesis told himself. *Their children won't come to any harm.* Sleeping Dragon took the life of every man in Kehin Nim, and a few stray women who got in his way or who showed a bit too strong a Source for his comfort. The children and the cowering women were left to their fates, condemned to watch their homes and fields burn under the unrelenting fire of the warlock's magic.

For three days, the *Mountain's Breath* toured Ghelk. Around the city of Dahn Fah, Danilaesis butchered herds of sheep and set the wheat fields there aflame. In the port of Jhan Mai, he sank fishing boats, punching holes in their sides with bolts of aether and letting the Aliani Sea rush into them. By the time they reached Tehn Mar, the Ghelkans had spread rumors of Danilaesis's rampage. They laid an ambush, and he found five sorcerers and a hundred troops lying in wait. When they escaped, Danilaesis had to change into fresh warlock garb; the black fabric was soaked through with blood so that it clung and dragged at him.

The *Mountain's Breath* flew low over the hills of central Ghelk, cutting across the countryside on their way home. Their lack of altitude was meant to hide them from the airships of the Megrenn Alliance. Poor copies of the Kadrin vessels though they might have been, Danilaesis was growing fatigued from the constant fighting and wanted no battle he did not choose on his own terms.

"What about the barrels, warlock?" Captain Gelleoth asked as they flew.

Danilaesis shrugged. He caught Captain Gelleoth looking at the top of his head strangely, and ran his fingers through his hair—they came away stained red. He wiped the blood-stained hand on his pants. "Fine. Go ahead. Bring us over Hemuhn Lake on our way back, and we'll dump them in."

He looked down at his hand, still smeared with blood that clung to the tiny crevices in his skin and to the whorls of his fingertips. *I am Danilaesis Solaran, Warlock of the Empire and blood-stained right hand of the empress.* His formal title had never seemed more appropriate. Fatigue got the better of him, and he found the thought helplessly amusing for no reason he could explain. He chuckled, then laughed out loud and could not stop until he had forgotten why he started.

The crew of the *Mountain's Breath* looked at him strangely. He held up the offending hand for them to see, and laughed himself silly once more. *Come on, it* is *funny, isn't it?*

Chapter 19

"You can't be your own man, if you're someone else's." -Ganrin Draksgollow

Draksgollow wrinkled his nose at the smell. The tunnel stank of human excrement and blood. Dead kuduks had been hauled away, the wounded carted off on express trolleys for the nearest hospital. There were no wounded humans; the ones too injured to escape had been finished off by Draksgollow's soldiers. They had won, but it had been costly.

He scratched at the stubble of his patchy beard. "Where did they get these things?" he muttered to himself. It was light in his hand, dense but not very large. It seems incongruous that the strange guns the humans had carried would punch holes in his steam tanks like an awl through leather. There was copper wound all around the barrel, which was made of brightsteel instead of plain carbon steel. Perched atop the barrel was an optical scope more appropriate to a rifle than a pistol. It made him wonder at the gun's range, that whoever made it saw fit to attach one. Most hand-held firearms weren't accurate enough at long range to warrant the addition of optics. Workmanship-wise, there was no question in Draksgollow's mind: kuduk quality.

"Arvernus, ask around a bit on the side, see if any of them spark scientists have been working on anything like this," he said over his shoulder. He knew that Arvernus was still hanging around, shadowing Draksgollow as he had all day. "Melt down my metal leg if I've got half a clue how a load of human miners got these in their stinking mitts."

Down one of the side passages, bodies were lined up like thunderail ties, all on their backs, heads on the same side—those that still had them—and spaced with enough room to walk between them. Draksgollow kept the strange gun in his hand while he walked the line. He heard grumbles from some of his men, mostly the mechanics and metalworkers from his workshops, not the soldiers. Hauling bodies and putting them out for display was gruesome work; it should have been left to humans, as far as they were concerned.

"Any sign of him?" Draksgollow asked. Three of his soldiers held newspapers in hand, comparing the ruined human faces to the one in the headline flashpop.

"Got three, might be him, on account of I can't say it's not with what's left to look at," one of them replied.

"I won't call it him unless I can see that face, that dumb, staring, ox face from the flashpop," Draksgollow replied. "Sick of seeing that mug on every slow news day or every time there's a rebel attack and they don't got any other flashpop to run. If we're gonna make a thump around here, we need that head in a jar. I want to put that on Councilor Dorsheen's desk and see the look on her face."

"That what we're doing now? Trophy hunting humans?" the soldier inspecting bodies asked.

"We're using the machine for the greater good. We're all going to be rich, soon enough," said Draksgollow. "We can be anonymous, but that only lasts until we slip up once. We get caught, and we're villains. We polish our image up a bit first. When someone sniffs out what we're actually doing, they shrug and think to themselves, 'huh, so that's how they did it.'"

"Yeah, but this one human …"

"Aww, blast it!" said Draksgollow. "What's one human or another? This one on all the papers, people will know that one. We ventilate a bunch of miners; they'll all say: 'Yeah, but where's that Mr. Coin-Eyed Gawper, the one from the flashpops? They ain't got *him* yet?' We bring his head and plop it on a newsman's desk; they'll see someone's doing something about it." He hadn't thought of it until he said it, but a newsman was a better choice that Councilor Dorsheen. There must be rules to being famous written down somewhere, and letting someone already famous make big news for you … that couldn't be the way to make a name for yourself.

"Yeah, but if he weren't here, where we gonna find him?"

Draksgollow looked down at one of the bodies and spat on it. "One problem at a time." He looked down the copper-wound barrel of the gun in his hand. "One problem at a time."

The Katamic Sea washed against the side of the *False Profit.* The deck did not yet feel right under his boots, but Denrik Zayne was home. The crew went about their work with a hustling efficiency that he demanded. Even after the disgrace of losing a ship, the story of sinking one of the Mad Tinker's smokers was enough to maintain his legend. If he happened to let slip rumors that perhaps the destruction of Tinker's Island was part of his revenge, then so be it. No one in Tellurak was going to gainsay him.

Footsteps sounded behind him on the deck, but Denrik knew who it was. Long habit had made him learn the gait and heft of every man aboard his ships. A captain could not be seen constantly looking over his shoulder. "Mr. Tanner …"

"Liking your new ship so far?" Tanner asked.

Denrik sneered, but Tanner would not have seen it from behind him. "It serves. I like it well enough, I suppose."

Tanner sidled up beside him. "You don't love her, though."

Denrik remained silent and hoped that Tanner would let the matter drop.

Tanner sighed theatrically. "Guess you're just gettin' too old to love a new ship. You know, you'd keep 'em longer if you didn't go around firing cannons at everyone."

"Do you have some purpose in coming to see me, Mr. Tanner?" Denrik asked. He wondered for the hundredth time what had possessed him to take on the annoying Kadrin twinborn.

"I heard about Dan," Tanner said. He sounded melancholy, not angry. That, at least, was a good sign. "I suppose that was your idea?" Denrik snapped his head around and fixed his glare on Tanner, who held up his hands in surrender. "Not accusing. Just … curious. Never had the grapes to do it myself, but I knew it'd happen sooner or later."

Denrik turned his attention back to his crew's preparations on deck. "It was Anzik's plan. The boy reads too much if you ask me. Asymmetrical warfare, he called it. I plotted entire wars, but I always thought of the twinborn connections as a parallel. I hadn't thought to use the Mad Tinker's machine to switch duels."

"Boy's smarter'n his old man, huh?" Tanner said. Denrik could *hear* the stupid grin on his face.

"Indeed."

"So … I … just wanted you to know …" Tanner said. "No hard feelings, ok?"

"Why is it that you're here, Mr. Tanner?" Denrik asked. "You've never shown especially much disloyalty to the Kadrin Empire before …"

"I spent three years traveling with a madman of a warlock. A warlock who's going to be charging up for a war like a monohorn with its danglies caught in a bear trap. Not much point getting' caught up in that. He'll march me off to get killed just to see more of your folks die. Rumors are already travelin'; he's just bent on blood."

"Yes, Jadon has told me of the raids. This time, we'll end them for good."

"Well then, take that as your answer. I know enough of what's going on that I want nothing done to me 'for good.'"

"As straight an answer as you've given me in ages, Mr. Tanner," said Denrik. "Now if you don't mind, I have a ship to run."

"Sure, boss," Tanner said with a mocking salute—Kadrin style, with fist to temple. "If you need me, I'll be checking on the whiskey and cards to see if they're in proper order. You know … new ship and all."

Denrik listened to him go. Let the buffoon drink himself stupid and rob his men at the Crackle table. He was bound to have drunkards and gamblers among his crew even with the vetting he'd given them. It was just a hazard of the occupation that many good sailors turn to piracy because of unfortunate vices that make them unwelcome on respectable ships. Tanner fit in better than most passengers he took aboard.

The man was a puzzle. He seemed to flit along in life, looking out for himself. Then on rare occasion he would show himself to be a better man than he let on. He had volunteered to save Anzik and Jadon both when kidnappings had taken both twins from him. Ostensibly Tanner had used the quest to find a way off Denrik's ship. He hadn't expected to see the Kadrin twinborn once he let him go, but Tanner had returned—in both worlds, with both boys. It was a debt that never seemed to be repaid, for whenever he thought the ledger balanced between them,

Tanner would need some small favor, and a tiny voice within Denrik could not refuse the man who had saved his son.

Now, it was the betterment of Veydrus. Tanner seemed to have finally realized the depravity of the Kadrin Empire and decided to work against it. Or had he? Denrik had to be careful until he was certain.

"Father?"

Denrik flinched, startled. Of all the footsteps on the ship, only his son's could be silent enough to surprise him from behind. "What is it, Jadon?"

"The runes worked like you said. It feels like Tellurak now. No more floating when I try to walk."

Denrik grunted. The moon, of all places for the Mad Tinker to take refuge. It fit his moniker. Only in a fever dream could Denrik have conceived of people living on the moon. In a world where machines could transport your enemies to you in an instant if only they knew where to look; it was an inspired choice of hiding spots. He hated having to credit the man who sank the *Fair Trader*, the man whose little fleet of smoking ships had harassed him for years, with such a coup.

"How are the goblins doing?" Denrik asked.

"We haven't made direct contact since Madlin went to Veydrus," said Jadon. "But we've been watching over her. There are thirty-five thousand two hundred eighteen goblins working on building … buildings. I don't know what they're meant to be yet, but Madlin is directing them."

"You didn't ask the tinker?" Denrik asked with a frown.

"No," Jadon replied. "He and I don't talk much. I suspect he doesn't trust me because I'm your son. I try not to provoke him."

Denrik scoffed. "You're not afraid of that weaselly tinker, now are you? Anzik was able to kill the twin of Danilaesis Solaran with little enough trouble."

"That was an ambush. I knew what I would face," Jadon replied. "I was the stronger of Source and mind, so a victory under even equal terms was all but assured. We need Cadmus Errol for our plans, so I cannot strike against him unless I am sure he has betrayed us. That means that most likely I will be the one ambushed."

"But still …" said Denrik.

"He is a clever one," Jadon replied. "A man who not only thought to hide on the moon but discovered the means to get there. I have postulated eighteen ways he might get the better of me, despite my advantage as a sorcerer."

"Humor me," said Denrik.

"He could change the settings on the world-ripper just before I step through, sending me into the void between worlds. He could use one of the coil guns against me—possibly with specific modifications to circumvent shielding spells. He could reprise my own trick and open a portal that would bring Danilaesis Solaran into my presence. He could use any one of a number of different ways to kill me in my sleep, including pumping anesthetic gas into my room, planting explosives in the room below—"

Denrik waved him off. "That's enough. You have a point. Hopefully the bastard doesn't know where Kadris is to even *try* bringing Danilaesis Solaran into this."

Jadon cocked his head. "Moon."

Denrik sighed. Jadon had a point; a man who would think to hide on the moon would have the breadth of thought to find the most notorious sorcerer in Veydrus. Language barriers aside, it would not even be difficult.

"Just keep a close watch and make sure the goblins don't double-cross us or harm Madlin Errol. If anything goes wrong with the goblins, as long as we have her help, we can get *some* number of those guns."

"The dragon is the bigger worry. The goblins will obey the bargain."

"Dragons are always the worry whenever they're involved," said Denrik.

Draksgollow sat at the head of the table. All down the sides were the best mechanics, machinists, and assistant tinkers he employed. He even had two of his rune-carvers handy. Not a single one of them was under the age of fifty, and grey was the most common color of beard around the table. Experience. That was what he needed. Fresh blood, fresh bodies, fresh ideas were all well and good, but he needed older eyes on this problem, eyes that had seen it all.

What needed seeing were the six coil guns scattered around the table. They passed the coil guns around, each man looking them over with a critical eye. Draksgollow gave them time undisturbed though they grumbled to one another as they passed the weapons around. Identical guns would get the same man's eye on them for minutes at a time even after he had seen three or four just like it. It was the way men like these were made, and Draksgollow wouldn't have them any other way.

"Well?" he asked at length, once most of the coil guns had been returned to a cluster at the center of the table.

"Can't see how it can possibly work," said Stipsin.

"Work's consistent, except the wrapped copper wire is a bit unruly," said Temmuth. "You got schematics for it?"

"I want to take one apart, see what's under that wire wrap," said Eithur.

"Runes are shit," said Sak, with a dismissive wave. "I'd send these all back, have 'em ground smooth and redone."

"What about the runes themselves, though?" Draksgollow asked. "Forget the layman's-grade carving job for a minute; you got any idea what they do?"

Sak shrugged. "Nope. I can make another one, does it the same though."

Draksgollow nodded. "Good enough. And yeah, I've got three more of these under lock and key, you boys can tear these down to bits and bolts to figure out how they're made. I want a hundred a day coming out by the end of next month."

There was silence around the table.

"Yer full of it," said Stipsin.

"I ain't," Draksgollow replied.

Another silence followed.

"What's so big about these, anyway?" Sak asked. "Why you need so many, so soon?"

"Boys, I seen a steam tank turned into a sieve by one of these," said Draksgollow. "We dug a half inch ball bearing out of two feet of rock; got put there by one of these. That ain't natural. But blast me, I want 'em, and I want a lot of 'em."

"What for? We goin' into the munitions business?"

"Step back a second, boys," Draksgollow said. "You seen the papers, you know what we've been up to. World's going down the incinerator chute, and these rebels are greasing the slide. More of 'em poppin' up every day, seems like."

All around the table, men nodded, beard braids bobbing.

"Well," said Draksgollow, "I finally figured out what we need to do about it."

"What's that?"

"We need a new crop of humans," Draksgollow replied. "Got a whole world filled with 'em, on the other side of that machine. We just get us rid of the humans we've got … maybe keep a few, just to train the new ones … and replace 'em wholesale."

"That's a lot of humans," said Sak.

"We'll have a lot of guns," Draksgollow replied, holding up one of the coil guns.

Chapter 20

"The moon is a ball of basaltic and igneous rock, devoid of air and water. Even if we should find some vessel by which to reach it, the environment is entirely unable to support life. Keep your dreams of fanciful cities upon the moon in the cheap newsstand novels where they belong. " – Astronomer Bendavik Wethbarry

The world hole opened without fanfare. There was neither ceremony nor lingering. As soon as the machine sprang to life, Rynn ushered her charges through and into the lunar headquarters. Jamile had won her argument with Cadmus, and he had consented to populate the facility with a small staff, as well as one additional guest.

Greuder came first, the only one of the group who looked eager to be coming. He looked all around, including up at the ceiling, before continuing in to make way for the others. "I'd swear I was dreaming, if I was the dreaming sort," he said, shaking his head. "You've cooked up a wonder here. That's for sure."

Kaia followed shortly behind, giving the Mad Tinker a quick nod of acknowledgment before hustling past. A pack slung over her shoulder was all the luggage she said she needed.

"Well, would you look at this place?" Kupe said as he wandered through the world hole. He wore a close-fit wood jacket and a matching wool cap, the short brim pulled low just above his eyes. Carrying nothing, he chose to keep his hands in his pockets as he gawked, eyes drawn to the inlet and outlet world-rippers that showed a jungle river at either end of the chamber. He turned back toward Rynn. "'Don't tell anyone,' she says. Girl, if I'd have told anyone about this place, they'd cuss me out for being drunk."

As a few workers carried supplies and the staff's personal effects into the headquarters, Kupe took the opportunity to introduce himself. "You must be Jamile," he said with an endearing smile. He took her hand and kissed it. "Your sister told me all about you."

Jamile allowed herself a tight smile. Kupe just didn't understand the idea of twinborn, and it didn't seem worth the trouble it would take to explain it. "I hope it was all flattering."

Kupe winked. "Didn't do you justice. I think she might be jealous, cuz you're the prettier one."

Cadmus ignored the newcomers for the moment, aside from a brief handshake and a word of greeting as he passed Greuder on his way to the viewframe. He stopped short of passing through and spoke to Rynn as if the hole were a physical barrier between them. "How goes the work in Veydrus?"

Rynn opened her eyes wide and shook her head slowly. "I can hardly believe it. Those goblins are like sponges. The old one I met first seems to be the exception, but most of them don't take much initiative or show a lot of original thinking. But you wouldn't believe how quick they pick things up. Four or five of them speak passable Korrish already."

Cadmus held up a hand to stop her flood of praise for the goblin people. "Production?"

Rynn shrugged. "Spark is new to them, wholly new. I don't think any of them considered lightning anything more than a destructive force, and it's taking them—"

"I don't care if they understand it. I just want them working."

"Whose plan was this, anyway?" Rynn asked.

"You tell me the little rodents are brilliant. Then, on the next hand, you're trying to give them the academic underpinnings of a whole new branch of science. We want hard-working goblins, making weapons to free Korr. I don't want to worry that they'll figure out how world-rippers *actually* work before we do and make their own. I don't want them deciding they can wipe humans off the face of Veydrus."

"Bit late to be thinking of *that*, now isn't it?"

Cadmus pushed his spectacles up higher on his nose. It was a nervous habit Jamile had noticed; he didn't do it often, and never, it seemed, because there was anything wrong with how the spectacles were serving him. "It's a juggler's dilemma. All these balls we're keeping in the air … they *are* going to fall. It's just a matter of when, and in what order. I won't abandon the humans of Veydrus, but I'll look after my own people first. The time may come though when we have a goblin problem to deal with."

"Or a dragon problem?"

Cadmus shrugged. "In that world, they'd appear to be the same thing."

"So," Kupe said, slinking up behind Cadmus. "Goblins and dragons, huh? Did I just get shipped off to the bedtime story division?"

Cadmus glowered at him. "I suppose I should have expected wandering ears from you. Must be a hazard of the occupation."

Kupe cocked his head to the side. "How's that again?"

"You're a newsman, I hear. I imagine listening to conversations that don't concern you are second nature."

"Oh," said Kupe, a broad smile replacing the bemused look he had a moment before. "You musta been around too many kuduks. They use that term for anyone that works at the paper. Mostly they're thinkin' reporters, though. Me? I don't write for the papers … shoot, I don't even read much past the headline of the day so I know what to shout about. I just bring 'em around and hawk 'em."

"So … you're one of those tunnel-rat news haulers who takes in a few tenar a day passing out papers," Cadmus said. "And you're the one who we're using to help recruit?"

"Yep," Kupe said, thrusting his chest out and standing up on his toes for a second.

Cadmus turned to Rynn, and there was an unasked question in his eyes.

"We need to keep him out of sight," said Rynn. "He needs an air of mystery around him, and …" Rynn looked at Kupe with a mild frown and pursed lips.

"Mysterious, huh?" Kupe asked. "We're makin' me more mysterious? I like the sound of that."

Rynn glanced sidelong at Kupe before addressing Cadmus as if the news hauler hero wasn't there. "And the more he talks to people, the harder that is to keep up."

"Hey!"

"It's true, Kupe," Rynn said. "You're a news hauler and everyone's best friend. You practically soiled yourself the one gunfight you were in. You can't shoot straight, and in a fair fight, I'd put my money on Jamile over you. The only way you get to pretend you're a hero is if people don't know you."

Kupe wouldn't meet her eyes. "I got ya," he muttered. Jamile felt like she was watching someone beat a puppy. Kupe slunk off and followed the luggage trail out of the main chamber. She watched and waited until he was gone, well out of earshot, before she insinuated herself between Cadmus and Rynn.

"What did you do that for?" Jamile demanded, pointing a finger squarely at Rynn's chest.

"Do what for?" Rynn asked. "Kupe's spouting off like some warrior king every time we bring him around to a new group of rebels. He can't keep that up on ship, and if he did, he'd get himself killed trying to back up his own boasts. You're not the one listening to him. You'd think he was a bareknuckle fighter, a crashball enforcer, and a military genius all rolled into one. Except he's a newsboy turned actor. I put him up on stage because I need to convince would-be rebels that we need to work together and not just act like a bunch of scattered gangs."

"I meant why'd you hurt his feelings," said Jamile.

Rynn was quiet for a moment and glanced away. "If he gets his feelings hurt that easy, we can't have him around the *Jennai*. He's bad for morale when people see him sulking and worrying, and he's only good at the hero act when he's had a couple drinks in him."

"Can't you just get him liquored, then?" Cadmus asked.

"Cadmus!" Jamile scolded. "That's terrible."

Cadmus shrugged. "Plenty of men do it willingly. It was just a thought."

"You have a lot to learn about dealing with regular people," Jamile said.

The corner of Rynn's mouth twitched before resuming its abashed look. "I think this is where I duck out." She stepped back from the viewframe and shut down her world-ripper. The world hole disappeared.

"What did you mean by that?" Cadmus asked. "Normal people?"

"People who aren't twinborn, or tinkers, or soldiers … just normal people."

"You just listed most of the people I know," said Cadmus.

"Well, you employed people who were as much like you as you could find," said Jamile. "Your twin was cooped up with a crazy old daruu. You never really saw normal humans."

"There was a serving girl from the kitchens at my patron's estate in Eversall …," Cadmus said.

Jamile raised her eyebrows and grinned. "And …?"

"I got her to help me work on the prototype for the original world-ripper," Cadmus said. "Smart girl, once you got her out of the kitchens for a while."

Jamile walked away, smiling despite herself. "You're hopeless, Cadmus."

The dormitory of the lunar headquarters was so new that the rock was still dusty from the auger. Jamile had made a cursory attempt to clean it in anticipation of their new arrivals, but the rock was porous and the powdery residue had worked its way into every pore and crevice. She hoped, as she walked down to see how her new neighbors were faring, that they didn't mind having a bit left to clean up for themselves.

Kaia was unpacking her clothes as Jamile poked her head in. The room was furnished with a bed, table and chair, wardrobe, and dresser, all pillaged from one of the finer hotels in Korr. Aside from a whiff of snooty kuduk perfumes, it was pleasant enough.

"How are you holding up this time around?" Jamile asked.

Kaia flipped a lock of hair over her ear as she looked up from folding a blouse. "I get my own room this time, instead of a cot in the corner of the pantry. I'm not going to be sick because my stomach thinks I'm falling. There's someone here to talk to besides the tinker … yeah, I'm holding up."

"Think you can stick with it this time?"

Kaia smiled. "Don't worry about *me*. I'd go see how that big, strong hero is holding up across the way. Heard him muttering to himself, but I didn't dare knock."

"Why not?"

"You know …" Kaia replied. "Because. Just … because."

"I see," Jamile said with a wink. "You don't want to intrude on his moment of quiet reflection."

Kaia looked everywhere but at Jamile and nodded. "Something like that."

"Well, I'll go see how he is."

Jamile shut the door behind her and knocked on Kupe's. The doors were taken from the same hotel as the furnishings, ripped from the stone and mortared in place at Cadmus's direction. *We'd have taken the whole hotel if the world-holes were big enough.* When Kupe didn't answer, she knocked again.

"Kupe, it's—"

"I know who it is," Kupe replied through the door. "This place ain't that big for guessing games. Just hold on a minute."

She heard the rustling of fabric from the other side of the door. A second later she stopped herself and pulled her ear away from the door, worried that if Kupe opened the door suddenly, it might look as if she had been listening at it.

When Kupe pulled the door open a moment later, she was glad she had thought ahead. *Rynn's paranoia is rubbing off, I guess.* Kupe stood bare-chested, his hair disheveled, wearing a different pair of trousers than he had when he came through the world-hole.

"What's it?" he asked, chest heaving from—apparently—rushing to put clothes on.

Jamile averted her eyes and took a step back. "Sorry, I didn't mean to catch you indecent."

Kupe gave her that lopsided smile of his. She shouldn't have noticed it, she realized, because she *wasn't* looking at him. "You didn't. Come on in. Sosha never mentioned they were tight-eyed where you were from. I'll throw a shirt on, if it makes you feel better."

"Please," Jamile replied.

She felt foolish turning her back while Kupe finished dressing. She was a nurse, after all. He was far from the first man she'd seen unclothed—and Kupe could have only been considered unclad by the most prudish of definitions. But that was medical. This was … well, if she didn't know better, she would think that Kupe was waiting half-dressed on purpose, wanting to be seen. *But maybe not by me? Kaia is cute as a thimble.* Jamile had been raised by her aunt, a woman who had always kept an eye for couples. It was her pastime and guilty pleasure, seeing young people get together. *When did I get to be so old?* Jamile wondered. *Either of them has three years on me, easily; Kupe maybe five. It's Rynn's influence. That girl is as old as Cadmus inside.*

"All set," Kupe informed her. Jamile turned to find him looking every bit the news hauler, with his plain brown trousers, held up by suspenders, and a white button shirt with the sleeves rolled to the elbows. He even had his cap on once more, hiding the mop of wavy brown hair that hadn't seen a comb since she'd known him.

"I just wanted you to know that Rynn's an insensitive clod, and that she does that to everyone now and then," said Jamile.

"Think I ain't known the type?" Kupe asked, hooking his thumbs behind his suspenders. "I just maybe ain't used to hearing that outta a girl, is all."

Jamile sighed. "Rynn's not very much like most girls. I blame Cadmus."

"It happens," Kupe said. "My old man was a news hauler. He breaks his leg one day trying to catch a trolley, next morning I show up and I tells 'em I'm Soger's boy, and I'm takin' over his route."

Jamile smiled. "So you turned out just like your father, too."

Kupe winked. "Nah, my old man was a drunk. Drink did him in years ago, scraping whiskey off the bottom of my wages." Something caught in the edge of Kupe's vision, and he tilted his head to look past Jamile. When she turned, there was nothing there. Taking one of Dan's lessons to heart, she let her eyes drift into the aether for a moment and saw a tall, strong Source slinking away down the hall.

"So you're not a drinker?" she asked, ignoring their almost-visitor.

"A drinker?" Kupe asked, incredulous. "Course I am. Everyone's a drinker if they've got the coin or got friends who'll spot 'em some. I just ain't a drunk."

"Well, if you're looking to pick up a new trade, I think Cadmus might be willing to take you on," said Jamile. Cadmus, of course, had said nothing of the sort to indicate he would, but that was an argument for later. "I don't know that you'll be delivering many more newspapers. He might be gruff, but he'll take a hard worker any day."

Kupe ran a hand up under his cap and scratched. "You're right on that one. I seen Kaia on that machine. She can sort 'em out faster than I ever could."

Jamile gave Kupe a sly smile. "Maybe she could teach you her way."

Jamile crept across the main chamber of the lunar headquarters, not skulking, but trying to avoid Cadmus's notice nonetheless. Whether she succeeded or not, he never let on. If there was one thing that Cadmus Errol excelled at, it was ignoring distractions. Many people would have said it was his tinkering or his talent for invention, but those all came from a singular ability to focus on one thing to the exclusion of all others. Once, that had bothered Jamile, but for now she was happy to be among the ignored.

She crossed on the far side of the river segment that bisected the room, the space between the near world-ripper viewframe and the cavern wall acting as a bridge. It was strange to be able to cross a river by going around it, but she chalked that up to yet another oddity about the whole situation. Another of those oddities lay down the corridor on the far side of the chamber.

Jamile heaved a sigh of relief, letting it out along with the breath she found herself holding. Anzik's room was the only thing down this way, at the end of a short tunnel bored especially for him in anticipation of Madlin's deal. She raised a hand to knock, but before her knuckles hit, a voice stopped her short.

"Come in," Anzik called through the door.

Jamile opened the door and peeked in. "I hope I'm not disturbing you."

"But obviously not as much as you hoped to speak with me," Anzik replied. Rynn had always complained that he never blinked, but Jamile was more put off by the fact that he looked at your mouth when he talked to you, instead of looking you in the eye. "By your tone, you seem not to be here for any urgent matter, which would imply that you place a low value on my time and privacy."

Jamile backed away a step, reaching for the door. "I'm sorry, I—"

"You are, however, correct in assuming that I am not pressingly engaged at present. If you have questions, I will consider them."

"I was just wondering why you didn't come say hello to the new residents," Jamile said.

"Technically, there was no question."

"Why?" Jamile asked.

Anzik shrugged. "I changed my mind. I don't need to know them."

"You live here too, you know," Jamile said. "Just because you and Cadmus don't get along, doesn't mean you can't make friends with the rest of them."

"I shouldn't have altered the gravity," he said. "There was no need. It was a request; I could have refused, or not sought help from my father on how to do it. I lured them here with the comfort of the world they came from, something familiar. This place wasn't meant for them; the strangeness might have been for their own protection."

"That's silly. Why would they need protection?" Jamile asked. Her eyes scanned the room, wondering if he was hinting at something dangerous that he might have brought with him. Clothes, a few books, little else. The Veydran boy showed no propensity for sentiment or leisure.

"Why do you boil the water?" Anzik asked, pointing out the open door.

"Well, because it's river water from a jungle. There are probably illnesses in it," Jamile said, trying not to get bogged down into discussions that required a Korrish understanding of biology and bacteria to follow. "Boiling makes it safe."

"Because it's not your world," Anzik replied. "There is no water here, so you bring it. It comes from yet another world, so you can't drink it. You boil it. Then you say it's safe. Now you say that gravity is wrong, and I fix it for you. How many other anomalies are here, uncorrected, threatening us?"

"Is this why you sit alone all the time?" Jamile asked. "Thinking this convoluted, philosophical bunk?" She shook her head. "Now don't go getting the wrong idea here, Mr. Sorcerer-from-another-world, but I think a boy your age ought to have himself a bit more fun. Say what you want for that crazy warlock you killed, but he lived his life."

Anzik looked off toward the wall, elevating his nose subtly, lending him a look of disdain. "I am betrothed to Princess Anju of Ghelk. I am in no position to sully myself in idle amusement."

"Oh," Jamile replied. Her little meddling spree had just been thrown clear off the tracks. "I didn't know."

"The event is yet some time from now," Anzik replied. "Ten years at least, perhaps twelve or more. I am … older than her."

"Well, don't let me bother you any longer," Jamile said, excusing herself and leaving the strange young sorcerer to himself.

Jamile left Anzik to whatever it was he did, sitting there alone all day staring at the walls. A boy his age should be drooling at every girl he sees, making a fool of himself, and trying to prove that he is ready to be an adult by acting in the most childish fashion. In short, he ought to have been more like Dan, minus the whimsical attitude toward murder. The way he was just didn't seem healthy. He didn't try to prove he was grown up; he had apparently skipped childhood. He accepted his arranged betrothal to a girl who, by Jamile's quick math was probably just learning to read, without any hint of resentment or rebellion. His self-restraint was borderline clinical. Her former patron, Dr. Coalear, had treated men who had suffered some great tragedy and closed themselves off from the world. Most often, he referred them to the sanitarium. Jamile knew Anzik needed help, but she wasn't qualified to offer it. That sat poorly in her heart.

"The philosopher enlighten you?" Cadmus asked, startling Jamile as she padded through the main chamber, hoping not to be noticed. The rush of water ought to have covered the sound of her footsteps. Whatever puzzle lay under Cadmus's drafting pencil ought to have kept his eyes occupied. He had been waiting for her.

Jamile offered a nervous smile. "Not any more than usual. Eziel knows what that boy's childhood was like, to make him this way."

Cadmus pulled off his spectacles and rubbed his eyes. "Street-corner prophet, except they don't believe the gunk they spew."

"He did make it feel like we're not halfway to floating to the ceiling with every step. That ought to count for something."

"He brokered a deal that has my daughter working for a dragon," said Cadmus. He pointed to the viewframe of the world-ripper that was not dedicated to bringing them air and water. Madlin lay sleeping in the corner of a shack of raw timbers, atop a pile of half-sized blankets. "Look at her there, sleeping like a—"

"Like a university maid?" Jamile finished for him. It was not what he was about to say, Jamile knew, but she didn't like where he was heading. "Face it, Rynn's been through worse, and Madlin will be fine."

Cadmus frowned. It looked strange without his spectacles on, like he was a different person. "Fine would feel a lot better if she were on this side of the viewframe."

"You really shouldn't keep watch so closely," Jamile said. "She should get some privacy. How about you show me what you're working on?"

Cadmus pulled on his spectacles. "Since when have you had any interest in tinkering?"

"Since Rynn stopped showing me everything she's working on. I guess I got used to seeing little pictures of things that don't exist yet. It was like knowing the future." Jamile peered over Cadmus's shoulder at the page of scratchwork sketches and notes. "Is that a coil gun?"

Cadmus harrumphed. "So, you've been paying attention all this time, huh? Scale is a bit different on this version. This one is for the *Jennai*."

"Oh," said Jamile. "The *Jennai* needs a big old gun on it more than it needs showers or a proper hospital station? I mean, look at all the wonderful things you made for this place: the water pump, the river from another world … *we* got a bathtub, at least."

"Necessities. We're at war, Jamile, and in wartime, you only worry for the barest necessities so you can concentrate on winning. When we've won, I'll build all sort of things, things like you're asking for, I promise." Cadmus smiled. It was a weak smile, but there was sincerity behind it.

"Does it bother you?"

"Hmm?"

"That the things you make cause so much suffering?" Jamile asked.

The Mad Tinker slumped back in his chair. "Suffering? I worry more about the suffering I allow. The beaten slaves, the uneducated children, even the shaver who comes home at night worn to bare metal with barely enough coin to feed his family to show for it. I worry about girls like Rynn, sleeping in boiler rooms, associating with gangs for protection, wasting their potential." He hung his head and rested his forehead on his hand, his elbow covering part of the drawing of the new cannon for the rebels' airship.

Jamile surprised both of them when she put her arms around him. He brought a hand up and put it on her arm, as if telling her it was all right to stay as she was. It had been an impulse. He just seemed to need someone right then. No one looked after him. No one but Rynn and Madlin ever seemed even to try. *What is it like, taking on the problems of all the world, thinking that you can fix them if only you build the right machine? What keeps you from seeing the enormity of all this, and just giving up?* If only there were some way she could ask him. If no one knew that answer, there was always the risk that one day it *would* all get to him, that he would just reach a limit to what he could endure on his own. *If I don't, who will?*

"Cadmus," Jamile said softly, still holding him. "Has anyone thanked you for all you do?"

"Not often," he replied.

"Thank you," she said. "I don't know what we'd do without you, and I don't want to find out. If you need someone to talk to—about Madlin, or the war, or what happened with Erefan—I'll always listen."

Cadmus turned, gently extracting himself from her embrace so that he could look her eye to eye. "Can I buy you a drink? They just restocked this place."

Jamile smiled, but shook her head. "I don't drink."

Cadmus snorted. "Neither do I as a rule."

Chapter 21

"Pure as native stone." –daruu expression

The domed chamber was dominated by a central table of marble polished to a mirror shine. Carved all around the edge were runes that spelled out: "We guide. We advise. We protect. We serve." Humble words for a table surrounded by the men who held power among the daruu. King Dekulon and five of his trusted advisors sat around it, with several empty chairs interspersed. Kezudkan wondered idly whose spot he was taking by occupying one of them.

"Thank you for joining us this morning, Kezudkan Graniteson of Korr," King Dekulon greeted him. "These are men whom you may trust with any secret you wish to share with me. These are Kenuk, Pillar of Finance; Sarbuun, Pillar of History; Braklan, Pillar of Defense; Zepdaan, Pillar of Runes; and Lunjak, my successor."

Kezudkan nodded to each man in turn, already having forgotten their names. *Still a patriarchy, it seems. Did the kuduks snuff that out as well?* "Good to meet you all. I am honored."

King Dekulon smiled. "Now that we have the formalities behind us, let us talk. These are learned men, and there is much we wish to know. New is not something we see often here."

Kezudkan's old eyes could still judge a stone or two, and he glanced around the chamber, sizing it up. "I can see not. This room was hand-shaped, oh, I'd say around six hundred years ago."

The king smirked, and glanced around the room in kind. "Would you care to guess higher? This is the oldest untouched stone in the kingdom. It has been as you see it for over eight thousand turns of the world."

"But how—"

"By the stones," said the Pillar of Runes. "I can only imagine the sorry state of your world's infrastructure if this room appears so young."

"Now, now," King Dekulon chided. "There is no need for disparagement. We are here to learn about one another. The mere fact of Citizen Graniteson's presence indicates that there are ways in which our kinsmen have surpassed us."

Kezudkan hung his head. "Perhaps, though I can only wonder at the cost that has been paid for them when I see a place like this."

"Perhaps a more general overview of your world might be the best beginning," suggested the Pillar of History.

"Well," said Kezudkan. "That's not a topic I get asked with regularity. Let me think where to begin …" He paused a moment to straighten himself in his chair.

"Well, geographically, Korr and Veydrus are the same. Same mountains, same valleys, same seas. Not as much of Korr is covered in forest, compared to what I've seen here, up above; we've cut most of it down over the ages. A lot of the mines are used up, and mining becomes more profitable every year as the metals get scarcer or have to come from farther away. We've got airships and thunderails to make travel easier. There are—"

"Pardon me," the Pillar of Defense cut in, "but what is a thunderail?"

"I … well … hmm." Kezudkan stopped a moment to think. *Muddy cracks, how can I explain it without explaining a dozen different concepts that make it work?* "It's a sort of machine." There were slow nods as the daruu indicated that they had passing familiarity with the concept. "It runs on steam … heated water from a furnace it carries with it … forces wheels to turn, wheels that the thunderail sits upon. It makes it move."

"It seems ill fit to the name," King Dekulon said with a chuckle. "Perhaps 'furnace wheel,' would convey it better."

"Well, the thunder part I imagine comes from the sound it makes. You can feel it coming from across the deep."

"It is a large machine, then?" the Pillar of Defense asked.

Kezudkan scoffed. "Hundreds of people can ride on one, and it can haul a like amount of cargo."

"Remarkable," breathed King Dekulon. He turned to his advisors, looking each of them in the eye. "You see? This is why I wanted to learn of their world. Think if we could ride these thunderails to the other deeps."

"The machine that brought him here seems more promising," the Pillar of Runes said. To Kezudkan's eye, the Pillar of Runes was the eldest among the Veydran contingent, and the one with the hardest set to his eyes.

"Impatience is uncalled for, Zepdaan," said the king's successor. *Interesting that the first thing he says is critical of one of his own. Is it his job to spare the king from having to scold?*

"Apologies," replied the Pillar of Runes. "But we have a device that can drop a man in our midst, despite all our defenses. I wished to focus on the practical."

"I agree," added the Pillar of Defense. "How does this machine of yours work, Citizen Kezudkan?"

"I don't have the dustiest notion," Kezudkan replied. The king and his advisors exchanged looks, but to their credit, there was no burst of outrage. *I expected a kuduk response. I expected Draksgollow's response.* "I found an ancient cache of books, written in a language I could not decipher. I was able to puzzle out its function and construction from detailed diagrams, despite not understanding the annotations."

"So you did not invent this machine," stated the Pillar of History. Kezudkan sensed that the historical record of the world-ripper machine had just demoted his contribution to a footnote.

"An artist draws a building; an architect creates it. I was the architect," Kezudkan replied. "Elements were missing; details had to be calculated. I can take credit for neither the underlying principle nor the grand concept of its purpose, but

I did create it … with some assistance from my human." He ground his teeth for adding that last bit. Something about the presence of the Pillar of History sitting there across from him nagged at his conscience. It was enough to make him wonder whether magic was at work on him, or whether he merely could not summon the deceit necessary to lie to his own people on first meeting them.

"So the daruu of Korr have friendly relations with the native humans?" King Dekulon asked, sitting up straighter in his chair. "I had been waiting until later to ask, but the question presented itself at the mention of a human assistant."

Kezudkan tugged at the collar of his suit coat. By the king's reaction, he had some fondness for the creatures. "Not as such, Your Majesty. I owned Erefan, the human in question."

"So we are dominant in Korr?" asked the Pillar of Defense. He looked in turn at King Dekulon and his successor, then the Pillar of History. "In some great war of ages past, we were victorious?"

Kezudkan closed his eyes and let out a long breath. "No." A long, somber silence hung over the table. *I suppose they want me to elaborate.* Kezudkan would have been just as happy avoiding the conversation to follow. He looked down at his clasped hands. "We lost. The humans outnumbered us, but each of us was worth ten of theirs. Their magic was strong, but primitive; ours was elegantly crafted, but our practitioners too few. In the end, neither of us won."

"Then who?" asked the Pillar of History.

"The kuduks."

"What's a 'kuduk?'" asked King Dekulon. By the puzzled expressions around the table, the ignorance was endemic. Kuduks had not arisen in Veydrus.

"Though they have purged it from their own histories, and those of the humans, daruu records have survived to tell their origins," said Kezudkan. "They are the result of an unfortunate crossing of the two races. They are stronger and heartier than humans and breed nearly as rapidly. They could work no magic of their own, but with equal numbers and superior strength, they helped us overwhelm the humans."

"So … you *did* win?" asked the Pillar of Defense.

Kezudkan shook his head. "The war devastated the populations of all three races. The kuduks recovered their numbers, as did the humans, though they now are a beaten and subservient people. We never have."

"Revolting," said the Pillar of Runes.

"I would not have thought it possible," said the Pillar of Finance, the first words the man had spoken since the introductory pleasantries.

Kezudkan frowned. "It is a sad state, but I hardly see how—"

"Cross-breeds, Mr. Graniteson," said the king's successor. "Braklan gets caught up in the strategic details, but the creation of an entire race of mongrel humans sickens me." He glanced around the table. "I think I speak for us all." Wizened daruu heads nodded in agreement. King Dekulon simply sat still, his face hardened into a scowl.

"The kuduks rule," Kezudkan said, raising his palms in a helpless gesture. "Our kind live well. We can work runes, and they can't. All the machines that rely on runes for some of their function, they need us for. A few humans can manage rune replenishment, but there aren't enough to go around. The kuduks need us."

"So, they view us as useful servants, instead of mere slaves?" King Dekulon asked. Kezudkan shrugged. "Unacceptable."

Kezudkan blinked. "I'm no man's servant."

"In all Korr, how many daruu kingdoms are there?" King Dekulon asked. "Do we have a homeland?"

"None, I am afraid," Kezudkan replied. "But we are ruled with a light hand, given preferential treatment in the legal system. Our word is taken as more reliable than a kuduk's, even by their own judges."

"Their own judges …" echoed King Dekulon. He shook his head and stood from the table. Kezudkan leaned forward, prepared to lever himself to his feet in accord with etiquette. But none of the pillars rose from their seats, so he kept his weight on his buttocks and spared his back and knees the pain.

King Dekulon stood beside his successor, who looked up to meet his monarch's eye. "Lunjak, am I a wanton king? Am I prone to rashness, or impulse?" The successor shook his head somberly. "What is my formal title?"

"You are King Dekulon the Ninth, Chosen of the Stone Itself, Ruler and Protector of the People," the successor recited in the resonant voice of a professional herald. It carried a weight of ages of tradition.

"This, we must correct," King Dekulon said. He turned to the Pillar of Defense. "Braklan, gather the Iron Guard."

The Pillar of Defense stood. He was a grizzled old daruu with an age-pocked face and one shoulder lower than the other. "As you command."

Kezudkan stared in shock as the Pillar of Defense left the room. *What have I started here?*

Gederon lounged at the controls of the world-ripper, his feet up on a crate as a footstool. The council meeting in the viewframe was like watching stalactites form. A bunch of stiff old daruu sat around a table, barely moving as they spoke. Gederon kept one eye on the conference while most of his attention focused on the book in his lap. *Rumbles of the Rail* was one of the latest in a series of thunderail adventures of which his uncle disapproved. Of course, Uncle Kezudkan disapproved of anything remotely entertaining, from music to theater, including books that were written in languages he could understand.

Gederon had seen those books, or at least his uncle's handwritten copies of the mysterious texts that had given birth to the world-rippers. The value of those books was plain, even if he could not tell nut from bolt of what they meant. There was no denying the result, since he had seen the machine work. It was just that, if it didn't make your brain hurt from the strain, Kezudkan could not abide any form of leisure.

A sudden motion in the viewframe drew Gederon's attention. The king stood and paced the chamber. Well, pacing might have been an exaggeration, Gederon realized, when the king stopped three chairs over and spoke with one of his advisors. It was an animated exchange. The king was the only young daruu in the group, and the only one who appeared possessed of passion. Another of the advisors rose from his seat, faced the king and gave a formal reply.

"Soft rocks, Uncle. Can't you build a machine that will write out what people are saying without having to hear them?" The conversation might have been worth listening to, by the reaction it got. Not that Gederon could have made out a word of it.

Uncle Kezudkan pried himself from his chair with the aid of his cane. Once he gained his feet, Kezudkan took the cane and tossed it up, catching it midway point of the shaft. That was one of several signals the two of them had worked out for Gederon to open a hole.

Squirming into an upright position in his seat, Gederon kicked the footstool crate aside. He adjusted the location of the viewframe from the vantage he had chosen for observation to one convenient for transport. There was a spot just behind Kezudkan that looked suitable, and its proximity was bound to make his uncle seem to be more in command of the situation than if he left it over in the shadows near the wall.

Pulling the lever, Gederon changed the viewframe from image to passage. The gathered advisors' eyes widened in awe as they stared into Korr. "Welcome, esteemed guests," Gederon said as he stood from the controls. "I am Gederon Ironvein, nephew of Kezudkan."

Kezudkan swept a hand toward the world hole. "After you, Your Majesty."

"King Dekulon, I must insist on checking the stability of the portal before you traverse," said the Pillar of Runes.

A wry smile appeared on the king's lips. "No, I think not. I shall be the first of our kind to set foot in this new world."

Wasn't new this morning, Gederon joked privately.

"It is, of course, your decision," said the successor with a bow.

"Now *that* ought to worry me more than Zepdaan's misgivings," said King Dekulon. "Were I the suspicious sort, I might wonder what deal you had made with our Korrish friend."

"Then I am indeed fortunate that you are not," the successor replied with a wink and a smile. Gederon knew few daruu as jovial as these seemed. Most of them were so stiff you could use them as anvils.

King Dekulon stepped through first, decked out in gold chain regalia and a crown set with eyeball-sized rubies. Gederon found himself wishing he had worn a clean shirt. He muttered his way through polite introductions, trying to at least remember the titles of their guests, if not the landslide of unfamiliar names.

"So this is Korr," King Dekulon said once both feet were on the poured-stone floor of the workshop. "Remarkable. And this must be the great machine."

"Uh, yessir," Gederon replied. "This is it. I work it. My uncle showed me how."

"Is it very complicated to use?" the king asked as Kezudkan and the royal advisors filed through into Korr.

Gederon rubbed one hand with the other as he shrugged. "Naw, it's not so bad with a little practice. Knobs do all the hard work. These switches turn it on and off; knobs aim it."

"Show me, if you please, some of these kuduks I have heard about," said King Dekulon.

Gederon looked to his uncle, leaning to catch his eye past the Veydran king.

"Go find him one of Draksgollow's workshops," suggested Kezudkan. Gederon's eyes grew wider, prompting for clarification. "The old Cavinstraw workshop is still running."

Gederon and his uncle knew that Draksgollow had done as the two of them had and had relocated to an undisclosed location. The lesson of the ambush on Erefan and the attack on his base in Tellurak had been that both men regarded secrecy as their primary defense.

Gederon flipped through Kezudkan's notes, scanning the pages until he found where the coordinates were scribbled. Of course, Kezudkan's scribbling was still immaculate, nearly as good as Gederon could manage with concentration. He returned the viewframe to just an image, and began dialing in the workshop as its target.

The daruu gaped as they watched the view shift through the swirls of the aether until it was showing Korr instead of Veydrus, then dart off for the distant city where the kuduk tinker had once kept his primary workshop.

"Breathtaking," said King Dekulon. "I should commission a statue of this moment."

"Who could possibly do it justice?" asked the Pillar of History. "Even Tarferen can't sculpt stone to shift in such a dizzy blur, and that seems to be the predominant sensation of this display."

"We should have brought a poet, not such prosaic minds as ours," said King Dekulon. "A poet could find a way to convey the sensation without its presence. A sculptor could carve what he feels."

"What is this piece doing?" asked the Pillar of Runes. He had wandered over and was standing by the dynamo, eyes inches from the crackling spark that was being fed to the world-ripper.

"It is called a dynamo," said Kezudkan, "and it is one of those missing bits from the text that I had to create for myself. It provides spark, which is the primary power source for the machine."

"These are kinetic runes," said the Pillar of Runes, squinting for a closer look. "I don't see anything that accounts for the lightning."

"We call that spark," said Kezudkan. "We create it by moving lodestone rapidly through loops of conductive wire. It is a recent advance, only coming into common use in the past fifty years or thereabouts. The possible uses are unlimited."

"Why not use lightning runes directly?" the Pillar of Runes asked.

Gederon perked up. He had asked this same question once. "Because my uncle doesn't know—"

"It's a very efficient system," said Kezudkan. "We avail ourselves of science to get more from our efforts than we put in. It is also adaptable to other means of rotation, such as hydraulic pressure or steam turbine."

Gederon caught a subtle glare from his uncle and kept his mind on his task. He homed in on the workshop, trying to keep an ear on what proved to be a historic conversation. Not that Gederon had any particular fondness for *reading* history, but this was different—he was about to *be* history.

"Got it," he reported. The delegation from Veydrus turned their attention fully to the viewframe. The workshop was larger than the one they stood in, with far more ancillary machinery for the processing of metals into crafted products. The world-ripper there looked the same as the one Gederon was operating, but it was inert at the moment. Of greatest interest to the Veydrans were the kuduk workers.

"They … look like humans," the Pillar of History remarked.

"More like humans than like us," said Kezudkan. "But they aren't built like axe-handles, the way humans are, and they don't bleed all over the place like humans do when they get injured. If you look at the faces—Gederon, bring us in closer on one—you can see the bone structure is more similar to our own."

"I see it," said King Dekulon, squinting at the viewframe. "I've met with humans, and they are a bit thinner in the face and limbs—and look at the noses." The king turned away and put up a hand to shield his view. "That's enough. Return the machine to where we departed."

"So soon?" Kezudkan asked.

"Indeed."

Kezudkan nodded to Gederon, who set to work on the dials once more. *And a setting where we could maybe pull a lever for a place, and it would just go there, instead of having to do the dials every time. Save us a lot of work, that would.*

"Is there some problem?" Kezudkan asked, his hands spread wide.

"Citizen Graniteson, it is you who has the problem," King Dekulon said. "One of these marvelous machines is in the hands of those mongrel creatures. This, I cannot allow."

"They're well-armed," said Kezudkan, "and if I must say, skittish. And they've got guns. We can go back there and I can show you what I mean."

"We have been made aware of the goblin style weapons," said King Dekulon, "but we cannot allow a machine that can penetrate our defenses to remain in the hands of creatures such as those."

Kezudkan shook his head. "They don't even know you exist. I haven't told anyone but my nephew."

King Dekulon rested a hand on Kezudkan's shoulder. "I believe you, and I believe that you could and would keep this secret. But I am king, and sworn to protect the daruu people. Nowhere in my oath did I limit my protection to the daruu of my own world. I will not sit by while my people live under the rule of those monstrous abominations. So to start with, we are going to confiscate that copy of your machine."

Kezudkan raised a brow. "How do you plan to do that?"

By the time they had returned the viewframe to the council chamber in Veydrus, the aspect of the room had changed. The Pillar of Defense stood proudly at attention, still as stone while he awaited the return of his king. Arrayed around him were sets of museum-quality armor, standing in ranks. Kezudkan had seen similar suits on display as antiquities, harkening back to ages long past. Historians had said that they were ornamental, meant to be worn in celebrations and ceremonies. Too impractical. Too ornate. No one would have made armor so beautiful if they intended it to see battle.

Yet here they were. The Iron Guard, King Dekulon had called them. Twenty doughty warriors, covered helm to boot in steel. No two were adorned alike. Some bore spiked protrusions at the elbows and knees, others backward curved blades along the forearms. The helms bore all manner of decoration, from stylized bestial faces to tiered fortifications that looked like siege towers. Colors ran amok among the ranks, with enamels and precious metals mixed together producing artwork fit for formal dinnerware or decorative vases. The shields they carried varied in heraldry, but were alike in size and shape, each tall enough to cover from floor to shoulder when set down, and broad enough to span shoulder to shoulder of the widest among them. Each of the Iron Guard carried an axe forged from an alloy Kezudkan could not immediately identify. The blades were curved like a crescent moon, and the back was formed into a squat hammer, lending the weapon heft behind its strikes.

"These are the greatest warriors of my kingdom," said King Dekulon, waving his hand toward the image in the viewframe. "You will find none better. If you would, open the portal."

Kezudkan nodded to his nephew, who obeyed without hesitation. There was a tiny flinch from the Pillar of Defense, but not a single one of the Iron Guard budged from his spot. King Dekulon stepped through into the council chamber to address his troops.

"Men, I have called you here for a unique defense of the daruu people," said the king. "We have just discovered a new world, one in which our people are sorely beset. They are ruled by a race devolved from a sinful mixing of human blood with daruu. Now, our new friend, Citizen Kezudkan Graniteson, has come to us for aid. We will not fail. There is a device, much like the one you see behind me, in the control of this mongrel race. You will follow me into this new world, and from there to where this device is located. You will wrest control of this device from the mongrels and aid Citizen Kedudkan in relocating it under our control. Is that understood?"

"Yes, King!" twenty voices responded in unison.

Kezudkan felt a tremor in his innards; it worked its way up his spine and into his head. It was glorious. Days long past, returning to Korr with a promise of vengeance, of justice long overdue. Some vague worries gnawed at him, but in the moment, he was swept up in the martial spirit of his kin.

King Dekulon stepped back into Korr, and with a few small gestures, cleared a path in Kezudkan's workshop. The Iron Guard fell in behind him, marching through in lock step without hesitation. The Pillar of Defense was the last one through. "Close the portal," King Dekulon commanded. Gederon complied. "What you see in this gate is now just an image. Watch, as the view changes, and we will see your destination in a moment."

The Iron Guard stood silent save for the occasional scrape of metal as heads turned to watch the swirling images fly past. They smelled of oil and polish, up close. Neither agile, nor stealthy, Kezudkan clopped around the assemblage with his cane and sidled up beside the Pillar of Defense. "Might I have a quiet word aside with you?" The Pillar nodded.

Eyes followed them out the door and into the hall beyond, but no one made mention or objected to their departure. That measure of trust buoyed Kezudkan's spirits. He hoped that the results of his discussion would not dash them.

"What is it?" the Pillar of Defense asked.

"These look like fine lads," said Kezudkan. "Disciplined, impressive, fearless. I just … I wonder if we might be digging a bit too deep without checking our supports."

The Pillar of Defense smirked. "You've probably never seen a true warrior."

Kezudkan closed his eyes. "Warrior? Oh, I fear my world might have made warriors obsolete. Technology does most of the fighting now. Guns that can punch holes in armor stopped us making armor hundreds of years ago. Those kuduks have steam tanks as well, rolling machines that are armored thicker than those soldiers of yours, with the strength of gears and pistons pushing them. Without even runes on that armor, I don't see how they're going to survive. I don't want their blood on my conscience."

"You needn't worry about runes," the Pillar of Defense replied. "I'm no expert on their creation, but all that armor is runeforged."

Kezudkan's brow furrowed. "What's that now?"

"The runes are carved and imbued as they are forged, and the runes end up inside the metal. No work of simple, carved runes can be so powerful. Same goes for their axes. If these kuduk things think as you do, they are in for an unwelcome surprise. Come. Watch."

The two of them returned to the workshop in time to see Gederon find Draksgollow's backup workshop once more. King Dekulon looked past his Iron Guard and caught Kezudkan's gaze. "Citizen Kezudkan, please explain what they are seeing though this portal and what they must strive to preserve. Also, anything you can tell them about kuduk physiology that might be of immediate relevance."

Well, Draksgollow, it looks like this one is being taken out of my hands. We never quite got on, and now we surely never will. No hard feelings.

Kezudkan described the machine, pointing to commonalities that the Iron Guard saw in the workshop around them. He told them what levers to watch out for and what parts were crucial to secure. Under no circumstances were they to allow any of the kuduks to pull the levers on the machine. He gave a quick synopsis of the kuduks' weapons and told them about kuduk hardiness compared to humans. The Iron Guard listened stoically; they watched where he pointed things out, but not a single question came from their ranks.

"Are you all satisfied that you know your mission?" asked King Dekulon.

"Yes, King!" came the unified reply.

I have to get myself some of these.

"Fall into ranks," the Pillar of Defense ordered. "Two wide by ten." The Iron Guard arrayed themselves for the offensive.

"Open the portal," King Dekulon commanded.

"Best of luck," Kezudkan added.

Gederon threw the switch, and the Iron Guard poured through the hole like an avalanche. The bustle of the workshop turned into chaos in an instant. Still paranoid about sudden holes opening in their midst, the kuduk workers kept guns close at hand. The first few workers fell to daruu axes before they knew what hit them, but before the whole host of the Iron Guard were through, the first shots were fired in defense of the workshop.

Old joints crying in protest, Kezudkan lurched out of the line of fire. "Gederon, close it!"

Gederon looked to King Dekulon and received a royal node before obeying. *Rotten little ingrate. That royal interloper didn't pay your university tuition.* But Kezudkan's anger faded swiftly once the world-hole had closed and he had taken no bullets during the brief delay.

Without sound, the battlefield was a surreal scene. The Iron Guard bulled their way through the workshop, using their massive shields as both battering ram and city wall, closing in on gun-toting kuduks until they were in range to cut them to pieces with their axes. If they called out orders and instructions to one another, there was no telling beneath the all-encompassing helms. It looked as if they were one entity with a score of axes and a steel carapace that repelled all attacks.

It's only a matter of time. Rifles and pistols were impressive enough to stop with steel armor, runes or no runes apparent upon them. They would face a real challenge as soon as the kuduk workers roused the mercenaries to the defense.

And there it was. With the remaining workers playing a game of rat and human around the metalworking machinery, the first of the roto-gun fire blasted into the room from the hallway. Kuduk mercenaries waded in, with tri-barrel weaponry slung low, held in both hands. The muzzles flashed a staccato, and sparks flew from the armor and shields of the Iron Guard. Stray bullets crashed around the room, riddling equipment with holes and dings, shattering spark bulbs, and sending the remaining kuduk defenders diving for cover.

The Iron Guard pressed forward, slowly but inexorably. Their shields shook from the hail of copper thrown in their direction, but none gave way. No holes appeared to show that bullets had pierced them. The mercenaries—no fools or heroes among them—fell back before the Iron Guard closed to axe distance. Kezudkan knew what that foretold.

"Move the view," Kezudkan ordered. "We're going to need a view of the corridor outside."

Gederon complied without delay this time, and swung the view around until they were watching through the doorway from just behind the leading troops of the Iron Guard. The steam tanks were coming. Twelve of them.

Kezudkan held his breath, wondering how his kin would react when the steam tanks plowed into the ranks of their elite troops. The vehicles were not monstrous in size, nothing like the thunderail he had described to the Veydrans. Still, each stood taller than the tallest human and as wide as three daruu across.

"Turn the machine on," King Dekulon ordered. "I wish to hear this."

"Wait!" Kezudkan shouted. "Don't do—"

"That was an order of his majesty, King Dekulon," stated the successor in a firm tone, glaring at Kezudkan. Gederon obeyed.

Instantly, they were awash in the ominous grumbling of the approaching steam tanks, the grinding of the drive chains against the stone, the cough and hiss of the steam engines that powered them. In the background, they heard the screaming and occasional gunfire that marked the end of the kuduk workers' defense of the workshop.

One of the Iron Guard in the fore raised his axe high. "HOLD!"

The three lead troops, including the one who shouted, blocked the doorway fully, facing down the oncoming tank. In unison, each lifted his left foot and stomped down, then repeated with the right. Each foot thundered against the stone. The Iron Guardsmen set their shields against the ground and hunkered behind them, leaning their weight forward.

The steam tank hit the wall of shields with a crash. The Iron Guardsmen rocked back, but none gave an inch of ground; not one foot budged. Drive chains scrabbled for purchase. Roto-guns mounted on the steam tank lacked the angle to fire across its own nose. The troops kept their footing and set to work with axes, blade biting into the steel flesh of the metallic beasts. With the sounds of resistance dying away in the background, more of the Iron Guard pressed in to attack over their fellows' ducked heads.

Kezudkan watched in fascination as twenty daruu warriors—the finest of Dekulon's kingdom—hacked a battalion of steam tanks to scrap metal over the course of several minutes. When the guardsmen reformed into ranks as King Dekulon came through the hole to inspect the battlefield, none of them appeared badly injured. A few armor spikes had been bent or broken. Enamel paint was chipped in hundreds of places from bullet strikes. The Iron Guard was covered in blood, but most of it was on their axe blades or had splattered from their enemies.

The world-ripper had received some bullet-related damage, but Kezudkan promised that it was all reparable. He oversaw the task of hauling it into Veydrus under the supervision of the Pillar of Runes, who saw it as an aether converter and therefore under his purview.

Kezudkan bore all of it with a bemused sense of wonderment. In the course of a day, his view of the world had been dug out from under him. *We're going to take back Korr.*

Chapter 22

"It's twice the work to undo something as it is to do it—if you can undo it at all." -Cadmus Errol

Madlin stared out over the valley. Her trek to the hilltops had become a morning ritual, seeing the changes from the day before. She wished she had thought to take flashpops from the same vantage every day and lay them out in a row. Two months … two months was all it had taken. However, for the first morning, the view was essentially unchanged. The work in the valley had moved indoors. Facilities that had grown like weeds from the valley floor now lay complete. Goblins and oxen that had carried lumber and the ingredients for poured-stone now hauled raw metals and firewood for the furnaces.

It had taken half of her time in Veydrus to figure out how to teach the goblins Korrish manufacturing. In the end, she had given in on all but the most essential processes. Instead of drawing the copper wire through dies, goblin sorcerers heated it to a molten liquid and poured it through funnels. Trigger assemblies were hammered into shape by jewelers and blacksmiths working in tandem. For the barrels, Madlin had gone to the trouble of designing rudimentary steam-powered lathes so that they could get a straight bore.

Metallurgy had been the least of her troubles. The goblins professed complete ignorance of brightsteel when she explained it to them. But, like the poured-stone, all it took was a detailed formula with percentages, and their metalworkers took care of the rest. The results were crude since the goblins lacked the sophisticated measuring and metering equipment of a Korrish foundry, or even the foundry on Tinker's Island. But the goblins made viable alloys, and they got better with each batch.

It scared her. She had the ultimate in trainable workforces at her disposal, but when she stopped to think about it—something she preferred to avoid—they were not hers at all. They belonged to Fr'n'ta'gur.

"How long before I get to take my quarter share?" Madlin asked.

"We await word of Fr'n'ta'gur's acceptance of the weapons." As was his habit, K'k'rt stood with one foot in her shadow. The goblin tinker was equal parts translator, assistant, and liaison to the dragon's priests. Since her initial meeting, Madlin had not seen the dragon in person.

Madlin pulled one of the goblin-made coil guns from inside her jacket. It was poorly formed by Korrish standards. The wire gauge was inconsistent; the barrel ribbed with marks from the lathe; the optics never quite able to focus. But it worked. The one in her hand she had fired herself and pronounced it a success.

"I'm going to *show* Froontagger how acceptable they are if he doesn't approve me getting my share." Madlin leveled the gun toward the mountain and peered through the sight. Much as she pretended they could shoot through anything, a few hundred feet of stone were more than it could handle.

"Fr'n'ta'gur," the goblin tinker corrected her.

Madlin shrugged. "Whatever. You clip all the vowels you want, I can't talk like that."

K'k'rt pinched the wisp of beard that dangled from his chin and nodded thoughtfully. "His proper name is Faaraunatagur. Blech, is that ever a torment of the tongue. But it is more respectful than that … that *thing* you called him."

"This isn't about names, or languages," said Madlin, "it's about bargains. And that overgrown lizard is kicking my pipes. Keep it up, one of them's going to burst."

K'k'rt chuckled. "This is why I keep company with humans, I think. You stood in the presence of a creature a thousand times your size, who was born a hundred generations before you, and who could devour you in a single bite. And you would point a tiny gun at him and threaten him. That takes a sense of humor about life, I think."

Madlin shoved the coil gun back in her jacket. "You're the expert. When do you think he's going to make good?" she asked.

K'k'rt sighed. "You must think like a dragon. Fr'n'ta'gur will make sure he gets his share. How can he ensure that?"

Madlin bent low and took K'k'rt by the front of his shirt in both hands. "You better not be telling me that your dragon is going to double-cross me."

"I'm telling you nothing," K'k'rt said, with a hint of a nervous chuckle. "I was merely asking you to consider that a change in perspective might offer new insight."

Madlin let the goblin tinker go with a shove and stood to tower over him once more. "I want you to get word to the priests. I want to know when I get my share."

Rynn and Sosha sat across the table from one another in the corner of one of the *Jennai's* dining halls. It was between standard meal times, which meant fewer people, but not a lack of food. The kitchen staff probably grumbled about it behind her back, but Rynn could always get a hot meal. The two women shared a platter of fried pork cubes with a honey molasses sauce for dipping.

"You've got to keep Cadmus on the level," Rynn said.

"Easier said," Sosha replied. "He's been wound like a watch spring since you went through to Veydrus."

"I just need you to keep a clamp on him. He gets any crazy ideas about a rescue; he could ruin everything. It's a delicate situation. Those goblins are like rats;

they get brave with such huge numbers. And I'm getting a distinct impression the dragon might be planning on leaving us empty-handed."

"Rynn, you're not doing much of a job convincing *me* we shouldn't mount a rescue," Sosha replied.

Rynn popped one of the pork cubes in her mouth, not worried about talking with her mouth full. "We've got the world-rippers, and the dragon doesn't have any idea just how valuable those are. Rescue is trivial. What I need is my father to stop following me everywhere with the viewframe. I think some of the little runts are able to sense when it's around. I see a lot of puzzled stares over my shoulder, and when I look, nothing is there."

"That's going to be a hard sell. Cadmus doesn't do much without the viewframe open, looking in on you," said Sosha.

"Isn't he still working on new designs?"

"Yes, but it doesn't stop him working within a turn of the head of watching you. Everything's all placed, so what he needs is all right there for him. He set it up that way."

Rynn slumped back in her seat, taking another of the pork cubes to chew on as she thought. "We need another project for him. One that needs the world-ripper in use. Maybe get Kaia to work on it, training and that sort of thing." Madlin's eyes widened and she stopped chewing. "Kupe."

"What about him?"

"Let him train Kupe," said Rynn. "Turn him into a proper leader. My father's been giving orders so long he hardly thinks about it anymore, but he was head of the largest company in Tellurak. He got men to do what he wanted even before he had the money to just bully them into doing it."

"I don't know …" said Sosha. "Kupe's not exactly leader material, I think."

"You never knew me when I was younger," said Rynn.

"I *only* knew you when you were younger," Sosha replied with a smirk.

"Blast it! You *have* been keeping Cadmus company; you're even picking words apart like him."

Sosha shrugged. "It's me and Greuder by turns, really. He won't talk to Anzik unless he needs an answer out of him, and Kupe and Kaia spend most of their attention on Kaia and Kupe. Your father's got a lot on his mind, but when you get him to relax a little, he's really quite pleasant company."

"Well, whether it's you or Greuder, you've got to stop him watching over my shoulder all the time."

"Why the sudden urgency?" asked Sosha. "You've been there months now."

"Because," said Rynn, "I'm hoping to get another meeting with the dragon. If the goblins might be aware of the viewframe's location, I worry that the dragon will, too. I don't want to play our hand early, in case we need to surprise the dragon with the world-ripper sometime soon. So whatever you have to do, get my father away from that world-ripper."

Sosha gave the kind of smile that just curled the edges of her lips and never showed in the eyes. She didn't look directly at Rynn. "I'll manage. Don't worry."

Madlin sat with her arms wrapped around her knees, on a bench that had to have been considered short even by goblin standards. The priests had insisted on her taking a bath before entering the dragon's presence and had dressed her up in orange robes. She found it curious that they had human-sized garments on hand or had made suitable for her in advance. Madlin certainly hadn't given them enough notice to have sewn it from a bolt of fabric before she arrived. The garment was lightweight, silky soft and left her feeling naked. Her gun belt lay in a bin that one of the priests had carted off, along with the rest of her personal possessions. She had persuaded them to leave her the spectacles she wore, but nothing else was allowed.

I guess I've slipped down the ladder a bit since my first meeting. Either that, or the priests just got their way this time. Without her pocketclock, she had no idea how long they had kept her waiting. It had been an hour, at least. That was just another of the ploys to make her feel uneasy before her audience. It was working. Madlin considered flagging down one of the priest and telling him that she had changed her mind. The longer she thought about it, the fewer ways she could think of where she came out ahead in the encounter. *I'm not likely to intimidate something that size. It already has what it wants from me. It might only be keeping me around because it wants to make sure I can fix the guns or the factories if something goes wrong. If I manage to upset it enough, it could kill me before Rynn can open a world-hole.* Despite ordering Jamile to keep Cadmus away from watching this negotiation, Rynn was ready at the controls with just a twist of the world dial separating her from a quick intervention.

Madlin was beginning to feel like the fulcrum between two great forces. Unfortunately, all the leverage was on one side. *That's what I really need. A lever. No, not just a lever, some huge force on the opposite side from the dragon.* Madlin wracked her brain for an adversarial force that the dragon could wrap its reptilian brain around. Surely Rynn and Cadmus could figure out a way to harm the dragon, but the dragon might not believe the threat. The Megrenn might be displeased enough at being cut out of the bargain that they might be plausible but perhaps not enough of a threat. The Kadrins? If the dragon had any inkling of what had passed between her and the Kadrin warlock, the gambit would likely end in her death. K'k'rt had made it clear how tolerant the dragon was of deceit.

Madlin needed a threat, and it needed teeth. She looked up suddenly. *Of course … teeth. I need to give these coil guns to one of his rivals.*

Worry had settled into an uneasy, pent-up energy by the time the priests arrived to take Madlin to her audience. Even seated on her little bench, she was taller than them. When she stood amid her ceremonial escorts, she felt like she was shepherding children.

As she followed them down the wide tunnel to the dragon's lair, she rehearsed her threat. *I only want what I've been promised. If you don't make good, someone else will. If you kill me, we'll send another in my place.* A chill in the subterranean air made her shiver, the supplicant's robe doing nothing to keep her warm. Her bare feet didn't help either, with the heat from her body sucked into the smooth stone through the exposed flesh. *Next time I come to see you, dragon, I'm telling your priests to piss off.* Rules were meant for those who couldn't break them and get away with it.

Rynn managed to distract herself from the thought of the dragon itself until she reached its treasure chamber. The goblin priests pushed and shoved and chittered away at her until she realized they were trying to get her to kneel. She was about to comply when an impulse came over her. Setting her feet, she put a hand to the shoulder of one of the prodding goblins and shoved him to the ground. He hit the stone with a rustle of priestly vestments and a look of astonishment. Madlin knocked over another of the priests before the rest backed away.

"Faaraunatagur," Madlin shouted into the dark recessed of the cavern, remembering the name K'k'rt had told her. "Call off these pests of yours!"

Fr'n'ta'gur's chuckle shook the cavern floor. The dragon spoke something in harsh, unintelligible syllables, and the priests scattered, bowing and pronating themselves as they scurried for the exit.

"I despise beggars," Fr'n'ta'gur said in clear, sub-bass Korrish. "What is it you come to discuss?"

"I'm here to find out when you plan to keep to your end of the bargain," Madlin said. Her head was fuzzy as she forced herself to confront the monstrosity verbally. *No deceit, no weakness, no backing down … no getting sick all over the pile of gold.* "We've got hundreds of weapons piling up in warehouses. One quarter of those are mine by terms of our deal."

Avalanches of coins rang like piles of chain, and Madlin could *feel* the presence of the great beast approaching. It was a tingle, like the feeling of aether through her when a sorcerer cast a spell nearby; only this was both larger and more subtle. An ocean wave instead of a river.

"I see no discrepancy," Fr'n'ta'gur replied. "Indeed, one weapon in four will be given to you in payment for the secret of their construction."

"Yesterday's inventory said there were eight hundred eleven completed coil guns," said Madlin, staring into the darkness, waiting for the first light to hit the dragon. "That means two hundred two of those are mine, even rounding in your favor. I want them delivered."

The first glint of light from the corridor caught teeth. Madlin's breath caught in her throat as the monster's head loomed over her as it approached. "I can see your dilemma. However, your view is shortsighted. Do you expect that eight hundred eleven weapons are all my goblins will make?"

"N-no."

"Neither do I," the dragon replied. "I expect far more than that. Far more. I have armies to equip. Six hundred and nine weapons would be insignificant."

"So?" Madlin asked. "Make more."

"They will do exactly that," Fr'n'ta'gur replied. "They will build, let us say, eight hundred thousand."

Madlin's eyes widened. She had grown too used to thinking on the scale of the rebellion. They had hundreds of troops. In the coming months, with the help of Kupe's notoriety, she had hoped their numbers would swell into the thousands. What would she do with two hundred thousand coil guns? The rebellion would have to reinforce the *Jennai* just to pack that many guns aboard and keep aloft.

"So you see," Fr'n'ta'gur continued as Madlin struggled with the sudden shift in expectations, "you are barely one tenth of one percent finished with your task."

"My task was to show your goblins how to build coil guns, not to be their shop foreman for the rest of my life," said Madlin, mustering her reserves of indignation. "I want my cut now, paid as we go."

The dragon bared its fangs in what Madlin sincerely hoped was a smile. "No."

Madlin backed up a step, but the dragon still hovered over her, its neck stretching off into the gloom beyond her vision. "I didn't want to resort to threats, but I *will* have my share. I need those guns, and I'm not waiting years for them."

"Amuse me, Madlin Errol of Korr," Fr'n'ta'gur said, twisting his head around and lowering it until it was behind Madlin, blocking the way out. "Threaten me."

Madlin turned to look into the nearest eye of the beast—she was too close to see both of them. "I'll find another dragon and teach *his* goblins to make coil guns. I'll find one of you lizards who'll pay his debts."

Fr'n'ta'gur hissed, louder than a thunderail coming to rest at a station and venting its boiler. The dragon's tongue flicked between its teeth, coming within inches of touching Madlin. She stiffened but held her ground.

"You think I would let you leave?" the dragon asked. "You have a debt as well, and until it is paid, you will not leave this chamber. The artisans can come here to consult with you. You will learn what it is to deal with dragons. I will not be threatened. I will not be dictated to. I will not be deprived of my rightful share."

"No," said Madlin. "I am going to sleep in my cot tonight, down in the valley below. I am going to get to work tomorrow morning, same as ever, overseeing the factories. And tomorrow night, I'm going to count up the inventory, set one gun in four aside, and take them to my troops."

"And if I just ate you? If I trusted that my artisans could keep making the weapons without your help?" Fr'n'ta'gur asked, drifting closer to her. His breath smelled of charred meat.

"Then you'd find out about the vengeance of a man who breached the barrier between worlds without even knowing magic, and what he would do to the creature that killed his only daughter."

"So, you believe you bargain from a position of strength?" Fr'n'ta'gur asked, drawing away from Madlin a few feet.

"If I die, I swear before Eziel, you'll die, too," Madlin replied. *Not to mention Rynn's vengeance though I'd rather not take the time explaining that one.*

The dragon's eye widened. "Worshipers of the war god? How interesting. Have the old gods taken refuge in your world?"

Madlin was tempted to reply that they had, but she remembered K'k'rt's warning. She had yet to lie to Fr'n'ta'gur and preferred not to test his powers of observation. "We follow the creed. Lord Eziel, grant us vengeance upon our enemies. Let us share our strength as comrades and become fearsome to our foes. I am your servant, teach me to kill in your name."

"Grammar was not the war god's specialty," Fr'n'ta'gur replied.

"You knew him?" Madlin asked.

"Of course not," Fr'n'ta'gur replied. "How old do I look?"

Madlin shrugged. He was the only dragon she'd ever encountered. He could have been a hundred years old or a million.

"A true servant of the war god *would* be prepared with vengeance, and you honestly believe you could achieve it," said Fr'n'ta'gur. "Very well. Your piddling requests for your proper lodging I grant you without condition. Your greater request for an earlier split of the spoils of our collaboration will require one thing."

"What's your condition?" *Why do I have the feeling I'm going to hate this, whatever he says?*

"You will prove the worth of them in battle, against a foe one of my kin was unable to overcome."

Yup. That's why.

Chapter 23

"You know, Father, you've gotten predictable as you've gotten older. I'm the one who comes up with the innovations now. You just tinker on old designs." -Madlin Errol

Madlin sat in the back of a wagon, having refused the goblins' suggestions that she walk the distance from Fr'n'ta'gur's mountain to their destination. If there was one thing that changed in the aftermath of her encounter with the dragon, it was that Madlin no longer allowed any of the goblins to boss her around. The only point on which they seemed never to budge was allowing Madlin access to the warehouse of completed coil guns. *I can steal as many as I want—once—with the world-ripper. Then, they'll figure out a way to protect them. They also might either try to kill me or stop making the weapons.* It still rankled her, seeing the goblin troops carrying more of the weapons than she had in the entire rebellion. The final count before the march had been three thousand eighty-five. *Seven hundred seventy-one of those are mine, by rights.*

The trip was eerily familiar. The trek from Buou had started farther north, but their destination was nearly identical. It seemed that no matter the world, once that vein of gold was discovered, someone built a mine there, then a great city atop its ruins. K'k'rt had given her a brief history of the city of Raynesdark, the westernmost major stronghold of the Kadrin Empire. It was thousands of years old, and the mines beneath had been emptied of gold centuries ago. It still produced exotic minerals that the goblin metallurgists used but which the humans of Veydrus did not. Madlin listened patiently as K'k'rt tried to explain, in child-like terms, what bauxite, chromium, and nickel could be used for. Of course, K'k'rt's Korrish was primitive, and he didn't know the proper terms, but Madlin knew what came from beneath that mountain better than he ever would. It had been home, at least in Korr. She knew miners who dug those ores loose from the earth with pickaxes, paid only two bowls and a loaf a day.

So many times in the days the army traveled, Madlin found herself turning to a phantom Jamile, or worrying over a memory of Dan. All she saw were goblins, oxen, and the strange six-lizards that the high-ranking officers rode, saddles perched on the creatures' heads. K'k'rt was one of those. Though technically he was not a member of the army, he was respected as an elder. The tinker had confided in Madlin that *she* was technically an elder, should she ever need a bit of leverage when arguing with the officers. Only a pair of sorcerers and one of the generals was over the age of sixteen.

Madlin sighed as she stared at the distant mountains, unchanging as they drew nearer, or at least growing so slowly that she couldn't notice. K'k'rt said they would be at the base of the mountains by nightfall, but he could have told her a week and she wouldn't have known any differently.

Except for Rynn. Madlin hadn't gone into the expedition blindly. Rynn had been using the *Jennai's* main world-ripper for days, sweeping the countryside for scouts, mapping the city of Raynesdark, taking count of troops and looking in detail at the fortifications. She had told none of this to her allies. Let the goblins think they were on their own, that she was trusting in them and in her invention to protect her. Let Anzik think that she was waiting to see Raynesdark for the first time upon her arrival. The enigmatic young sorcerer likely would have guessed that she would scout ahead through a viewframe, but she wasn't about to tell him and remove all doubt. Nor was she about to share the knowledge she gained, at least not without negotiating a price. Given freely, the knowledge of the stronghold was as likely to be used against her somehow, as it was to gain her anything.

The casual consideration of betrayal was new to Madlin. All her life, she felt she had known who to trust. The rebels, her gang friends, her father's workers, she trusted all of them with her life. She had never been betrayed by a kuduk because she had never trusted one. *When did I start becoming so distrustful? Dan?* The murder of the unbalanced warlock lad was certainly the first time she felt the guilt of double-crossing someone. *No. Naul. First human who ever sided with the kuduks against me.* She wondered whatever became of him. Had he delivered the "music box" that Madlin had entrusted to him, brought it to his kuduk patron, and been killed? Had he realized at the last minute that he had his freedom, if only he took it? Madlin shook her head. She had never investigated. The gift she had given herself was the uncertainty of not knowing that she'd sent Naul to his death.

The rumble of wagon wheels and the bestial noises from the goblins' pack animals formed a relaxing monotony that threatened to lull Madlin to sleep. She tried to judge the size of the mountains, remembering her views of them in Korr, from the thunderail, and from a wagon in Tellurak. But the memories did not come with a ruler or a sextant, or any other measuring device.

K'k'rt's chuckle snapped Madlin awake. "Do you have your optics?" the goblin tinker asked. His lizard mount was walking beside and behind Madlin's wagon, and he had guided the creature's head around in front of her. The lizard was walking without looking where it was going, which Madlin took as a sign that they were either very stupid creatures or very smart ones.

Madlin cocked her head in reply, confused by the question. She pointed to the spectacles, which were not exactly hidden on her face.

"No, the long-sight one on your weapon," K'k'rt said. "Look to the east, then turn thirteen degrees right."

Madlin drew her coil gun and sighted down the scope. It was her own gun, not one of the goblin-made weapons with the shoddily-ground glass. They were getting better, she had to admit, but they weren't yet up to Tinker's Island standards. In the tiny circle of view, she saw a lot of dark grey rock. She panned to the right, unable to judge precisely how far thirteen degrees might be. Through the scope, it was hard to miss.

It looked so much smaller than it had in the world-ripper's viewframe, but there it was: Raynesdark. The poor, beset crossroads of two worlds' ambitions, about to become a battlefield because of Madlin. All she could see of it were the two staggered walls—one above the city protecting it from the glacial ice, one below shielding it from view from the west—and a few taller buildings, one of which was the ruler's dwelling. Rynn had been all through the building, which was half buried into the side of the mountain, covering the entrance to the old gold mines. It was stark, unadorned stonework, grand in scale but juvenile in its simplicity. Raynesdark had a deep, which surprised her more than anything else she found about it. It was a single, massive vaulted cavern with forges vented up through to the sky. There were offshoots that looked to have been built from old mine tunnels, and a few that appeared to be active mines. The inhabitants were only mostly human. Rynn had seen her first ogres in those deep mines. Gigantic, dull-eyed humanoids, they provided brute labor for the Kadrins; Rynn suspected that they would provide muscle in battle as well.

Had she wanted to, Madlin could have arranged for Rynn to do any number of things to sabotage the Kadrins' defenses. With access via the world-ripper, she could have arranged assassinations, undermined the city wall, poisoned the water supply, or pillaged the armory. But something Anzik had told her kept nagging at her thoughts. *The Kadrin Empire keeps its power by magic.* Dan was a symptom of a larger problem with the empire: sorcerers bred for generations to produce stronger and stronger bloodlines. If one of those sorcerers caught her with an open world-hole, there might be no end to the trouble that resulted.

Of course, Madlin also didn't care whether the goblins prevailed. So that was an even better reason not to risk aiding them. The coil guns worked. She knew they would function to the dragon's satisfaction.

"It's just a wall," K'k'rt said. "Unless you see something more than these old eyes could make out."

Madlin blinked and lowered the coil gun. "No, just thinking."

K'k'rt chuckled. "Getting the palm sweats before a battle. You wouldn't be the first."

Madlin snorted. "Please. I've been to more battles than you've ever seen."

"Oh, I hadn't realized I was in the presence of such a grizzled old warrior, elder Madlin."

"You know," Madlin replied, "for someone who claims that speaking my language cramps his tongue, you sure talk a lot."

K'k'rt laughed out loud, slapping his knee repeatedly. "Exercise doesn't do an old body like mine any good, but it seems my tongue is younger than the rest of me."

Madlin sighed. The city was still well out of range for the coil guns. The wagons dragged on. "So what now?"

K'k'rt shrugged. "For such a young human, you are quite impatient. We wait."

The arrayed goblin forces prepared for the assault on the Kadrin city of Raynesdark. Madlin had never seen the whole group at one time, strung out as they were over the course of miles of wagons. Now, as tents popped up and cooking fires lit the dusk, the plains below the mountain city teemed with scrawny, grey-green invaders. Madlin crouched at the flap of her tent, too tall to stand inside it. It was an annoying precaution, but a sensible one for her safety, having her in the same tents as the army. Even poking her head out to peer through the optics on her coil gun seemed risky. There was always the chance that some sharp-eyed bowman or sorcerer aided by magic would catch sight of her and make her a target. Rynn had made and runed a steel plate jacket for her, but Madlin resisted the urge to open a world-hole to receive it. Her better protection was anonymity.

Up on the walls, in the evening's fading light, Madlin could just make out movement. The city's defenders must have known that the goblins were settling in after a long journey, not preparing for an immediate assault. *Sorry fellas. You may just be doing your job up there, but you're doing it for the wrong side.* At least, everything Madlin had heard told her that it was the wrong side. When she had started out her rebellion, it had been the right thing to do. Humans. Kuduks. Daruu to a lesser extent. She knew who she was fighting for, who she was fighting against. A few holes in some knockers were a cause for celebration. Dead humans were mourned. Now she was surrounded by goblins, about to attack a city of her fellow humans. Except that *these* humans—in fact all humans of this world—seemed to place little value on that fellowship. She had needed allies, and to secure them, she had taken sides. In so doing, Madlin had set in motion this series of events that led her to Raynesdark. There was no way she could have foreseen it, but she was the cause nonetheless. The human blood spilled was on her conscience. The goblin blood, Fr'n'ta'gur could keep on his own conscience—if dragons even had them.

The clank of spoon in bowl brought Madlin's attention back to her immediate surroundings. "Still looking through that thing?" K'k'rt asked. He handed her a bowl of the sugary mush that the goblins seemed to use for any meal that had to feed thousands. Madlin wondered if they even had a more sophisticated cuisine.

"Thanks," she replied, juggling her coil gun and the bowl until she managed to holster her weapon. "Just wanted a better look, I guess."

K'k'rt chuckled softly. "Second thoughts about attacking your own kind?"

"You think it's funny?" Madlin snapped.

K'k'rt cocked his head. "Oh … that. Nervous habit. I seem less threatening if people see me as pleasant-faced."

"You mean lighthearted."

K'k'rt shrugged. "Same thing, I imagine. I have spent far too long—most of my ember years—balanced on a blade. I used to be a sorcerer who tinkered for amusement. I was younger, back then." He drew a thin blade from his belt, little more than a pocket knife, and twirled it in his fingers. It spun, darting around nimble fingers, twisting and reversing. Then it fell to the turf. K'k'rt muttered something in his own tongue and kicked the knife away, stumbling as he overbalanced.

"What was that all about?" Madlin asked.

"I used to be able to do that all day, without even paying heed to it," said K'k'rt. "I used to have the fingers of an assassin, or a harpist. I was quick with my spells. Now, I'm a shepherd of vengeful humans, a promise-maker to dragons, and not much of a sorcerer at all. You'd laugh too, if it kept them all at bay."

Madlin sat down in the dirt beside the tinker, still poised at the opening of her tent flap. "What's gotten into you? Battle too much for you?"

"I was here the last time," K'k'rt replied. "My magic was growing difficult even then, six winters ago. But it was enough to sneak me away. I saw it all though before I escaped. The cannons smashing the Kadrin wall. The glory of Ni'hash'tk breathing fire down on their city, routing their forces. I saw the demon arrive and the two of them quit the battlefield together, to watch us mortals fight it out. I watched the demon kill her, and destroy the high wall, dropping an avalanche over our forces. As far as I know, only myself and the human sorcerer who taught me to make cannons survived."

"So, history coming full circle?" Madlin asked. "You're worried it'll only be you and me walking away from here?" She winked at him, trying to cheer him up.

K'k'rt sighed. "No, I think this time is different. The demon is dead. Ni'hash'tk is dead. And Fr'n'ta'gur is not the fool she was. History repeats so that we can do better each time. But …"

There it was. "But what?"

"You have a plan to escape if this goes badly," K'k'rt said. It was always difficult to tell, given his shoddy Korrish, but Madlin heard no hint of a question.

"What if I did?" Madlin asked, staring K'k'rt right in the eye. Sitting next to him, they were of like height.

"The machine that sent you will snatch you back," K'k'rt said. "You had the same plan when you argued with Fr'n'ta'gur. I have known madman humans, but you do not strike me as one of them. At the first sign of danger to you, you will sneak away."

Madlin remained silent. *Assume all you want. I don't have to tell you anything.*

K'k'rt leaned close. "I want you to rescue me as well."

Madlin pulled away, trying to get a full view of the wrinkled, grey-haired goblin as if seeing all of him would make his request any less bizarre. "What?"

"I can be of use," K'k'rt continued. "Even if we sneak back, if the danger passes, I can cover your story. I can be a valuable ally."

"You aren't on my side," Madlin said. "You're keeping watch on me for the dragon, making a deal for your friends in Megrenn, and coming out ahead. I know where we stand."

"We stand on the edge of a blade. I've been on it for a long time, but you're new up here. You'll want an expert."

Madlin kept silent once more.

"Don't answer me now. Eat your meal and get some sleep. The attack will launch before the dawn."

Rynn found herself wandering the corridors and catwalks of the *Jennai* with no destination in mind. Madlin lay sleeping in an undersized tent, waiting for the sound of goblin signal horns to wake her for the battle. Rynn was no good at waiting, so she stalked the far corners of her ship, looking for distractions. There was activity even in the dark hours, though the most interesting construction happened in the daylight hours. Despite the scarcity of daylight as the sun crept over the western horizon, she headed to the belly of the ship—or more precisely, below it.

The great scaffolding that hung below the *Jennai* was all new. Rynn slung herself down by one of the larger support beams, and onto the makeshift walkway that ran to either side of her father's latest project. Below her, clear to see through the metal mesh of a floor, was the sunset reflected from the sea a half mile below them. It caught her breath short every time she looked down, but there was not a spot anywhere along the scaffold where there was a gap large enough for her to fit through on purpose, let alone by accident. The welds were sound; she had checked them herself. She had even carved levitation runes on a belt she wore, ready to be activated in case of a fall. For all that, the feeling of doom when looking straight down from such a height never faded.

The enormous cannon was a product of Cadmus's recent paranoia. The design and oversight of its construction had kept the Mad Tinker busy, but it was a ludicrous waste of resources. The bore was large enough for workers to crawl down on hands and knees. The copper wire had not been wound around it; the gauge was so thick it had to be hammered into shape around the barrel. Cadmus had constructed six dynamos to power the weapon. It was covered in split runes, ready to come together and make the barrel as massive as the whole of the ship for a brief moment as it fired. It was ludicrous on a scale that Madlin had rarely seen from her father. She had nicknamed it the World Ender Cannon, Version 1.

The problem was not that a coil gun wouldn't work on such a scale; on the contrary, Rynn was convinced that it would. The problem was that there was very little worth firing such a weapon at. The *Jennai* had been harassed by kuduk airships from one nation or another from time to time, but between their own liftwing airships and the hundred or so handheld coil guns they had aboard, the crew had always handled the situation.

As a rule, machines don't like to fly. The science of keeping one in the sky was finicky, and it didn't take much convincing to send one back to the ground where it belonged. While the World Ender Cannon, Version 1 would certainly make short work of any vessel it hit, a far smaller bore would have been just as effective and much easier to build. Not to mention the small matter of aiming something mounted ventrally the length of the ship. *How many coil guns could we have made with all this copper?* Goblins or no, it seemed like a waste of resources. That was what puzzled her.

Cadmus Errol was not a wasteful man. He never had been, and it seemed like a peculiar time to start. There was a war to be fought, and Cadmus's gun was a solution to a battle they had already won. The skies belonged to the rebels. Wherever the *Jennai* went was their home. Cadmus knew that as much as Rynn did. As she ran a hand along the wrapped copper coils, strolling the length of the barrel, Rynn tried to imagine what you could do with a gun like the World Ender.

The target would need to be slow-moving, preferably stationary. It would need to be well protected, something that would justify putting this much power behind it. Ideally, it would be of use to us in the rebellion against the kuduks.

Rynn stopped, the springs in her tinkers' legs bouncing her once as they settled. A chill ran through her as she put the pieces together. *He wants to destroy the deeps.* Perhaps her flippant moniker for the cannon was not so far off the mark. It would explain the chuckle from Cadmus when she named it. If a coil gun could put a half-inch steel ball a few inches into rock, how far could this monstrous weapon send a three-foot diameter steel shot though stone? It had six times the power of a world-ripper … the math just eluded her. She had no idea.

Rynn slumped against the side of the scaffolding. *He's going to try to wipe them out.* In moments of anger, Rynn had wished for the extinction of all kuduks, but when her temper cooled, she could not sustain that wanton vitriol. They weren't *all* bad, and even if they were, that wasn't justification for wiping out their whole race. Rynn had proven that the rebellion could evacuate humans from the deeps. Get that operation working on a larger scale, and they could pull the humans to safety and bury the kuduks—and daruu, she supposed—beneath the stone of their own cities.

"You all right?" a voice called from the far end of the catwalk. Sosha. Her dark skin made it hard to pick her out in the fading light, but the voice left no doubt.

"Yeah," Rynn shouted back. "Just out for a walk while I wait for the rusted goblins to attack." She leaned back against the scaffold as Sosha approached.

Sosha wasn't dressed for the night air, shivering in a light dress. Wherever she had expected to find Rynn, it hadn't been outdoors. "What are you doing down here?"

"Just checking on my father's bloated coil gun," Rynn replied, patting the coil-wrapped barrel.

Sosha nodded. "You could almost fire a person out of that thing."

"Don't even say that," Rynn snapped. She glanced down, even though her tinker's legs were hidden by her trousers, she knew exactly what lay beneath.

"Sorry," said Sosha. "I just wanted to see how you were faring. Big war starting tomorrow, right?"

"Any time now, actually," Rynn replied. "Goblins plan to start it in the middle of the night."

Sosha tugged her arms tightly to her body and shifted behind Rynn for shelter from the wind. "Good thing it's you there, not me. I'd be all in pieces by now."

"If this is where you try to get me to admit that I'm scared, you can quit it," said Rynn. "I'm heading up to the world-ripper as soon as Madlin wakes up. Anything goes wrong, I pull her out of there. I hope you're a bit more subtle when it comes to getting Cadmus's mind off his troubles."

Sosha snorted. "Mad Tinker or not, he's still a man. He's dense as stone about anything as squishy and non-mechanical as feelings. He's actually much easier to manage than you are. He doesn't push me away or avoid me."

"I don't need any help; I've still got Madlin. Ever since my father got one-worlded, he hasn't quite been the same."

"He doesn't feel as invincible anymore," Sosha said. "He's not so dead-sure certain he's going to win."

Rynn bobbed her head. "Yeah. That sounds about right. He stopped acting like he was carving his own tunnel to his destiny."

"How about you come inside," Sosha suggested, jerking her head toward the near end of the catwalk. "I'll put on some tea and we can stay up, watching the battle."

Rynn eyed her suspiciously. "Fine. But I just want you to know I'm on to you." Sosha smiled and Rynn chuckled as they headed for the kitchens.

Madlin awoke to the sound of a war horn. There was no preparing the slumbering ears for the sound, even knowing in advance how the goblins would begin their assault. What amazed her upon peeking out her tent flap was that the sound was not the wake-up alarm, but the call to charge. Somehow the entire army had prepared themselves for an assault without waking her. Madlin was under no illusion that they did it to spare her a few moments of extra sleep, but nonetheless, she was astonished at the stealth the small creatures could employ—and the organization.

Fumbling amid her belongings, Madlin found her coil gun and sighted through the optics. Nothing. There was starlight to see by, but cooking fires that had burned throughout the night kept the camp better lit than the walls. *Why would they leave the fires burning? Won't that make them easier to see from the city?* Goblins milled around the fires, cooking, chatting, acting as if there was no army massing to assault the walls. Someone who could only see by the firelight might think the goblins were well settled in their camp. *A trick, then.* Madlin filed that away in her mind, should the goblins ever be on the other side of a wall from her.

"Settle in for the show," she muttered to Rynn. Madlin could taste the ginger tea Rynn shared with Sosha, but the sensation was already fading. Rynn was more likely to see through the world-ripper's viewframe than through their twinborn connection.

The horn sounded again, playing three notes. There were no whoops, no battle cries, no wordless snarls of bared ferocity. The goblins simply moved forward as a mass, as if someone had rolled a sack of marbles down a shallow slope, gathering speed until the whole army was at a dead run. Madlin's vantage was high enough that she could see the army flowing into the plains and up the low road that wound back and forth up the mountainside. It might have taken half an hour for the first of them to make the mountain's base, but Madlin was too engrossed in the spectacle to check her pocketclock.

The first she saw of the actual battle was surreal. The night was lit by a plume of flame erupting from the goblin ranks. So far from the action, she could barely hear the tiny, chittering shouts of alarm. Even after the initial burst, the flames lingered, clinging to distant, frantic forms, rushing around in their final chaotic moments. The defenders on the wall had struck first, with magic.

From the ranks of goblins, a volley answered. Whoever was commanding the goblin forces had ordered waiting until the goblins were almost to the wall before unleashing their secret weapons. All along the wall, Madlin saw blue glowing ripples, like pebbles thrown into a pond, each representing the strike of a single shot from a coil gun. Madlin wished she could take a flashpop, but the still image, rendered in two-tone color, would have come off as a paltry imitation of the wondrous sight.

"Good. You're awake," K'k'rt's voice came from beside her. The old tinker settled himself in the dirt next to her, looking out at the battle. "Best view you're likely to get."

Madlin caught herself just before she corrected the goblin tinker. Rynn had the best view anyone could get; Cadmus very likely had one to match. But there was nothing to be gained telling K'k'rt that. "Yeah, well, pretty as it is, I'd like to see those little blue splashes *stop*."

K'k'rt sighed. "Indeed. Both our lives here are at an end if those devices of yours don't work."

"They'll work," said Madlin. *Rusted little ingrates!* She scolded the guns. *Blast down that wall!*

"It's not working," Cadmus said, pointing at the starlit wall of Raynesdark. Here and there, collections of goblins went up in flame as the sorcerers high atop the wall alternately cowered and lobbed destruction down into the mass of goblin flesh that swarmed up the road below them.

"Give them time," said Jamile. "It looks like it's weakening." The blue ripples reverberated wherever one of the coil gun shots hit.

"Bah, you're just imagining what you want to see," Cadmus snapped. He adjusted the view frequently, shifting their vantage all around the battlefield, keeping a close watch on the integrity of the wall.

"This is incredible," said Kaia, staring into the viewframe. She sat with Kupe and Greuder at a side table, sharing a bowl of candied chocolates.

"Sure are a pissload of them little buggers," Kupe observed sagely, drawing a snort from Greuder.

Cadmus shook his head. "We need that wall to come down. I'd rather the dragon be impressed over false pretenses than try to argue with it over production quotas and delivery schedules. Time for the backup plan. Battle stations!"

Jamile's eyes shot wide. "What?"

Kupe, Kaia, and Greuder looked to one another with no hint of a clue among them.

Cadmus stood from the controls and stalked across to the controls for the other world-rippers, the ones that bracketed the ends of the room, beginning and ending the tiny chunk of tropical river that flowed through Korr's moon. "Kaia, take the controls. Keep a sharp eye in case things go wrong. Greuder, put a hand on that lever … yes, that one right there," Cadmus said, pointing. "Be ready to pull it when I give the signal."

"Cadmus, what are we doing?" Greuder asked.

"Jamile, get on the controls of that machine," Cadmus ordered, ignoring Greuder's question. "Once we shut down the river, I want eyes on that wall from your viewframe." He waited for Greuder to get into position. "All right … NOW."

Cadmus and Greuder shut down their world-rippers simultaneously. The river sloshed in its artificial banks and turned into a shallow pond. There was no longer a flow into or out of the lunar headquarters.

"Ain't we going to suffocate?" Kupe asked. "I thought we needed air from those."

"Don't worry," Kaia told him. "We have enough air for a while."

Cadmus was already spinning dials, sending the view in his world-ripper's viewframe blurring past. There was no visual aim; he was working entirely by memorized coordinates, entering them as quickly as his hands allowed. When it stopped, most of the other occupants of the chamber were busy with other tasks. But not everyone.

"Lord Eziel, preserve us," Greuder said, his voice hollow. There in the center of Cadmus's viewframe, twitching around as the Mad Tinker fine-tuned the angle, was the cannon. They were staring down the three-foot diameter barrel of the World Ender Cannon, Version 1, as Rynn had dubbed it.

Jamile looked over her shoulder. "Cadmus! What are you doing?"

The Mad Tinker hopped down from the control console with a spyglass and a plumb line in hand. He hustled across to Jamile's world-ripper, where she had paused somewhere over the western Kadrin Empire as she gaped across the chamber. "What does it look like we're doing? Providing artillery support. Kupe, in that cabinet over there, get goggles and earmuffs for everyone."

"Is that thing loaded?" Jamile shouted.

"Of course," Cadmus said. "Where were you when the crane was filling the hopper?" He began taking measurements, sighting down the length of the barrel, which was lit by reflected moonlight from the Sea of Kerum. "Status, Kaia."

"Nothing yet," Kaia reported. "Still just splashing blue magic puddles against the side of the wall."

"Cadmus," Jamile said. "What if that thing misses? I'm not twelve feet from this viewframe."

"It won't miss." He peered around to the front side of the viewframe, checking where Jamile had brought them. The view showed the battle from overhead, somewhere above the goblin encampment. "Good. Good. Now just move it into the wall, lined up and down the length."

"Um, Cadmus," Greuder said. "Are you sure this is the best idea?"

"Thank you, Kaia. I'll take over from here," Cadmus said as he jogged over to the primary world-ripper. "You go take the controls of the one opening onto the barrel."

Kaia nodded, eyes wide, chest heaving. She was a good soldier though and did as she was ordered.

In moments, Cadmus had reoriented his own world-ripper to the other end of the World Ender Cannon. There was a console there, much simpler than the ones for the world-rippers. It was dominated by a large lever with a bright red grip. Cadmus opened the world-ripper, and the Korrish night air rushed into the lunar headquarters.

Kupe came back, arms piled with goggles and earmuffs. He scurried among the residents, handing them out to each of them. "Just, um, how loud's this gonna be? We talking thunderail whistle? Pistol shot by your ear? What?"

Cadmus had his goggles on before he answered. "I have no idea." He turned to Kaia and Jamile. "On my mark, open those world-holes."

Cadmus stepped into Korr, to the console on the scaffolding below the *Jennai*, and flipped one of the smaller switches.

Klaxons blared, shattering the relative peace of the night aboard the *Jennai.* Rynn jumped in her seat, and Sosha hunched down and covered her ears at the sudden, deafening noise. The battle scene in the viewframe was momentarily forgotten.

"What the rusted, bloody bolts is going on?" Rynn shouted over the noise.

"Your father," Sosha replied. "You might want to hold onto something."

Rynn didn't ask; she just grabbed hold of the control console with both hands. Just then, the ship lurched. There were groans and screams of tortured metal, and the floor tilted beneath their feet. A moment later, the sound stopped and the ship slowly righted itself.

"What just happened?" Rynn asked.

Sosha pointed to the viewframe. "Look."

The wall of Raynesdark, which had been repelling everything Rynn's coil guns had thrown at it, burst at the base like split wood. Splinters of rock blasted out into the ranks of onrushing goblins, and a furrow appeared along the wall's base. It looked for all the world like some gigantic creature—or perhaps a three-foot diameter steel ball—had burrowed beneath its surface.

On a hilltop, west of the plains just below the Kadrin city of Raynesdark, and the old goblin's heart skipped a beat. The ancient gods themselves had returned and had struck down the wall of the Kadrin city, the blow hammering like the thunderclap. He felt it in his chest, in his guts; it passed through him as it must have passed through everyone on the battlefield, human and goblin alike.

The pretty little echoes of aether, rippling out from where the walls rune-enhanced strength was tested, were no more. K'k'rt did not doubt that the shots were still being fired. The wall just had no more strength to resist them. The remnants of the wall hung together for some time, superior masonry causing the undamaged sections to function as a sort of arch, supporting the section whose base had been gutted. Under withering fire from the goblins below, that section—along with the rest of the wall, and the defenders beyond—fell not long after.

"What was that?" he asked.

Madlin shrugged. "We won."

Cadmus stepped through the world-hole and back into the lunar headquarters. Pulling the switch, he shut them off from Korr once more. The chamber was filled with a cloud of Veydran rock dust, and the trough of water was littered with shards of granite, but the World Ender Cannon had blown most of the debris ahead of it.

"What … just … happened?" Greuder asked, coughing on the dust.

"Kaia, Jamile, get that river flowing again," Cadmus ordered. "Then check back in on the battle and make sure there are no surprises."

"No surprises, he says," Kupe muttered.

Cadmus found a blank sheet of paper and a pencil and cleared himself a spot on the side table, pushing aside a dish of candied chocolates. He had revisions to make to the cannon.

Chapter 24

"Wars keep things interesting." –Rashan Solaran

Servants bowed and stepped aside to remove themselves from Axterion's way. The green-veined black marble halls depopulated ahead of him as rumor spread that he was in a stomping mood. Unfortunately for the aged High Sorcerer, the thick carpets ruined the effect of a proper stomp. The object of today's stomp was oblivious enough that the he needed all the help he could get.

When he reached his destination, the halls were deserted. A moment's view in the aether showed him a strong but slovenly ward protecting the door. Danilaesis's handiwork, for certain. It was not, however, Danilaesis's bedroom. Axterion was down in the servants' wing of the palace, a place that was unused to guests of his importance. Guests of Danilaesis's caliber appeared to be more common.

Undoing the ward was a trifling matter for someone who had been making and breaking them for over a hundred winters. A moment later, Axterion was pounding a fist on the door.

A startled yelp and hushed words, muted by the intervening door, were his only reply. Axterion could have peered into the aether, now that the ward was gone, and taken a quick count of the occupants of the door beyond. But the voices and his initial suspicions agreed that there were but two, and he left it at that.

"Get out here, you halfwit Seventh Rank," Axterion shouted through the door. "There is a meeting in the Inner Sanctum, and against my better judgment, your presence is required."

Axterion stepped back. Experience told him that there would be no response before the door opened. It was just the way this sort of thing went. He waited.

When the door peeked open, one of the younger gardeners emerged, a girl not much older than Danilaesis. She was barefoot, and her dress was crooked across her shoulders. As she tried to slip past, she looked to the floor, not even in the direction of Axterion's feet. He caught her by the chin and stopped her, turning her face toward him and up.

"Look me in the eyes," he ordered. The girl hesitated, but complied. "Wider." She blinked, but forced herself to look at him with eyes wide as a doe's. He let her go. "You're fine. Go on and dress yourself properly. Whatever duties he relieved you of, consider yourself unrelieved." Whatever means Danilaesis had used to bed her, he had not compelled her with magic.

The girl bowed and scurried away. Axterion watched for a moment, wondering how long it had been since he'd chased girls so young. A lifetime. Maybe two.

"So what's the commotion that's got you fetching me yourself like some messenger?" Danilaesis asked, pulling on a pair of trousers. "We weren't done, you know."

Axterion harrumphed. "I can only keep telling myself that you'll grow out of it." He pointed to one of the two bunk beds that took up most of the servants' room. "Those things are sleeping quarters, not a training yard."

"Why would I ever want to grow out of it?" Danilaesis asked with a grin. "I'm going to have to track her down later and make good on a few promises. I can't go around sullying my name."

Axterion sighed and looked up to the ceiling, if nothing else, to avoid watching his grandson dress himself. "You know, your father was much the same, and he grew out of it. Took a few wives, but they finally broke him of the habit. I'd blame him for the way you are, but the impudent drunkard would just blame me in turn."

Danilaesis gave his grandfather a knowing look. *Dull as a spear tip, that one. Blast me, was I ever this much trouble?*

"Come on," Axterion grumbled as Danilaesis finished donning his proper attire.

"So, you going to tell me what's going on?"

"Yes. In the Inner Sanctum, along with everyone else. I might have more breath in these lungs than I did a season ago, but I don't intend to waste it repeating myself to every wayward sorcerer who has to get himself fetched out of the servants' wing."

Axterion strode the palace halls without looking back. He knew Danilaesis followed him. The boy had many faults, but a lack of curiosity was not among them. They made their way to the Tower of Contemplation, at the northwest corner of the palace. Older than the rest of the structure, it was a habitat all to itself, with its own staff separate from the main palace, and bustling with sorcerers administrating the empire's magical assets. A long, spiral set of stairs wound around the interior or the tower, stopping at landings that led off into libraries, laboratories, and lounges. A levitating platform was provided for the elderly and infirm among the tower's visitors; Axterion used to be its primary rider. Now, reinvigorated with youth, he took pride in setting a punishing pace for his grandson up the stairs.

"You're not going to make me fall behind, you know," Danilaesis told him from a few stairs below.

"This isn't a race," Axterion replied without turning back. "There is work to be done, and important matters to discuss."

"When was the last time the Inner Circle met for anything that mattered?" Dan asked. Axterion could picture the insipid smirk on the boy's face.

"About an hour ago."

When they reached the top of the stairs, a pair of tower guardsmen pulled back their halberds to allow Axterion and his grandson passage into the Inner Sanctum. It was all very formal and highly unnecessary. Had Axterion been a reformist, he would have done away with the guards, and shipped them off to one of the army battalions. But there was little enough continuity in the Kadrin Empire these days, so he left them in place.

The rest of the Inner Circle was already present. Danilaesis took a spot normally reserved for petitioners, at the center of the chamber, where the surrounding sorcerers, behind their elevated desks, could look down on him. He was joined by General Varnus and Empress Celia. The Inner Sanctum was the only place in the empire where she did not rule.

"Good," said Axterion as he took his seat at the head of the circle of desks, opposite the door. "Dispensing with the pleasantries, let me be blunt … We are at war."

"You think I didn't know about Warlock Danilaesis and his raids?" Empress Celia asked, holding her chin high, trying to appear dignified from eight feet below the Inner Circle's sorcerers.

"Of course," replied Axterion. "We've been goading them. Everyone here knows it. But this is another matter entirely. The goblins have taken Raynesdark."

"What?" several sorcerers of the Inner Circle cried out. There was chaos as a dozen questions flew around the room. One sorcerer tried to talk over the next, and even Empress Celia's shrieking demands to be heard were drowned out.

One sound, discordant among the outrage, the confusion, and the fear, finally managed to draw the attention of the squabbling sorcerers. Danilaesis, Warlock of the Kadrin Empire, was laughing.

"Oh, you poor, unlucky bastards," Danilaesis said when he gained enough control of himself to speak. "Forced to rely on your favorite target of torments to save you all. From now on, no more classes, no more getting dragged out of bed, no more rules about when and where I can keep my sword with me. I'm going to win your two wars; don't fret yourselves stupid. This is going to be fun."

Draksgollow sat around the table with a few of his new generals. They weren't the rabble he'd hired, or former machinery operators who had been elevated out of loyalty instead of skill. The men who shared his meal were loyal to his new cause. Quotes in the newspapers, rumors in the right sort of public houses, Draksgollow had dredged up the malcontents among the militaries of Korr. Some had been dismissed for brutality; others were deserters from active duty. They shared one trait in common: they hated humans, and rebel humans most of all.

"To another successful purge," Draksgollow toasted, raising his mug. Few kuduks had developed a taste for alcohol; it was a predominantly human vice. But when they were stolen from human scum, recently dead by their rifles, the taste was not the point. "May many more follow."

"I gotta hand it to you, Drak old boy," said General Bradet, a snarl-bearded former artillery sergeant with the 81st division of the Ruttanian army. "That contraption of yours is gonna make mushing these rebels to crack-fill a whistle in the tunnels."

General Knorlen nodded from behind his mug. "Almost makes this vinegar drinkable."

"You sure this ain't piss?" asked General Yurgenn. "If I'd have been about to get rolled up under a tank's wheels, I might piss in the barrels."

One step above animals. Half a step above humans. Draksgollow chuckled into his own mug, but not because he found Yurgenn amusing. *Still … right size wrench turns the bolt. Can't be picky when hiring exterminators. Nice, polite fellas won't take the work.*

Draksgollow had spent his life among grimy men, men who didn't let a little grease on their sleeves stop them from doing their jobs. Now he was moving on to a time where he needed men who felt the same way about blood: wash it off at the end of the day and put your feet up.

"Excuse me, sir," one of the world-ripper technicians poked his head into the room, drawing scowls from the generals. He handed a clipboard to Draksgollow, piled with pages of scribbled notes. "Today's reports."

Draksgollow brushed it aside, refusing to take hold of it with his non-mug hand. Normally he'd have leafed through it himself, right then and there, but he had an image to craft. "Give me the short version."

The technician shook his head. "Still no sign of him."

The generals chortled at Draksgollow's expense. "That daruu done stuck a rat in your pipes, ain't he?" General Knorlen said.

"Can't blame a fella," Yurgenn replied. "I'd be steamed, too, if some old statue of a daruu nicked a machine like that. Surprised one of them relics knew how to turn the spark on."

There was a laugh around the table at the daruu's expense, and a few crude jests added in amidst the mirth. Draksgollow kept up his smile and played along. "There won't be stone enough to hide behind once I find that rusted thief. I want my machine back before Kezudkan Graniteson makes it public and claims he invented it."

King Dekulon stood with his hands clasped behind his back, a gesture Kezudkan hadn't possessed the flexibility for in over a century. The elder daruu stood leaning on his cane, overseeing the installation of the pillaged world-ripper. The chamber was an oddity in the daruu kingdom—it was brand new. Freshly excavated and purpose-built to house the machine, it was the cozy stone hideaway that all Kezudkan's other bases of operation had failed to become. It wasn't just the workmanship of the octagonal chamber and its domed ceiling—though its form was flawless. It wasn't the attention to detail, the minor embellishments in the stone, or the subtle flow of one feature to the next. No, it was the *feel* of the stone, the ancient, beloved companion of a civilization that knew it for what it truly was: the flesh of the world. The stone here knew Kezudkan accepted him as one of its children.

The world-ripper looked at home as well. The complex spark routing was hidden within steel cabinets, but the jumble of wires was hidden from view, run beneath the stone, which the artisans flowed over and around the conductive wires, insulating them more securely than anything Draksgollow's kuduk workmen could have managed. The viewframe sat nestled in a stone cradle that fit it as close as paint. At the console, which was set into one of the walls, a stone chair melded with the floor, allowing the feeling of being tucked in the world's embrace. It was sized to Kezudkan's exact measurements, as a sign of respect for the device's creator.

Of course, all the parts had been disassembled, thoroughly cleansed of kuduk blood, and blessed before they were brought into the chamber.

"I don't know what to say, Your Majesty," said Kezudkan.

King Dekulon turned and smiled, then returned his attention to the daruu who were completing the installation. "You may say whatever comes to mind. This world of yours, Korr … the more I hear about it, the more I find it distasteful. This … this is how a master craftsman's works deserve to be treated." The king swept a hand over the whole of the room.

"Until I came here, until I saw all this—all of this, not just this one chamber—I had thought myself well off. I had no idea what had been taken from me, the years spent living a life whose upper bounds had been set by creatures with the vision of swine—gluttons of coin, and content to live in tunnels not fit for a sty."

A tremor shook the chamber. Kezudkan looked to Kind Dekulon but saw only surprise on his face. "There should have been no tremor," said the king. "The magma chamber to the north is calm, and Veydrus is exceptionally stable here. If you will excuse me, I must find out what has happened." The king graced Kezudkan with a nod and hurried from the chamber with all the speed possible while maintaining an air of dignity.

Kezudkan watched him go. He did not feel it was right to give the king leave even though Kezudkan was the elder by a wide margin. Dekulon was king and would go where he pleased within his kingdom. Resisting the urge to tag along was a war between curiosity and his aching bones, and Kezudkan's joints had been reigning champions of such contests for ages. With a long breath, Kezudkan returned to looking over the shoulders of a small crew of artisans—he could not even demean them by calling them workmen—who were putting the final pieces together. The whole lot of them was sharp as cracked obsidian, picking up on the written diagrams easily and putting together a machine they had never before laid eyes on. He had not found a single flaw in their work.

"It's finished, Citizen Graniteson," the lead artisan reported some time later.

"Well then, let's have a look see," said Kezudkan, easing himself into the chair at the controls. The aches in his back subsided as the curves of the chair supported him just where he needed it most. He let out a relaxed sigh. "Oh … maybe in just a few moments. I think I'm going to enjoy this chair for a bit."

His respite was short lived, for the king returned like a rockslide, the Pillars of Runes and Defense trailing behind him. Whereas the king had left the chamber in a state of confusion, he had returned in a state of alarm. "Is the machine working?" he asked. The question carried the subtle undertone that it had better be.

A nod to one of the artisans got the daruu to flip the switches to light the viewframe. The webwork of copper wires disappeared, giving a clear view of the wall behind it. Of course, this was because the dials were all set to zeroes. "It seems to be, though we haven't opened a hole yet," Kezudkan reported.

"I wish to see the surface. There is a human city above us which seems to have been the source of the tremor." The king did not look at Kezudkan, nor at his advisors, but stared into the viewframe, waiting.

Kezudkan grunted as he shifted himself forward to better reach the controls. It only took a few quick twists to bring them up the mile or so to the surface. The scene that unfolded before them was a tableau of carnage. Bodies lay everywhere amid the shattered ruins of the city. The rocky debris that littered the ground was clearly stonework, and there was evidence of runework on some of the unbroken faces. All of that was noteworthy, but what caught everyone's attention were the creatures moving amid the wreckage, carrying spears or pistols.

"What are those things?" Kezudkan asked.

"I don't know," replied the Pillar of Defense. "Some new sort of weapon, I imagine."

Kezudkan shook his head. "No, the little green creatures crawling everywhere. What are they?"

"Those are goblins," replied King Dekulon. "They have plagued this region before. They live in the mountains far to the west, mountains claimed by their dragon overlords—mountains we are not welcome beneath."

"Those things they're carrying are called guns," Kezudkan clarified for the benefit of the Pillar of Defense. "I don't know what goblins are, or where they got those weapons, but I doubt they were enough to topple a wall that size. I mean … just look at it." Kezudkan adjusted the viewframe to better make his point. The wall was a massive edifice, easily twenty feet think. To think that even with runes to reinforce it …"

"Nevertheless, something destroyed a wall that we helped those humans rebuild after the last time the goblins attempted to invade," said King Dekulon. He turned to address the Pillar of Defense "Draklan, prepare for an influx of refugees. Zepdaan, once we have the human survivors within our tunnels, seal the entrance where the old human mines end. Make it look like ogres dug those walls."

"What about those ogres?" the Pillar of Defense asked. "They might not all have died in the fighting."

King Dekulon was silent for a moment. "Allow them."

The two pillars of King Dekulon's advisory council left the chamber. The artisans had slipped out during the excitement, leaving the king and Kezudkan alone.

"You'd risk getting involved in that mess," Kezudkan said, "just to save some humans?"

"Not all humans are created equal," King Dekulon replied. "Some of them are capable of nobility. You have made quite a remarkable device. Thank you." The king turned on his heel and left Kezudkan alone with his world-ripper.

With nothing else to occupy himself, and not wanting to get dragged into involvement in the immanent refugee debacle, Kezudkan settled in to watch these goblin creatures survey the aftermath of their own victory. They were spry, nimble creatures, with limbs so thin it seemed they should snap under their own weight. That they could have smashed a walled human city reminded Kezudkan that he was in a world whose rules were not the same as the ones he knew. It was not likely to be the last surprise he received.

Poking around in the ruins, the goblins seemed to be looking for something. A few times they spotted a survivor. Their own, they carried off down the mountainside to an encampment below. The humans they found, they fired their pistols at. Kezudkan brought the viewframe closer, close enough that he could see the coil guns for what they were. They looked just like the ones that had been popping up among the human rebels of late, according to the newspapers.

"So Erefan," Kezudkan muttered to himself. "Is this where you got the idea for those weapons you armed your rabble with?"

As Kezudkan began wandering the rest of the battlefield, something caught his eye. There was a lone figure, taller than all the goblins, dressed in a leather waistcoat and wearing goggles. A human! While the goblins had been killing all the human survivors they found, this one female human was welcome in their midst. She and one of the goblins appeared to be discussing a chuck of masonry that the human held in both hands.

The human woman stepped forward and vanished from Kezudkan's view. He rubbed at his eyes, half expecting to see her there when he opened them, but the goblin was gone as well. He scanned the area, even reversing the angle of his view in case someone else had a world-hole open. But she was gone.

Kezudkan decided it was time to shut down the machine for the night.

It was dawn by the time Madlin and K'k'rt picked their way to the ruined wall. In the shadow of mountains whose proper name she had never learned—the goblins called it something incomprehensible—goblin soldiers searched the rubble for the wounded and sorted them according to allegiance. Goblins went to the surgeons, humans to the spear point of the end of a coil gun. The hilltop where Madlin had watched the battle was catching the first rays of sunlight. It seemed appropriate that her recent past was lit while she trudged forth into the dim grey middle world of not quite utterly dark. Her coil guns weren't ever intended to take human lives. She tried not to watch or to hear the click-sizzle-crack of their firing.

Cadmus's ludicrously oversized cannon had done the work of a thousand sappers tunneling beneath the wall, drilling out the foundation over a span that Madlin estimated at a hundred fifty feet. Even her optimistic assessment of the handheld coil guns would not have expected them to tear such a huge chunk from the city in so short a time. It proved to her once again that her father was a madman of the most prestigious sort. He had devised a plan to rescue her that didn't involve whisking her away from trouble, but rather solving the problem she faced, and he had done it right before her eyes without her realizing.

I came up with the system to bring fresh air and water to the moon; he builds it into a weapon. Madlin thought about the precision with which the two world-ripper viewframes in the lunar headquarters aligned, and wondered how long ago Cadmus had planned for something like this. At the time, Madlin had taken the exactitude as merely a symptom of his extreme attention to detail, his desire for perfection in the things he created. *Maybe if you make things well enough, it just opens more options.*

"What are you hoping to find?" K'k'rt asked as Madlin turned over pieces of broken wall. She climbed atop piles of rubble that were anything but stable, and the goblin tinker followed gamely a few paces behind her. Madlin might have felt badly for him, but she had not asked him to follow, nor was there a particular glut of sympathy left in her after the massacre.

"Evidence."

K'k'rt chuckled. It sounded out of place amid the misery all around them. "I think Fr'n'ta'gur will take a conquered city as evidence."

"I can't dump a conquered city in his heap of coins and demand my payment now, can I?" Madlin snapped. "I want a chunk of wall that shows what the coil guns did to it."

K'k'rt tugged at her sleeve and beckoned her down. Curious what he wanted, Madlin obliged by leaning close. "You and I both know that this was not the work of your weapons."

"So?" Madlin replied. "I want to prove the guns work. You want them ripping walls to shreds; build one a quarter mile long with a three and half ton bullet."

K'k'rt's brow frumpled. "I don't know your measurements. How long? How heavy?"

Madlin looked up into the pink-tinged clouds and did some quick math in her head. "A barrel roughly two hundred fifty times my height long, with a shot weighing sixteen of me."

"Not possible," K'k'rt replied. "You'd need the aether of a dragon to power it."

"I can show you," said Madlin. "Just help me find a piece of that wall we can take to your dragon."

K'k'rt made a show of helping, but he seemed more intent on watching Madlin. He peered over some stones and prodded others with a toe. Given that he was probably the equivalent of seventy by human standards, Madlin could forgive him not digging amid the rubble with his bare hands.

Madlin lifted one promising specimen, and it came away dripping blood. Lying beneath were the crushed remains of one of the Kadrin soldiers. Dropping the stone, Madlin lost the previous night's dinner over the ruins. She closed her eyes, willing some other image to replace what she just saw. Through bleary eyes, she stumbled away to compose herself on hands and knees.

"Here," K'k'rt said, handing her a flask. It was goblin-sized, no more than a single swallow for someone Madlin's size. She twisted the cap free and swished the stale, warm water around in her mouth, then spat it onto the rocks.

"Thanks," she said, still queasy.

"And to think, your people are carnivorous. How did you ever survive to become civilized?" K'k'rt asked. "You ought to have starved in the wild. Did your gods feed you meats without telling you where it came from?"

"That's not meat!" Madlin shouted. The effort threatened to find something new in her stomach to heave forth. "It was one of my own kind."

"It's meat now, even if you would not eat it. We don't eat our own dead either, but the dragons do. I wonder … does that make us lesser creatures. The dragons accept death. Is denying it a mortal folly?"

Madlin shook her head, more to clear it than to answer the goblin's question. "Let's just find a rock with evidence of a coil gun's penetration and get out of here."

"I'm afraid there will not be a caravan back home for some days. The messengers have already left, and they would not have tolerated our presence slowing them anyway."

"Just shut up and find a rusted rock."

It took another twenty minutes, but K'k'rt happened upon a piece of masonry that looked promising and called Madlin over. "Inspect this one, and see if it fits your requirement."

Madlin lifted a chunk of granite too large for the elderly goblin to manage. She turned it over in her hands. *□his is perfect*□There were runes from the wall's defenses on one flat surface, and along the shattered edge, a perfectly smooth trough. A shot from a coil gun had split one of the runes and left an unmistakable mark from its passing. "Yeah, this will do it. Come on, let's get out of here and show your dragon that my guns work."

"My aching knees could use a break before we head down the mount—"

K'k'rt stopped and gaped as the world-hole opened. "How did you activate it from here?"

Madlin stepped through into Korr, where Rynn sat at the controls of the world-ripper, goggles down and a scarf wrapped around her face. There was no one else present in the hold of the *□ennai*. "You coming?"

K'k'rt nodded and stepped tentatively through after her, and the hole closed behind them.

The taproom of the Savage Swordfish was packed. The regular patrons had been shoved out, told they weren't welcome and to come back some other night. The crews of Denrik Zayne's pirate fleet were in town, and all of Marker's Point were going to know about it. Men from the *Merciful* traded jests and boasts with sailors from the *□um □hark*, and the crew of the *□alse □rofit* told the men of both that they could shove those boasts in their ale-holes.

Captain Denrik Zayne sat at a table with three guests, and no man called into question the choice of his companions, even if it left Captain Zhi-Yin of the *□um □hark* at a table with his own men. Zayne knew that he had the reputation to do as he liked, the loss of the *□air □rader* notwithstanding. He soaked in the room, the feeling of being among all his loyal crewmen—and the disloyal ones as well. Money did not buy loyalty, but the credible promise of money soon to come bought enough for his satisfaction. Those with whom he shared his table were a different sort. That night, he chose to drink with those whose loyalties had nothing to do with money.

"This is most unlike you, Captain Zayne," teased Captain Stalyart of the *Merciful*. "You might confuse people into believing you are a man of good humor and jovial disposition."

Denrik sneered and tilted back a bottle of whiskey. After a gasp, he said, "So I'll burn a village to remind them. A village with orphans in it."

"Are you sure that will be enough?" Stalyart persisted. "This is quite a rowdy and festive occasion."

"Sick orphans."

"What're we doing here, anyway?" Tanner asked. "You been clam shut about it for a week now. What's the big surprise?"

Denrik nodded to his son. "Go ahead. Tell him."

"We've got a war started," Jadon said.

"Yeah," muttered Tanner, sloshing the last of an ale around the bottom of his tankard. "Tell me something I don't know."

"You don't know that I got the goblins to attack the Kadrin Empire," Jadon said.

Tanner blinked. The ale-stupefied expression on his face told everyone at the table that he had, perhaps, misheard. "What's that now?"

"Raynesdark," Denrik said. "Except this time, it fell. It seems that Madlin Errol's hand-held cannons fared better than my own import of ship-based cannons. Of course, there is no longer a demon guarding the Kadrin Empire, so I'm sure that was no small factor."

"Jealous of your own son, Captain?" Stalyart asked. He shook his head, belying the grin on his face. "For shame."

"With the help of the transference machine, I'll be able to take the rest of the Kadrin Empire," Jadon said. "It's just a matter of time now."

"It's got to be her idea, or you've got to be *bloody* sure you get control of them all," Denrik said. "They keep even one hidden machine; they could doom us."

"Sounds like they'll be plenty of doom to go around," Tanner said, closing his eyes and swallowing the last of his ale. He let the tankard slam down on the table to get the barmaid's attention.

"Is there going to be a problem with this, Mr. Tanner?" Denrik asked. "You were eager enough to be rid of your warlock companion. The empire is no better. I don't have any quarrel with the peasants—most of them will be fine … better off, even. The rot of corruption at its heart though, is going to finally be ripped from it."

Tanner looked around for a barmaid and caught one's attention. Seconds later, his empty tankard had been traded for a full one. He took a long pull from it before he answered. "No. You go on, do what you need to do. I'll play along."

"Mr. Tanner, cheer up. We're going to free the world."

Chapter 25

Two figures sat atop the glacier wall, overlooking the ruins of Raynesdark, their feet dangling a hundred feet above the rubble-strewn streets. Below them, countless goblins filled the city, poring over the shattered buildings and corpses, beginning the process of setting the captured city in order. Crews worked on clearing the debris from the streets, removing corpses, scrubbing blood and dust from the areas that had just been cleared, and inspecting the buildings for stability. Not a single one of them was aware that they were being watched.

"So, was it everything you hoped it would be?" Juliana asked, staring down at the destruction even as the goblins sought to put things back to rights.

Kyrus's face was somber except for a hardened set to his eyes. "Of course not. I still remember saving this city once. It really wasn't that long ago."

"A lifetime," Juliana replied, kicking her feet absentmindedly against the wall.

"Six winters, approaching seven," Kyrus said. "I bargained for the stone folk to help rebuild that wall the goblins just destroyed."

"Madlin and her father destroyed it."

Kyrus shrugged. It made no difference. "This will all work itself out. When it does, they'll have a peace of their own, not one I imposed on them. But …"

"But what?" Juliana asked.

"I do wonder, at times like this, whether I'm being selfish," said Kyrus. "The demons don't want another Tallax because they'll have someone to answer to. That whole book could be a lie, you know. Have you considered that? Illiardra admits she was the one who wrote it, and who was around that long ago to gainsay her?"

"Do you really think the book is a fabrication? A convenient lie she prepared over five thousand years ago? I don't think even the immortals are that far-sighted."

"What if they were?" Kyrus asked. "What if they knew someday another sorcerer like Tallax would be born? Statistically, it was only a matter of time."

"They should be more worried about the Mad Tinker," said Juliana. "That science of his was frightening. You at least have your conscience keeping you in check. What if the next weapon he builds is even more powerful? I think he'd rather destroy the world than lose it."

"Rashan was like that," Kyrus said. He held up a palm and a tiny, translucent sphere appeared, resembling a globe. "He wanted the Kadrin Empire to rule all of Veydrus … he didn't even want it for himself, just the knowledge that he had delivered the victory. I still have yet to find a historical analog for a conqueror like him."

"You know I couldn't just let them all die," Juliana said softly.

"When I said we couldn't interfere in the mortal's wars, I never mentioned non-combatants."

"So you don't mind me shielding the peasants, sneaking them down into the lower mines?" Juliana asked.

Kyrus shrugged. Unable to suppress a smirk any longer, he let Juliana see it. "Of course I don't."

"Well then," Juliana said. With a flourish, a newspaper appeared in her hand, written in the language of the stone folk—the language of Korr. "Read this."

Kyrus took the paper. The picture on the front was of a crowd of kuduks carrying placards. The image was grainy, but he could make out slogans such as "Dead Humans = Safe Deeps," "Free Humans Are Rebel Humans," and "Collar And Shave." The headline read: HARDLINE ANTI-HUMAN MOVEMENT GAINS TRACTION.

Kyrus read through the article. "Looks like some of the kuduks want all humans either chained up or shot." He shrugged and handed the paper back to Juliana.

"Dead humans in Veydrus, dead humans in Korr. Did you know, that kuduk Draksgollow is planning on wiping out *all* the Korrish humans? He's planning to replace them with slaves from Tellurak."

Kyrus smiled. "It'll never happen."

"It'll never happen because you'll see you were wrong and stop it, or because you think it'll never get that far?"

"I just won't bet against a man who can destroy a runed wall without even using magic."

Other Books by J.S. Morin

If you enjoyed World-Ripper War, why not go back to the beginning, and experience the journey of mundane scribe Kyrus Hinterdale who discovers what it means to be Twinborn—and the dangers of getting caught using magic in a world that thinks it exists only in childrens' stories.

The **Twinborn Trilogy** is available for sale on Amazon

War-Bringer
Prequel

Firehurler
Book 1

Aethersmith
Book 2

Sourcethief
Book 3

About the Author

Born in New Hampshire in 1977, J.S. Morin found himself captivated by the wonders of fantasy novels at a young age. He was introduced to the genre via the works of R.A. Salvatore, Ed Greenwood, and Margaret Weiss and Tracy Hickman. He loved exploring other people's worlds, from Shadowdale to Hyrule. He also quickly found Dungeons and Dragons to be a creative outlet for stories, characters, and new worlds of his own creation.

His other passion was for building and designing things, and when it came time to choose a career, he went down that road. A Mechanical Engineer by day, he spends his evenings with his wife in their New Hampshire home, enjoying the simplicity of life in a quiet state.

By night he dreams elaborate dreams of visiting fanciful worlds, performing acts of heroism, and solving intriguing puzzles, which inspire him to craft stories that he hopes will help shape the lives of the next generation of fantasy readers. He hopes to avoid finishing growing up.

17966976R00127

Made in the USA
Middletown, DE
17 February 2015